HOT AND BOTHERED

Her eyes were dark and luminous as midnight ponds. "W-what are you doing to me?"

He grinned. "Maybe what you want me to do, darlin'?"

"Please," she panted, "remove your hand."

She was squirming, and Lucky relished it. "I don't think so," he replied huskily. "I'm your husband now and I'll do what I please." To demonstrate, he moved his hand to her other breast, teasing the nipple with a fingertip.

She shuddered. "You—you're trying to—"

"Get you hot and bothered?" he offered. "Oh, yeah, darlin'. *Very* hot and bothered."

Other *Love Spell* books by Eugenia Riley:

BUSHWHACKED BRIDE
THE GREAT BABY CAPER
STRANGERS IN THE NIGHT (anthology)
EMBERS OF TIME
LOVERS AND OTHER LUNATICS
TEMPEST IN TIME
A TRYST IN TIME

EUGENIA RILEY

Bushwhacked Groom

LOVE SPELL

NEW YORK CITY

LOVE SPELL®

November 2004

Published by

Dorchester Publishing Co., Inc.
200 Madison Avenue
New York, NY 10016

ISBN 0-505-52588-7

Printed in the United States of America.

This book is dedicated, with love,
to our newest family member—
my nephew, precious Justin David,
born June 23, 2002,
with warm congratulations
to proud parents, Jen and Jeff.

Bushwhacked Groom

Prologue

Buck Hollow, Colorado
The Present

"You know, darlin', here in the West, when a man catches his woman cheating on him, he can still shoot both the low-down sinners and the jury will salute him."

The two occupants of the sagging bed at the Buck Hollow Motel jumped awake at the sound of the charged voice of the vengeful man who loomed in the opened doorway with antique Colt pistol in hand, his tall, hard frame and black Stetson backlit by an angry red Colorado dawn. A bitter cold spring wind blew in after him, heightening the terror of the two transgressors cowering in the darkness.

"L-lucky!" gasped the voluptuous blonde clutching the cheap sheet to her neck. "What are you doing here?"

Lucky glared at his so-called "girl," Misti Childers, trembling next to his so-called best friend, Bobby

1

Stringfield. "Under the circumstances, darlin', I should be asking that of you," he drawled. His gaze shifted to the wild-eyed naked man who shivered next to her, the coarse hairs of his brown crew cut standing on end. "Though it's pretty obvious what you've been doing, eh, Bobby?"

Bobby gulped. "Now, Lucky, this ain't what you think it is—"

"No?" Lucky mocked. "Don't tell me you two are out on a scavenger hunt, chasing up Bibles in motel rooms, naked as two jaybirds?"

Bobby held up a quivering hand. "Lucky, if you'll just put down that gun—"

Lucky's derisive laughter cut him short, followed by dead silence as he cocked his revolver. "Thanks for reminding me, partner. You know what? Think I'll just let my granddaddy's pistol do the talking for me."

Both went wide-eyed. "Lucky, no!" Misti wailed.

"Please, man, I know you're pissed, but—"

Both protests ended in screams as Lucky opened up fire, shooting several holes in the mattress. With grim satisfaction, he watched the two fornicators go diving off the bed in opposite directions, their white butts flashing in the dim light. He took gleeful aim at the floor by Bobby's feet, and chuckled at the sight of the coward dancing about crazily, trying to avoid the barrage of bullets. Meanwhile Misti stood paralyzed, hollering at the top of her lungs. Lucky pivoted, his well-aimed shot cutting across the cheap carpeting and streaking between her widely spread legs, sending her into a tortured jig, as well.

What a sight they were! he thought with vindictive

pleasure. The two looked as ridiculous as a couple of drunken, naked fools doing the schottische on a huge ant bed. He was continuing his fun when an ominous click warned him he was out of ammunition.

Through the acrid haze of smoke, he glanced over to see the two regarding him in frozen terror. Reaching into his pocket for bullets, he began calmly reloading. "Know what, folks? If I were you, think I'd hightail it before I have time to refill this cylinder."

At that, Misti seemed to recover herself. Face red with anger, she waved a fist at him. "You're the one who'd best head for the hills, you rotten SOB! You're going to jail for this, do you hear me, Lucky Lamont? Or have you forgot my uncle Bub's the county sheriff?"

"Yeah!" added Bobby with bravado.

Lucky fired a shot through the ceiling that left both cringing. His voice came cool and hard. "No, I haven't forgotten, honey. Now scram before I change my mind and kill both of you no-good backstabbers." As Bobby reached for his jeans, he waved the pistol. "Don't bother with clothes, either. You'll want to present *all* your evidence to good old Uncle Bub, right?"

At this insult, Misti squealed in frustrated rage, then another shot from Lucky sent both of the cowards shrieking past him out the door. Lucky watched them skedaddle into the parking lot, darting about like two cockroaches panicked by a sudden light, their naked forms skidding past the scandalized eyes of an elderly couple just emerging from their sedan. As the oldsters watched openmouthed, the two streakers dashed across the two-lane highway toward a gas station that sat framed by breathtaking Broken Buck Mountain.

EUGENIA RILEY

Lucky relished their humiliation. 'Bout time the two traitors got a taste of their own. Should he go shoot the miserable dogs? Hmmmm. They were clearly headed for the hills. Had they suffered enough already?

Naw, he quickly decided, *not nearly enough*.

"Hey, what the hell is going on here?"

At the sound of an irate male voice, Lucky turned to watch old Mr. Winston emerge from the motel office. A thin, bent man in checked shirt and jeans, he hobbled forward in a painful, arthritic gait, an expression of fury gripping his whiskered face.

Lucky lowered his pistol. "Sorry, Mr. Winston. Just taking care of a little business."

Arriving at Lucky's side, the old man's horrified glance moved from the pistol to the smoke-filled, bullet-riddled room. "Lucky Lamont, you low-down snake! What do you mean, shooting up my motel? Your granddaddy would have your hide for this."

"Sorry, sir." Lucky shoved the Colt into his waist. "But it was a matter of honor. My woman was running around on me."

"Well, no wonder, with a temper like yours."

"Look, sir, I'll pay for any damages—"

"Damages, my butt!" Winston snapped back. "You'll rue the day you trashed the Buck Hollow Motel, you little shit. I'm calling Sheriff Childers, then fetching my shotgun to hold you, you no-account saddle bum."

Watching the old man quickly hitch-step back toward the office, Lucky reflected ruefully that there were just too many people with short tempers in these parts. Tipping his hat at the elderly couple who still

4

stood frozen like statues in the parking lot, he beat a hasty retreat and drove off in his pickup truck.

You're the one who'd best head for the hills.

Two hours later, riding his nutmeg yellow horse Gypsy out in the mountains, Lucky was galled to remember Misti's words—and, especially, to realize their truth. After shooting up the motel, he had been forced to turn tail and run, humiliating though it was.

Lucky Lamont wasn't a coward, but he was a realist. Between old Mr. Winston being riled as hell and Misti being the sheriff's niece, his goose was cooked pretty good, he reckoned. Even Granddad would have boiled his gizzard over this prank, and Grandma would have wrung her hands and beseeched the Almighty to redeem him.

Lord, how he missed his folks. As Gypsy crested the hill, he reined her in and stared at the old homestead in the hollow below. The white cottage where he'd been raised was now a ramshackle, falling-down shack covered with vines. Once a cozy ranchstead nestled between soaring, snow-capped mountains, the whole enterprise had now wasted away just like his grandparents had, the barn a sagging heap, the corral teetering on its posts, the pond dried up, his grandma's beloved vegetable garden overrun with brambles and weeds.

Lucky shuddered slightly in the frigid air and pulled his jean jacket more tightly about him. Even the birds seemed to be hiding on this chill spring morning.

A lump rose in his throat as he gazed off to the east,

at a knoll with two simple stone crosses. He galloped over to the small cemetery and dismounted, pulling off his hat. He fought the sting of tears as he knelt and pulled the dandelions off Grandma's grave, then Granddad's. The mingled smells of earth and greenery, powerful scents from his youth on the land, tugged at his senses.

Virgil and Bessie Lamont. They'd raised him here, these two wonderful people. Lucky had never known his parents. His father had deserted his mother shortly after conceiving him; after his birth, his mom had descended into wild ways and had run off with some drunken fool, both of them getting killed in a traffic accident. His grandparents had stepped in and done justice by him, adopting him, raising him righteously, taking him to the Baptist Church each Sunday. It would have been an idyllic upbringing for any child; but Lucky in particular had thrived here on this ranch and in the nearby town of Buck Hollow, with its economy based on hunting and fishing, its conservative values and community spirit. He'd bought into the entire baseball and apple pie philosophy, adopting his granddad's code of honor—that men should be men, and women should remember their place.

Of course, Lucky had never actually met a woman who knew her place, aside from his own grandmother. By the time he'd been in high school, he'd realized that his granddad was a relic, a man of another time, and his grandmother a jewel from a gentler age. But Lucky loved and respected both greatly, and had never told them about all the sex-crazy cheerleaders who had jumped his bones in the back of his pickup truck.

After graduating from high school, Lucky had continued to work the spread with Granddad. He'd hoped eventually to marry an old-fashioned, God-fearing woman like his grandma, though where he would find her, he had no idea.

Then times had turned tough. Granddad had been a smoker all his life and for years had suffered from debilitating emphysema. Three years ago when Lucky was only twenty-two, Granddad had passed away. Grandma had never been the same afterward, and had followed her husband to heaven that winter, quietly slipping away in her sleep. Lucky had been alone, devastated, faced with a stack of bills from the two funerals and his granddad's last illness. Ultimately he'd been forced to sell the family homestead to settle his grandparents' debts. Now he worked for the rich rancher who'd bought him out, and the land he loved was no longer his.

And he'd lost all faith in the goodness of life. He'd quit attending church, for what cruel God would snatch away from him not just the true parents of his heart but the home for which all of them had sacrificed? He'd begun to hang out in honky-tonks, pick up women, get in fights, even land in jail on occasion . . . Hell, even his granddad's good friend, old Mr. Winston, now considered him bad news, no doubt that was why he'd called Sheriff Childers.

Lucky knew he'd been searching for something ever since his folks' deaths—for a friend he could count on, a woman to share his life with, a sense of home and belonging. Instead he'd found Misti, his tramp of a new girlfriend, and Bobby, his traitor of a best friend, the man he'd thought he could trust, the one he'd bunked with at the Flying T. Both of them had let him down—although in some ways Bobby's betrayal had hurt even worse than Misti's. By now Lucky pretty much expected most women to be whores; but what did a man have without the loyalty of his friends?

And what would his granddad advise him to do now? Again a tear threatened to well up as he gazed at the graves. No doubt Granddad would understand his anger toward Misti and Bobby, since he'd always been a firm believer in the double standard. But he'd still advise Lucky not to run from his fate, but to turn himself in to the law. After all, he hadn't actually shot anyone. He might get county lockup for thirty days this time—perhaps an even longer stretch, with Misti's uncle being the sheriff and all—but it shouldn't be too bad.

But first, before he faced the music, he'd spend one night out here on the range, camping beneath the stars just as he and his granddad used to do. He'd ride on out past the old ghost town of Mariposa, where no one was likely to follow him, then turn east to Reklaw Gorge, the old outlaw stomping ground and hideout. Tonight the earth would be his bed, a rock his pillow, the small flask of whiskey he carried the source of his warmth.

Shit, he thought ruefully, this might well be his last excursion for ninety days to six months.

He spurred Gypsy and rode on, across plateaus and into valleys, passing magnificent stone dikes, rushing streams and pristine meadows, mountains green with aspen, balsam and firs. The day had warmed slightly, and he spotted mule deer munching on weeds, horned larks flitting through the purple and pink wildflowers, a hawk circling overhead. The sun was bright, the sweet scent of nectar intoxicating, the rush of his heartbeat making him forget his troubles for a moment and just feel grateful he was alive.

Closer to the ghost town, he spotted evidence of the abandoned gold and silver mines in the area: a broken-down train trestle zigzagging across a mountain pass; an abandoned sluice sagging on its supports; a crumbling stamping mill slouched in a distant valley. Beyond the next pass, Mariposa itself was just as he remembered it, a long line of deserted shacks, dust and tumbleweed, yucca plants spiking through the splintered boardwalks, shattered windows rattling on weather-beaten facades and old doors creaking in the wind. He stared at the gray, sagging saloon, the roofless abandoned church with steeple still proudly intact, the old schoolhouse that stood battered but brave. The wind whistled a low dirge. He sighed. Once upon a time this place had been full of life and hustle and bustle. Whenever he passed through, he wondered what it would have been like to have lived here a century ago. Hell, in so many ways he was a man of another age, a man of the Old West, just like his granddad. Maybe he belonged in a place like this, a place where time didn't seem to exist. There was a time, he reflected ironically, when women were women, when they honored and obeyed their men and shared their old-fashioned values. Was it too much to hope for to find a woman who respected her man—and herself?

Evidently it was, and he'd be spending a good spell in the calaboose contemplating this very injustice.

After he rode out of town and turned east, the landscape grew increasingly craggy as he approached Reklaw Gorge, the old Cheyenne burial ground and outlaw hideout. The place was rumored to be haunted. Lucky recalled that the ghostly legends had gained new momentum five years earlier when a young university professor had disappeared from a stagecoach dispatched on an outing from the now-defunct Broken Buck Dude Ranch. Lucky remembered reading about the bizarre event in the *Buck Hollow Rag*. Even though Jessica Garrett's three companions and the driver had reappeared a few days later, bringing back with them a journal purportedly written by the professor herself and claiming she was now happily living in the late 1880s, the woman's parents had been appalled to hear that their daughter had supposedly vanished into thin air. Not to mention the fact that all four stagecoach survivors had come back dazed and crazy. Why, they'd even claimed outlaws had attacked them and kidnapped Professor Garrett. All four men had been committed to a psych ward for observation, and several families had sued the Broken Buck for negligence, forcing the dude ranch into bankruptcy.

Lucky chuckled at the memory. The whole episode had been crazy as hell as far as he was concerned. But then, sometimes strange things happened here in the hills of Colorado.

Indeed, as Lucky nudged Gypsy onto a ridge overlooking Reklaw Gorge, he caught a curious sight on the first step of the zigzag dike stretching beneath him. There on an outcropping of volcanic rock was perched the relic of an old stagecoach. He drew closer and dismounted, staring over the rim at the heap of wood and cast iron. Funny, he'd ridden this way before but had never seen this strange conveyance.

The carriage was obviously old as the hills, a faded yellow, its shell riddled with bullet holes and the washed-out letters L.L. inscribed on its doors. L.L. Damn! Could this be a reference to Lila Lullaby, the infamous Colorado City cathouse madam, another legend in these parts? Lucky was amazed. Could this actually be the celebrated old "parlor wagon" the whore had used to fetch her girls out to service the miners? The one the dude ranch had later bought and renovated for taking guests on excursions? The very vehicle from which the young professor had disappeared? Had the ranch proprietor, Woody Lynch, abandoned it here sometime after his enterprise had failed?

"Well, I'll be damned," Lucky muttered.

Now intensely curious, he lowered himself onto the ledge to have a closer look at the rattletrap conveyance. One wagon wheel was missing, and three others stood rusty and askew. Through one partially opened door he caught a glimpse of moth-eaten, burgundy velvet upholstery, and holes in the roof and floor. A musty, aged smell emanated forth from the interior.

Lucky could only shake his head. Had Woody Lynch really put the stagecoach here, or was this somebody else's idea of a joke?

He was closing the door when he flinched at the sound of hoofbeats approaching from above. He scrambled back onto the ridge, only to watch a stranger gallop toward him from the south. Reverting to instinct, Lucky drew out his pistol. As the rider grew closer, he caught a better look. Dressed in jeans, a sheepskin coat and a beige Stetson, he appeared to be in his late twenties and was pudgy, with a potbelly and a round baby face. A harmless enough looking character, definitely not the sheriff or anyone else Lucky knew from these parts. Still, under the circumstances he should exercise some caution.

Twenty yards from Lucky, the stranger pulled his mount to a halt and grimaced comically at Lucky's pistol. "Hey, mister, that's a pretty unfriendly greeting," he began in a high-pitched voice.

Lucky stood his ground, waving his Colt menacingly. "Who are you and what are you doing out here?"

The man gulped. "Cool down, will you, neighbor? I'm Grover Singleton, and I'm here visiting with my folks at their ranch south of Buck Hollow."

"Singleton?" Lucky asked with a frown. "Never heard of any Singletons in these parts."

"My family hasn't lived here very long." The man extended a hand in pleading. "Look, mister, would you mind lowering that gun? You're making me nervous as hell."

"You still haven't told me what you're doing way out here."

As the man's brown horse snorted, Grover Singleton glanced around in bewilderment. "Well, I went for a ride and got lost. Then I spotted your horse and hoped I'd found someone who could steer me back in the right direction."

Lucky gave a laugh. "Since I've never heard of your people that's unlikely. Don't you have a cell phone?"

"Nope." He grinned sheepishly. "Truth to tell, I ain't that fond of modern technology."

Lucky had to smile, for he'd clearly met a kindred spirit. "Me neither. I like to get away from civilization, not bring it closer."

"Amen." The stranger cleared his throat. "Still, if I don't return to the ranch soon, my folks are bound to worry. Can you at least tell me how to get back to Buck Hollow so I can call them from there?"

Lucky shook his head ruefully and shoved his pistol into his waist. This numbskull was no threat. "Sure. Why not?"

The man grinned in obvious relief and dismounted. Stepping closer to Lucky, he eyed him curiously. "When I rode up I saw you climbing up from that gorge. Any reason?"

"As a matter of fact, yeah. Come have a look at this, stranger."

Lucky pointed out the broken-down stagecoach to his companion, then answered Grover's many questions, relating his own theories about the Broken Buck Dude Ranch and how the stagecoach might have gotten stranded here. Grover appeared fascinated, chuckling over the account of the female professor who had supposedly been abducted across time by an outlaw gang. By the time ten minutes of jawboning had passed, Lucky found he was actually enjoying Grover's company.

Afterward he gave Grover directions for getting back

to Buck Hollow. "Head southwest toward that high mountain peak," he directed, pointing off into the distance. "That's Broken Buck Mountain. The town lies directly beneath it."

Grover was gazing off at the mountain. "Thanks; sounds pretty easy."

"It is. Anything else I can do for you?"

He shook his head. "No, but let me give you a ten for your trouble."

"Naw, no problem."

But the man was already reaching inside his jacket—only to pull out a black revolver.

"What?" Lucky cried, backing away.

Watching Lucky reach for his own gun, the other man yelled, "Freeze, mister! Don't even think about it!"

Lucky gulped, his fingers paused in midair as he eyed his adversary in mingled shock and disbelief. A dramatic change had come over Grover Singleton's features; a mask of surly anger had replaced the jovial facade. Even his voice had gone low and was full of menace. And his steely automatic was pointed at Lucky with deadly intent.

"Pitch that weapon into the gorge right now or I'll drop you where you stand," the man ordered.

"What the hell—"

"I said drop it! Careful-like. Use two fingers."

Lucky stared.

"Ya think I don't know how to use this gun?" Grover asked, striding forward aggressively. "I'll have you know I'm a county deputy from Colorado Springs."

At that Lucky snorted a laugh. "A baby-face like you is a lawman?"

14

Grover fired a shot that whizzed past Lucky's cheek and practically shattered his left eardrum.

"Well, you don't have to get so testy about it," Lucky retorted with a grimace.

"Your weapon!"

Gingerly Lucky retrieved his grandfather's Colt, then pitched it over the embankment. He rubbed his smarting ear. "What the hell burr do you got on your ass, mister?"

"The burr is, you tried to kill my sister," Grover practically spat back.

"Your sister?" Lucky was amazed.

"Yeah. Misti Childers."

"Misti? You're her brother? I didn't even know she had one."

"Our parents divorced when we were young, and my ma remarried and raised me in Colorado Springs. When Misti called me this morning to tell me what you did, I came straight out here to track down and kill the low-down coward who'd scared the wits out of my baby sister."

Lucky's face heated with anger. "Did your baby sister tell you what she was doing? That I found her in a cheap motel room, screwing my best—"

"Shut up!" A muscle jerked in Grover's cheek. "I don't care if she was screwing in a lightbulb. Nothin' excuses attempted murder."

"Oh, yeah? In these parts when a woman cheats on her man it excuses a lot more."

Grover waved his weapon. "You got a lot of bluster for a man about to meet his maker."

Damn, this was serious! Lucky thought. He'd gone

from a potential ninety days in lockup to a looming death penalty. Lucky sized up his opponent, deciding the man looked entirely too nervous to be predictable. Grover's jaw was twitching, his hand quivering on his weapon. If Lucky tried to jump him, he might well get shot for his troubles. "Look, can't we work this out?"

"You should have thought of that before you scared the bejesus out of my sister." Grover stepped back, while never taking his eyes off Lucky, and pulled several lengths of twine from his saddlebags. "Now back up."

"Back up?" Lucky stared over the rim of the gorge. "There's nowhere to go but down."

Grover grinned. "Yeah. That's the idea."

Lucky backed up as far as he could, gulping.

"Now turn around."

Lucky complied, and felt his hands being tied from the back.

"Now step down to that stagecoach."

Tossing the stranger a mystified glance, Lucky again did his bidding, though it was far from easy trying to skid down the steep slope with his hands bound.

Jumping down beside Lucky, Grover flung open the stagecoach door and jerked his head toward the interior. "Get inside."

A sick, terrifying prospect seized Lucky. "You're not thinking of—"

"I said, get your butt inside that coach!"

In short order, Lucky found himself inside the dusty stagecoach, his tall form doubled over on the floorboards as he felt Grover binding his feet, then tying them to his hands. The door slammed and he heard his assailant's mocking voice. "Happy trails, partner."

"Holy hell, you can't mean—"

"Good riddance, you sonofabitch."

Oh, God, Lucky thought desperately, this couldn't be happening! But it was. Even as he cringed in horror, the stagecoach creaked into sickening motion, then went tumbling off the embankment, crashing repeatedly as it careened down the long stair-step expanse of dike.

"Sheeeeee-it!" Lucky screamed, his body mercilessly banged and jostled and pitched. Then, even as he thought things couldn't possibly get any worse, he felt the entire crumbling conveyance being launched into sheer, thin space, and then . . .

Everything went black.

The bastard had it coming.

This was Grover Singleton's vengeful thought as he watched Lucky Lamont plunge to his death as the stagecoach crashed into the gorge below in an explosion of dust and noise. His sister Misti would be tickled pink to hear the no-good scoundrel had met his maker. Besides, Misti had offered to buy him an antique Winchester rifle he'd coveted for ages if he'd only give the SOB his comeuppance. And he had, in spades.

Now to be sure . . .

Gingerly Grover maneuvered his horse down the steep embankment into the gorge, then quickly galloped over to the old stagecoach's final resting place. Dismounting, he approached the pile of rubble and moved aside several boards, searching for his victim.

Shit! What was this? No body. Nothing at all but shattered wood and twisted metal. His gaze scoured the wall of dike above him, but he spotted no sign of a corpse anywhere. Sneezing at the rising dust, he began rummaging again. He checked through the stack of debris several times but still found no hint that a human being had ever been there. What the hell? What would he tell Misti now? Where on earth was Lucky Lamont?

Had Lucky gotten lucky after all?

Chapter One

Mariposa, Colorado
The Past

"I've just about had my fill of your tomfoolery," Cole Reklaw scolded his children as he angrily paced the parlor.

Molly Reklaw cowered on the long horsehair sofa along with her four brothers, all of them watching their irate father prowl about while lecturing them soundly. In his mid-fifties, Cole Reklaw was a daunting figure with his tall, lean frame, graying dark hair and grim though handsome features. At the moment he was more menacing than a snorting bull, with boots shaking the floorboards and hands gesturing passionately. Even Ma and Grandma seemed wise enough to keep their distance; both women peered anxiously from the corridor.

How Molly wished *she* had a hole to hide in! For the

19

five Reklaw children had gotten in real trouble this time. Molly's four older brothers looked a sight and reeked of stale tobacco and cheap whiskey. Zach, the eldest, had a black eye; Vance sported a cut on his chin, Matt bandaged knuckles and Cory a swollen nose. The four had stayed out all night, getting into another fight at the local saloon and landing in the county jail.

As for eighteen-year-old Molly, usually she was the apple of her daddy's eye, but this morning things hadn't gone particularly well for her, either. Even as Pa was busy paying the saloonkeeper for damages and convincing the sheriff to release her brothers from jail, Grandma had caught Molly out behind the shed smoking a cigarette. Molly's pleas—that this was, after all, the year 1911, and surely women would soon get the vote—had fallen on deaf ears. Grandma had hauled Molly inside by her ear—and thus the five Reklaw children were receiving their tongue-lashing in unison.

"I can't believe I've raised such a bunch of rascals," Cole ranted. He pointed an accusatory finger toward his daughter. "You, Molly, out smoking behind the barn—"

"It was the shed, Pa."

"Never mind! My point is, you were behaving like some cheap floozy, when your ma raised you better."

"But menfolk smoke," she retorted, forever the rebel. "Why can't I?"

"Because you're a lady. Or you're supposed to be."

Molly jerked a thumb toward her brothers. "Well, at least I didn't land in the hoosegow like these fools."

"Hey, who are you calling fools?" asked Zach, glowering at his sister.

"Speaking of which," Cole added, "you boys are no better than her, bustin' up the saloon—"

"But Pa," protested Matt, "them Hicks boys insulted us bad, calling Cory here a pantywaist for volunteerin' at the library. 'Sides, you always said boys'll be boys and we need to sow a few wild oats—"

"Not by becoming habitual felons," Cole chided. He eyed his sons narrowly. "And by the way, Sheriff Hackett mentioned to me that there was another train robbery out near Dillyville the other day. You boys know anything about that?"

All four went wide-eyed at this pronouncement. "No, Pa," insisted Vance. "This is the first we've heard of it."

Cole appeared unconvinced. "Are you boys forgetting that this family had to be exiled to Wyoming for almost a decade due to these sorts of shenanigans?"

"Pa, we ain't robbed no trains," Zach argued. Hopefully he added, "But we did hear Dirty Dutch Dempsey was getting his gang back together."

"Oh, don't give me those old rumors," scoffed Cole. "Dempsey escaped the Colorado pen over twenty years ago, and he's gotta be dead as a post by now."

Vance snapped his fingers. "Then it's probably them Hicks boys, always up to no good."

"And you're not?" challenged his father.

"Sheriff Hackett should have locked up all them Hickses ages ago, only he favors Bart and Winky's widowed ma," argued Zach. "'Sides, begging your pardon, sir, but the sheriff probably only asked you 'cause you used to be an outlaw yourself—"

"Don't try to lay this on me." Cole shook a finger at his son.

"No, sir," replied Zach, gulping.

"Pa, the real problem is, you keep treating us like children rather than grown men," protested Matt.

"Because you act like children."

" 'Sides, all of us are squeezed up in that rickety old bunkhouse like rats in a trap," added Vance. "It's time for us boys to move out on our own. You always said one day you'd divvy up the ranch among the four of us—"

"Hey, what about me?" protested Molly.

"Aw, you're a girl, and you don't count," answered Matt, waving her off.

"Yeah, you'll marry up," declared Vance. "Let your future husband provide you a spread."

"So you four sidewinders get to cheat me out of my inheritance?" Irate, Molly turned to her mother. "Ma, is that fair?"

Jessica Reklaw, a lovely, auburn-haired middle-aged woman wearing a Victorian-style yellow muslin dress, stepped inside the room to face her husband. "Cole, Molly has a point. If we do divide up the ranch one day, it needs to be among all five children."

Cole smiled at his wife while scratching his graying head. "Maybe so, honey, but the way these holy terrors are carrying on, that won't be any time soon."

"But Pa," pleaded Zach, "at least let me have my portion now. I'm the eldest. If you'll just turn over the lower five hundred—"

"The lower five hundred?" cut in Matt. "So you get the best piece of land on the whole ranch, with the best water, the best grassland?"

"*I* want that parcel," put in Vance.

"So do I," added Cory, who was usually the quiet one.

"Me, too!" declared Molly.

Bickering broke out among the children. At the sidelines, their father listened for a moment in scowling silence—then, curiously, Cole Reklaw smiled. "You know, maybe for once you troublemakers have had a flash of inspiration. Maybe that's not such a bad idea, after all, all of you with the same portion of land."

"What?" cried Matt. "You're going to give it to all of us? Why, we'll kill each other over it."

"Sure 'nuff," agreed Zach with a vehement nod.

Grandma, a huge, sagging-jowled, silver-haired woman, lumbered into the room with her typically painful gait, dragging her heavy dark skirts behind her. "Cole Reklaw, the boys is right. Have you up and lost your mind? You're gonna give the lower five hundred to them five and let 'em plow each other under over it? You know, I'm still hoping for a great-grandchild or two one of these days, before I fly off to the sweet bye and bye, and that ain't never gonna happen if we have to bury all five of these heathens."

"Heathens?" protested Vance. "Grandma, you know right well Ma makes us all read the Bible and to go to church on Sundays."

" 'Heathens is as heathens does,' " Grandma pronounced piously.

"Pa, you're not really going to give it to the five of us, are you?" interjected Cory with a stricken expression. "You'll never hear the end of the wrangling."

Cole chuckled. "I agree, son. My point is that all five of you want that same parcel. So I just may use it as an opportunity to make you grow up"—he nodded toward his mother—"and give Ma a shot at those great-grandchildren she covets."

"What do you mean, Cole?" Jessica asked with a puzzled smile.

He glanced lovingly from his wife to his mother. "Ma, remember how, twenty-three years ago, you established a contest for my brothers and me, announcing that the best-behaved would win Jessica's hand?"

Ma's jaw dropped open and she swatted Cole's arm. "You ain't saying you want them four whelps to fight it out over their *sister?* Why, of all the evil, unclean, perverted—"

"No, Ma, no," Cole reassured her, laughing. "They won't be fighting over their sister but the land."

"Huh?" Ma asked.

With seven sets of eyes fixed intently on him, Cole continued. "What I'm suggesting is, what if I offer the lower five hundred as a prize to the first one of these five devils to grow up, marry and produce a grandchild for Jessie and me?"

Grandma lit up, playfully batting Cole's arm. "Well, now you're talking! Son, that's a right fine idea. Make them whippersnappers work for their portion. Like history repeatin' itself, eh?"

Jessica appeared appalled. "I think the whole thing sounds diabolical."

Cole winked. "What else do you expect from me, honey?"

"Cole, really," she scolded.

Meanwhile the "devils" also began objecting. "Are you saying we got to marry up now, Pa?" demanded Zach.

"Yes, marry and produce an offspring if you want that land—just like I fought to win your ma." Cole proudly put his arm around Jessica's waist.

"But your bride came from across time," protested Vance. With a cynical eye-roll, he added, "Or so you say."

Molly shot Vance a forbearing look. Years ago their ma had told all five of them the astonishing story of how she had traveled back in time to be with their pa. Ma had made them all swear never to divulge this bizarre family secret. She needn't have bothered. Although Molly's three elder brothers did believe that their pa and his outlaw brothers had bushwhacked their ma off a stagecoach, they'd totally dismissed her "haywire" assertion that she had first traveled across time in that very vehicle. They had decided her story was a fairy tale, like Santa Claus or the Easter Bunny. Though Cory had been a little more open-minded, he'd still ultimately sided with his brothers.

But Molly knew better. Unlike her boorish siblings, she was a believer in all things possible in the universe. Plus, she was educated—Ma had seen to that. Granted, she hadn't taken to their ma's set of *The Harvard Classics* with the same relish as Cory, but she loved tales of adventure and had voraciously devoured every dime novel she could get her hands on—everything from tales of Deadwod Dick and Calamity Jane to all of the Horatio Alger stories. She knew all about the exploits of Colorado legend Dirty Dutch Dempsey, the outlaw turned prison escapee whom Zach had mentioned. She also loved science fiction, Jules Verne and H. Rider Haggard. Heck, how could her moron siblings believe in time travel, when they'd never even opened H. G. Wells's *The Time Machine*?

Her father's voice cut into her thoughts. "You mean you men aren't capable of finding wives?"

"Pretty women are scarce as hen's teeth in these parts," protested Matt. "There's the Trumble sisters, but old man Trumble has had it in for us ever since the family moved here and Grandma refused to let him court her."

Grandma harrumphed. "You hush up, Matthew Reklaw. You think I want to spend my waning years washing out Ezra Trumble's stinky undergarments or rinsing his false teeth? I have plenty else to do around here, I'll have you know. You five have practically been the death of me already with your reckless ways."

"Well, like we told Pa, we ain't sowed all our wild oats yet," contended Zach.

"To heck with your wild oats," pronounced their father. "You four need to start thinking about brides and babies." He glanced meaningfully at Molly. "And you, a groom and a baby."

For a moment all five children scowled at their father, then Matt spoke up. "Pa, you're being unfair."

"Too bad, then. You children want the land, you play by the rules and win the game."

"Well, I ain't playing," declared Matt, setting his jaw.

"Me neither," added Zach.

"Well, I am," declared Molly with a grin.

"What?" her brothers cried in unison.

Molly shot to her feet, only to see her siblings staring murderously at her. "You four are nothing but a pack of sissies," she accused with a superior air. "It takes a real woman to win a tough fight, and I'm the lady who's going to do it."

"You a lady?" jeered Matt.

"Yeah, what man is gonna want a pistol like you?" added Vance.

Although dressed in jeans and a shirt, Molly promptly simpered, doing her best imitation of a blushing belle, complete with dimples and fluttering eyelashes. "Hide and watch, fellas."

Vance popped up. "Well, if you think we're just gonna sit here while baby sister tries to best us—"

"Yeah!" seconded Zach, following suit, with Matt and Cory jumping up soon after to add their own affirmations.

"Well, well, good for the five of you," pronounced their smiling father. "Let the contest begin."

"Yeah, bring on them great-grandbabies!" added Ma, clapping her hands.

"Oh, brother," groaned Jessica.

Molly grinned at her four brothers. Clearly the game was on.

Chapter Two

Perhaps one day her hero would come.

This was Molly Reklaw's thought an hour later as she sat on her palomino horse, Prissy, on a ridge overlooking the eastern edge of Haunted Gorge, ofttimes called Reklaw Gorge in this region. Sanchez, ranch handyman and Molly's faithful escort, was perched on his mount beside her.

After the scene in the parlor, Molly had grown weary of bickering with her older brothers and had ridden away. It wasn't easy being the youngest of the five Reklaw children, not to mention the only girl, with four unruly older brothers to bully her and boss her around. Truth to tell, she and Cory had a special bond, though it was fragile at times. He was the youngest male, the sweet one, if boys could ever be called sweet, but he lived in the shadow of his more strong-willed older brothers. As for Zach, Vance and Matt, they could be real hornets at times. Why, just last week the ruffians had thrown cattle chips at Molly and chased her under the house, all because she'd claimed she could outshoot them all. Well, she could! Her ma had always told her a woman could do *anything* she set her mind to—certainly anything a man could do. In fact, Molly had been named for Molly Brown—one of her true heroines—and everyone knew that Molly was a humdinger.

Only problem was, this Molly was sorely outnumbered.

Thus the only peace she knew was out here on the range. For several years now she'd been periodically watching this old Indian burial ground where spooky things were known to happen, including the strange events that had brought her parents together. Crazy though it seemed, she was waiting for her own special someone to appear.

This was a fanciful side to Molly's nature that, so far, only her mother really knew about. She'd tried to confide in Sanchez, but every time she spoke of her ma traveling through time and her pa bushwhacking his bride off Lila Lullaby's old parlor wagon, the poor Mexican would start crossing himself and muttering to the heavens. Being Molly's guard, he had no choice but to tolerate her eccentricities—but how her brothers would laugh if they knew she was sitting here waiting for a man to appear. Molly, the original hellcat, indulging in such romantic foolishness.

Molly wasn't sure she believed in true love, but she was a believer in destiny. Ever since her folks had told her how they'd really met—with her ma traveling back here from the future to meet her pa—the story had en-

thralled her. Along with the world her ma had cheer-
fully left behind to be with her pa. Well, if *she* lived in
an age of refrigerated houses, horseless carriages
faster than a Rocky Mountain avalanche and rockets to
the moon, it would take more than dynamite or one of
those newfangled nuclear bomb blasts to banish her
from such a paradise.

Thus as a child Molly had woven a fantasy that
someday her hero would come and take her off to that
fabulous world of the future, where women were no
longer chattel and men knew their places. That
prospect still held its appeal today, though she'd miss
Ma, Pa and Grandma—Cory, too, she supposed. And
actually, following the family powwow this morning,
the idea of winning the lower five hundred in a contest
against her obnoxious brothers, besting them once
and for all and establishing a place of her own, where
she was queen, was equally tempting.

For Molly had another dream. Though she had little
use for men, their seed was another matter. Tomboy
though she was, she purely loved babies, and had all
her life. Her uncle Billy and aunt Dumpling were still
completing their brood, and only yesterday she'd
rocked their three-month-old twins out on the porch of
their house. She adored the babies' smell, their soft
skin, the cooing sounds they made, the way their tiny
arms wrapped around her neck . . . And the process of
making those babies must not be half-bad, either, as
often as Billy and Dumpling seemed to do it.

Now all she needed was a suitable male of her own.
Hopefully one of those fellows from the future that her

ma had described as "wimps," a man who would let his wife wear the pants in the family.

"Señorita, *mira, alli!*" declared Sanchez at her side.

Her thoughts scattering, Molly frowned at her escort. Whenever Sanchez became excited, he reverted to his native Spanish. When she turned her head in the direction he had pointed, she became appalled and fascinated herself.

What the hell . . . ! As Molly watched in amazement, a decrepit horseless stagecoach materialized on a high ledge opposite them, came tumbling over the ridge and went crashing down the zigzag line of dike into the valley below. Molly grimaced at the earsplitting sounds of wood shattering and metal screeching. If she hadn't seen it with her own eyes, she never would have believed it! Within twenty seconds the crazed runaway had exploded at the bottom of the gorge, and all that remained was a pile of splintered wood and twisted metal, awash in a haze of rising dust.

Molly's mouth hung open. "I'll be a horse's . . . Did you see that, Sanchez?"

The Mexican was busy crossing himself. "*Madre de Dios!* A stagecoach with no horse or driver, flying like a bird. It's the haunted *coche.*"

"The haunted . . . ?" Molly's eyes grew huge. Sanchez might not be the same believer in destiny that she was, but he, like everyone in these parts, had heard the legend of Lila Lullaby and her hussy wagon. "You can't mean Lila Lullaby's old parlor wagon? The same one that brought my ma and pa together?"

Sanchez gulped. "*Por favor,* señorita, you are driving me mad with your *loco* talk."

"But it makes perfect sense!" Molly went on in rising excitement, her gaze fixed on the wreckage. "Here I was, wishing for a bridegroom, and that old cat wagon comes flying right along, just like it did for my pa." She peered over the rim. "The wood is faded, but even from here I can see a yellowish cast. How amazing. Wonder if anyone's inside?"

Sanchez was staring at her in disbelief. "Señorita, no one could have survived that fall."

"Are you sure?" Molly grinned, her curiosity thoroughly piqued. "Come on, quit being a stick-in-the-mud. Let's go investigate."

With Sanchez protesting every step of the way, the two guided their mounts down the steep mountainside into the gorge, then galloped toward the pile of debris. Molly was the first to dismount, eyeing the heap of wood and metal from several angles. She dislodged a piece of faded wood with chipped yellow paint, and spotted the washed-out monogram, L.L.

"My God, it *is* Lila Lullaby's old parlor wagon!"

"*Caramba!*" muttered Sanchez, again crossing himself.

Then Molly heard a moan from somewhere inside the rubble. "Sanchez, did you hear that?"

He was backing away while violently shaking his head. "Santa Maria! *Es un espectro!*"

Molly waved a hand. "For Pete's sake. Of course it's not a ghost. Come on, you lazy saddle tramp, help me. There's someone trapped in there."

Though his eyes were huge, Sanchez dutifully obeyed,

hunkering down beside Molly. The two hurriedly pitched aside boards and metal, searching for the source of the groans. Soon they uncovered the body of a man.

"Well, I'll be damned." Molly stared down at the unconscious stranger, who was quite handsome, with thick, curly blond hair and a noble face. But he was dressed in typical cowboy garb, a checked blue shirt, faded denims and dusty boots. "Looks like some no-account wrangler," she muttered to Sanchez in obvious disappointment. "Though he's a comely one. 'Spose he's still alive?"

As if to answer, the stranger thrashed around a bit and grunted, though he still didn't open his eyes.

Sanchez leaned over, retrieved an item from the rubble and handed it to Molly. "Señorita, look at this."

Molly frowned at the odd-looking, thin leather wallet. She flipped it open, only to gape at a strange collection of cards, made with some hard, smooth, fantastical-looking and -feeling material. Some of the cards were stamped with words and numbers, and one small card held the cowboy's image—like a tiny photograph, but all done up in colors!

Molly pulled it out and stared at it in stupefaction. There was the stranger, grinning at her with his bright blue eyes, straight nose and bold, sensual mouth. "Colorado Driver License," it said. It listed the man's name—"Lucky Lamont"—and his place of residence in Buck Hollow, a town she'd never even heard of. Her eyes froze on the date of his birth: January 15, 1979.

1979! Could it be? That was almost seventy years in the future! Frantically digging further in the wallet, she found a typewritten receipt for a pair of dress boots with the date April 2, 2004.

2004! Oh, God, did this mean . . . ? But what if the items were faked?

Not likely, she quickly realized. For who could have created that amazing photograph and those cards made of that slick, astounding material? Flipping through the rest of the wallet's contents, she found stubs for rodeo tickets—also dated April of 2004—and outlandish-looking paper money, ten- and twenty-dollar bills labeled with "Series 2001" and "Series 2004."

At last she realized only one explanation made sense.

"Great jumping Jehoshaphat!" Molly cried, staring from the receipt to the man. "He's not some no-account saddle tramp! He's from the future—the year twenty-aught-four—and he came across time in Lila Lullaby's hussy wagon, just like my ma did for my pa."

"Señorita, *por favor*," pleaded Sanchez. "You are talking out of your head."

"No, don't you understand?" she cried. "He has to be from the future. It's like history repeating itself, Lila's stagecoach bringing me a man just like it brought my pa his woman—"

But then Molly became distracted by a bellow of pain. She glanced downward just as the stranger opened his gorgeous dark blue eyes and scowled up at her. He shook his head as if to clear it, then stared at her harder, speaking in a deep, though hoarse, voice. "What in hell is going on here?"

Molly laughed, totally delighted with herself. "You should know that, mister. My hero has arrived. And you're going to win me the lower five hundred."

Chapter Three

What in blue blazes had happened to him? This was Lucky Lamont's desperate thought as he stared up at the young woman standing above him, scrutinizing him inch by inch as if he was a prize bull in a pen. Who was she and what was the nonsense she was spouting about him being her hero and winning her the lower five hundred?

Not that he could even think very well at the moment. Every inch of him blazed with pain from the brutal ride he'd taken down the dike in the driverless stagecoach. A board poked him in the back and a huge chunk of cast iron lay crushing his legs. He was stunned that he'd even endured the breakneck plunge.

Indeed, had it not been for the agony he felt, he'd never have believed he was still alive. But somehow he had survived, unless he was already in heaven and this was an angel standing above him.

A cherub in blue denim, he thought humorously,

though she did have the face of an angel. A strong chin, wide mouth, delicate little nose, large green eyes, long dark lashes and high arched brows. She was dressed, however, like a cowgirl, in her jeans and matching gabardine shirt, a wealth of lush auburn curls spilling from beneath her western hat and dangling about her shoulders.

Next to her stood a small, mustachioed Hispanic man in an outdated poncho and sombrero. He was crossing himself and muttering to the Virgin Mary in Spanish. Beyond the pair, two range horses munched on the nearby grass.

Who was this odd pair? He'd never before seen them in these parts. But then, he'd encountered some curious types today.

"You all right, mister?" his rescuer asked in a lilting feminine voice. "That was some fall you just took."

"Who are you, honey?" Lucky replied in strained tones.

"Hey, don't you be calling me *honey*," the young woman chided. "It's not fitting until we're officially affianced."

"Officially affi . . . *what?*" Lucky's protest was lost in a grunt of pain as a metal chunk shifted on his legs.

She sank down on her haunches beside him. "Hey, stranger, you aren't going to die on me, are you?"

Through the haze of his pain, Lucky somehow realized that the length of twine connecting his hands to his feet had snapped during the harrowing ride, but otherwise he remained bound. Raggedly he replied, "If someone doesn't untie me and get this g'damned axle off my legs, I may."

"Hey, you don't have to resort to cursing," she said primly.

He spoke through clenched teeth. "Lady, you crawl under this torture device and see how long you're spouting hearts and flowers."

She stood, turned to the Mexican and snapped her fingers. "Sanchez!"

"*Sí*, señorita." Convulsively crossing himself, the little man stepped forward, eyeing Lucky with trepidation.

"Come on, let's get to work," the woman ordered him.

"Easy now!" Lucky exclaimed, as aghast at the thought of them trying to free him as he was at his current plight.

Undaunted, both knelt and began trying to extricate him, tossing aside scraps of wood and chunks of iron. Within seconds Lucky was in everlasting hell. With each shift of metal or wood he suffered the torment of the damned. Though he winced and grimaced aplenty, he was too proud to cry out. But when they rolled the heavy, twisted axle off his legs, the agony was so exquisite that he bit his bottom lip.

The woman dusted off her hands and regarded his ashen face with a frown. "Whoa, mister, don't you go swooning on me. You're as white as one of my grandma's antimacassars."

"Her *what?*" He sucked in a tortured breath. "Can't you please untie my hands and feet?"

She appeared skeptical. "We'll see to that directly."

Lucky was incredulous. "What? What the hell? How do you expect me to get up, trussed up like a g'damned turkey?"

She shook a finger at him. "Mister, I said no profanity. I declare, you swear worse than my brothers."

"What brothers?"

The Mexican extended his hand. "Perhaps I may pull you up, señor?"

Lucky moved tentatively, only to yelp in pain. "Not with the two broken legs I think I may have."

"Two broke legs?" the woman repeated, looking him over with a scowl. "Well, we'll just have to fetch you home so Grandma can set 'em."

"Who's Grandma?"

"I know you had a rocky ride through time—"

"Through *what?*" What psych ward had this woman escaped from?

"Just don't you go thinking having a busted limb or two will get you out of marrying me."

Lucky stared at her, unable to believe what a whack job this woman was. Again he wondered if he had died—and gone to Looney Tune hell. "Marry you? Are you nuts?"

"Nope, and I'm taking you straight home so my pa can fetch the preacher. Ain't no way I'll let my no-account brothers best me in this contest."

"What contest?"

"We'll be wed before sundown, even if we have to roll you to the altar in a wheelbarrow," she finished with determination.

Lucky remained stunned. "Just who in the hell are you and why do you think I'm going to marry you?"

"I'm Molly Reklaw—"

"Reklaw? You mean like the gorge?"

"Yeah, like the gorge. And you're going to marry me because you're my destiny from across time."

"Your what? What time?"

She tossed him a superior smirk and waved his wallet at him. "The year twenty-aught-four. Isn't that where you came from . . . Mr. Lucky Lamont?"

What the hell did this lunatic mean, where he came from? "Right," he mocked. "And this *is* the year 2004, in case you hadn't noticed."

The woman laughed while the Mexican turned a sickening shade of green and began silently praying. "Mister, it's not the year 2004 but the year 1911, and you've come back in time to be my hero."

Lucky had thought he couldn't possibly be any more flabbergasted than he already was, but he was wrong. "Your *what?* The year *what?*"

"Don't you know how to say anything but *what?*" she mocked. "You sound like a darned Victrola with a stuck needle." She waved him off matter-of-factly. "Don't worry, my ma will explain it all to you. It happened to her, too, you see."

Lucky could barely speak. "You're a crazy woman!"

She clenched her jaw at that, and Lucky felt a surge of self-satisfaction that he'd managed to rile her. "Now don't you go insulting me or my pa will bust your chops," she scolded, then turned to the Mexican. "Sanchez, help me hoist my fiancé over my horse."

Lucky was so horrified by the prospect of being "hoisted" that her reference to his being her fiancé went almost unnoticed. "Please," he pleaded, shuddering at the anticipated torture, "you can't move me right now. Why, I could have a fractured spine, or—"

"Oh, quit your bellyaching," the woman shot back.

"You must be made of tougher stuff than that if you survived the journey across time, not to mention the plunge into this gorge."

Lucky couldn't believe she was actually going to do this. "Won't you at least untie me?"

"Nope. My daddy bushwhacked his bride back to the ranch and I think I'll do the same with my groom." She flashed him a simpering smile. " 'Sides, you ain't exactly taken to the notion of wedding me, have you, handsome?"

"No shit!" he roared back.

"Hey, I said no bad language. You want my grandma to think I've brought home a foul-mouthed heathen?"

It was on the tip of his tongue to say he couldn't care less what her grandma thought. But then she and Sanchez began to *hoist*—and Lucky screamed.

Every muscle in Lucky's battered body that hadn't been abused so far was tortured during the interminable ride to the crazy woman's ranch. His long, lanky body lay dangling over her lap, and the saddle horn was gouging a hole in his belly. His face was pressed against her knee, his nose slammed repeatedly against her shin even as he smelled the scent of her womanly skin and absorbed her heat. A terrain covered in rocks, grass and Colorado wildflowers bounced past his aching eyes as his sorer-than-hell body was repeatedly bumped, jostled and slammed.

"Lady, please, show some mercy," he pleaded. "You're killing me."

"Oh, hush, or I'll gag you, too."

Lucky ground his teeth at this possibility. Clearly there was no reasoning with this she-devil; she was a lunatic.

After what seemed forever, he felt her horse descending into a valley, where cattle grazed and fields of fledgling wheat and corn waved in the distance. At last the horses came to a halt in a dusty yard, and as Lucky sneezed and groaned, he caught sight of chickens scurrying about in a barnyard, and steps leading to a whitewashed house where two brown-and-white cattle dogs dozed on the porch. Then the vixen who had captured him dismounted, unsheathed a rifle and fired it into the air; she followed that with an earsplitting rebel yell that had the poor Hispanic man muttering blasphemies.

Oh, God, what was next? A firing squad?

Even as his ears were still ringing from the rifle crack and shriek, the dogs began to howl, and he heard the thunder of running footsteps and watched a group of people pour out of the house amid shouts and expostulations. This had to be the family she'd spoken about. He spotted an attractive middle-aged couple in antiquated clothing and four handsome young men in farm attire—three were dark-haired, while the fourth and smallest was auburn-haired like his captor. Lumbering along at the end of the entourage was a huge old woman with a fiercely set, grumpy face—undoubtedly Grandma of the antimacassars. He could not believe the bizarre costumes these folks wore, or their primitive surroundings. Had he landed among some oddball religious sect?

Even as he was contemplating this, one of the mongrels raced over to sniff him and lick his nose. Lucky mouthed an epithet, and the dog whined and scurried away.

"Molly, what the hell is going on here?" demanded the middle-aged man.

His captor patted him on the rump, making Lucky churn in impotent fury. "Daddy, I've won the contest. I've brought home my bridegroom."

"You've what?"

Everyone began talking at once then, and more warm bodies surrounded Lucky. The second dog licked his ear, while the plump old grandma leaned over to peer at him with her garish features. "You've brought home your bridegroom, eh? Why, this fella's all beat up, like he's been to hell and back."

"No, lady," Lucky all but spat. "I've landed in hell."

That comment caused several family members to snicker. Then his captor's father demanded, "Molly, who is this man? Where did you find him, and why is he lying hog-tied across your saddle?"

"His name is Lucky Lamont, Daddy, and I found him in Haunted Gorge, just like you found Ma," she declared proudly. "He tumbled over the ridge in Lila Lullaby's old parlor wagon, and he was already hog-tied, all set to fetch home and marry."

"You're lying!" accused one of her brothers.

"No, I'm not, Matthew. Ask Sanchez here. We watched this stranger crash into the gorge. He's the one I've waited for from the future. I found him there just like Daddy found Ma."

Her father scratched his head. "This doesn't seem possible, does it, Jessie?"

An attractive middle-aged woman with auburn hair stepped up to join him, her expression awed. "Cole, do you really think it could happen—again?"

Before he could answer, Molly yanked Lucky's bill-fold from her pocket and handed it to her mother. "Here, Ma, have a look for yourself. It'll tell you all about how he's from the year twenty-aught-four."

"Two thousand four!" the woman gasped.

As she opened the wallet, a brother protested, "Pa, I don't care where the hell this cowboy is from. Molly can't just hog-tie some wrangler and force him to wed her. Ain't she gotta win and woo him just like us boys'll have to do with our own chosen ladies?"

Frowning at Lucky's driver's license, the woman corrected her son. "Vance, how many times have I told you not to say *ain't?*"

"Aw, Ma, when we talk all educated like you the men in town tease us."

"Well, the ladies you court won't mind your displaying an ounce or two of refinement," she chided.

"Still, don't—I mean *doesn't* she got to court him fair and square?"

As a brief silence fell, Lucky was not about to lose his cue. "Folks, would someone *please* get me the hell off this horse before I barf all over this barnyard?"

At last everyone seemed to realize his plight. The old woman patted him on the back. "Yep, let's see to this here poor fella before he hurls his biscuits." She shook a finger at Molly. "Granddaughter, this is no way to treat your future husband. I should give you a good brooming for this."

"Ah, Grandma, he's hardly dying."

"*Yet,*" Lucky intoned painfully.

Molly's dad whistled at her brothers. "All right, men, let's get him inside."

Breathlessly Lucky added, "Just be right careful, and—"

Before he could finish his sentence Lucky once again felt his battered body being heaved—and once again he screamed.

Chapter Four

"Well, he looks a prime specimen, if a bit busted up at the moment."

Would the indignities never end? Now Lucky lay on an old-fashioned feather bed in a front bedroom furnished with country-style antiques and kerosene lanterns, while the two females he'd learned were called Grandma and Jessie pulled off his clothing. They'd already dispensed with his boots and socks, and now Jessie was reaching for his belt buckle.

He grabbed her hand and eyed her with menace. "Hey, lady, I can tend to that myself."

"Just quiet down, son," she scolded back, matter-of-factly unbuckling his belt. "I've raised four sons and you don't have a thing I haven't seen before." Contradicting herself, she gasped. "Ma, look at this zipper! How amazing! I haven't seen one of these since—well, since before I made my journey back here."

"Well, I'll swan, Jessica."

Jessica! My journey back here . . . At the women's words, Lucky felt a sudden chill. Hadn't the professor who had disappeared five years ago also been named Jessica? Did that have anything to do with the fact that these crackpots seemed to believe they all lived in the year 1911?

Grandma was also peering downward, her eyes huge. "Why, of all the outlandish . . . Do you suppose Molly's right and this here fella really is from the future?"

Jessica, too, looked awed. "I never would have thought . . . but after looking at his wallet and this . . . well, I must admit it's looking more and more possible."

By now Lucky was thoroughly perplexed, not sure what to believe. And although he was not a particularly modest man, his face was also burning. These two women, babbling away about the future, were likely as crazy as the minx who had kidnapped him, and their frank perusal and blunt talk were tormenting the hell out of him. "Will you two ladies kindly quit staring at my crotch?" he managed, mortified to hear his voice crack.

Both of the ladies burst out laughing. "Full of piss and vinegar, ain't he?" asked Grandma. "He'll be a right good match for our Molly."

"Possibly," mused Jessica. She reached for the zipper. "Now relax, son, so we can have a look at your injuries."

He seized her wrist. "Hey, lady, that ain't where I'm injured."

"I know," she soothed in motherly tones. "But we can't exactly look at the rest of you without pulling off your pants, now can we?"

Lucky was reduced to pleading. "Ma'am, please, just

show me to your phone and I'll be out of here in two shakes."

She shook her head. "I'm afraid we don't have a telephone here on the ranch."

"Though they do have some of them newfangled contraptions in town," added Grandma.

"Newfangled?" Lucky repeated in bewilderment.

Jessica's lips curved with amusement. "Don't worry about that now. So your name's Lucky Lamont, eh?"

"Yes, ma'am." Much as Lucky hated to admit it, this woman had a calming effect on him.

She carefully unzipped him and began tugging down the tight jeans. "Well, Lucky, you seem to be one lucky fellow." She ran a hand down one leg, then the other. "You're bruised up, but no signs of anything broken here."

"He's well endowed, too," put in Grandma with a grin.

"Ma!" Jessica scolded, while Lucky turned every shade of purple.

Unrepentant, Grandma scowled at Jessica. "Well, we need to make sure he didn't lose none of his essentials when he crashed into that there gorge. All his childmaking equipment looks intact to me." She pointed at Lucky's briefs. "And as skimpy as that undergarment is, it leaves nothing to the imagination, if you know what I mean."

Both women took another look.

"Will you two *please* quit staring at my privates?" Lucky implored.

The ladies only laughed again, then removed his shirt and began seeing to his many cuts and scratches, cleaning them with soap and water. Although at first the soap stung, causing him to grimace and grind his teeth, once the cool compresses were applied, Lucky had to admit the ladies' ministrations felt good.

Their touch was a damn lot more soothing than that of the hellcat who had hauled him back here.

Afterward, Grandma dried her hands. "He'll live but could use a good soaking in Epsom salts. I'll go ready a bath for him while you tug off that underwear."

The woman lumbered out of the room, and Lucky glowered at Jessica, pressing his hands to his crotch. "Touch it and I'll kill you, lady."

She winked. "Don't worry, son, we'll allow you a little dignity."

Scant little, Lucky grumbled to himself.

As if reading his thoughts, she touched his arm and spoke solemnly. "Lucky, I know a lot has happened to you, a lot of bizarre things you can't possibly understand right now. In time, I'll try to explain it to you. You see, it all happened to me, too. It has to do with your destiny."

Lucky eyed her askance. What the hell was going on here? *Was* she the same Jessica he had heard about, the one who had disappeared? If so, had the same wacko cult kidnapped her, as well?

"I had a bath, too, when I first arrived here."

Half an hour later, every step was torture as Lucky hobbled through the bedroom toward the back door, leaning on Jessica, a skimpy towel tied at his midsection the only barrier between propriety and the altogether. He couldn't figure out which smarted more, his body or his pride. At least Jessica had allowed him some measure of privacy when she'd returned for him, turning her back while he slipped off his briefs and donned the towel.

Much as he found his current situation absurd, he remained amazed that this slender, middle-aged woman had such a soothing effect on him. She was pretty, too, with her graying auburn hair and classically lovely features. She seemed well educated . . .

Just like the Jessica Garrett who had disappeared would have been, he thought with another chill. But hadn't that Jessica been much younger—still in her twenties, if memory served?

She swung open the back door and helped him step down onto the porch. With a grimace he glanced about. The expanse of gray-blue deck was large and sheltered, protected on two sides by the whitewashed back walls of the house and on a third by a huge trellis teeming with fragrant honeysuckle.

Then he caught sight of Grandma, who stood proudly grinning in the center of the porch next to a steaming tub.

"Well, there you are," she greeted.

Taking in the small proportions of the tin tub, he managed a pained grunt. "You expect me to take a bath in *that?*"

"Sorry, son, but we ain't got any of the so-called *modern* stuff they got in town," Grandma replied. "No indoor plumbing, no electricity and none of them god-less horseless carriages, neither."

Lucky was stunned. "Damn—how far out in the country do you folks live?"

Jessica laughed. "Don't worry, Lucky. You'll catch on to everything in due course. Now go have a good soak in the tub."

He eyed her askance. "Looks more like a torture chamber to me."

"We'll help you in," she offered.

He grabbed his privates. "Not on your life!"

"If we leave, will you promise to get in?" cajoled Grandma.

Lucky glanced from her fiercely determined face to Jessica's. "Okay, then."

"Okay?" Grandma stepped forward to elbow Jessica. "Ain't he a hoot! He's talking that new slang like they do in the Springs, eh?"

Lucky rolled his eyes.

"Come on, Ma," urged Jessica. "Let's give the poor man some privacy." She turned to give him a quick once-over. "Looks like you're about the same size as my Vance. I'll lay out some clean clothes for you in the bedroom. After you're done, I imagine Mr. Reklaw and I will want to have a word with you."

"Yeah," Lucky muttered.

"Call if you need anything," Grandma added pleasantly.

Lucky flashed the women a stiff smile. "I think you folks have done enough for me already."

After they left him, Lucky struggled to gather his wits. These people were clearly whacked as hell, living in primitive squalor with no electricity, indoor plumbing or phone. He needed to get his butt away from this funny farm, pronto.

But how? After that jarring upside-down ride on hellcat's horse, he wasn't sure exactly where he was. Plus he couldn't just hightail it for the hills in his current state of undress. Though Jessica had mentioned laying out some clothes for him . . .

He tiptoed over to the bedroom door and eased it open. He froze. Jessica was there, gathering up his dirty duds, placing his wallet on the dresser; but so far she hadn't yet laid out any fresh garments. He might as well take a quick bath and soak his wounds in the Epsom salts. Then he'd sneak in, grab the clothes and make tracks before anyone caught on.

He hobbled over to the tub, dropped his towel and painfully lowered his large body inside. The position was awkward and hellish, with his knees folded up practically to his chin, but the hot, medicated water felt wonderful on his scratches, cuts and bruises. No doubt this would help limber him up to make a run for it.

Of course he had no transportation, and according to the lunatic Grandma, they didn't even possess a car on this primitive farm. Should he steal a horse from the barn? He grimaced. To this day, horse thieves were looked on poorly everywhere in the West. At least they weren't lynched on the spot anymore, although he didn't doubt these kooks might string him up.

Then he remembered about his wallet. He knew he had at least fifty dollars; surely he could leave that as "horse rental," with perhaps a note promising to return the animal as soon as he got back to the Flying T. Yes, that was the best way to handle this crazy predicament.

Lucky was still plotting his escape when he heard a shrill feminine voice yell, "You're letting him *what*? All by his lonesome?"

Without even contemplating the matter, Lucky *knew* this was the voice of his she-devil tormentor, Molly. A second later she burst out onto the porch, only to freeze at the sight of him in the tub. Lucky was tempted to jump up and strangle the minx; then he felt himself harden at the sight of her. She stood there so flushed and breathless, tendrils of auburn curls framing her face, her tight pants and shirt clinging to her shapely body. His outrage and horror were soon replaced by fascination and lust. Could she spot the heat in his eyes? He prayed she'd mistake it for anger.

She recognized something all right, for she gulped, then drew her chin up proudly. "Don't you go getting no thoughts of hightailing it, mister. I've got plans for you."

"You can take your plans and—"

Even as Lucky was blessing her out, Grandma rushed out onto the porch with broom in hand. "Granddaughter, have you no sense of decorum?"

Molly turned on her. "You left my affianced here alone where he could escape."

"I'm not your damn affianced!" Lucky yelled from the tub.

Molly glared back.

"Now look what you done," Grandma scolded Molly. "You went and got him all worked up again. How's he going to skedaddle, anyhow, him in the altogether and nekkid as a jaybird? You're just a wicked girl aiming to have yourself a peek before the parson blesses your union."

To Lucky's immense satisfaction, Molly blushed. "I am not!"

Grandma switched her legs with the broom. "Get yourself inside, Granddaughter, before I give you a serious brooming."

"Oh!" She dashed inside, chased by the broom-wielding Grandma.

Before Lucky could even absorb this ridiculous happening, Jessica stepped outside again, expression contrite. "Lucky, I'm so sorry about the intrusion. I've tried to raise my daughter properly, but she has her father's blood flowing in her veins as well, I'm afraid. You know, when I first arrived here, back in the year 1888—"

"Eighteen eighty-eight!" Lucky gasped.

"—Mr. Reklaw interrupted my bath, too." She winked. "Could be that destiny does have something in mind for you and my daughter."

Lucky could only stare at her.

With a knowing smile, Jessica turned to leave, and Lucky shook his head. So much for Jessica being a kindred spirit. These folks were all sky western crazy.

Then Grandma lumbered out with a steamy bucket— a *very* steamy bucket. Who in hell would charge in next? A welcoming committee from town—wherever that was?

"Sorry 'bout my granddaughter's manners," Grandma muttered, wiping her sweaty brow.

"She has manners?" Lucky scoffed.

She offered a crooked grin. "Thought you could use some more hot water as a sort of peace offering."

Lucky half-panicked. That water looked *really* hot. "No, ma'am, I'm fine, I'm . . . aaaaaaaaah! Sheeeeee-at!"

After pouring out the scorching brew, Grandma was

already happily plodding away. "Told you it would make you feel better, young fella."

Lucky was gasping, struggling to recover from his near scalding, when a large calico cat, obviously quite pregnant, crept out onto the porch and meowed at him plaintively, swishing her tail and beseeching him with large green eyes.

"You, too, eh?" he drawled. "Can't a man take a bath in peace around here?"

The cat mewed again; then Molly dashed back onto the porch, scooping her up. "This is Jezebel the fifth," she told him pertly. "She's about to have . . . *babies,* if you know what I mean."

With a saucy grin and a wink, she was gone.

Chapter Five

"So, Pa, are you going to go fetch the preacher now so handsome and me can get hitched?" Molly demanded.

Sitting in the parlor an hour later, amid a family powwow, Lucky could scarcely believe his ears. Did this crazy woman still actually believe he would marry her—after all the hell she'd put him through?

And as if her wacko assumptions weren't enough to deal with, he was still reeling from trying to take in his bizarre, antiquated surroundings—like the ancient horsehair sofa where he sat with the madwoman's brothers, the old rocking chairs where the women were settled, the primitive stone fireplace where Molly's father stood brooding, with several old Winchester rifles hanging above him in blatant menace. Lucky felt as if he'd stepped right into a rerun of *Lonesome Dove*. Nowhere had he spotted a telephone, a television, a computer or any other signs of modern civilization.

On top of all this, the four brothers—whom he'd learned were named Zach, Vance, Matt and Cory—kept shooting surly glances his way, although Cory, the auburn-haired one, didn't seem quite as antagonistic as his siblings. Why were they all so pissed off at him? He was the one who'd been hurled into a ravine, then kidnapped by their loco bird of a sister. They clearly weren't motivated by brotherly protectiveness, given the fierce rivalry he'd already observed between Molly and her brothers.

Even as Lucky glowered at the maddening female, her pa glanced grimly from her to Lucky. "Look, young lady, you can't just drag home any old saddle tramp and assume your ma and I will let you marry him."

As Lucky bristled at being called a saddle tramp, Molly wheedled, "But Pa, he's the one I've waited for—my destiny from the future."

"Not that *future* hokum again," scoffed Vance.

"Yeah, not that," seconded Matt.

"Yeah," Lucky rejoined. "And does anyone care to ask me whether I want to be here, much less marry *her*?"

His tone was not missed by Molly's father, who shook a finger at him. "Young man, you watch your lip around my daughter and stay out of this discussion. It's family business."

"But your haywire daughter wants to make me part of your crazy family!" Lucky retorted.

As Cole took an aggressive step forward, Jessica stood and touched his arm. "Cole, Lucky has a point. He's a part of this, too, now."

"Yeah," put in Zach from next to Lucky. "And if he don't want to marry her, you shouldn't force him, Pa."

"Yeah," seconded Vance and Cory.

"But he has to marry me," protested Molly.

"Why?" sneered Matt. "So you can win the land?"

"Sure, why not?" she shot back.

"What land?" demanded Lucky.

For a moment no one spoke; then Grandma took the reins. "You see, sonny boy, my Cole here set up a contest to help his rambunctious brood grow up. The first one of 'em to wed—and produce a grandchild—will win a prime parcel of ranch land, the lower five hundred."

Lucky was stunned. "You've got to be kidding me. You mean after being shanghaied by this wildcat, I've become some kind of prize in a g'damned contest?"

At his profanity, the boys guffawed, Jessica gasped and Ma frowned massively. "You watch your mouth, sonny, or I'm fetching my broom to teach you some manners," she scolded. "I'll have you know this is a *genu-wine* contest, just like the one Cole and his brothers fought over Jessie here, twenty-odd years ago."

With a horrified glance at Jessica's smiling face, Lucky shot to his feet, then winced at the pain. "Why— why, that's downright sick. What's wrong with you folks? You can't just go around using men and women in contests, like studs or brood mares."

Now Cole did charge forward, his face livid, his fist clenched at Lucky. "You heed your tongue around my wife or I'll hang you by it."

Lucky faced him down with a sneer. "Go ahead, sir. Actually, I'd prefer a healthy lynching to dealing with a bunch of psychos like you."

For a moment there was a tense silence as the two

men confronted each other. Then Grandma laughed and clapped her hands. "Got grit, don't he, son?"

Surprisingly, Cole grinned back. "Yeah, he does. But that doesn't mean he's the right man to marry my Molly."

"My God—when will you wackos get it through your heads that I don't *want* to marry her?" Lucky all but shouted. "I don't even want to be here."

Grandma waved him off. "Oh, you're just the bridegroom. You don't count."

"What?"

Shooting Lucky a rebellious glance, Molly firmly set her jaw. "Hell, I don't know what we're arguing about, anyhow. The deed is done—and old handsome here has already compromised my virtue."

Lucky was appalled. "Quit calling me handsome. And quit lying, too."

But Cole frowned darkly as he stepped toward his daughter. "Daughter, what do you mean, this man compromised your virtue?"

Molly appeared smug enough to burst. "Well, when we pulled Handsome here from the rubble of the stagecoach, he pinched my butt."

At this, the boys split their sides laughing, and Lucky's jaw fell open.

"He did what?" thundered Cole.

"I did no such thing!" shouted Lucky. "Lady, I was half-dead, too puny to pinch a petunia."

Cole glanced in consternation from Lucky to Molly. "What's going on here? One of you has to be lying."

"Well, it's not me," Molly swore, "cross my heart and hope to die."

"She'll be dead by sundown," drawled Lucky, " 'cause I'm gonna murder her."

"You shut up," barked Cole.

Zach jumped up and into the fray. "Pa, can't you tell baby sister here is fibbing a blue streak, just to get her way and win the land?"

"Yeah!" agreed Matt and Vance.

"You're just being sore losers," Molly accused her brothers.

"Stop it, all of you." Cole stood rubbing his forehead in obvious frustration. "Heck, I don't know what to believe. I'll have to ask Sanchez whether this insult ever occurred."

"But he didn't see it, Daddy," Molly quickly put in.

"Because it didn't happen!" yelled Lucky.

Cole held up a hand. "All right, enough, all of you. We'll discuss this matter again later when everyone cools down. We're not going to act hastily—"

"Meaning you're not going to go get the parson?" Molly wailed.

"Not right this minute, daughter. And definitely not until we get some things straight around here."

By now Lucky's temper was boiling over. "Look, people, I've had enough of this hogwash. I'm not gonna marry the squirrel lady here, do you understand? So, if someone will please just take me back to Buck Hollow—"

"Buck Hollow?" repeated Cole with a mystified look. "I've heard of Broken Buck Mountain, but never a Buck Hollow."

With an expression of awe, Jessica stepped up to join them. "But Cole, there was a town called Buck Hollow, Colorado, in the world I left behind. It was a tourist town, built in the nineteen-forties, beneath Broken Buck Mountain." She flashed Lucky a smile. "You know, Lucky, maybe Molly's right that there's a reason you've come here."

He rolled his eyes. "Lady, I got nothing against you, but every time you and your daughter start up with that destiny hogwash, you sound about ten beans short of a burrito."

"Hey, don't talk about my womenfolk that way," scolded Cole.

"It's all right, dear," Jessica reassured him with a wise look. "Obviously it's going to take Lucky a while to accept his—well, what the Fates have in mind for him."

Lucky ground his jaw. "Is someone going to take me to town or not?"

"I'll take you to Mariposa," volunteered Cory.

"Yeah, sure you will," mocked Lucky. "It'll do me one helluva lot of good to be dropped off at a ghost town."

"But Mariposa's not a ghost town," protested Matt.

"Like hell it isn't."

"Silence, all of you," scolded Grandma. She turned to Lucky. "Young fella, Matthew and Jessie are right. Mariposa ain't no ghost town, and Buck Hollow ain't been hatched yet. But the truth is, you're in no condition to travel. Now, if you'll just rest up a spell and try to ease your mind a mite—"

"Right, you folks have such a soothing manner about you," Lucky mocked.

"Then maybe in a week or so, we'll take you on in to Mariposa."

Lucky threw up his hands.

"And in the meantime, we can plan our wedding," added Molly gaily.

"When hell freezes over!" Lucky retorted.

"Pa, are you going to keep allowing her to do this?" demanded Vance. "Just assuming she'll get to marry this stranger, and against his will?"

"Yeah," seconded Matt. "Ain't that contrary to the rules—I mean, forcing him and all? What if us boys tried to hog-tie our brides and drag 'em to the altar? You'd never allow that, right? So how come she gets to have her way with this drifter without a 'by-your-leave'?"

Drifter, Lucky thought ironically. Now, that was an apt description. He'd drifted about as far from civilization—and sanity—as a man could get.

Cole smiled wisely. "Sons, you're right. I'm not going to force Lucky here to wed Molly." He glanced from the fiercely glowering Lucky to the smirking Molly, then chuckled. "But knowing my daughter as well as I do, I fear this whole marriage idea won't be *against his will* for long."

After the family war council, Cory and Matt helped Lucky hobble to the necessary out back. By now he was exhausted and in terrible pain, a fact not lost on Grandma, who poured half a bottle of foul-tasting patent medicine down his throat on his return. Fortunately, the snake oil concoction was at least two-thirds alcohol, and within moments after collapsing on the soft feather bed, he had blissfully passed out.

"Just a song at twilight . . ."

The next thing Lucky heard were the lilting strains of

a woman's voice, singing "Love's Old Sweet Song." He grimaced in the half-light and creaked out of bed, wrapping himself in a quilt to cover his ridiculous drawers—a garment that resembled a gauzy nineteenth-century version of warm-up pants. A cool evening breeze wafted over him, ripe with honeysuckle.

Then he saw her, and his heart quickened. Molly, the hellcat and temptress, sitting there pretty as a picture on the porch swing, dressed in a low-cut yellow gingham gown that showed off her flawless curves. Her rich auburn hair was caught back with a pale blue ribbon, the strands catching gold fire from the setting sun. Swinging gently, she was petting the pregnant cat, Jezebel.

What a vision she was, perched there just like an angel, when he knew she was the devil in a dress. In her own way, she was every bit as treacherous as Misti.

Still, he couldn't take his eyes off her. His loins twinged in potent response, just as they had when she'd interrupted his bath earlier. Damn, that was the last thing he needed—to be lusting after a crazy woman when he should be running like hell.

That was when she noticed him, stopped singing and sashayed over to the window, pertly tipping her face toward him. "Well, hey there, handsome. Quite a rest you had. How ya feelin'?"

Lucky scowled, clutching the quilt tightly about him. "Don't you go trying to sweet-talk me."

She chuckled. "But you look mighty fetching with those bedclothes wrapped around you."

Lucky was hardly immune to the vixen's teasing, a fact that was confirmed by a second rush of heat to his privates. "Well, take a good look, lady. It's all you'll be getting."

She pouted. "Would it be so horrible to marry me, cowboy?"

"By God, if you don't have a one-track mind."

"Well, would it?" she wheedled.

"Anything short of leaving the state you're in would be torture."

She tossed her curls. "Well, I know better. I saw you staring at me just now—and earlier."

"Yeah," he sneered, "I'm not a man to turn my back on my enemies."

She chuckled, wagging a finger at him. "That's not the look I caught you giving me. That look was hot and naughty, like you were aiming to—"

"Strangle you?" he provided pleasantly.

"Well, *something* physical," she teased back.

He glared.

"Cowboy, why are you being so ornery?"

"No reason I can think of," he shot back. "Certainly not having every bone in my body near busted when I was hurled into a canyon, then being kidnapped off to live with a bunch of lunatics who think the Old West has risen again."

She appeared perplexed. "Just what are you saying?"

He muttered to the heavens. "I'm saying you're delusional, lady. I'm saying I'm not going to let you use me. I'm not gonna let you marry me just so you can win your crazy contest with your brothers."

"But if you don't hitch up with me, what else can you do?" she cajoled. "Seems to me you blew in here just like tumbleweed, and now you're stuck. You got no horse, no roof over your head, not even a pot to piss in—"

"Lady, I don't need you to rescue me!"

"All right, then, simmer down." Expression turning coy, she tried a different tack. "I ain't saying you got no grit, seein's how you did survive that stagecoach crash—"

"No shit."

"So why don't you tell me a little about where you came from."

"Like what?" He eyed her narrowly.

Her expression grew rapt. "Well, you came from the future, just like my ma, didn't you?"

He waved a hand. "Please don't start up with that nonsense again."

"But it's true, isn't it? Why don't you just admit it?" Fervently, she continued, "All my life my ma's told me her stories about the future—the zooming automobiles, buildings hitting the sky, rockets flying to the moon. Now we're seeing it all happening with the Wright brothers' flight, those shiny horseless carriages and the newfangled skyscrapers they're building in Chicago and New York. Heck, last fall we saw a genuine airplane fly over the ranch—some French fella, it made all the papers—and Pa took us all to see the new nickelodeon in Colorado Springs. Why, we even know what germs are now, thanks to Louis Pasteur—"

As she spoke Lucky's jaw slowly dropped open. "My God, are you totally out of your mind? Just what year do you think we're living in, anyway?"

"Like I told you, it's 1911."

"And I'm Zane Grey," he ranted. "The Wright brothers and Louis Pasteur—give me a break."

She waved him off. "Cool down, stranger, before you give yourself apoplexy. I asked Ma about you at dinner, and she said you're just confused right now, and you'll see the lay of the land in time. I'll get those stories out of you soon enough."

Lucky could not believe he was having this absurd conversation with this nutty woman. "Oh, I'm plenty perplexed, all right. And has it occurred to you that you shouldn't be pushing my buttons while I'm in my current state?"

"You got buttons?" she teased, looking him over in an unabashed manner that made his face go red. "Why, darlin', I'm just dying to pop 'em."

"Damn it, woman."

"Whew, if you don't got a temper on you." She winked. "That's why I've decided to give you till tomorrow to marry me."

And she sauntered off down the steps, swinging her fanny at him. Lucky bellowed curses, then yelped as his knees buckled beneath him.

"This has been some day, hasn't it, darling?" Cole asked.

Sitting in bed in her nightgown, Jessica Reklaw smiled at her husband, who stood across from her at the dresser, naked down to the waist, washing up in the soft glow of the lantern. Their twenty-three years together had been wonderful ones, and Cole remained a strikingly handsome man, every line on his face beloved to her, every tuft of gray hair a monument to his manhood.

"Has it ever," she replied vehemently. "Especially with Lucky showing up here in such an outlandish fashion."

He frowned pensively. "Yes, it's strange how he arrived—right after I issued my challenge."

Jessica snapped her fingers. "You know, you're right; it was almost as if you'd summoned him here. How amazing. It certainly never occurred to me that we might have a new visitor from across time. I've been asking myself all day what his presence here means. He seems a decent enough young fellow. And to think he came here in Lila Lullaby's old stagecoach, just like I did."

"Yeah, that's pretty spooky. So you really think he came here from the twenty-first century?"

She nodded. "His clothing, the items in his wallet, the things he says . . . I just don't think he could have faked all of that, Cole. In fact, I've been dying to question him all day—"

"So maybe you can learn more about your time—like what happened after you left?" Cole cut in tensely, giving her a pained look.

She stood and went over to hug him, taking a towel to wipe moisture from his beloved face and inhaling his stirring scent. "Darling, *this* is my time. Never doubt that. But, yes, Lucky's arrival here has definitely aroused my curiosity. If it's true that he's come here from the year 2004, five years after I left the present, then he surely knows some things about the future that I don't know. I want to find out more about him—for Molly's sake, for all our sakes. But right now, he's too confused, too much in shock, just like I was when I first arrived here."

"He's fit to be tied, all right," Cole concurred with a chuckle.

"I need to help him understand what has happened to him, but there's no point trying to reason with him as long as he's so determined to fight every step of the way." She squeezed his arm. "Cole, when he feels better, you need to take him around, show him Mariposa, so he can see for himself where he really is."

"Good idea. You know, I almost feel sorry for the poor boy. Molly really has her sights set on him, insisting on an instant wedding and all."

Jessica sighed. "She's so headstrong, Cole, just like you."

Cole tweaked her nose. "And her ma isn't stubborn?"

"Well, I sure wouldn't jump at the chance to marry a stranger."

"Like me and my four brothers did?" He nestled her closer and spoke with fond remembrance. "Nabbing you off that stagecoach, fighting over you . . ." His voice dropped a sexy notch as he nuzzled her hair with his lips. "Doin' some friendly persuading—"

"Until the best man won," she finished ecstatically, kissing his strong jaw. "Although I'm very proud of your brothers, too. Twenty-three years ago all of you were outlaws. Then you found wives, we all moved to Wyoming—"

"And Gabe, Luke and Wesley remain there as prosperous citizens to this day," Cole finished. "Still, I'm glad we decided to return here a decade later, and Billy and Dumpling came with us. Wyoming was a raw, beautiful land, but when Ma kept bellyaching about missing Colorado and the old homestead . . . Plus, poor Dumpling's pa took ill, after caring for both spreads all that time . . . Anyway, it was good to settle back here once the coast was clear."

"You mean, once the statute of limitations ran out. And speaking of legal matters . . ." She sighed. "I was so disappointed to see the boys land in jail again."

He nodded grimly. "I know. I plan to make it clear to my sons that the next time they indulge in a donny-brook like that, I'm not going to come rushing down to the jail to bail them out." He paused, grinning ruefully. "Otherwise, guess I can't be too hard on them, being a former hot-blood myself."

She wrinkled her nose at him. "You still are one."

"And plenty proud of it," he quipped.

"I just fear our children are too much like you, Cole," she fretted. "This business about the robberies—"

"That is a strange one," he agreed. "Especially to hear of trains and stagecoaches being stuck up in these modern times."

She rolled her eyes at that. "Well, if memory serves me correctly, Mr. Reklaw, the last recorded stage-coach robbery in this country won't be until 1916, in Nevada."

Cole grinned ruefully. "You know, I never have quite gotten used to the idea of being married to a walking history book—especially one that opens into the future."

She chuckled. "I'm afraid it doesn't help me that much with *our* futures, though. I just pray our sons aren't involved in these holdups. I don't think Cory would break the law, but as for the others . . ."

He kissed her chin. "Cheer up, sweetheart. I have a notion this contest may help distract the boys, and could even force them to grow up."

"If they don't end up hating each other over it," she fretted. "The whole competition idea still makes me uneasy."

He squeezed her close. "Darling, don't worry. Truth to tell, this won't be much of a contest. I'm banking on Molly."

"Why, Cole! I know she's the apple of your eye, but to hope she'll win over our sons—"

"But our sons weren't sent a potential spouse from across time, were they?"

"Yes, that's true," Jessica admitted with awe. "Not to mention, Molly is the only one of our four children who ever really came to believe that I actually traveled through time. Mind you, Ma may have given the idea lip service, but as for the boys . . . well, we just had to drop it with them, remember?"

"Molly's the only true believer, all right," he conceded. "And I'm figuring that if Destiny brought you and me together, then—"

"She and Lucky may belong together, too," Jessica finished wisely. "Don't think I haven't been pondering that all day. But we must be careful, Cole. The Fates could always fool us."

Cole winked. "No lie, honey. Why do you think I've been holding the reins on my headstrong daughter? There's no way I'm gonna let her rush into wedlock and possibly make a huge mistake."

"I agree we should take our time till we figure out what Lucky's presence here really means." Jessica frowned. "What should we tell folks about his being here?"

Cole shrugged. "Oh, a variation of the truth should work—you know, that he was passing through and took a fall off his horse on our range."

"And what a fall," she added drolly.

He tenderly caressed her cheek. "We didn't tell anyone the truth about you when you came here, and we shouldn't about Lucky now. We'll need to keep our own counsel, especially when it comes to the folks in town."

"Amen," seconded Jessica. "If we spilled the beans in Mariposa, we'd be locked up in the loony bin, and they'd throw away the key."

"And you know," Cole added wryly, "our guest from the future would agree with them completely."

The two fell into gales of laughter, ending in a kiss. . . .

Chapter Six

Amazingly, Lucky awakened in something less than agony, to the slow ticking of the ornate bronze clock on the dresser. How long had he been passed out this way? A glance at the window revealed the first rosy rays of dawn filtering through, and a sweet breeze ruffling the lacy white curtains. He'd pretty much slept around the clock then, thanks to Grandma and her potion. And if he'd had any hope of awakening back where he'd come from—awakening to *sanity*—it was dashed now. He was still stuck in the same wacky limbo in which he'd fallen asleep.

With a pained grunt, he crept out of bed and put on the strange clothes he'd been given yesterday—the odd jeans with the button fly, the long-sleeved, green-checked shirt that looked homemade. He slipped on his own well-worn brown cowboy boots and made his way out the door, across the porch and to the necessary.

He emerged in the morning briskness to the sight of

a glorious Colorado dawn, with mule deer grazing in the valley beyond and hawks soaring overhead, against a rugged Rocky Mountain backdrop. He could hear the calls of horned larks and mourning doves.

What he didn't hear were any sounds of civilization—at least not the civilization he remembered. Not a truck engine revving up or a tractor groaning its way across a field. Not the distant blare of a stereo or the hum of an AC unit. This place truly seemed suspended in time. Though Lucky wasn't a technology buff, he actually found himself missing the comforting drone of CNN in the background and the binging of the microwave.

Where in hell *was* he? Nothing about the terrain or the house looked familiar. Even more critical, how would he find his way home? If what these people said was true, he was not only miles distant from home but nearly a century away.

This last he refused to believe. These fruitcakes must be lying to him. Even this Jessica person, though she had her motherly appeal, was too ultimately far-fetched to be believed. He needed to get the hell away from these crazies, find some folks who had their heads on straight and could direct him back to the Flying T . . .

He was hobbling around toward the front of the house to get a better look at the farmstead when the sound of *"Chee, chee, chee!"* interrupted his musings. Out in the barnyard he spotted his lovely nemesis feeding the chickens. Again she looked too pretty for words in a low-cut, pink muslin gown that did nothing to hide the lush contours of her breasts and the trim lines of her waist. She was throwing seed to an attentive flock of chattering hens.

Lucky was about to duck around toward the front porch when she spotted him. Dimpling charmingly, she called out, "Morning, handsome."

"Morning," he grumbled back, about ready to give up on trying to rid her of her obnoxious habit of calling him "handsome." He strode closer and found even the strong barnyard odor could not dampen the effect on his senses of seeing this vision of femininity—damn her little hide!

"How you feeling?" she asked.

"Better, no thanks to you."

She glowered. "Hey, I'm the one who rescued you yesterday—"

"And half killed me on the ride back here."

"Well, you couldn't have been too messed up, since you're already up and rambling about." She regarded him slyly. "Were you hoping to give me the slip?"

Lucky ground his teeth; that notion had certainly crossed his mind numerous times. "You think I'm gonna steal one of your daddy's horses?"

"He'd shoot you if you did."

"How hospitable of him."

She gave a shrug. "You up to getting hitched today?"

Lucky's glare was eloquent.

She rolled her eyes. "I see you're just as ornery as you were yesterday."

"Yeah, that pretty much happens every time I get shanghaied by a crew of psychopaths . . . and it takes some time to pass." He rubbed his unshaven jaw. "What's got you up so early, anyhow?"

"This is a farm—or have you already forgot? Someone has to scatter feed to the chickens."

"If anything's scattered, lady, it's your brains."

"You think I don't have chores around here?" she demanded.

He laughed. "All gussied up in pink muslin? Tell the truth, now. You got up early and got yourself dolled up just hoping you could entice me so I'd go along with your crazy scheme."

"Cowboy, you can't think I'm that conniving," she flirted with a grin.

"You and Scarlett O'Hara."

"Scarlett O'Who?"

"Never mind."

She sashayed closer, tempting him with her bright green eyes and smiling, rose-hued lips, and despite himself, Lucky drew in a harsh breath. As he watched in fascination, she drew a teasing hand down her lacy bodice—puckering a nipple in the process—then trailing her shapely fingers past the trim lines of her waist to the tempting folds of her skirt.

Lucky's privates twinged painfully and he almost groaned out loud. Her gesture was blatantly sensual yet enticingly naive.

She spoke in a low purr. "Handsome, do you really think I'd wed you in this here pink, rather than virgin's white?"

"Virgin, eh?" Lucky gulped, unable to help himself. He was riveted.

"Are you insulting my maidenhood now?" she demanded with a pout.

74

Lucky wasn't sure how to respond to that, especially since he couldn't even recall the last time he'd met a bona fide "maiden." "Just tell me why you're all prettied up."

"Well, truth to tell, my aunt Dumpling and uncle Billy and their young'uns are coming for dinner today. I know they'll enjoy meeting my affianced—"

"I'm not your g'damned affianced!" he exploded.

"And Aunt Dumpling will just love helping me plan my wedding," she finished cheerily, ignoring his flash of temper.

Lucky knew there was little point in arguing further. Muttering "Damn crazy woman," he turned and strode off for the house.

Lucky returned to his room to find shaving gear—an old-fashioned, hand-held blade, a basin of warm water, a crude bar of soap and a linen hand towel—laid out on his dresser. Some kind soul—probably Jessica—had put the items there. Mumbling, "She's got to be kidding," he tried his best to trim his stubble with the antiquated equipment, yelping numerous times when he nicked himself with the less than sharp blade. By the time he finished, the smells of ham and strong coffee were enticing him toward the kitchen.

Rubbing his sore face as he stepped into the large, stone-floored room, he spotted Grandma and Jessica, both in homespun dresses and aprons, busy making coffee, flipping flapjacks, ham and eggs at an antique cast-iron stove. The other kitchen fixtures consisted of a primitive drain board with a pump, two large pie safes and a crude porcelain icebox, much like the antique one his grandparents had stored on the back porch.

Lucky could only shake his head. Another scene from a B western.

"Mornin', ladies," he greeted.

Jessica turned with a smile. "Lucky. Good morning to you. You feeling better?"

"Yes, ma'am."

"Did you find the shaving paraphernalia I left you?"

He rubbed his smarting cheek again. "Oh, yes, ma'am."

Grandma guffawed. "Just look at him—all scratched up like a rooster caught in chicken wire. Ain't nobody learnt you how to shave, sonny?"

"Not with a blunt object," he replied dryly.

"Huh?" Grandma asked.

Jessica was laughing. "Sit down, Lucky, and I'll bring you some coffee."

"Yes, ma'am." He took a seat at the long trestle table and sipped the strong brew from a blue enamel cup. Within seconds Cole strode in, dressed for the range in jeans and a long shirt, followed in quick order by the boys, who filed in one by one, cleanly scrubbed, from the bunkhouse. They took their places, barely acknowledging him with stiff nods.

Lucky was astounded at the feast the two ladies served up—flapjacks with hot syrup, fried eggs and ham, biscuits with cream gravy. Although the fare was definitely mouthwatering, Lucky was stunned at the massive amounts the other men consumed. He could only watch in mingled fascination and disbelief as

Zach wolfed down five pieces of ham and at least as many eggs, and Matt devoured four huge biscuits soaked in gravy.

"Eat up, boy," Cole directed him, heaping his own plate with more pancakes. "You need to regain your strength."

"Sir, I've already had three of everything."

"Pa, is he gonna ride with us today?" asked Matt.

"Naw. This boy needs a little more mending time before we show him the range."

"Bet he's a pure greenhorn," jeered Vance.

Now Lucky felt compelled to defend himself. "I'll have you know I've been working the Flying T for three years now, and rode my grandparents' spread before that."

"Flying T?" scoffed Matt. "Never heard of it."

"All right, boys, leave Lucky in peace," scolded Jessica.

Matt was about to protest when Molly came dancing in the back door with a basketful of flowers. "Ma, I got done feeding the chickens early so I picked some black-eyed Susans for you."

A stunned silence fell as every member of Molly's family regarded her in amazement. "Daughter, what are you doing all scrubbed and starched so early in the day?" her father asked.

"Are you implying I don't bathe?" she shot back impudently.

"Ain't you coming with us to the range today?" Cory asked his sister.

Molly preened, then winked at Lucky. "Naw. Now that I'm an affianced lady, I'm gonna stay here and help out the womenfolk."

While Lucky muttered to himself, all of Molly's brothers broke up laughing. "You, a lady with a fiancé!" scoffed Zach. "Might as well be Vance or me putting on airs and a frilly dress."

"Do you boys have some peculiar notions you haven't told us about?" she mocked back. Amid chuckles, she turned to her mother. "Ma, you and Grandma could use my help today, couldn't you? I mean, with Uncle Billy, Aunt Dumpling and the cousins due here at high noon."

"Noon?" put in a confused Lucky. "I thought you said those folks were coming for *dinner*."

Everyone but Jessica stared at Lucky in mystification. "Lucky, dinner here is at noon and supper at five o'clock," she pointed out tactfully.

"Ah, yes, dinner," Lucky replied with a scowl. "Come to think of it, I can remember my grandma sometimes used to refer to lunch as dinner, too."

"And of course you'll join us, Lucky?" Jessica added graciously.

" 'Course he will," retorted Molly before Lucky could speak.

"Molly," scolded Jessica, "let the man answer for himself."

While Molly scowled, Lucky smiled at Jessica. "I'd be honored to join you for dinner, ma'am."

"Wonderful," she replied, turning to Cole. "And you men bear in mind you need to be back by eleven-thirty to scrub up."

The boys exchanged conspiratorial looks, then Vance whined, "Ma, do we gotta be here? Zach, Matt, Cory and me sort of had other plans for this afternoon."

"And what are those?" their mother asked.

"Ma, it's a secret," put in Cory with a self-conscious expression.

Jessica's eyes danced with amusement. "Very well, boys. Just clear this clandestine mission with your father."

"Yes, ma'am," chanted the brothers in unison.

"You boys aren't aiming to go rob a stagecoach or a train, are you?" demanded Cole with a suspicious look.

"No, sir," Matt denied vehemently. "Didn't we already tell you we're not involved?"

"Then where are you bound this afternoon?"

Miserably, Matt replied, "We'll just—we'll explain it to you while we're riding out to the range, all right, sir?"

"Very well," conceded their father.

Molly gave her brothers a dubious glance, then turned to her mother. "So, may I help out you and Grandma?"

"Of course Ma and I would be happy to have your assistance, dear," Jessica responded.

Molly beamed. "And while I'm at it, I'll just keep an eye on old handsome here." She winked at Lucky.

Everyone else laughed, and Lucky sorely wished he was up to riding the range.

Chapter Seven

After the men left, Lucky lingered over a third cup of coffee. He had to admit Molly amused him as she tried to "help" her ma and grandma prepare dinner. Obviously, she hadn't a clue how to cook, much less maneuver herself around a kitchen. He chuckled as she singed her fingers on a cast-iron skillet; he laughed at the sight of Grandma slapping her hand as she would have dumped a tablespoon of salt, rather than a teaspoon, into the yeast roll mixture.

But when she started washing and pitting fresh cherries for the pie filling, he found her actions mesmerizing and all too sensual. In awe he watched her delicate fingers dip the fruit in water to wash the ripe balls, her teeth pluck the stems, her slender hand grip the corer she used to remove the pits. Each time she licked the red juice from her fingers, his cock hardened and his throat tightened, especially at the thought of her licking *him* that way.

Hells bells and sciatica, as his grandma used to say. What was he doing pining after this loco woman? She wanted to wreck his life and destroy his sanity. He'd be better served cozying up to a black widow spider.

But fascinated he was—by Molly's body language, the voluptuous way she moved, the little wisps of hair clinging to her damp cheeks and brow due to the heat of the stove. When she sashayed over, inundating him with her sweet female fragrance, tempting him with her bright, mischievous eyes and plopping a pitted cherry in his mouth, he all but came unglued.

"Good, eh?" she purred.

"Yeah," he barely managed, sucking on the luscious fruit. "Sweet."

She swung away, flashing that delectable derriere at him.

Damn! Would the torture ever end? Remembering another adage from his grandma—"If you can't stand the heat, get out of the kitchen"—Lucky decided he'd best make himself scarce before he did something foolish, like haul the siren up over his shoulder, caveman style, carry her off and take what he craved.

Painfully pushing himself to his feet, he muttered, "Ladies, if you'll excuse me, I think I'll go stretch my legs."

All three turned from their labors to stare at him. "Sonny, don't you think it's a bit soon for you to be gandering about?" asked Grandma. "Seein's how you near busted them same legs yesterday?"

He gave a shrug. "The exercise will be good for me— you know, prevent blood clots and all that."

"Huh?" questioned Grandma.

Molly stepped forward. "I'll go with you."

Lucky ground his teeth. Couldn't this vixen understand that it was *her* he needed to get away from? "Including to my first stop—the outhouse?"

As Jessica and Grandma laughed, Molly blushed, and Lucky felt a surge of satisfaction that he'd managed to embarrass her for a change.

"Molly, give Lucky a little space," put in Jessica wisely. "We can't keep guard over him every second."

"But he'll hightail it!" she protested. "I already caught him outside once today, like a sneaky old weasel."

"Hey, I wasn't going anywhere," Lucky protested, "except perhaps to get the hell away from you."

"Oh!" she cried.

"In that case, granddaughter, perhaps you should think about mending your manners so your young man will want to stick around," scolded Grandma.

"I'm not her young man," snapped Lucky.

Molly waved a hand in exasperation. "See what I mean? He's stubborn as a stuck door and determined to fight this every step of the way."

"Reminds me of someone I know," quipped Jessica.

Molly frowned at her mother, and Grandma narrowed her gaze on Lucky. "You gonna steal one of our horses, cowboy?"

"No, ma'am."

"Then skedaddle."

"Yes, ma'am."

"Grandma!" wailed Molly.

"Granddaughter, he's got no horse and he ain't gonna limp all the way to town."

"Ma is right," Jessica added firmly. "Have a good walk, Lucky."

"Yes, ma'am," Lucky replied, not giving Molly a second look as he quickly hobbled out the back door.

In the yard, he did glance back, saw the curtain move at the window, then quickly slip back into place. Damn it, the little she-devil was watching him. Guess he had no choice but to go visit the outhouse, even though he wasn't in need of another pit stop. But if he went off in another direction, she'd no doubt come chasing after him, tattling to the others that he was a lying SOB—and he'd already had his fill of her insolence and interference this morning.

Inside the cramped little necessary, he spent a most unpleasant and all too aromatic five minutes leafing through the outlandish 1910 edition of the Sears, Roebuck and Company catalog, marveling at everything from nursing flask fittings to silver snuffboxes to cattle dehorning clippers. Well, if these crackbrains really wanted to convince him he was living in the year 1911, they were leaving nothing to chance.

When he emerged, he was pleased to note the kitchen curtains remained in place. He was eager to explore the rest of the ranchstead—and perhaps find some trappings of the world he'd left behind. He limped to the front of the house and glanced around slowly and carefully.

Damn. This was a working farm, all right, but decidedly primitive with its stone and wood barn, the quaint little springhouse with charming cupola, the woodshed, corncrib, smokehouse and cellar. He strode over to the crude pigpen, separated from the rest of the homestead for obvious reasons, and watched the gray and white swine wallowing in the muck. Despite the stench, the sight of five little piglets suckling at the sow was a sweet one to him. His gaze scanned the fields of budding wheat and corn in the distance, the brown and white cows grazing on spring grasses.

He shook his head, feeling the same disorientation that had nagged him ever since he had arrived here. Nothing was making sense—not the fact that this farm was an archaic yet fully self-contained operation, nor the absence of any fixtures from the present, nor the fact that all the inhabitants thought they were living in the year 1911. And although Lucky was accustomed to living with few frills, even he was daunted by the prospect of never again watching HBO or driving his pickup truck or going off to town to see a movie.

Surely all of this was just a really bad joke—like the living farm from hell. Where was his reality, his world? How would he get back there?

And most disturbing of all, why was this hellcat of a girl enticing him to stay here?

He remembered Molly and her ma arguing that this was his "destiny," that he was meant to be here now. To be brutally honest, he should be dead now—and at times he still wondered if he wasn't. That breakneck plunge into the gorge should have ended his life, or at least rendered him a quadriplegic. Instead, other than being sore as hell, he was fully intact. It made no sense—but then, nothing much was making sense right now.

Was there indeed a reason he was here? If so, the

reason seemed a curse. Was he being punished in the afterlife for shooting up the Broken Buck Motel somewhere back on earth?

Lucky lingered far from the house until the sun was high in the sky. Not wanting to be late for dinner and raise everyone's ire, he strode back to find a curious sight at the front of the bungalow. A throng of adults and children was gathered around a large, horse-drawn surrey. He recognized Cole, Jessica and Molly, and then his gaze was drawn to the visitors, gathered in the yard, laughing and embracing other family members.

Damn, new arrivals straight out of *Little House on the Prairie*. First there was a plump, middle-aged woman in a nutmeg-yellow calico gown that trailed the ground; her thick blondish-gray curls hung from beneath a huge slat bonnet. Next to her stood a slight, silver-haired man with sharply hewn but handsome features and a handlebar mustache; he was dressed in an old-fashioned brown suit with a satin vest and a red bow tie. Around the yard scampered three tow-headed boys in overalls, homespun shirts and button-top shoes; they appeared to range in age from around six to twelve, and were happily shrieking as they chased the two dogs.

Then the group spotted him, and all turned to stare.

Lucky gulped. How he hated being the center of this confounding group's attention! But his torment was not about to end. The large woman, whom he could now see held a plump baby in each arm, shrieked with joy and hurried toward him.

She spoke all in a rush in her country twang, giving Lucky no opportunity to respond, leaving him to stare in consternation at her pretty and still youthful, freckle-dusted face. "Why, hey, precious, ain't you the sweetest thang?" she drawled. "No wonder my niece Molly is gonna marry you! Here, darlin', have a twin!"

And as Lucky stood frozenly, a round blond infant in a frilly pink gown was deposited in his arms. "Ma'am, I—I can't—"

The woman ignored him, caterwauling to Molly, "Molly Reklaw, get your pretty self over here and take Farley." She winked at Lucky. "You got little Fanny there, handsome. After purely a dozen tries, I got me my girl child."

"Thank heaven," intoned her husband, and everyone laughed.

Lucky extended the squirming infant. "Ma'am, could you please—"

Molly skidded up to join them, scooping up the blue-gowned baby boy with a sigh of delight, then flashing her dimples at Lucky. "Ain't he precious, Lucky? Kinda reminds me of you, with his blond hair and blue eyes. Wouldn't you like to have one of these yourself soon?"

Lucky blushed crimson, glowering at Molly.

"Now don't you go embarrassing him, Molly girl," the woman scolded with a grin. "Why, he's already turned three shades of red." She elbowed Lucky. "Don't worry, young fella. You'll get the hang of holding Fanny there. Whenever we come over, everyone gets a twin to pass around."

"Yes, ma'am," said Lucky, again extending the baby toward her. "However, if you don't mind—"

He was ignored as Jessica stepped up. "Lucky, let me introduce you to everyone. This is Cole's brother, Billy Reklaw, his wife, Dumpling, and their sons, Abel, Jeb and Cal. I see you've already met the twins."

"Yes, ma'am. But would one of you ladies kindly—"

"Well, everyone, shall we go eat?" interjected Cole, grinning and clapping his hands.

"Where are my brothers?" asked Molly.

Her father smiled sheepishly. "Actually, I'm not supposed to tell."

"Cole, really," scolded Jessica.

"Don't worry, honey, this time there's no mischief-making involved," he reassured her.

Dumpling batted Cole's arm with a glove. "Then why are you keepin' us all in suspense, Cole Reklaw?"

Amid laughter, he conceded, "Very well, I'll confess. The boys decided to go courting for the afternoon. The Trumble sisters, Sally, Nelly, Bonnie and Ida May."

"So that's what those little devils are up to," laughed Jessica.

"Tarnation!" cursed Molly. "I just knew those varmints would try to beat me out."

Grandma was scowling fiercely. "Why, the whelps. Bet they went to the Trumble homestead just to spite me. They know right well how I feel about old Ezra."

"But Ma, his daughters are lovely," Cole pointed out.

"They may be comely as mountain columbine, but that don't mean I'm for hitchin' up our two families," Ma retorted stoutly. "Why, Ez is cantankerous as a mule, deaf as a post and dumb as a bale of hay. Not to mention he's older than Methuselah. Why, I hear tell he got all them girls off'n his fourth wife after he plumb wore out the first three—and her, too, before he was done with her."

"You're just riled because Ezra had the gall to propose to you, Ma," teased Cole.

She harrumphed. "Darned right, I'm galled. Why, I'd just as soon hitch up with a frog in a union suit. If you ask me, there's something peculiar about that whole Trumble clan. They've been standoffish ever since they settled here. Like the way old Ez keeps them girls under lock and key—"

"Well, they are the prettiest fillies in the county," interjected Billy. He winked at Molly. "Excepting for my darling niece here."

As Molly simpered, Lucky felt impelled to bring her down a peg or two. "You know, I can't say I blame the boys," he interjected. "The Trumble girls do sound mighty tempting. Maybe I'll just tag along the next time the men go courting."

Molly kicked Lucky in the shin and he yelped in pain.

The others laughed, and Dumpling bragged to Cole, "Ain't Molly a pistol?"

"Yeah, she's definitely a girl after her daddy's heart," Cole agreed. "All the spirit of a champion, that one. I'm afraid old handsome here hasn't got a chance."

"Now wait just a minute, all of you," Lucky chided, growing exasperated. "I'm getting sick and tired of all of you assuming that I'm . . . aaaaaaah!" His words ended in a grimace as he felt something wet and warm trickling down his shirt and the front of his pants. He scowled at the baby he held; she gurgled back, grinning toothlessly at him.

The others broke up with hilarity. "She got you!" teased Molly.

"Looks like old handsome peed on hisself," added Billy, slapping his sides.

"You don't have to look so damned surprised, cowboy," Molly went on. "A body would think you have no idea how babies work. What a tenderfoot you are."

At last Lucky found his voice. "Ain't you folks ever heard of Pampers?"

Except for Jessica, they all stared back at him. Evidently they hadn't.

"Come on, I'll help you change her," offered Molly. "Ma always keeps some extra diapers in the guest room."

"You want to come with me to my bedroom?" he asked in disbelief.

Dumpling shrieked with laughter. "With Fanny and Farley there to chaperone, we won't worry about you, will we, Cole and Jessie?"

Cole frowned, but Jessica nodded. "Dumpling is right. You two go on and change the babies."

"But leave the door open," Cole added sternly.

Realizing he had little choice but to comply, Lucky started off with Molly. He slanted Cole a resentful glance, only to be rewarded by a look of pure menace.

Then his gaze swung back to Molly. She winked. "After I change these babies, how 'bout I change you, handsome?"

"How 'bout you jump in the creek?" he retorted, but the vixen only smirked.

* * *

"Will you kindly finish up so I can change into some dry jeans and a shirt?" Lucky asked irritably.

Standing near the dresser, still sopping wet and feeling supremely awkward, Lucky glowered at Molly, who was kneeling by the bed. For the past ten minutes she'd been playing with the two infants, cooing to them, singing to them, nuzzling their bellies and faces, making both shriek with laughter and wave their plump little arms and legs, taking her time and tormenting *him* as she dressed them in dry diapers and embroidered linen shirts. Though he hated to admit it, the domestic scene fascinated him, and despite his drenching by Fanny, he found the twins to be as cute as a couple of bugs. Lucky had never had a brother or sister and hadn't even been around babies very much. All of this left him feeling vulnerable, and aggravated at himself for being so charmed by all of them—but especially Molly.

She hurled him a saucy look. "So you want to change, do you? Who's stopping you?"

"You are." Watching her grin from ear to ear, he felt himself blushing again and could have kicked himself. " 'Sides, I shouldn't be undressing in front of—er, these children."

She hooted. "These two are too young to know the difference."

"But you would."

"Oh, yeah. I would." She looked him over and licked her lips.

He groaned, striding forward. "Woman, do you have any idea what you're doing? Tempting a full-grown man like you are?"

She stood to regard him forthrightly. "Yeah. We need to get this marriage business started, handsome, so I might as well just tempt away. Heck, my brothers are already off a-courting, and I intend to stay at least five lengths ahead of 'em in this race."

Lucky remained incredulous. "And it doesn't matter to you at all that I'm a stranger who has no interest in marrying you?"

She gave a shrug. "One man is about as good as another, as far as I'm concerned. 'Sides, you're not just any old stranger but my destiny."

"That's a load of crap."

"Hey, watch your language in front of these young 'uns."

"I thought you said they were too little to know the difference."

"They can understand your tone of voice."

He rolled his eyes. "My point is, you know nothing about me, not really."

"And whose fault is that?" she demanded, pouting. "You won't tell me anything about yourself or answer my questions about where you came from."

"Perhaps I never will," he flung back at her. "Fact is, I could be anyone—a deadbeat, a swindler, a murderer, a thief." Moving closer to her, he smiled nastily. "Why, I might just strangle you in your sleep."

She hooted with laughter. "Mister, I got three wild-as-hell older brothers, not to mention a daddy who's a reformed outlaw, and I've been holding my own with all of 'em for eighteen years now. You think I can't handle *you*?"

"Don't bet on it," he growled.

Undaunted, she tossed her curls. "Good try, cowboy, but you don't scare me. Tougher men than you have tried and failed. 'Sides, I think you're much more trustworthy than you let on."

"And why is that?"

"You wouldn't steal one of our horses. That makes you a man of honor."

"Yeah. Being lynched for horse theft is not how I'm planning to exit this hellhole for the hereafter."

She grinned. "And as often as you invoke the name of the Almighty, I'd say you got religion, too."

"What little you haven't made me lose."

She continued to grin at him and looked so maddeningly impish that Lucky was hard-pressed not to haul her close and kiss her. He was forced to clench his fists at his sides just to restrain himself.

Get a grip, he warned himself. If he didn't watch out, he'd soon get in so deep with this loco woman, he wouldn't be able to retrieve himself.

Fortunately, one of the babies chortled, breaking the tension. He nodded toward the bed. "Can we go in to lunch—er, dinner—now? They look dressed."

She held up two pairs of crocheted booties, one pink, one blue. "They ain't got their shoes on yet. Care to do the honors?"

"Sure, if it will speed things along," he grumbled. Lucky grabbed the booties, knelt by the bed and began trying to tie them on wiggly little feet, while Molly stood watching him and giggling at his awkward attempts.

He cast her a surly look, then paused, feeling a lump in his throat despite himself. "Damn, their little feet are so tiny, so soft, and they smell, well, so sweet-like—"

"That's baby smell," she amended, leaning over to meet his eye. "No finer smell on this earth."

Lucky found himself staring into her vibrant, slightly flushed face. With her auburn curls hanging loose and free and her bosom generously exposed, he felt himself harden painfully.

Hastily he snatched his gaze away and began fumbling with Farley's booties.

But Molly continued to linger close to him, too close. "Tell me, cowboy, have you ever held a newborn? I have. Nothing softer this side of heaven."

"Yeah," Lucky muttered hoarsely. He dared not look at Molly then. They both knew precisely what she was offering him, and he was far from immune. Indeed, to his shock, he was tortured by yearning, a craving to tumble her and give her just what she was begging for so brazenly. He'd never have thought a familial moment could affect him so, haunting him with visions of having his own home and family, perhaps even regaining his faith and everything else he had lost . . .

But not with this she-devil!

He finished the task with trembling fingers, then stood, depositing a baby in each of Molly's arms. Still avoiding her gaze, he spoke gruffly. "Get out of here while I change."

"Sure you don't need any help?"

"I said make tracks, sister."

She chuckled. "We'll be waiting for you in the kitchen, cowboy."

She sashayed away with a baby on each hip, and Lucky collapsed onto the bed.

Chapter Eight

At dinner, with the family gathered about the long trestle table, the twins dozing in a cradle near the hearth, and the dogs devouring cooking scraps by the back door, Molly observed Lucky covertly. He looked awkward as he passed around mashed potatoes, gravy, corn on the cob, and a huge plate loaded with beefsteak. He kept directing blistering, resentful glances her way. No matter. She knew she had him where she wanted him now—all hot and bothered. He'd given himself away when he'd stared at her bosom while she'd fed the chickens, when he'd gulped at the sight of her with a baby in her arms, when he'd stood in the bedroom with jaw tight and fists clenched, eyes blazing as he'd watched her change the twins. When she'd teased him, she'd even noticed a telltale bulge at the front of his jeans, and the sight of it had made her mouth go dry.

And those steamy glances he kept casting her way

were definitely affecting her, too. Every time his gaze scorched her, she felt funny little twinges in her breasts, her privates, the sensations achingly pleasurable. She was fascinated by her own responses but daunted by the prospect of giving this stranger so much power over her.

Molly had only been kissed once, a sloppy, distasteful affair, when Chester Snyder had waylaid her behind the schoolhouse in town and planted a wet smack on her mouth. Totally disgusted, Molly had knocked him to his knees.

But the prospect of this handsome stranger grabbing and kissing her elicited a totally different response, making her heart go all aflutter, and she felt both confused and intrigued by this exciting but peculiar response. As he'd argued only moments earlier, she barely knew him. How could he already bedevil her so?

But entice her he did. She wanted to know more about him and his world, and it galled her that he wouldn't answer her questions. Yes, he had been through a shock, and yes, she supposed she was nervy to expect him to marry her, just like that. But none of that fully explained the extent of his anger toward her. She needed to chip away at his defenses and wipe that perpetual glare off his face.

For the moment Lucky's frown had shifted to Pa and Uncle Billy as the two men monopolized the conversation, discussing politics—whether or not Teddy Roosevelt, a favorite of theirs, would run for president again next year. "Mr. Taft just ain't got his grit," Uncle Billy pronounced. "We need old Teddy's big stick and hard-charging manner back in the White House. And them rambunctious children of hisn was fun, too."

"Yeah, I chuckled when I read how Quentin dropped a water balloon on his daddy's guards, and how Archie played with his pet badger," put in Aunt Dumpling. She paused, winking at Cole. "And speaking of unruly offspring, I hear your four eldest landed in the hoosegow again the other night."

Cole gave a groan. "Yeah, they mixed it up with those obnoxious Hicks cousins at the saloon." He flinched. "No offense, Dumpling."

"None taken," she assured him. "Even though I used to be a Hicks myself, Dulcine and them five cousins is from the white trash branch of our family." She nodded to Lucky. "No class."

"Yes, ma'am," he soberly agreed.

"Our boys have been arguing that the Hicks cousins may be responsible for the robberies we're having in these parts—or even that the Dempsey Gang may be riding again," Jessica interjected.

"And we're hoping the boys aren't just saying these things to cover their own tracks," added their father grimly.

"I'd bet on those no-account Hicksses," pronounced Dumpling.

"And I'd bet on my brothers," put in Molly cynically.

"Now, Molly," scolded Uncle Billy, "you know your ma and pa raised your brothers righteously, even if they is full of prunes." He smiled at Jessica. "They'll settle down in time, Jessie, you'll see."

"Let's hope so, Billy. For now, I'm just praying old

man Trumble won't kill them for going courting in the middle of the week."

Amid laughter, Dumpling turned her beaming smile on Lucky. "So, young fella, how exactly did you come to be among the Reklaw clan?"

Molly almost chortled as Lucky appeared to go blank, but her pa quickly spoke up. "As I mentioned earlier, Molly found Lucky out on the range. Evidently he'd taken a bad fall from his horse. She and Sanchez fetched him home so the women could care for him."

Dumpling gasped ecstatically, turning to Molly. "And you decided on the spot that you wanted to marry him? How romantic. Love at first sight and all that?"

"Yeah, love at first sight." Molly smirked at Lucky.

"She means love at first sight of the lower five hundred," he drawled back.

"Huh?" asked Dumpling.

Cole shot Lucky a dark glance, then told Dumpling and Billy about the contest he'd established—and explained how Molly was, so far, first at the draw.

Afterward, Dumpling hooted her delight. "Good for you, honey," she declared, patting Molly's hand. "We females gotta win over these menfolk, even if it kills us."

"Yeah, I know," grumbled her husband.

Batting Billy's arm, Dumpling turned back to Lucky. "Where you from, young fella?"

"He's from these parts," Molly answered for him.

"And your people?"

There Molly hadn't a clue; she waved a hand at Lucky.

"My grandma and grandpa raised me, but they've

both passed on now," he grudgingly explained to Dumpling.

"Why, bless your little heart." Dumpling reached out to pinch his cheek. "All you're needing now is a fine new family like the Reklaws."

"Yeah," Lucky muttered, "they're a swell bunch of folks."

Her husband spoke up sternly. "Dumpling, quit pestering this young man and let him eat his vittles, will you? You're preening at him so, I'm suspectin' you've taken a shine to him."

As the others laughed, Dumpling guffawed. "Billy Reklaw, hush your mouth. You know darn well my heart is yours alone, especially after putting up with your temper these twenty-odd years, not to mention bearing you ten young 'uns."

"Just don't forget your place, darlin'," he teased back. "I can still wallop that pretty behind of yours."

"And I'll smack you good for that comment once we're alone," she retorted.

He winked. "You mean a kiss, darlin'?"

"No, I mean a slap upside the head!"

Amid gales of merriment, Dumpling spoke again to Lucky. "Don't fret, sugar. I know a virile stud like you needs a feisty young filly like Molly here to keep him satisfied. Can't wait to see the two of you hitched—and the sooner, the better, I'm saying."

At this, even Molly winced, realizing her aunt had gone too far. She watched as, face burning, Lucky shot to his feet, his fingers trembling as he hurled down his napkin. "Look, will all of you please just stop it? Since yesterday I've had my body busted up, my dignity assaulted, and I've landed among a passel of lunatics who think good old Teddy Roosevelt is still charging up San Juan Hill. But that isn't the half of it. Why in hell do you crazy people keep assuming I'd want to marry a manipulative little she-devil like her?"

Fixing a glare on Molly, Lucky turned and stormed out the back door as fast as his hobbling legs could carry him, leaving stunned silence in his wake. Even Molly felt slapped by the venom of his diatribe.

"Got a temper on him, don't he?" Dumpling muttered, fanning her face.

"Oh, yeah," agreed Grandma.

Molly continued to seethe. How dare Lucky insult her, reject her, call her names that way, in front of everyone? To her mortification, she felt hot tears stinging her eyes. This utter stranger had actually hurt her with his comments, she realized. Indeed, she could not recall any man's words ever smarting so.

Glancing at the four elders who now regarded her with pity, Molly burned with humiliation. She vowed she would give Lucky Lamont his comeuppance if it killed her.

And she knew just how to do it. Taking full advantage of the conflicted emotion churning inside her, she allowed huge, heartbroken tears to well up from her eyes and start streaming down her face.

The others watched in horror. "Oh, no!" wailed Dumpling. "He's gone and made her cry."

Cole was on his feet, face livid, jaw tight. "That does it! No bastard makes my baby girl cry."

Billy popped up, too. "Damn right, brother. You need any help stringing up the scoundrel?"

99

Jessica's hand shot out to grip Cole's wrist. "Cole, no. Both of you men just settle down and let's finish our dinner. We can address this matter later on, once everyone cools down."

Molly sprang up. "Well, I'm giving that snake his comeuppance right now." She stomped toward the back door, then flung over her shoulder, "And don't none of you dare come watch."

Molly well knew they'd all do exactly the opposite.

Storming into the backyard, she spotted Lucky striding about angrily, waving his hands and muttering to himself. She caught the words "damn loco woman," and charged toward him, skirts flouncing and curls flying. "How dare you insult me, you low-down coward!"

He turned aggressively, then blanched. "Hey, what's that on your face?" he asked gruffly. "You been crying?"

Molly felt red shooting up her face at the realization that he knew he had shamed her. His expression of concern should have enraged her, but instead she felt even more vulnerable, close to breaking down entirely. Nonetheless, she drew herself up with as much dignity and courage as she could muster. "Never mind that. I want you to come back inside right this minute and apologize to my entire family for insulting me, then apologize to me, too."

All signs of sympathy fled from his features. "In your dreams, lady."

"Damn it, why are you acting this way? What do you want?"

"To get the hell away from you wackos."

Though Molly wasn't precisely sure what *wacko*

meant, his tone told her enough. "So you really don't want to marry me?"

He laughed in disbelief and flung his arms heavenward. "You finally got *that* through your thick head."

She paused, tapping her foot in frustration, her wounded pride warring with angry determination. She realized this stubborn drifter had her all but thwarted.

Then a delicious strategy occurred to her, a way she could make him pay—and enjoy every second of it.

She chortled and shook a finger at him. "I get it now. No wonder you don't want to marry me—or tell me anything about yourself."

"What do you mean?" He eyed her suspiciously.

"You must be one of them *sissy-fied* fellas who likes boys."

"What?" he cried, his eyes wild.

Savoring her victory, she stepped closer and spoke in a low, tormenting hiss. "Yeah. Like Sidney Riddle in town, with his sack coat, ascot and jeweled walking stick. Everyone knows he only likes to do it with other fellas. You one of them fancy-pants types?" She looked him over with contempt. "Hell, you're pretty enough."

"Why, you little shit!"

Never had Molly seen such rage gripping a man's features. A second later, she was hauled up hard against Lucky's lean frame. His mouth slammed down on hers and his tongue plunged fully inside her mouth. To her further horror and fascination, his strong hands gripped her buttocks, pushing her against something very stiff and tantalizing.

Molly burned from head to toe, but not from embarrassment. What Lucky's scorching looks had done to her could not compare to the storm of excitement she felt with his masterful mouth ravishing hers, his tongue probing, retreating, then plunging again, his fingers digging into her bottom, forcing her into his heat, making her throb inside. She ached for him all over!

Then, as quickly as the kiss had started, he shoved her away, triumph and a darker emotion gleaming in his eyes. He spoke hoarsely, raggedly. "There, lady, you got it, now? I like to do it with *girls*. But you're the last girl this side of Hades I'd ever want to do it with."

For a moment they just glared at each other. Molly felt appalled yet equally fascinated, almost hoping he would grab her and kiss her again. Then both tensed at the sounds of gasps. Molly turned to see Ma, Pa, Grandma, Aunt Dumpling and Uncle Billy, all standing on the back stoop, regarding them in openmouthed disbelief.

Molly almost shrieked with joy at her good fortune. Deliberately bursting into tears again, she ran back to the stoop and thrust herself into her father's arms. Convulsively she cried, "Pa, Lucky grabbed me and kissed me and shoved his nasty tongue down my throat!"

"He shoved his *what?*" cried Dumpling.

"Yeah, and he pinched my butt, too."

Clutching Molly close, Cole had gone white with anger and was shaking a fist at Lucky. "Young man, you've got a lot of explaining to do—"

"But, sir, she provoked me."

"She's a lady, and that's no excuse."

"Yeah," added Billy with a fearsome scowl. "Brother, should I go fetch your shotgun?"

"Oh, yes," chortled Dumpling, clapping her hands in glee. "We'll be having us a wedding afore sundown."

At the mention of a wedding, Molly turned triumphantly, just in time to see Lucky's jaw drop almost to the ground.

Chapter Nine

"Pa, you just gotta make Lucky marry me! You just gotta!"

Inside the kitchen, Cole Reklaw frowned and watched his daughter pace about, her features murderously set. For long moments now he'd been trying to reason with Molly, while out in the backyard, his brother Billy stood guarding the "scoundrel" Lucky at gunpoint.

Damn, but things were in such a lather. Cole badly needed time to gather his thoughts regarding the wisdom of his daughter's demanded shotgun wedding to this drifter, and unfortunately Molly wasn't cutting him much slack. Of course Lucky Lamont had insulted his daughter terribly and deserved to be horsewhipped for his sins; but for her doting father, that didn't necessarily mean she should rush headlong into marriage with a stranger—whether fortune was at play here or not.

She sure had that wild Reklaw blood in her, he

thought with a mingling of pride and exasperation. When Molly set her sights on something, there was no stopping her. But she had to be made to understand that this marriage business was a serious matter, and nothing to be embarked upon on a whim.

When Cole had established the contest, he'd been well aware that they lived in a small, close-knit community, where he knew all of the young men who might be suitable candidates to wed his daughter; it had never occurred to him that she'd take a shine to a vagabond, even if it did appear that Lucky was from another time and there might well be something to this Destiny business. Jessie seemed convinced it was so, but to be honest, he'd never seen a more contentious pair.

Then he smiled, remembering how he and Jessie had started out on equally rocky footing—and what a glorious outcome had followed. Nonetheless, some caution was definitely in order.

"Well, Pa?" Molly prodded.

Cole fought a grimace at the sight of the outrage and pride gripping her beautiful face. "Molly, honey, your ma and I just want what's best for you. This young man is a stranger. We hardly know him—"

She folded her arms over her bosom. "We know he grabbed me like I was some whore and insulted my womanhood. And it's your duty as my daddy to make things right. That means you either gotta make him marry me or you gotta shoot him."

"Defeated by my own code of honor, am I?" Cole asked wryly.

She nodded adamantly. "Yes, sir. You got no choice now."

He moved closer, reaching out to smooth an errant auburn curl away from her brow. "Molly, girl, you know you're the apple of my eye."

At last she grinned. "Yeah, I know."

Oh, the little stinker! Fighting a smile, Cole continued sternly, "But your ma and I don't want to see you make a huge mistake."

"Meaning what?"

"Meaning you haven't really thought through all the implications of marriage—'til death do you part and all that. You regard Lucky as no more than a means to an end. This is not what I intended when I established the contest, honey. I was hoping all of you children might use this as an opportunity to grow up and find the right spouses, mates you could really get to know—and love for the rest of your lives. I had no idea things would take this reckless turn, and frankly, I'm beginning to regret establishing this competition at all. I know you too well, honey. You don't really want this rambler; you just want to win."

Ire sparkled in her eyes. "Oh, I want him, Pa. I want him in the worst way."

Cole chuckled. "You know, I'm almost feeling sorry for the poor fella."

"Sorry for him? After he assaulted my—"

Cole held up a hand. "Your pride? Yes, daughter, I think I've got your story straight there."

She tapped her foot. "It wasn't just my pride he riled—"

"I know. It was your desire to win against your brothers at any cost."

For just an instant, Cole thought he detected a twinge of guilt flicker across her face, then her chin came up. "So what if it was? Great Jumping Jehoshaphat, Pa! Just what do you think my no-account brothers are gonna do to try to beat me out? Hitch up with anything with titties, that's what they'll do."

Cole whistled. "Mind your language, daughter."

Undaunted, she went on, "'Sides, my friend Janey Struthers went out to Wyoming as a mail-order bride without a never-you-mind, hadn't even met the man she wed. At least I know the arrogant, infuriating son-of-a-bitch I'll be marrying."

Cole couldn't help himself, he shook with silent laughter. "How can I say no when you speak of him with such eloquence and affection?"

"Pa, are you giving me my way in this or not?" she demanded with a scowl.

He gave a long sigh. "You're sure this is what you really want, daughter?"

"Yes, sir."

"Have you ever heard the old adage 'Be careful what you wish for'?"

"Yeah." She grinned. "I may just get it."

Cole gave a groan. As usual, Molly had an answer to his every argument. Before speaking with her, he'd actually feared she might be biting off more than she could chew with this Lucky character, but as the conversation had progressed, he had felt more and more sympathy toward the object of his daughter's designs.

Still, he was not about to ride posthaste for the parson as Molly was insisting. "Very well, then," he conceded. "Mind you, I'm not making any promises, but I will have a word with your young man. Go tell your uncle Billy to bring in the prisoner."

Cole could only shake his head as Molly whooped with glee and went tearing out the back door.

How in hell had he gotten himself into this appalling predicament?

In the yard, Lucky stood glowering by a Douglas fir while Billy guarded him at gunpoint and regaled him with tales of shotgun weddings in these parts. In the background the two dogs and the pregnant cat listened to the oration in apparent fascination.

"Now Tildy Jessup and Owen Tanner, that was a funny one," Billy was saying as he puffed away on a cigar, holding the shotgun loosely in his other arm. "You see, Tildy's pa caught her out in the springhouse cavortin' with old Owen. Wilbur blasted the miscreant out of there in a hurry, let me tell you. After the fireworks, poor Owen stood repeatin' his vows with his pants still smolderin' from the buckshot."

"Yeah, that's just hilarious," Lucky snapped.

"Then there was the time the mayor caught the new preacher kissing Edwina Ann Morton—the two of them was rolling around in the church baptistery, would ya believe? Edwina Ann's a distant cousin of our'n, did you hear tell? Anyhow, after them two was corralled up, there was nobody to perform the nuptials—seein's how the preacher was the bridegroom, and all—so me and Cole, we had to ride out to Dillyville to fetch in the circuit judge. Ain't that a hoot?"

"You trying to scare me?" Lucky countered nastily.

Billy fixed a fearsome scowl on the younger man. "Maybe I'm aimin' to impress on you how lucky you are, young *Lucky*, to get to marry my pretty niece—"

"Instead of meeting my maker?" Lucky snarled back.

"There are worse fates for a man in this world," Billy rejoined piously.

"Well, *excuuuuse* me if I can't think of one."

Billy was about to reply when both men tensed at the sound of loud female hooting coming from within the house. Seconds later Molly burst out the kitchen door, looking flushed and breathless. "Pa's ready to talk to old handsome now!" she yelled at her uncle.

Lucky muttered curses.

Billy regarded his niece with veiled humor. "Should I come along to guard him? He ain't acted none too hospitable toward me so far."

Molly grinned at her uncle. "Naw, I'm sure Pa can handle a greenhorn like him."

Billy nudged Lucky with his shotgun. "Get on in the house now, junior. And no trying to hightail it, neither, you hear? I'll be keeping watch out here in the yard, so mind your manners."

Hurling Billy a nasty look, Lucky trooped off toward the back steps. He was angrier than he'd ever been in his entire life, but more at himself than Molly. He still could not believe that this slip of a girl had managed to maneuver him into what now would surely be a shotgun wedding. How could he have been so stupid?

He'd gotten in his licks, of course, had mortified and humiliated her with his brazen kiss—a kiss that had aroused him far too much. Still, ultimately, he had only himself to blame for letting her break his control that way.

Surely her pa would understand that, he thought with desperate hope. After all, a man could only take so many insults from a female.

The vixen smirked at him as he passed her on the stoop. He ground his jaw, silently vowing that he would find a way to wipe that impudent smile off her face if it killed him.

He barreled into the kitchen to see Cole standing at the side window, hands shoved in his pockets. "Well, sir? You wanted a word with me?"

Cole turned, smiling. "Seems my daughter is determined to marry you, young man."

"No way!" scoffed Lucky.

Cole shrugged. "Well, it's either that or I've gotta shoot you, she tells me."

Lucky gulped. "What? You'd really shoot me, sir?"

"You want to wait and find out?"

"Goddammit!"

Cole glowered. "Watch your language, young man, or my wife and mother'll be dashing in here to clean out your mouth with soap."

Lucky had to admit *that* was a daunting possibility. With considerable effort, he calmed himself. "Sir, excuse me, but this is ridiculous. A shotgun wedding, my ass."

"Didn't I just warn you about your—"

"Do you think we're living back at the turn of the century or something?"

"Well, yes." Cole appeared perplexed.

Lucky uttered a sound of frustration. "I can't believe you're allowing your daughter to deceive and manipulate you this way. Whatever you folks saw outside was totally staged on her part. Sir, she forced me into it—"

"Forced you to kiss her, eh?"

Miserably Lucky confessed, "She taunted me, called me a pantywaist, said I must like boys—"

"Boys?" Cole's eyebrows shot up.

Lucky felt a flush creeping up his face. "You know, sir, she said—uh—that I must only like to do it with other guys."

Cole roared with laughter. "Lord have mercy. I knew I'd raised a spitfire, but now I see I've underestimated my daughter."

"No shit!" Watching Cole's features darken with fury, Lucky quickly held up a hand. "No offense, sir, but with all due respect, that daughter of yours is dangerous."

"She's a determined one, all right."

"And there's only so much a man can take, before he—"

"Shows his woman her place?" Cole provided.

Lucky realized he was quickly painting himself into a corner. "Well, er, yes, sir, I mean, no, sir. That is, she ain't my woman, but she did need some showing—"

"And you hated every second of it, right?" Cole drawled.

Lucky frowned but didn't answer. Truth to tell, he had savored every second of the kiss but would *never* admit it.

Cole eased into a smile. "Look, young fella, there's no stopping my Molly when she's determined. Guess she's too much like me—"

"But she purely goaded me into this," Lucky reiterated. "Surely you can see that."

"Yes, I believe she might have. But you took her bait, didn't you?"

"Damnation," Lucky muttered. "So I've been had?"

"Reckon that's about the size of it."

Lucky glowered.

"She's a good girl once you get past all the bluster," Cole went on. "If I were you, I think I'd quit fighting so much and try to get to know her better, to make the best of things."

Lucky clenched his fists. "Look, get it through your head, Mr. Reklaw. All I want is to be free of you folks."

"Free? But where would you go?"

"Back to my life at the Flying T."

Cole sadly shook his head. "Son, there is no Flying T, and it's about time you accepted the notion that your life is gonna be here."

"Bullshit."

He sighed. "What will it take to convince you to stick around?"

"I haven't a clue, sir."

Cole frowned for a moment, then smiled. "You know, my wife made an apt suggestion."

"I can't wait to hear it."

"What if I take you around, show you the town and convince you that you really are living in another century now?"

Lucky gave a disbelieving laugh. "You mean you're actually gonna persuade me we're all living in the year 1911?"

"Yeah. What if I can make you accept that? Will you stop fighting your fate so much then?"

Lucky spoke with absolute conviction. "Sir, if you can convince me of that, I'll marry your haywire daughter."

"Will you?"

"Hell, I'll marry your ma." Watching him glower, he hastily added, "But *only* if you can convince me. Otherwise, I want your word that you'll let me go."

Cole beamed. "You've got it, son. I'll let you go with fifty dollars and a horse, no less. Shall we shake on it?"

"Yes, sir."

As he shook Cole's hand, Lucky waited for the expected wave of elation to sweep over him. This was a bargain he surely could not lose. There was no way they were actually living in the year 1911, and soon he'd be free of these lunatics.

Then why did he feel such a sense of impending doom instead?

Chapter Ten

While Lucky pondered his fate, the four Reklaw brothers were approaching the Trumble farmstead several miles north of the ranch. It had been a painstaking journey through high mountain passes and on toward a misty valley beyond.

Cory Reklaw didn't have a good feeling about this spur-of-the-moment courting excursion. He was the youngest of the four, the one who most resembled their ma, with his auburn hair and green eyes, the one who shared her more moderate temperament and love of books—while his three older siblings were their pa reincarnated, both in their dark good looks and in their wild, unruly ways. Although his brothers often teased him about being a sissy and a mama's boy, Cory was much more inclined to believe what Ma told him—that he was the only one among the four who had any sense.

Cory was also the only one among the boys who really believed his ma had traveled through time to be with his pa—which he supposed also meant that Molly's "fiancé" might have accomplished the same outlandish feat. When Molly had been younger and Ma had told her stories of the future, Cory had often secretly crouched outside his sister's bedroom window, listening in fascination to the astonishing and marvelous tales. Moreover, Molly was not the only one who enjoyed the works of Jules Verne and H. G. Wells, who saw possibilities beyond their own limited reality.

Only Cory knew he never dared voice his true feelings on the subject, even to his ma, or his brothers would roast him worse than a wiener at a Fourth of July picnic.

He'd definitely seen enough of his brothers' hot-headed exploits to have a healthy fear of their tempers. Time and time again, he'd implored the other three not to rush headlong into trouble, and time and time again, he'd failed—including the other night, when they'd mixed it up with their long-standing rivals, the Hicks cousins, at the saloon, and all four Reklaws had landed in jail.

His pleas had made little difference then, just as his arguments earlier today had been jeered at. He very much feared they'd get off on the wrong foot with old man Trumble and his daughters. And he really liked the girls—particularly Ida May, whom he'd waited on a time or two at the Mariposa library. Once he'd even helped her select a novel—*Daisy Miller* by Henry James—before her scowling father had dragged her away.

Now, spotting the neat two-story farmhouse emerging in the hazy hollow below them, he cleared his throat and tried one last time to convince the others. "Boys, like I told you, I've got a bad feeling about this courting business. Hasn't Ma always told us wooing a future wife is nothing to be embarked on in haste?"

"Yeah," answered Vance, "but just look what baby sister is doing, beating us to the punch with that drifter. Hell, she'll likely have the knot tied with him before we get home tonight."

"But Molly's a girl," Cory argued. "Girls can get away with murder—leastwise, that's what Ma has always told me."

"Well, baby sister ain't beating us out this time, not while I have breath left in my body," asserted Zach. "And quit quoting Ma to us, you little pantywaist."

Cory bucked up his fortitude. "Boys, my point is, we haven't thought this through. We're going off half-cocked to court these four sisters when we know Mr. T. will likely forbid us to see them—"

"Yeah, he's had it in for us ever since Grandma gave him his comeuppance," grumbled Matt.

"Well, would you want to marry old man Trumble?" asked Cory.

While Zach and Vance hooted with laughter, Matt went red-faced. "Hell, no! Just what are you insinuating, you little pissant?"

"I'm saying we can't just each of us up and grab a sister and go get hitched, like a bunch of barbarians."

"Why not?" asked Vance.

Cory waved a hand. "Well, for one thing, we don't even know which one of us is going to court which sister."

116

"Ah, that's easy," blustered Zach. "We'll just go by ages. I'll take the eldest, Sally. Vance, you get Nelly, Matt can court Bonnie and Cory, you get the pudgy runt, Ida May."

"I don't think she's pudgy, or a runt," Cory protested.

"Good. You're welcome to her, then."

Cory could only shake his head as the group arrived before the two-story Victorian farmhouse. All dismounted and tied their horses at the hitching post; Vance was the first to go vaulting up the steps and knock on the door. Following along, Cory could have sworn he spotted a curtain moving in an upstairs window, a flash of blond curls. And had he heard a giggle?

A moment later a gaunt, bearded, elderly man with bushy eyebrows and fearsome features opened the door and scowled at the four as he lifted a hearing horn to his ear. "So, it's the Reklaw boys, eh?" he greeted in a loud, strident voice. "What are you four whelps doing on my porch this fine spring afternoon?"

Vance had the grace to remove his hat. "Afternoon, Mr. Trumble. We've come to court your daughters, sir."

"What?" the old man cried, ire shooting from his dark eyes. "You say you're here to *wart* them? How dare you!"

As all four men struggled not to smile, Vance said forcefully, "No, sir. No. We've come to *court* them."

The old man harrumphed. "Court 'em, eh? Why, that's even worse! Of all the gall! What makes you pipsqueaks think you have my permission to spark my daughters?"

Vance gulped. "Well—er—"

Trumble advanced, sneering at the boys. "You ain't

even asked me, you know. Just showing up here without a never-you-mind."

"Well, sir, we're asking now," put in Matt bravely.

Trumble snorted. "That ain't how you ask, young fella. You should make a proper appointment, or speak to me in town. Did your ma raise up a bunch of heathens?"

"No, sir," insisted Zach. "You know we all attend church every Sunday, just like you and your girls do."

" 'Pears it hasn't done you much good."

The three older Reklaw boys glanced helplessly at one another. Cory knew he had to step in. "Sir, we apologize for just showing up like this, but we really were hoping we could see your daughters—er—just for a few minutes."

"Where's your calling card, young man?" Trumble demanded.

"Er—we don't have any."

"Well, how can I tell you boys whether or not you're received if you don't even got no calling cards?"

All four Reklaw brothers appeared stumped. "But sir," pleaded Matt, "just let us have a moment—"

"Young man, what makes you think you have anything at all to offer one of my daughters?" Trumble demanded.

"Why, I've plenty I'd like to offer your Bonnie," Matt spouted back. "The lower five hundred . . ." He paused, grinning. "If she'll just give me a baby right quick."

Cory winced as Trumble cursed violently, then slammed Matt across the jaw, knocking him to his heels. Horrified, Cory watched his brother go crashing down the steps, landing with a moan in the swept yard.

Meanwhile, their host was bellowing blasphemies

and bashing Zach and Vance with his hearing horn. "Filthy-mouthed hooligans! Where's my shotgun?" he shouted, whirling to go back inside.

This was all the prodding the Reklaw brothers needed. The three who remained upright vaulted down the steps and hauled Matt to his feet. Then all four jumped on their horses and galloped away.

Hearing the sounds of feminine laughter, Cory glanced back to see the four lovely Trumble daughters framed in a second-floor window. All were tittering and waving. Great. Not only had they made complete fools of themselves, but the four sisters, ladies they'd hoped to impress, had witnessed their downfall.

"Well, that was right productive, boys," Cory drawled to the others.

"Shut up!" Matt snapped back, rubbing his jaw.

But Cory was too indignant to be silenced. "Didn't I tell you boys what Ma said—that you can't just go snatching up some lady like a caveman?"

"If you don't stop quoting Ma, we're gonna string you up," threatened Zach.

Cory waved a hand. "There you go again, behaving like savages. Has it ever occurred to you boys that the only way to win this contest might be to *listen* to our mother?"

There; the others had no replies, though their angry looks spoke volumes.

The sun was low in the sky by the time Cory and his brothers arrived, dusty and bedraggled, at the ranch house. Before they could even dismount, Molly came dancing down the steps. With secret mischief in her eyes, she teased, "Well, don't you four look a sight? Where you boys been? You missed all the excitement."

"Well, maybe we had some of our own," sneered Vance as he slipped off his horse.

Molly frowned at the sight of Matt hobbling toward the front steps. "You boys get in another fight at the saloon?"

"That's none of your business," Matt snarled.

"So, be a prickly pear, then," she taunted back. "I'm still gonna tell you my good news."

"Oh, yeah?" scoffed Zach.

"Yeah." She preened to each one in turn. "Handsome and me are gonna get hitched. It's all official now."

All four of Molly's brothers snapped to attention. "What?" demanded Zach.

"You're lying!" accused Matt.

"No way you did all that in one afternoon," protested Vance.

"Oh, no? Just go ask Ma and Pa."

"We will," vowed Zach.

As his three older brothers stormed toward the house, Cory lingered on the steps with his sister, shaking his head at her superior look. So she had already hoodwinked the drifter into a proposal of marriage. He had to hand it to her—Molly was one smooth operator.

"So you did it, eh, sis?" he teased. "Convinced that cowboy to marry you, just like that?"

"Well, I have my ways about me," she gushed, smoothing her hair with a hand. "Still, I reckon it was more Pa's shotgun that persuaded handsome, right after he shoved his tongue in my mouth."

Cory laughed. "Wonder whose idea that was?"

"Why, old handsome's, of course."

"Sure, I just bet it was."

She winked. "So, how did it go, courting the Trumble sisters?"

"You knew?" Cory raised an eyebrow.

"Pa told us after you left. Now I want to hear all the juicy details."

He just bet she wanted to hear. "Well, maybe I'm not in a mood to chat."

"Cory, please . . ." she wheedled.

He wagged a finger at her. "You may have that cowboy of yours bamboozled, but I'm wise to you, sis. Don't expect me to help you win this contest over the rest of us."

"Well, hell, I tried." She grinned. "Reckon I'll go air out my hope chest."

Cory was still laughing as he followed Molly inside the house.

Jessica turned from the sideboard at the din of her three eldest sons storming into the kitchen.

"Ma, is it true?" Zach demanded. "Has Molly already convinced that low-down sidewinder to marry her?"

Laughing, she wiped her hands on a kitchen towel. "Boys, really, no firm date has been set."

"You're already discussing dates?" Matt cried, crestfallen.

Glancing at her son, Jessica grimaced at the sight of his bruised jaw and ripped shirt. "Matt, what on earth happened to you?"

Matt gulped but did not reply.

"Old man Trumble knocked him down the front stoop," explained Vance.

"Well, I'm not surprised," Jessica said wearily.

"What?" cried Matt.

She rolled her eyes. "Didn't you boys just show up there in the middle of the week, without an invitation?"

"Well, we wanted to court his daughters," grumbled Zach.

"Your father explained that to me. But there's more to courting than just following your noses. Why, just to intrude that way—"

"That's what I told 'em, Ma," put in Cory self-righteously as he stepped inside the kitchen to join the others. "How they were going off half-cocked and not thinking this through."

"Amen," agreed Jessica.

"Old man Trumble wouldn't let us see his girls, any-how," griped Vance.

"Gee, what a shock," murmured their mother.

"Well, our intentions were honorable," spouted Zach with a dark look. "Old man Trumble knows we all have marriage on our minds."

"I'll just bet he does," Jessica concurred.

"And I told him I'd provide well for his Bonnie—if she'd just give me a baby right quick," added Matt.

"You didn't!" Jessica gasped.

Matt rubbed his jaw. "And that's when the geezer knocked me three ways to sundown."

"Well, I can't say I blame him."

"Ma!" protested Matt.

Jessica balled her hands on her hips. "Boys, I've told you and told you that when the time comes for court-ing, you must show the proper respect. Sunday after-

noon is the appointed time. Going-to-meeting clothes
are in order, as well as modest gifts of candy or flowers."

"But, Ma, he even demanded we show calling
cards," protested Zach.

"A fine idea," Jessica agreed. "We can go into town
and get some printed up."

Zach's jaw dropped open.

Matt was pacing about angrily. "But that'll take a
month of Sundays, and baby sister is already besting us."

"I told you nothing has been firmly decided."

"Hell, she'll have that sissy yoked up before the week
is out," put in Vance with disgust.

Jessica had to smile. "I'm sorry you're feeling so frustrated, boys. But if you want to win this contest, you'll
need to proceed with a little more finesse in approaching your future wives."

"But Ma, Pa bushwhacked you home and it worked
out just fine," complained Zach.

"Son, that was a very special incident, and frankly,
your father is lucky I didn't roast him on a spit. If you
really want to court your ladies, then you need to listen
to me, and start remembering some of those lessons in
good manners that you've all so conveniently forgotten." She smiled at her youngest son. "All except Cory,
that is."

Jessica's three oldest sons regarded her in surly silence—and Cory grinned from ear to ear. "Didn't I tell
you boys? Ma is always right!"

Zach snarled at his younger brother, then jerked his
thumb toward Matt and Vance. "Come on, boys, let's go
rub down the horses and see if Sanchez has any chili

left out at the bunkhouse. Sure beats the company in *here.*"

Watching her three older sons troop out, Jessica sighed, then turned to Cory. "Honey, I'm sorry the courting expedition was such a disaster."

"Well, I warned my brothers—and you did, too."

"I know, but I do feel badly for the boys." Jessica pensively eyed her youngest son. "What are your sentiments regarding this contest, Cory?"

"What do you mean?"

"I mean, do you want to win like the others? Do you favor one of the Trumble girls yourself? I know you've mentioned helping out Ida May at the library."

He grinned. "Yeah, I like her a lot, Ma. She's pretty and smart—and favors books, like I do."

Jessica bit her lip. "She is lovely, dear, but I don't want to see this absurd competition derailing your future. Of you five kids, you're the one I've always considered to be the most like me."

"Hey, that's quite a compliment." He affectionately hugged her.

"And you've also been the one who is most devoted to pursuing your education," she continued. "Indeed, I was hoping we might go visit the University of Colorado this fall, perhaps enroll you."

He nodded. "I'd like that, Ma. And of course we can do it."

"But what about Ida May?"

He winked. "By then, who knows? We might even be able to take her along with us—that is, if her pa will ever allow me to court her."

Jessica laughed. "Well, that is a thought. Actually, I

was really hoping we might take Molly—but with her already so fixated on marrying Lucky . . ."

Cory rolled her eyes. "Ah, Ma, don't worry about Molly. I don't think they offer many courses in 'The American Dime Novel' at the University."

"Yes, I suppose she does have rather lurid reading tastes," she rejoined dryly. "And I do think she and Lucky might be good for each other. I'm just afraid this whole business will deteriorate into a nasty war—especially between Molly and your older brothers."

Cory nodded. "I know, Ma. Me, too. Truth to tell, although I like Ida May, I'm involved in the competition mainly to keep my brothers out of trouble."

She patted his arm. "I pretty much figured that. Poor Cory. That's been your role all your life, hasn't it?— keeping the other boys from ruining theirs."

"Well, I can't let you and Grandma be the only crusaders in this family," he quipped.

"Thank heaven for that," Jessica replied, laughing and embracing him.

Chapter Eleven

Lucky could not believe his eyes and ears as he and Cole rode down the streets of Mariposa on two range horses. Only days earlier he'd seen this place as a ramshackle ghost town. Now he viewed a thriving community of the early twentieth century. Storefronts boasting signs emblazoned with everything from APOTHECARY to HABERDASHERY to DRY GOODS to SALOON lined the streets. On an adjacent square, a red brick Victorian complex housed the county courthouse, jail and library.

Citizens mingled on the boardwalks, gentlemen in old-fashioned suits, farmers in denim, lumberjacks in dungarees, ladies in long, straight gowns and feathered hats, little girls in pinafores and bonnets, boys in overalls and straw hats. Crude telephone poles laden with wire zigzagged past. In the cobbled streets he spotted all sorts of amazing conveyances—several antique carriages, a couple of drays hauling logs, a few riders on horseback and a couple of high-wheeler bicycles. He even spied a Model T Ford sputtering along, its mustachioed driver wearing a jaunty cap, an ascot, a sack coat and knickers.

What in hell was going on here? Some sort of movie production, maybe? He was half expecting to see Kevin Costner or Clint Eastwood come striding down the boardwalk.

Lucky regarded Cole in suspicion and amazement. "How exactly did this town come to be?"

"Mariposa was originally a mining town that sprang up when the Aspen Gulch Consortium made its strike at the eastern branch in 1883," Cole explained. "But there was mining in these parts for decades before that, thanks to those snakes in Colorado Springs."

"Snakes?" Lucky asked.

Cole's mouth was set with bitterness. "The Aspen Gulch Consortium. They're the sidewinders who poisoned the water and the land with metal runoff and murdered the miners by overtunneling. My ma lost two good husbands due to those vipers. My pa, Chester Lively, was killed in a cave-in, and my brothers' pa, Joseph Reklaw, died of miner's lung."

"Hey, I'm sorry to hear that," Lucky said sincerely.

"That's why almost three decades ago my brothers and I started robbing gold shipments from the Consortium—"

Lucky snapped his fingers. "And became the infamous Reklaw Gang, the one that later kidnapped Professor Jessica Garrett off the stage?"

Cole smiled wryly. "So you've heard of us?"

"Guess so."

"Well, we did bushwhack Professor Garrett, the very woman who's my wife today. And I take it you're opening up your mind a little about what has happened to you?"

He glanced about slowly and mumbled, "Looks like I may not have much choice."

"Anyway," Cole continued, "after Jessie came here, she, too, was appalled by the plight of the miners, and convinced the Aspen Gulch Consortium to close the mines down and pension the miners."

"How did she do that?"

He grinned. "Though some—er—hardball tactics involving the Colorado Springs press. Unfortunately, around that time the Colorado City sheriff got wise to me and my brothers' activities. After Jedediah Lummety almost nabbed us, we had to hightail it. We all got married, then pulled up stakes and moved with our wives to Wyoming."

"Hiding out, eh?"

"Right. When we left, we kind of expected the town to fade away. But a decade later, when my brother Billy and I decided to return here with our families, we were pleased to discover Mariposa had revitalized itself around farming and lumbering."

"Yeah, I guess not having all that pollution must have made a difference," Lucky muttered.

Cole motioned to Lucky to pull up his horse at a hitching post. "Come on. Let's take a walk," he suggested.

Hands shoved into his pockets, Lucky trooped along with Cole. As they passed a soda shop he glanced inside and spotted a soda jerk in white jacket and cap standing behind a bar with a huge, antique Coca-Cola plaque behind it; the man was serving ice cream sodas to two ladies wearing absurd feathered hats. Next they passed a bakery, where a plump woman was pulling loaves of bread out of a wall oven; Lucky had to admit the smell of warm baked goods wafting out the open door was tantalizing.

Cole motioned toward the general store ahead. "We'll stop in here. Jessica asked me to fetch home some flour and bacon."

They entered to the jangle of a bell and an over-abundance of sounds, sights and scents. Lucky couldn't begin to take it all in at once, so he started with the people: the aproned proprietor with gartered shirtsleeves and handlebar mustache, standing behind a counter stacked with tins of tobacco; the housewives perusing yard goods and grocery staples; the old-timers in overalls chatting around a barrel of pickles.

Next, the objects and wares: the antique wooden telephone hanging on the wall; the Victrola with huge shiny horn, displayed for sale in a front window; the fussy rows of ladies' satin slippers and button-top shoes; the cast-iron toys for the children; the jars of mustache wax and bottles of castor oil and other patent medicines; the old-fashioned mason jars and antique tin cans, offering foods ranging from pickled pigs' feet to "Son-of-a-gun Stew."

And the smells: tobacco and leather; old-fashioned talcum and pomade; spices and sawdust; pickles and molasses.

Lucky felt baffled, disoriented. Where were the symbols of modern life—the security cameras and video games, the coolers with beer and freezers with microwave meals, the racks of mass-produced groceries and staples?

Determined to get to the bottom of this, he strode over to the group of old-timers and addressed a bearded man with a potbelly and a pipe in his mouth. "What year is it, sir?"

The men guffawed, and the one he had addressed turned to Cole. "Who's this young whippersnapper you brung into town with you, Cole? Bit short on manners, ain't he?"

Cole strode forward. "Sorry, Walter. This is our house guest, Lucky Lamont. Had himself a bit of an accident the other day——"

"Did he fry his brains?" asked another old gent, amid more spurts of laughter.

As Lucky glowered, Cole held up a hand. "No, Lucky here fell off his horse."

"Weren't too lucky for him, eh?" interjected a bald oldster in overalls.

While Lucky ground his teeth, Cole explained, "Anyhow, he took a bad spill, and since then he's been——"

"A trifle tetched in the head?" offered Walter, prompting more gales of mirth.

Lucky had had his fill of these codgers and their jeering. "Would you geezers kindly stop breaking my butt and give me a straight answer? I want to know what year it is."

Walter whistled. "Got a temper on 'im, don't he, Cole? Well, young fella, it's the year of our Lord 1911."

"Bullshit."

"Hey, watch your lip, you little snot nose," Walter scolded.

Lucky jerked a thumb toward Cole. "How much did he pay you guys to do this?"

"Do what?" asked the bald one.

"To pull the wool over my eyes."

The man scratched his jaw. "Don't see no wool there, young fella—"

Exasperated, Lucky snapped, "Would you lose the farmer-in-the-dell routine? What I'm asking is, how much did he pay you to *pretend* you're living in the year nineteen-eleven?"

The man appeared mystified. "But we ain't play-actin', young man. This *is* the year 1911."

"And I'm Madonna in spurs."

Walter whistled. "He's a mite sacrilegious, ain't he, Cole?"

Before Cole could answer, Lucky turned aggressively on Walter. "Quit talking to him and give me some straight answers. We all know damn well it isn't 1911. Either you guys have pulled a fast one, setting up this practical joke, or I've just walked onto the set of a very bad spaghetti western."

"Spaghetti what?" Walter asked. "Cole, this youngster is loco."

"I told you he'd taken a bad fall."

Walter pointed to his head. "And now he has spaghetti for brains, eh?"

Before more chuckles could erupt, Lucky grabbed Walter by the lapels of his flannel shirt. "Okay, Rip Van Winkle, stuff the attitude and tell me what the hell year it is."

"Hey, cool down, young fella," Walter retorted, shaking himself loose. "Look, sonny, I know you don't want

131

to hear this, but it really is 1911." Watching Lucky go wild-eyed, he hastily pointed across the store. "Hell, don't listen to me. The *Denver Post* is right over there. Go see it with your own eyes."

Lucky gave Walter a nasty look, then strode across the store and grabbed a newspaper from the stack. He gulped at the date of the issue, from May of 1911, then quickly scanned the front-page articles: suffragettes staging another march in Washington, D.C.; news of the investigation of the Triangle Shirtwaist Factory Fire in New York City; a photo of Harry Houdini escaping a bank vault; details of an orphan train arriving at the Denver station; a picture of the Colorado governor John F. Shafroth greeting the Theodore Roosevelts during a visit to the state.

"You convinced yet?"

He turned to see Cole standing beside him, regarding him with amused indulgence, while the old-timers looked on, smirking, from across the store.

Despite the fact that his confidence was crumbling, Lucky slammed down the newspaper. "All of this could have been staged."

Cole waved a hand. "You know what, young man? I'm beginning to believe you are a good match for my Molly, since you're every bit as stubborn as she is. Look, I know this is a lot for you to absorb, but you must face the truth. What will it take to convince you you're really living in the year 1911?"

Lucky thought fiercely, then snapped his fingers. "Take me to Buck Hollow."

"I can't do that, son," Cole replied patiently. "As we've already told you, there is no town of Buck Hollow."

"All right, then. Take me to Broken Buck Mountain. It's gotta be due south of here. And the town lies right beneath the peak."

Cole nodded, then grinned. "Broken Buck Mountain, eh? Now that I can arrange."

A hard two hours' ride later, Lucky found himself sitting on horseback beside Cole, staring in bewilderment at Broken Buck Mountain. The dramatic peak loomed before them with its every well-remembered contour, its soaring pines and aspens, its haze encircling the snowy crest.

But the town of Buck Hollow was nowhere to be seen. Instead he viewed a lush valley where Colorado bluebirds chattered and a moose grazed, a stand of Douglas firs stood where the Broken Buck Motel should have been.

Damnation! Nothing was making any sense.

Except the possibility—indeed, the probability—that he *was* living in another time now, insane as that sounded. Of course he could ask Cole to take him by his grandparents' old homestead, but that was another long ride out of the way, and frankly, he couldn't bear the possibility that the beloved home of his youth was no longer there, either.

These crazy people were right. In fact, maybe they weren't so crazy after all. His entire existence was gone now, and he was lost in time, trapped in some never-ending nightmare or bizarre alternate world. It was unnerving.

"Well?" Cole prodded.

Lucky sighed. "Okay, guess I'm convinced." He cast

Cole a surly look. "Does that mean shotguns and flowers by sundown?"

Cole chuckled. "We'll proceed a bit more cautiously than that."

"Oh, yeah. That'll go over just swell with your lovely daughter," Lucky drawled.

"Son, believe it or not, Molly doesn't have the final say in my household."

"Sir, with all due respect, I don't believe you."

Cole broke up laughing as the two men turned their mounts homeward.

By the time Lucky and Cole guided their tired horses back onto the main street of Mariposa, a cold dusk had fallen and gaslights were winking on. At the edge of town they passed the small community church—the one Lucky had seen absent a roof only days before, now totally intact in its clapboard splendor. He watched the parson emerge, a portly little man with a trim mustache and balding head; he was attired in a traditional black suit with a clerical collar.

The preacher spotted the riders and waved. "Well, hello there, Cole! Who do you have with you?"

"Evening to you, Pastor Bledsoe," Cole called back. "This is our houseguest, Lucky Lamont. My daughter Molly has taken something of a shine to young Lucky, and as it happens, we may be needing your services soon."

"Oh?" As Lucky hurled Cole a nasty look, the little man stepped forward with an expression of avid interest.

"Yeah, looks like Lucky and Molly may be getting hitched soon."

"Well, splendid! Congratulations, young man!" the parson gushed to Lucky.

"Preacher, save the moonlight-and-magnolias routine," Lucky grumbled back. He turned to Cole. "I thought you said this wasn't set in stone as yet."

As the clergyman gave first Lucky and then Cole a perplexed look, Cole explained, "Yes, Lucky here has needed a bit of a nudge."

"Like with your shotgun?" Lucky provided with a sneer.

"A shotgun wedding, eh?" Glancing at Cole, the minister laughed nervously. "I'm not exactly unfamiliar with that term myself."

"Oh, yeah," agreed Cole with a grin. "We had us a fine shotgun wedding with you and Cousin Edwina Ann, eh?"

"Thanks to you and your brother Billy," the parson rejoined modestly.

Good Lord, this preacher was as crazy as the rest of these lunatics, Lucky thought with horror. To the preacher, he drawled, "That's right. Good old Uncle Billy regaled me with stories of all the shotgun weddings in these parts as he held me at gunpoint yesterday. Looks like the Reklaw brothers may have stuck it to you, too."

With a self-conscious chuckle, Pastor Bledsoe approached Lucky. "But young man, that shotgun wedding was the best thing that ever happened to me and my Edwina."

"Yeah, just like an overdose of arsenic, right?"

With a bemused expression, Bledsoe turned to Cole. "You know, Cole, perhaps some counseling might be in order here for the happy couple—"

"Happy!" Lucky exclaimed.

"—and as your community pastor, I'd be delighted to provide it."

Lucky's mouth dropped open.

"Hey, that's a splendid idea," agreed Cole. "You could impress on young Lucky here how serious this business is."

"You think I'm not taking it seriously now?" Lucky demanded.

"It will be my pleasure to advise him," said the minister enthusiastically.

"Oh, brother," muttered Lucky.

"Then I'll bring him by when we come back to town to see to the marriage license."

"Marriage license?" Lucky repeated, aghast. "Now you're talking about a marriage license?"

"Son, Mr. Reklaw is right," put in Bledsoe. "You really should get the paperwork started if you wish to wed in the foreseeable future. Old Dinkle, the county clerk, is slower than Christmas."

Cole nodded firmly. "So, after we run by the courthouse tomorrow—"

"Tomorrow!" Lucky shouted.

"—I'll bring Lucky by the parsonage."

"You're kidding me."

Cole waved a hand at Lucky. "Well, you heard the man. We need to rattle our hocks, since the clerk is slow as Christmas."

"But—*tomorrow!*"

"Maybe some stern talk from the good pastor will calm you down a mite," Cole added.

Lucky groaned massively. He was getting damn tired

of everything being out of his control. "And what about sweet little Molly? Seems to me she could use a good scold—I mean, a good counseling, too."

Cole grinned and slapped him across the shoulders. "Great idea, son. We'll bring her along, as well. Put you two lovebirds together and let you hash out your differences, eh?"

"Indeed!" seconded Bledsoe.

"Oh, hell," Lucky muttered.

"Then they're both all yours," pronounced Cole.

As Bledsoe beamed and effusively thanked Cole, Lucky wondered why he felt no sense of righteous vindication.

Chapter Twelve

At least the moon and the stars are the same. . . .

After the two men arrived home and tended to their horses, Lucky decided to avoid the house and the certain gloating of his "fiancée," telling Cole he needed a walk to clear his head and would return shortly. Cole, seeming to recognize that his guest needed some time alone, voiced no protest, merely nodding and striding toward the warm lights of the house.

Lucky climbed up the hillside and looked back down at the hollow where the farmstead lay slumbering. A chill had settled over the landscape, and Lucky pulled the sheepskin coat Jessica had given him more tightly about himself.

For long moments he gazed up at the sky, so clear and sparkling with thousands of stars. That luminous heaven was his touchstone, the most familiar and comforting respite in an alien world. How had he strayed so far from everything he held dear?

Since he'd arrived here, Lucky had somehow managed to hold off his overwhelming feelings through anger and defiance, through fighting his fate and refusing to believe he could actually be living in the year 1911. But now that he could no longer avoid the truth of his plight, the enormity of what had happened to him staggered him like a two-ton weight.

Of course, back in the present he had read—and seen—stories of time travel. But that was science fiction, right? Everyone knew that time travel wasn't *really* possible. Yet he'd somehow done the impossible and now seemed to be living a science fiction story—or was it horror?

Whatever joke the Fates had played on him, he wanted out, he wanted away—he wanted *back*—but there was no escape in sight. As far as he knew, he would be stuck here in Old West limbo forever.

He couldn't be meant to be here, as everyone kept insisting. He couldn't be destined to marry that little she-devil, even if she did stir his lust. He felt forlorn, adrift, without a friend or a path to guide him. . . .

"Lucky, talk to me."

At the sound of a female voice, Lucky whirled, expecting to see his adversary standing there. He expelled a sigh of relief as Jessica stepped up to join him; she wore a dark woolen dress and a heavy shawl.

"Evening, ma'am," he muttered. "For a moment there I thought you were your daughter."

"And you were not pleased?" she asked ironically.

Lucky stabbed the ground with the toe of his boot. "No comment, ma'am."

She smiled. "I guess you must have received a massive shock today when Cole took you into town."

"Now, there's an understatement," he concurred dryly. "But the bigger setback came when I saw that the town where I was raised no longer exists."

She touched his arm and regarded him with keen sympathy. "I know, Lucky. Cole told me, and I'm sorry you had to see all of that to be convinced. Just remember that I, too, was totally confused and disoriented when I first arrived back here, in the year 1888."

"The year 1888," Lucky repeated cynically, still not certain he believed her. Nonetheless, he felt compelled to ask the question that had been nagging him for days now. "So you are the *real* Professor Jessica Garrett, the one who disappeared from the year 1999?"

"I am indeed," she confirmed with a dry laugh. "Then you've heard of me?"

"Oh, yes, ma'am. There was an article in our local newspaper about how you disappeared—and how your colleagues reappeared a few days later with your journal."

She gasped. "So my associates all made it back okay?"

"Yes, ma'am."

"I'm so relieved to hear that. Do you know if they got my journal to my family up in Greeley?"

"I'm sure they did, although I really don't remember that many details."

"I understand." She sighed. "You and I do seem to have a lot in common, Lucky, in that we both came here in the same stagecoach."

He nodded. "Though my ride was a trifle rougher than yours."

"Indeed."

"I'd take you to see the vehicle, but it's a pile of rubble now."

"So I've heard."

"Wish it could take me back home," he added wistfully.

She appeared about to respond to that but bit her lip instead. "Well, I did want to tell you I was fit to be tied when I first arrived here—kidnapped off a stage and forcefully brought to this ranch by the Reklaw Gang, only to have Cole and his four brothers decide to fight over me, even as I was struggling to comprehend and accept the incredible things that had just happened to me."

"No kidding," Lucky replied. "Cole told me some of your family history today." He regarded her quizzically. "But after you got here, you decided this is where you belong?"

"Oh, yes," she replied fervently. "Lucky, it took me quite a while to accept my fate, but I finally realized that I belonged with Cole, that he was my destiny."

"Good old destiny again," Lucky drawled.

"Not that my feelings weren't torn," she continued. "And I'll admit there are things about the time I left behind that I sometimes still miss."

Lucky was pleasantly surprised. "Yeah? Such as?"

Her expression turned poignant. "Well, indoor plumbing, fast food, automobiles, air conditioning, watching TV, cruising the Internet. And though our isolation here has its advantages, sometimes I miss the instant communication of living in a world connected by satellites and CNN."

As she'd spoken, Lucky's jaw had slowly dropped open. "My God! You really *are* a fellow time-traveler—bizarre as that sounds."

"I know, Lucky. It's a very difficult notion to accept."

"Amen. But—how could you leave a world of cell phones and day spas and be happy here, in a world of kerosene lanterns and outhouses?"

She gave a rueful laugh. "Well put. I'm not saying it wasn't a sacrifice, but ultimately it was one I gladly made. However, I do miss my family, and sometimes I wonder what happened to the world I left behind." She glanced at him tentatively. "You know, don't you? I mean, at least you would know about the five years that passed after I left—and before you did."

He stared at her for a long moment, not certain how to respond. Days earlier he never would have dreamed he'd be having this conversation with Jessica. Should he tell her about the horror and tragedy of 9/11, the wars in Afghanistan and Iraq? Or even about the fun changes, such as Harry Potter fever sweeping the country and big-screen plasma TVs becoming the latest rage? He couldn't exactly discuss the sweet without the bitter, he realized.

At last he gently replied, "Ma'am, I think there's some things you're probably better off not knowing."

She gazed at him with concern and puzzlement. "Well, we won't press the issue for now. But please, just tell me what I can do to help you, Lucky."

He shook his head in irony. "Help me? Ma'am, I'm lost. I've lost my world, my faith, the grandparents I loved, and now I'm caught in some hellhole in time, engaged to marry some wildcat who only wants me as a sperm donor." Watching her flinch, Lucky added, "Sorry, ma'am."

"Lucky, I know you're frustrated," she replied patiently, "but please don't allow your stubbornness to make you discount all the possibilities you have here. I was really hoping you'd see much sooner than I did that you're only hurting yourself by fighting your fate."

"Yeah. Right."

"Besides, deep down, you and Molly are a lot alike—"

"Sure, like oil and water."

"You might balance each other out, teach each other something."

"We'll kill each other first."

"Lucky, I think you and Molly belong together, just as Cole and I do," she continued sincerely. "That's surely the reason the Fates brought you here. You can't avoid Molly forever, or deny what's happened to you."

"That's quite true," Lucky rejoined cynically. "Tomorrow your husband is taking the spitfire and me to town to apply for a marriage license—and for pre-marital counseling with the charming Pastor Bledsoe."

She fought a smile. "Yes, Cole told me."

Lucky angrily waved a hand. "And you didn't say anything to stop him? You're just gonna let me be bushwhacked all the way to the altar?"

"I don't think either of us can fight Destiny, Lucky—"

"Lady, *please,* give it a rest," he pleaded.

"I'm sorry, but I do think it's preordained."

"So much for your helping me," Lucky rejoined bitterly.

Jessica started to respond, but then, with a sigh, she turned and walked away. Lucky felt a twinge of guilt for being short with her, and almost went after her to apologize. Instead, feeling helpless, he stood staring at the stars for a long, long time.

Chapter Thirteen

The next morning Lucky found himself back in Mariposa, standing with Molly before the county clerk, a bad-tempered little man absurdly named Dudley Dinkle, who sported a high-pitched nasal twang and a tobacco-stained suit. Both his breath and his clothing seemed to reek of mothballs. Behind them in the small anteroom of the courthouse stood Cole, the forever-menacing overprotective father.

"Name?" the crotchety man asked Lucky as he began scribbling on the marriage license.

Glancing sourly at his "fiancée," who stood beside him wearing her customary smirk as well as an all-too-enticing peach-colored dress, Lucky cleared his throat. "Lyndon B. Lamont."

Molly tittered. "Lyndon? Your real name is Lyndon?"

At once Lucky wanted to kick himself. Why had he revealed his given name to Molly? After all, back in the present, he'd gone to great lengths to bribe one of the sweet young things who worked for the county into putting Lucky on his driver's license.

But then, his grandma had always loved Lyndon, and had suggested the name to his mother. Maybe it was just a sentimental slip—but that didn't mean he wanted to hear the name from *her* lips.

"Yeah, Lucky's my nickname," he told Molly tersely. "And if you really want to get me riled, try saying 'Lyndon' one more time."

She chortled. "But what kind of name is that?"

"I'll have you know I was named after a president."

"Which one?"

Lord, was there even any point talking with this infuriating woman? "Johnson."

"But President Johnson's Christian name wasn't 'Lyndon.'" She turned to Cole. "Was it, Daddy?"

"No. It was Andrew."

"I'm talking about a different Johnson!" Lucky burst out in exasperation. "The one from Texas. My grandma was from there, too."

"Huh?" Molly asked blankly. "Daddy, what's he talking about?"

Before Cole could respond, the clerk waved a hand. "Now, children, get aholt of yourselves, will you? You want to stand there and bicker all day or get hitched?"

Both the bride and groom glowered at him.

The clerk looked askance at Cole. "Why do these two want to tie the knot anyhow? 'Pears to me they hate each other."

Cole grinned. "Sounds like the basis of an excellent marriage to me."

"Ah, all of you Reklaws are haywire," groused the little man.

"Don't call me a Reklaw," retorted Lucky.

"Well, you're about to wed one—"

"That don't make me a Reklaw." Abruptly Lucky smiled vindictively, jerking a thumb toward Molly. "But come to think of it, it'll make *her* a Lamont."

"Oh," cried Molly.

The clerk rolled his eyes. "Just keep on dreaming, sonny. Now if you'll just put your John Hancock right here, and pay the fee—"

Grudgingly, Lucky took out his wallet and extended a bill to the man. "Here."

The man's eyes grew huge as he examined the alien bill. "What in Sam Hill . . . ? Sonny, are you trying to pass off counterfeit on me? I've half a mind to call the sheriff—"

Laughing, Cole snatched up the bill and handed it back to Lucky. "I'll pay the fee for these two."

Lucky glowered at him. "Why not? You and your crazy daughter are calling all the shots in this marriage business anyway, aren't you?"

The clerk reached out to swat Lucky's arm. "Just my point, young man. You're a Reklaw now, and all of you Reklaws are haywire."

Lucky almost slugged the codger then. Only the thought that the county jail might be more objectionable than being in Molly Reklaw's clutches stopped him . . . though just barely.

"Ah. Here's the happy couple."

Half an hour later, Lucky glowered at Reverend

Bledsoe as he entered the fussy Victorian parlor of the parsonage wearing a huge smile and carrying a large black Bible. After being dropped off by Cole, Lucky and Molly had seated themselves in stiff, high-backed chairs on opposite sides of the room, and had been staring daggers at one another ever since.

"Reverend," Lucky acknowledged stiffly.

He nodded and turned to Molly. "And Miss Molly? How are you today?"

She tapped her toe on the rug. "Just get on with it, Pastor Bledsoe. This counseling business is supposed to be for Lyndon here—"

Lucky shot to his feet. "Call me Lyndon one more time and you're toast, sister."

"Now, now, children." The pastor laughed nervously and sat down on the settee between the two.

Molly was contemptuously ignoring Lucky's outburst. "Like I said, he's the one that needs some educatin', but for some reason Pa insisted I come along, too."

"Yeah, imagine that," drawled Lucky. "Whoever would have thought you might need some training as a proper wife?"

Molly shot to her feet, her eyes flashing. The reverend frantically waved a hand. "Youngsters, please, please. Little birds in their nest should agree."

"Oh, brother," groaned Lucky.

"Tell *him* that," retorted Molly with a defiant jerk of her chin. "He's the one who's being so damned ornery about everything."

"Because I don't want to be forced into this sham of a marriage."

Molly sneered at him. "You know, handsome, women get forced into roles they don't want all the time. Like cooking for you menfolk, and mending your socks. About time a man got a taste of the same treatment, I say."

"Well, thank you, little miss suffragette," Lucky mocked back.

By now the reverend looked almost desperate, and Lucky and Molly appeared ready to lunge at each other. Then all were distracted as a door swung open and a pretty, plump woman bearing a tray moved inside, whistling, "Lead, Kindly Light." She wore a floor-length dress of sprigged nutmeg muslin, and her dark shiny hair was piled high on her head.

All three rose, the reverend appearing supremely relieved. "Ah, Edwina, dear, how kind of you to bring us tea."

"Your wish is my command, dearest," she responded, flashing her dimples at him.

"Molly, you know my wife, Mrs. Bledsoe. Lucky—"

"How do you do, ma'am?" he asked grudgingly.

She beamed her dazzling smile on him. "Just splendidly, young man, especially since I've heard the exciting news that we're soon to have a wedding at our church. All of you, do sit down and I'll serve you tea."

Exchanging hostile looks, Lucky and Molly resumed their seats.

Watching his wife attend to her duties, the reverend noisily cleared his throat. "Well, young Molly, as I was telling your father yesterday, marrying Edwina here was the best thing that ever happened to me—"

"You mean the best thing that ever happened to you with a shotgun at your back," grumbled Lucky.

Molly stuck out her tongue at him.

Bledsoe gave a squeaky laugh, then winked at his wife. "Well, in First Corinthians, the Gospel sayeth, 'Better to marry than burn.'"

As both Bledsoe and his wife fell into gales of laughter over this obvious private joke, Lucky fired back, "And in Lucky Lamont's book of favorite proverbs, it sayeth, 'Marry in haste, repent at leisure.'"

Molly tossed an antimacassar at Lucky; Edwina smiled and reached out to pinch his cheek. "Now, young man, it'll all work out for the best, you'll see."

"Yeah, just like the maiden voyage of the *Titanic*," Lucky mocked back.

As the others absorbed this remark in confusion, a muffled wail came forth from within the house. "Ah, I hear the baby," declared Edwina ecstatically. She winked at Lucky and Molly. "You two just wait. Having a young one will be the greatest joy the good Lord has in store for you. 'Be fruitful and multiply,' sayeth the Lord."

"Amen," intoned her husband.

"And while you're at it, win the lower five hundred," Lucky finished cynically.

Molly shot him a withering look, while the reverend and Edwina regarded one another in confusion before she hastily left the room.

Coughing, the parson opened his Bible. "Now, youngsters, according to the Book of Genesis—"

"Wait a minute," Molly cut in. "You ain't gonna read us all that Genesis hokum about Adam and Eve, are you? My grandma's already forced me to memorize half the Old Testament."

Before the preacher could answer, Lucky cut in snidely, "I think the parson should read it, so you can learn all about *your place* as Adam's rib—"

"Oh, yeah? Didn't Eve tempt dumb old Adam into being banished from the Garden of Evil—"

"*Eden*," Lucky corrected. "And bring it on, sweetheart, bring it on. I'd purely love to be banished. Just say the word, call off your father and the rest of your crazy family."

"Oh! Maybe I should ask Pa to fire a few shots into your worthless hide."

"Children, please, please!" beseeched the minister, mopping his brow. "Perhaps we can forgo the biblical lessons this time and speak in more general terms of the honorable institution of marriage, the foundation of the sacred union in harmony and trust—and, especially, *patience*. Then we can read over the marriage ritual itself, the obligations and the vows—"

"Oh, yeah, like to love, honor and obey," Lucky cut in with relish. "Ain't she gotta obey me, Preacher?"

"In a pig's eye," declared Molly.

"Well, that is the wording of the sacrament, young lady," intoned the preacher.

She harrumphed. "So, take it out. Or better yet, make handsome obey *me*."

Reverend Bledsoe's gaze implored the heavens. "Lord, grant me patience." To the couple, he said, "Just what is the problem between you two?"

"Other than my being shanghaied into this union?" scoffed Lucky.

"Yes. Other than that, why are you opposed to marrying this lovely young lady?"

Lucky glanced at Molly, who was simpering back at him. "Because she's the devil incarnate, beguiling and manipulative. Because she lied to me, to her parents, her grandma, everyone, to lasso me into this ridiculous marriage. Because I don't like her, much less love her—"

"Is that all?" interrupted the minister.

"Damn it, man, isn't that enough?" Lucky demanded. "Bottom line is, she's not my idea of a proper wife and never will be." With satisfaction, he watched Molly flinch at his emphatic words.

"Then what is your idea of a proper wife, young man?" asked Bledsoe.

Lucky cast Molly a baleful look. "Someone like my grandma, a helpmate who reveres her husband and knows her place—"

"You mean a mealy-mouthed little drudge?" interrupted Molly.

Lucky waved a hand. "See what I mean? She's got no respect for me—"

"And what have you done to earn my respect, cowboy?"

"Well, you sure as hell haven't earned mine, trying to use me to get a baby—"

"Whoa, children, whoa!" the parson cut in, his face crimson. "I can understand that you're feeling frustrated, young man—"

"Frustrated? Try pissed as hell!" Lucky shot back.

The parson loudly cleared his throat. "But—er, ultimately, isn't bearing the fruit of a blessed union at the heart of any marriage, just as my beloved Edwina indicated?"

"You don't understand, parson," Lucky retorted. "If the she-devil here produces an heir before her brothers do, her pa will award her the lower five hundred. That's all she really cares about."

The minister frowned at Molly. "Is this true, young lady?"

She grinned unabashedly. "Absolutely."

"And do you have objections to marrying Lucky here?"

She gave her fiancé a dismissive glance. "He'll do, I reckon."

The minister turned to Lucky. "Sounds like a fitting marriage of convenience to me."

Lucky was incredulous. "What? You gotta be pulling my leg, Parson. What about love, commitment, all those things you were just preaching about?"

"With the Good Lord sanctioning your union, all that will come in time," he rejoined piously.

"Oh, brother." Lucky was finding this clergyman every bit as loony as the Reklaws. "Tell me, Pastor, if I'd arisen straight from Lucifer's lair in the House of Hell, would you still be blessing this marriage?"

"Well . . ." He coughed, then nodded to Molly. "I do have a healthy fear of Cole Reklaw's shotgun—er, just as you should, young man, if you're wise."

Lucky slapped his knee. "My God, you people are incredible. 'Better to marry than burn,' eh, Pastor?"

"I'd say that's excellent advice." Bledsoe hastily opened his Bible and buried his nose in it. "Now, according to the Book of Genesis . . ."

Lucky flung his hands outward.

Molly popped up. "You learn him the Bible, Pastor. I'm already a good Christian woman—"

Lucky hooted. "Right. With a heart full of deceit."

A clenched jaw the only betrayal of her irritation, Molly continued, "As I was saying, I'm already a *good Christian woman*, so I'm gonna go help Mrs. Bledsoe with that baby." She smirked at Lucky. "Don't worry, cowboy, you'll get yours in time."

He glowered back. No doubt he would.

Chapter Fourteen

Well, the dirty deed is done.

This was Lucky's forlorn thought as he paced near the corral at sunset. Back on the front porch, his fiancée sat smugly on the swing, rocking to and fro, petting the cat while keeping a watchful eye on him. Even she lacked the gall to approach him now. No one in the Reklaw household dared to come within yards of him, not after Cole and Pastor Bledsoe had decided the wedding would be performed this Sunday after church.

This Sunday—damn it to hell! Well, the wildcat might force him to the altar, but that was the only cooperation she'd ever get from him, he vowed fiercely.

Inside the corral paced a young black stallion, not yet tamed. Lucky felt a keen kinship with the horse—who was, like him, all boxed in with nowhere to go. Like the stallion, he could probably jump the corral—

but what then? He had no home to return to. Hell, he had no *reality* to return to. He had left the age of *Harry Potter* and Victoria's Secret; now he was trapped in the era of Harry Houdini and bloomers.

Talk about culture shock.

Across the corral the horse stamped the ground and eyed Lucky warily with his brilliant dark eyes. Lucky felt a moment of connection, of bonding with a kindred spirit. He knew he could tame this proud beast, cajole him with some sugar, and the two could ride for the hills, taste freedom together, even if an alien freedom. Only he couldn't, for that would be breaking his word to Molly's pa. One thing Grandpa had drilled into his head was that a man's word was his bond, that he was nothing without his honor.

In 2004 he'd been backstabbed by both Bobby and Misti, and he would not break his word to Cole Reklaw, much as he despised the man's daughter. The most ironic part of all of this was that he had ended up in the clutches of a woman he distrusted every bit as much as he had Misti—all due to his own code of conduct.

He might go down in defeat on this one, but he'd go down like a man. . . .

Molly petted Jezebel and watched Lucky pace near the corral, looking every bit as defiant and trapped as the young black stallion he was watching.

She realized she'd only made things worse today, needling him at every turn. But he'd contributed plenty to the tension and hostility himself by insulting her right and left.

Was there no way to reach him, no way to persuade him to abandon his stubbornness and pride?

At last she drew a bracing breath, got up and walked over to join him at the corral. He turned at the sight of her with eyes blazing.

"What do you want now?" he demanded. "To gloat some more about having me at your mercy?"

Molly grimaced at his sharp tone. "I'm just trying to understand something, Lucky."

For a moment his features softened slightly—then he scowled again. "You—actually trying to understand? I never figured the word *empathy* would be in your vocabulary."

She frowned in confusion. "It isn't."

"Oh, yeah," he drawled. "That must be one of those pop psychology terms that hasn't come into common usage as yet."

"Huh?"

"Never mind—just tell me what you're *trying to understand*."

Awkwardly she explained, "Well, what I mean is—everything's settled now. We're getting married on Sunday."

"Yeah."

"Why can't you try to make the best of things?"

He laughed shortly. "Be a sport, right? You and your mother—like Pete and Repeat."

"Well, why can't you be a good sport?" she reasoned.

He groaned loudly. "Haven't you listened to a single word I've said since I landed in this underworld?"

"Yes, I've listened, and I'm sick of hearing you belly-ache about being trapped here."

"So what's your point? I *am* trapped."

"Haven't you ever heard of looking for the silver lining in a cloud?"

He crossed his arms over his chest. "Yes—but in this case, that silver lining seems to be a bolt of lightning."

She gritted her teeth. "Why can't you at least make an effort? You have a chance for a home, a family. Before you had nothing—"

"You have no idea what I had before," he cut in heatedly.

"Because you still won't tell me a damn thing about where you come from, or how you got here—"

Abruptly she stopped speaking as he seized her by the shoulders and spoke passionately. "You want to hear a story, Molly? Okay then, I'll tell you a story. It's about a woman who was low-down and conniving, just like you. Her name was Misti Childers, and she was the first person I thought I cared about after I lost my folks. Only she was a no-account whoring bitch—one I caught in bed with my best friend."

"I—I'm sorry," Molly stammered.

"When I caught the two fornicators together, I shot up the motel room where they were screwing. Then I headed for the hills—"

She gasped. "Did you kill—"

"No. Only the mattress."

"What?"

"Anyway, after I hightailed it, Misti's brother, a little shit named Grover Singleton, hunted me down, hogtied me, put me into that infamous stagecoach and pushed me into the gorge. Did I mention the ride damn near broke every bone in my body? Anyway, that's how I got here—thanks to *her*—and now I seem to be stuck here with *you*."

Molly was amazed. "My God. You mean she—your old girlfriend—started this chain of events? But I thought I wished you here—"

His cynical laughter cut her short. "Oh, I don't doubt that, either. Lady, you've all but wished me dead."

"And you think I'm like this woman who betrayed you?"

"Oh, yeah," he retorted cynically. "You're a woman who needs her daddy's shotgun to get a husband. What have you done but manipulate me and ruin my life? You and Misti—one and the same."

Molly was crestfallen. "But that's not fair. You can't blame me for another woman's sins. I'm not like her."

"And why not?"

"Well—I'm honest."

Lucky roared with derisive laughter, and Molly slapped him full across the face. For a moment he just glared at her, trembling. Then he cursed and hauled her close, kissing her punishingly. His hands roved over her back, her buttocks, his boldness shocking and enthralling her, making her nipples pucker and heat curl between her thighs.

Then she felt a shudder jolt him, and abruptly the kiss that had flared so angrily banked to pure, tantalizing heat as he teased his tongue in and out of her mouth, again and again, in a ravishing kiss that left Molly reeling. On and on it went, Lucky coaxing, seducing, shattering her with his sensuality, until she thought she might die of the intense need throbbing inside her. She was so aroused that she instinctively teased her tongue against his own.

She felt a second shiver rack him, then abruptly he backed away, breathing hard, eyes gleaming fiercely.

Molly desperately tried to read his feelings in his face but could detect no hint of softening in the intensity she spotted there. In a choked voice, she asked, "You don't know what you want, do you, cowboy?"

Afraid to wait for his response, she turned and fled for the porch, trying hard to keep up a brave front and not succumb to the tears that threatened.

At least now she understood Lucky's terrible anger. But in the wake of his admissions she faced another insurmountable hurdle: After all the horrible things that woman had done to him, how could she ever make him trust her?

Lucky stood struggling for breath, fists clenched at his sides, watching Molly retreat to the porch and turn to stare back at him defiantly. God, he had acted like a jerk. But she never should have approached him when he was in such a state.

Nonetheless, the blame was far more his than hers, and shame washed over him for the shabby way he'd treated her. When she'd pressed him for answers, he'd been harsher with her than he'd intended—and more passionate, too. He'd deserved the slap she'd given him, but that smack had also broken his control, prompting him to grab her and take the kiss he craved. Then, when she'd tantalized him with her tongue . . . heaven help him, he'd been ready to rip her clothes off right there. Thank God he'd come to his senses before things had gone too far. No benefit could have come from his taking his raging desires to their natural conclusion.

Funny, but despite his narrow escape, he didn't feel the least bit triumphant at the moment. Instead he felt confused and frustrated as hell. He could still taste Molly, still burned for her. She was a vixen, but *damn,* she was sweet.

She was going to drive him crazy. Already had.

Chapter Fifteen

In the bunkhouse, Cory Reklaw watched his brothers pace about like troops drilling. His siblings had been ranting and raving for over twenty minutes about the upcoming nuptials.

"I can't believe the little brat up and did it," declared Matt, kicking an iron bootjack out of his path as he stormed around the room. "She went and twisted Daddy around her little finger like always, and she's getting hitched to that no-account on Sunday."

"Hell, old man Trumble forbade us to court his daughters until at least then," cursed Zach, stomping about and almost colliding with Vance.

"And we ain't even got calling cards yet," added Matt in a voice shrill with frustration.

Vance waved a hand. "Anyhow, them women won't be at home receiving callers come Sunday. They'll be at the church with everyone else, eyeballing the sideshow."

"Yeah, watching *us* get our noses rubbed in it," agreed Matt as he shouldered past Zach.

Zach paused to snap his fingers. "Not if we do something about it."

"Like what?" asked Matt.

"Well, like shoot the low-down sonofabitch she's marrying."

Now Matt and Vance stopped dead in their tracks as well. "Brother, have you lost your mind?" asked Vance. "If we kill 'im, Ma will flat murder us."

"Yeah," seconded Matt.

"Not if she don't know," argued Zach.

The other two fell silent, scowling.

Cory, who had been listening to this exchange in appalled silence, sprang up from his perch on a bunk. "Have you three been eating loco weed? I knew you were all wild and half-crazy, but I never dreamed I'd hear my own brothers, my own flesh and blood, plotting an act of homicide."

Zach rolled his eyes. "Oh, hush up, Cory. I swear, you carry on worse than a woman. You sound as bad as that traveling melodrama we saw last Christmas at the courthouse."

"So do you," retorted Cory. "And I won't stand idly by while you plot to kill a man."

"Why not?" demanded Matt.

Cory was flabbergasted. "Why not? Well, it's wrong, for one thing. What has Lucky Lamont done to deserve a death sentence from the three of you?"

"He's marrying baby sister," replied Vance.

"That's not his fault. The man is being forced to."

"So we'll force him *not* to," mocked Zach, "owing to—er—a previous engagement with the Grim Reaper."

As the three laughed, Cory shook a finger at them. "Don't you boys dare try it or I swear, there will be consequences."

Vance surged toward him, his expression nasty. "Consequences? You gonna tell Ma on us, you sneaky little rodent?"

Cory was silent, glowering.

Matt loomed closer, seizing Cory by his lapels. "You know, you are the damned runt of the litter and the rest of us should have drowned you ages ago. Always so different from us. Always the sissy and tattletale."

"Yeah," agreed Zach.

"Now give us your word you won't squeal to Ma—or it's curtains for you," Matt declared.

Cory gave a sigh. "Very well. I won't tell her."

"A wedding dress in only three days," fretted Grandma. "Lord have mercy on us all."

In the kitchen, Molly stood in her lacy bloomers and camisole while Ma and Grandma both knelt at her feet with their sewing baskets, taking measurements for the wedding gown they'd begin frantically making that night. Grandma had hauled Molly into the house only moments before, and she'd had scant time to compose herself following the wrenching scene with Lucky. Then, too, she wasn't particularly happy to leave him unguarded—especially considering the state he was in.

Today he'd told her outright that she wasn't the kind of woman he wanted for a wife. Tonight he'd made it clear that he felt forced and trapped. But then he had kissed her with brash, wanton sensuality—both arousing and confusing her.

What was his problem? Did he at least desire her—or did he just want to make her suffer? Considering what that other woman had done to him, she suspected the latter.

But even though Lucky had insulted her horribly, Molly couldn't help feeling a stab of guilt in that she'd only made things worse—again. It unsettled her that his opinion had come to mean so much to her—and especially that he could make her *feel* this way. It gave him too much power over her. She'd best buck up her courage, or he'd be making mincemeat of her emotions in short order. . . .

Her mother's voice cut into her glum musings. "Now, Ma," Jessica soothed, "we've had that beautiful piece of white eyelet in Molly's hope chest for ages, along with blue satin slippers and that lovely length of Barcelona lace for her veil. Besides, we have the new Singer trestle sewing machine to do all the seams on the dress and lining."

Grandma harrumphed as she looped the measuring tape around Molly's slender waist. "Well, it don't seem fitting. A wedding gown should be sewn by hand. To use some newfangled machine will be bad luck, I'm telling you."

"You can do all the lace trim by hand, and I know it will look just divine."

"Will you two kindly stop your bickering?" Molly cut in irritably. "I don't care if I get married in a flour sack, so long as it's white."

"Why, Molly Reklaw, that's blasphemy," scolded Grandma.

"No, it's practicality," Molly shot back. "Now will you two finish up so's I can resume guarding handsome before he hightails it to the hills—and there ain't no nuptials to fret over?"

Grandma was about to reply when the back door swung open and Lucky strode in, only to stop in his tracks at the sight of Molly. His expression was tight, and a muscle worked in his jaw. Though her ma and grandma gasped, the bride-to-be was not about to cower before him—especially not after the way he'd treated her outside.

Instead, she proudly stepped forward to give him a better view of her lush curves, so enticingly revealed by linen and lace. "Well, hey, handsome," she crooned. "Want to come help Ma and Grandma measure me for my wedding gown?"

Lucky gulped and stared at her speechlessly, heat smoldering in his blue eyes—just the reaction Molly had wanted!

Then she heard a cry of outrage as Grandma heaved herself to her feet. "Granddaughter, remember yourself! You're behaving like a trollop." In short order she seized the gingham tablecloth off the table and draped it about Molly's shoulders, then soundly popped her granddaughter on the behind.

"Ouch!" Molly cried, grimacing and rubbing her smarting rear end.

Simultaneously, Lucky began to speak in strangled tones. "Ladies, I'm sorry . . . I mean, I didn't realize—"

Face red as an apple, he turned and fled the room.

Molly smiled victoriously, then turned to catch her ma's sternly disapproving frown.

Grandma sucked in an indignant breath. "See what I told you, Jessica? This girl is shameless."

Molly wondered if she should tell them about Lucky's insulting kiss, then thought better of it. "Grandma, I was just giving old handsome his due. He's been nothing but a bellyacher ever since he arrived here. You don't have to have apoplexy over it."

"Oh, no? I'll give you your due, you little Jezebel," Grandma shot back. "Jessica, where's my broom?"

"Grandma, please—not again!" Molly wailed.

That was when Molly decided that retreat was the better part of valor—even though Grandma caught her one stinging wallop on the derriere as she vaulted out the door.

In his room, Lucky stood pressed against the wall, breathing harshly. First Molly had goaded him into kissing her again—a kiss that left him still ravenous for more. Then he'd seen her half-clothed in the kitchen. Now he couldn't get the vision of her in her camisole and bloomers out of his mind. What a dazzling temptress she was, her curves so flawless, her skin so creamy and luminous, her eyes so large and seductive, her lips so sweet and red. She'd looked him over in a brazen way that had left no doubt as to what she was offering.

Shamelessly she'd enticed him, parading her wares and teasing him, even as he stood there with her essence still on his lips, trembling with frustrated desire. Damn her hide, she'd done nothing but taunt and torment him ever since he'd arrived here. And it was working—he had a hard-on more rigid than a Rocky Mountain peak, a fire in his loins that felt as if it would never stop burning.

So far Lucky had managed to be comforted by the thought that even though Molly was forcing him into marriage, she couldn't force him into her bed. At least on that one critical level, he'd win.

Now he had his doubts. She was leading him to the altar by his nose. Would she ultimately lead him to her bed by his cock?

Chapter Sixteen

"What the hell?"

Before dawn on Sunday morning, Lucky felt himself being seized from bed by several sets of rough hands. He caught a glimpse of three shadowy male figures surrounding him in the darkness; then a gag was stuffed in his mouth, a blindfold yanked about his head. Even as he struggled and uttered muffled protests, his hands and ankles were bound with stout twine and he felt himself being carried from the room, down the creaky central hallway and out the front door.

A blast of cold wind hit him as he was borne down the front steps and thrown facedown across a horse. Lord have mercy, this was a repeat performance of the nightmare scenario that had brought him to live among these wackos in the first place. What now?

Within seconds the group of four was riding off.

Lucky spent a hellish half hour slipping and sliding on his horse, several times almost crashing to the ground. Fortunately his bound hands were in front of him, and he managed somehow to steady himself with a hand on one stirrup and a foot on the other.

But riding so long in that unnatural position was pure torture. He wore nothing but a set of long johns, and the wind sliced through the knit cloth like splinters of ice. His belly took an incredible pounding and all the blood in his body felt as if it had been forced to his head. Several times he feared he would start vomiting and choke on his gag.

Then, following a dizzying uphill climb, the small group came to a halt. Amid the snorting and stamping of the horses, Lucky felt himself being hauled roughly to the ground. He was surprised his feet still supported him. He felt the cold steel of a knife blade cutting free his feet and then his hands. His gag and blindfold were yanked off.

Lucky coughed, then blinked in the bright light of dawn. He shuddered at the sight of Molly's three older brothers standing across from him: Matt wearing a snarl and holding a Colt pistol; Zach sneering and sporting a rifle; Vance glaring and pointing a shotgun at Lucky's middle.

"My God, have all of you gone loco?" he cried.

In reply, Vance tapped Lucky's belly with his shotgun. "Take a hike, stranger. Go back where you came from."

"My pleasure." Lucky turned, only to reel and stare wide-eyed at the steep, dizzying plunge of Reklaw Gorge, the canyon floor yawning at least a hundred and fifty feet below him. "Shit! There's nowhere to hike!"

"Now ain't that a shame?" mocked Matt.

Lucky whirled on the three men who had him cornered. "Look, guys, I enjoy a practical joke just as much as the next fellow. But this is serious. You need to knock it off or I could fall into this gorge."

"That's just what we have in mind," said Vance with a grin.

"What?" Lucky cried. "You three brought me out here to kill me?"

"Let's say, for you to have a little accident," drawled Zach. "Now take off."

"You actually think I'm gonna jump off a damn cliff just because you're asking me to?" Lucky demanded.

Matt cocked his Colt. "Would a bullet or two help convince you?"

Lucky could not believe these three maniacs actually expected him to leap to his death. He knew they were all rowdy and half haywire, but this was preposterous.

Furthermore, he was not about to give up without a fight. He faced down Matt with all the courage he could muster. "Then you're gonna have to fire that pistol to make me jump, junior. Should I turn around so you can shoot me in the back like the no-account coward you are? Or will you pitch that shooting iron into the gorge and fight me man-to-man?"

Matt blinked rapidly, obviously quite taken aback by Lucky's show of courage.

"Or you could always give me your pistol and I'll blow my brains out for you," Lucky added nastily, hoping these morons would go for his bait.

Matt was actually starting to hand Lucky his gun when Zach slapped him across the wrist. "Idjut! He's trying to hoodwink you."

"A toddler could con you three fools," Lucky scoffed.

"Oh, yeah?" Zach loomed closer, his expression nasty. "How 'bout a little shove, then?"

"How about it?"

After several more seconds of blustering, Zach backed away, cursing under his breath. "We told you to jump, stranger. Now jump."

"And I told you, you're gonna have to make me."

As Lucky continued to stand his ground, the three began muttering to one another. "This ain't so easy as we figured," Matt fretted to his brothers. "He ain't obliging."

"Well, we did ask him to jump off a cliff," remarked Vance.

"Guess the three of us will have to gang up on him, then push him over," mumbled Zach.

"But that would be murder," stewed Vance. "I mean, I don't mind bullying him a little, but shoving him, or even shooting him . . ."

"Pa surely murdered folks when he was an outlaw," argued Zach.

"Hell, we don't know that," countered Vance. " 'Sides, if he killed anyone, I'm sure it was well deserved. Like Cory said, this fellow only got hog-tied and shanghaied by Molly."

"Yeah, why aren't you murdering *her?*" Lucky demanded.

The three pivoted to glare at him.

" 'Cause she's family,"Vance snapped back. "Much as we hate to admit it."

By now Lucky was exasperated. "Look, you fools, have you ever thought about just *asking* me to leave?"

All three stared at him blankly. "Huh?" asked Matt.

"You don't have to kill me, just give me a horse and some clothing and I swear you'll never see me again."

"For sure?" asked Zach with a skeptical frown.

Lucky nodded vehemently. "I promised your pa I'd marry Molly, but I don't think even he would hold me to my word under these circumstances."

The three consulted among themselves for a few moments, then Matt flashed his brothers a relieved smile. "You know, the man is right. He don't want to marry her any more than we want him to." He fixed Lucky with a fierce look. "All right, then, mister, maybe we'll agree to your terms. But if we ever again spot you in these parts, it's the bone orchard for you."

"If you ever again spot me in these parts," Lucky intoned vehemently, "you can send me there with my blessings."

After a bit more consulting among themselves, Lucky's three captors agreed to cooperate. Vance gave him his shirt, jeans and boots; Zach gave him a hat and Matt handed him a canteen. Within minutes he was settled on his horse.

"Make tracks, stranger!" Zach yelled.

"With pleasure."

Lucky was galloping back down the path, the brothers following behind him, when he rounded a curve and practically collided with two more riders—Cole and Cory Reklaw, both of whom appeared sober as judges. The three men pulled up, their horses whinnying and stamping.

"Where do you think you're going this morning, son?" Cole asked meaningfully.

Snorting a laugh, Lucky jerked a thumb back toward Cole's older sons, who had also spotted the riders and were approaching with abashed expressions. "To perdition, if your three eldest sons had had their way. They snatched me out of bed and tried to murder me."

Cole frowned at the other three as they neared, raising an eyebrow at the sight of Vance in his long johns. "Is that true, boys?"

Miserably, Matt confessed, "Pa, we just tried to persuade him to take a little hike—"

"Yeah, off a cliff," Lucky finished.

Cole fought to maintain a stern expression. "I find your behavior contemptible. Your ma and I raised you much better than this. In fact, I can't even imagine what your ma and grandma will do when they hear what you tried to do."

All three men went ashen-faced. "Pa, do you have to tell 'em?" Matt pleaded.

"Especially Grandma!" added Vance. "She'll broom us half to death."

"No promises," Cole replied. "Anyway, I'll have to deal with you rascals later on. Go on home now with Cory. I'm going to have a chat with Lucky here."

After some more grumbling, the three galloped over to join Cory. All cast him resentful glances. "You broke your word," Vance accused.

"No, I didn't. You asked me not to tell Ma, so I didn't. I told Pa."

"Same difference," snapped Matt.

"Yeah," added Zach.

Observing the four riding off, still bickering, Cole ruefully shook his head. "Lucky, I must apologize for my sons' behavior."

"Behavior? Try attempted murder."

"Let's not exaggerate, now."

Lucky shouted a disbelieving laugh. "Sir, I almost got tossed in a ravine, before breakfast even, and that ain't no exaggeration."

"But you're all right now, so no harm done."

"Right. I'm still in the clutches of the same gang of psychopaths, so I'm doing just swell."

Cole's jaw tightened. "Look, son, I'm going to wear out all three of those scoundrels once we get home. You have my word this will never happen again. What else can I do to make this right?"

"Let me go!"

Cole scowled.

Lucky gestured at his mount. "I've got a horse, I've got clothes, just let me go. You folks have all but killed me, but no hard feelings, okay? Just release me from my promise to marry your crazy daughter and we'll shake on it and I'm outta here."

Cole was slowly shaking his head. "But where will you go, Lucky? You have no idea how to function here."

"No? Watch me!" Lucky scoffed. "Besides, *this* is functioning?"

"It's a life, a new beginning for you, a way you can succeed."

"Puh-leeeze," Lucky implored, "spare me the look-for-the-silver-lining lecture. Your wife and daughter have already delivered it several times."

"Obviously, then, you haven't listened. So, my question is, are you going to run like a sissy—or stay with folks who understand you?"

"Understand me?" Lucky repeated in disbelief. "You folks are understanding me straight into my grave. Besides, I'm no sissy."

"No?" Cole's dark eyes gleamed with sly wisdom. "Well, maybe I disagree. Maybe you're just not man enough to admit you can't handle my Molly."

"What? Can't handle her?" Lucky roared. "Your daughter—"

"Is the real reason you want to run, isn't she?" Cole cut in. "You can't admit you have feelings for her."

"Feelings for her?" he retorted. "Oh, yeah, I have feelings for her, all right. I'd love to wring her neck."

Cole shook a finger at Lucky. "You'll treat her right, or you'll have me to reckon with."

Lucky was exasperated. "Sir, why are you pushing this so? Can't you find someone else more suitable for that wildcat daughter of yours?"

"Possibly so. But Molly wants you, so that's that."

Lucky fixed his future father-in-law with a steely glare. "For the last time, are you going to let me out of my promise?"

"No."

"Then plow me under now."

Lucky spurred his horse, and Cole laughed as he followed suit.

Chapter Seventeen

Damned pantywaist of a preacher.

It was funny, Lucky thought, standing in church on Sunday afternoon next to the treacherous Molly, but ever since he'd arrived here, he'd relied increasingly on his grandma's old-fashioned sayings. He'd been used and abused three ways to sundown, tarred, feathered and ridden to the church on a rail. Ever since his grandparents' deaths, just being in a church had seemed a mockery to him; now this absurd wedding was the ultimate travesty, and he was caught like a grouse in a trap.

That was about how ridiculous he felt wearing this fussy old brown suit with the high silk cravat that seemed to be strangling him at the moment. All because this little sissy of a preacher refused to stand up to Cole Reklaw's shotgun.

Well, maybe he needed to amend that. As far as blame went, there was plenty to go around. He could blame Molly for her stubbornness and treachery, her pa for shamefully indulging her, even her brothers for not having the courage to shoot him.

And what about himself? Maybe he was a coward, too, but somewhere along the line he'd decided that this little hellcat wasn't worth dying for. Even if she looked sexier than hell in that virginal white dress with its high Victorian neckline, her hair styled in lovely curls around her head and shoulders—and behind that pristine, wispy veil, a smirk on that beautiful face of hers as she sealed his fate.

No, she wasn't worth buying the ranch for. The parson, on the other hand, had a duty to uphold right and wrong, to protect this community from the vengeance of a father's shotgun. Instead he was performing a farcical ritual, droning on about true love between a man and a woman, when this union was about as far removed from true love as was an elephant from an ant.

He glanced over his shoulder at the small church stuffed to the gills with rubbernecking townsfolk: In the front row, Dumpling Reklaw waved at him while juggling babies and Jessica offered a reassuring smile. Billy Reklaw also grinned; but Lucky's soon-to-be father-in-law only glowered, as did the four Reklaw sons. Lucky whipped back around just in time to repeat a vow he had no wish to keep. At his side he could swear he heard Molly snickering. His hands itched to throttle her.

Better yet, he should give the vixen just what she deserved. Take her to bed, rip her clothes off and give her much more than she had *ever* bargained for. Show her just what could happen when she tempted the *wrong* man.

But wasn't that what she really wanted? For him to lose control again—and give her a baby in the process? He was damned no matter which way he turned!

At Lucky's side, Molly was well aware of his glare. Earlier, when Mrs. Bledsoe had sung "Oh, Promise Me," he'd just about jumped out of his skin. Now she could hear frustrated little sounds rising in his throat as he repeated his vows. Clearly he was fit to be tied at having to marry her. Well, too bad—she'd won. If he wanted to be a sore loser, that was his problem.

But had she bitten off more than she could chew in wedding this virile, hot-tempered cowboy? He did look awfully handsome in that brown suit, the smell of his pomade and shaving soap devilishly seductive, his thick blond hair gleaming in the afternoon light, his magnificent scowl and glinting blue eyes only increasing his stormy sexiness. What would it be like having all that male ferocity directed at her? And would he try to take his due that night? She shuddered in both anticipation and dread at the thought, remembering his brazen, all too intimate kisses.

But, oh Lord, what if the opposite happened? What if he spurned her? That would be just like him, too, she realized with a sudden sinking feeling—especially now that she knew another woman's betrayal had started the chain of events that had brought him here. Knowing how much she wanted a baby, he might hold off just to spite her.

Then she'd just have to find a way to change his mind. Might even be fun, she thought with a certain perverse relish.

She repeated a vow, grinned at the parson and caught Lucky glaring daggers at her again. When the end came and the beaming parson gushed, "You may kiss the bride," Lucky turned and just barely brushed his lips against her own, then quickly swung away.

The last thing Lucky needed was a full-blown social following the wedding. But that was definitely what he got. Out in the pavilion behind the church, tables were laden with food, succulent fare ranging from fried chicken to barbecued ribs to ham, sweet potatoes and potato salad. A small table in the center of the area held a white, homemade wedding cake. Off to one side, three fiddlers sawed away at "The Blue-tail Fly" as several couples square-danced.

Lucky and Molly stood next to Cole and Jessica in an informal reception line as townsfolk trooped by, congratulating them. Lucky soon grew weary of being slapped across the shoulders by the men as they joshed him with, "Quite a pretty little gal you got there," and "Finest filly in five counties."

Oh, to be five counties away from here, and a hundred years!

Once the line tapered off, Cole strode over to speak with the musicians while Lucky stood with arms akimbo, ignoring his bride. As Cole returned, the fiddlers started up a slow waltz of "I Love You Truly."

Oh, *puh-leeeze,* Lucky thought. The song hit him as

the ultimate insult, making this occasion even more of a charade than it already was.

But his torture was not about to end, as everyone in the congregation turned to regard the bride and groom with hushed anticipation. Lucky noted that even Molly was eyeing him expectantly.

Lucky stood as immovable as stone.

Cole strode back over to him and spoke with low menace. "Ask your wife to dance, son."

Lucky hissed back, "You gonna force me to do *that* at gunpoint, too, sir?"

Even as Cole muttered a blasphemy, Grandma, wearing a ridiculous-looking purple silk dress and a large feathered hat, rustled up to regard Lucky with her fierce scowl. "Well, sonny? You gonna dance with my granddaughter, or am I gonna roast your bacon?"

Waving a hand in frustration, Lucky turned to Molly. "You care to dance?"

"Why, I'd be honored," she replied, simpering.

Clenching his jaw, Lucky led her out into the clearing, pulled her close and began to dance to the lilting waltz. A cheer rose up from the gathering, and Molly preened and gaily waved. Lucky could have skinned her alive. On top of everything else, she looked way too pretty, with her curls dancing about her face and her cheeks and lips so temptingly rosy, and she smelled like—well, like honeysuckle, and talcum and woman.

As if sensing his thoughts, she glanced up at him slyly. "Well, we're hitched now, eh, handsome?"

"Yeah."

"You ever gonna smile again, precious?"

He grunted. "Not likely."

She snuggled closer, causing him to recoil as the tantalizing contours of her breasts brushed against his chest. "Well, you'd better smile right now or I'm gonna kick you in the shin."

He pulled back and glared. "And maybe I'm gonna turn you over my knee in front of all these folks and teach you some manners."

She hooted. "While my pa's watching, you're gonna wallop me?"

"I am your husband now. Even he must respect that."

She dimpled unabashedly. "So you're finally acknowledging it. You're my husband."

Lucky mumbled something unintelligible.

"So, are you gonna smile or am I gonna kick you?" She gave him a sharp nudge with her slipper.

Lucky growled. "Just wait till I get you alone. I'll make you pay for this."

She only chuckled, saucily tipping her face toward his. "Oh, darlin', I'm counting on it. Now smile for the nice people."

Lucky flashed the crowd a frozen smile, and a new cheer went up.

GET TWO FREE* BOOKS!

SIGN UP FOR THE LOVE SPELL ROMANCE BOOK CLUB TODAY.

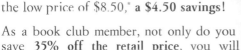

LOWEST PRICES EVER!

Every month, you will receive two of the newest Love Spell titles for the low price of $8.50,* **a $4.50 savings**!

As a book club member, not only do you save **35% off the retail price**, you will receive the following special benefits:

- **30% off** all orders through our website and telecenter (plus, you still get 1 book FREE for every 5 books you buy!)

- Exclusive access to dollar sales, special discounts, and offers you won't be able to find anywhere else.

- Information about contests, author signings, and more!

- Convenient home delivery of your favorite books every month.

- A 10-day examination period. If you aren't satisfied, just return any books you don't want to keep.

There is no minimum number of books to buy, and you may cancel membership at any time.

* Please include $2.00 for shipping and handling.

NAME: _____

ADDRESS: _____

_____

_____

TELEPHONE: _____

E-MAIL: _____

_____ I want to pay by credit card.

__ Visa __ MasterCard __ Discover

Account Number: _____

Expiration date: _____

SIGNATURE: _____

Send this form, along with $2.00 shipping and handling for your FREE books, to:

Love Spell Romance Book Club
20 Academy Street
Norwalk, CT 06850-4032

Or fax (must include credit card information!) to: 610.995.9274. You can also sign up on the Web at www.dorchesterpub.com.

Offer open to residents of the U.S. and Canada only. Canadian residents, please call 1.800.481.9191 for pricing information.

Chapter Eighteen

"We should have shot old handsome while we had the chance," grumbled Matt.

"Yeah, now Molly's flat beat us to the draw, and she'll be having that baby by Christmas," added Zach.

Off to one side, Cory stood with his brothers, the four watching the bride and groom waltz to "I Love You Truly." Watching his sister kick Lucky, and the latter flash the throng a stiff smile, he had to chuckle. "I wouldn't worry too much about those two having a baby any time soon. I've never seen a more unwilling groom."

"Yeah, but what's he gonna do once they're sharing a bed together, legally bound as husband and wife?" demanded Vance. "What nature intended for him, that's what."

"He'll have a bun in the oven in no time," added Zach with a sneer.

"You know, I find that a really crude comment,"

scolded Cory with a red face, "and furthermore, I don't think it's any of our business."

"The hell it ain't!" exclaimed Matt. "It's us who shoulda gotten hitched up to our women today, only old man Trumble won't let us within shouting distance of 'em. Problem is, there's way too many bachelors in these parts and not nearly enough pretty women." He jerked a thumb toward the pavilion, where Ezra Trumble and his four lovely blond daughters sat in an awkward row. "How many young men has that codger beaten away so far today?"

"At least six that I've counted," fretted Zach.

"Uh-oh," put in Vance, gesturing toward the crowd. "There go them low-down Hicks cousins, trying to beat us to the punch!"

All four scowled tensely as the line of five tall, skinny young men with straw-blond hair and overalls approached Mr. Trumble. "Don't worry, they'll get their comeuppance," Matt reassured his brothers. "Them Hickses are the ones that would have gone to the hoosegow last week, if it weren't for the sheriff lusting after Bart and Winky's ma." He sneered toward a middle-aged couple off to the side—a plump woman in a garish red dress and outlandish dyed ostrich feather hat and a potbellied man with a handlebar mustache, wearing a ten-gallon hat and a silver star. "Just look at old Sheriff Hackett preening away like a peacock with Dulcie Hicks."

"Yep, it's plumb disgusting," agreed Zach. "Oh, lookee there, boys."

Cory watched anxiously with the others as the troupe of Hicks cousins arrived before the Trumble daughters. As Jeeter Hicks grinned broadly and extended his hand toward Sally Trumble, old man Trumble sprang up and began shouting at all five men, even bashing Linus and Merle with his hearing horn.

"Whew!" exclaimed Matt with a grimace. "That geezer has some temper on 'im."

"He's just a stickler for manners," put in Cory.

"Yeah, sure," mocked Vance. "You know, I despise the Hicks boys as much as the rest of you, but what exactly did them fellas do wrong?"

"Isn't it obvious?" Cory asked, rolling his eyes.

"Not to me," Matt shot back.

"Well, Jeeter asked Sally to dance rather than asking her pa," Cory explained.

"What?" shouted Matt. "You think I'm dancing with that son of a bitch?"

"No, no, you need to ask his *permission* if you want to dance with one of his girls." Cory laughed.

"Oh," Matt muttered.

"Look, if you fellas want to try again, why don't you just let me do the talking?" Cory suggested.

"Sure; why not?" agreed Zach. "You're the only sissy in this family with any manners."

Forgoing an urge to admonish Zach, Cory directed, "Then all of you remove your hats and follow me."

"Yeah, straight to the funeral parlor, we will," groused Matt.

But the three others dutifully doffed their hats and trooped along behind Cory as he approached Mr. Trumble. As the oldster greeted them with a look sour enough to curdle milk, Cory bravely smiled; the three older girls tittered back, while Ida May shyly waved. He noted that all four women looked pretty as flowers in their best gowns of various pastel shades.

"Good afternoon, Mr. Trumble. Lovely weather, isn't it?"

"'Spect I seen worse," Trumble muttered back. "What's on your mind, sonny?"

"Well, actually, my brothers and I were wondering if we might have the honor of dancing with your daughters—with your permission, of course."

New giggles burst forth from the girls, and Trumble harrumphed. "Oh, you were? Hoping to dance with 'em? Rather fresh of you, I must say."

"I apologize for our rudeness when we came to call," Cory continued patiently, "but seein's how this is our sister's wedding, we were hoping you might show some mercy on us."

Trumble pursed his mouth stubbornly. "Well, I suppose it is something of an occasion."

"So, may we dance with them, sir?" Cory asked hopefully.

Trumble ruminated, then broke into a rare, sly smile. "Well, I might just agree, especially if your grandma will promenade with me." He jerked a thumb toward Eula, who stood conversing with Jessica and Cole. "Mighty handsome Eula's looking today."

All four Reklaw boys blanched. "Well, sir, Grandma can't dance with you right now," Cory hastily lied. "She's been ailing all winter."

"Oh, yeah? Don't look like she's missed no meals to me. What's her malady?"

Cory struggled to remember terms from his ma's

medical dictionary. "Er—she's been suffering from dropsy and phlebitis."

"You don't say." Trumble scowled at Eula. "Sounds serious."

"Yeah. But I know she'll be right pleased to hear you expressed your concern," Cory quickly added.

As the fiddlers launched into a new square dance, Trumble scowled a moment, then waved a hand at Cory. "Ah, go ahead and dance with my girls. Maybe I'll go pay my respects to your grandma whilst you do."

Watching his brothers grimace in horror, Cory evenly replied, "Yes, sir, why don't you do that?"

Trumble shook a finger at all four men. "But none of them scandalous waltzes, you hear? And keep a proper distance from my girls or I'm boxing all of your ears."

"Yes, sir," chanted the boys in unison.

One by one, the brothers stepped forward to offer their arms—Zach to Sally, Vance to Nelly, Matt to Bonnie. As the three older girls giggled and gushed and went off with Cory's brothers, he extended his hand to Ida May, and was pleased when she rose with an eager smile. She was the shortest of the four, slightly plump, pert and blue-eyed, with a darling upturned nose; she looked especially vibrant today in her enticing blue eyelet gown.

As Cory led her out to join the others, she confided, "Thanks so much for rescuing us, Mr. Reklaw."

"Please, call me Cory," he returned gallantly. "And may I call you Miss Ida May?"

She dimpled. "Just 'Ida May' is fine."

As he led her into the square dance, he murmured, "Well, Ida May, did you enjoy the Henry James novel I recommended at the library?"

Her eyes lit with animation. "Oh, yes. I found I really identified with Daisy Miller, as well as Mr. James's heroine Isabel Archer in *The Portrait of a Lady.*"

"Yes, James does portray fascinating female characters," Cory concurred. "Both women had such spirit and wanted to make independent choices, but were ultimately destroyed by the conventions of society—and by the constraints of domineering men."

Biting her lip, Ida May glanced awkwardly at her father. "Yes, I sympathized with them."

While guessing her meaning at once, Cory hesitated a moment before asking, "I do hope you realize not all men are tyrants?"

She regarded him with luminous eyes. "Yes, and thank heaven for that, Mr. Reklaw."

Cory knew he was blushing at her obvious compliment, but he didn't care. "Actually, Ida May, I've been meaning to apologize to you for the courting debacle last week. I also regret that your father can be—well, rather difficult at times."

"Now there's an understatement," she replied ironically. "I'm so sorry he slammed the door in your faces and knocked your poor brother down the steps."

"So you girls really were watching from the upstairs window?" Cory teased.

"Oh, yes. Truth to tell, you and your brothers are the first gentlemen who have ever had the nerve to come calling directly at the house—and now that you've met

the 'welcoming committee,' I'm sure you can understand why," she finished ruefully.

"I do, but don't blame your father entirely. The four
of us didn't exactly put our best feet forward, just showing up there, uninvited. Actually, the whole scheme
was my brothers' idea—not that I wouldn't have liked
to come along under, well, better circumstances."

Ida May glanced off at the other three couples,
laughing and dancing nearby. "Your older brothers are
a bit on the rash side, aren't they?"

"Amen to that."

Her gaze lingered on her sister Sally, who was tossing her blond curls as she made a turn with Zach. "Actually I think my sisters may suit them well. They're all
a great deal more high-spirited than I am."

He chuckled. "I've noted at the library that their
tastes run to dime novels—tales of Billy the Kid and
the Dempsey Gang—just like my sister Molly."

She lifted a delicate eyebrow. "They're certainly fond
of American folklore."

"Tactfully put." Clearing his throat, he added, "Given
your sisters' penchant toward independence, and your
father's, well . . ."

"Please, you may speak freely, Mr. Reklaw," she encouraged.

He regarded her with concern. "Well, I was just going to say that your father's strictness must really wear
on your sisters at times—and on you, too, of course."

"Oh, you have no idea," she confided. "Though it's
definitely harder on the elder three. Sometimes they
talk back to Father, and . . ."

Cory tensed. "Excuse my frankness, Miss Ida May, but I must know—does your father ever hurt you girls, or beat you?"

She chewed her lower lip again. "Pa sees that—well, we all remember our places."

Cory was becoming quite anxious. "Please, if he's ever tried to harm you, you must let me know."

She shook her head miserably. "I'm sorry, Mr. Reklaw, but that's really all I'm free to say. Besides, we girls do all right as long as we stick to our duties—you know, chores and church, mainly chores. I just wish my sisters wouldn't complain so much about how we never get to have any fun. And that Pa wouldn't make us . . ." She started to say more, then glanced toward her father again and clamped her mouth shut.

"Yes?" Cory prompted with a scowl.

She quickly shook her head. "Never mind. I'm running on way too much as it is. Can't we simply enjoy this occasion?"

At once Cory felt contrite, and knew it would be best not to pursue his questions now. "Yes, of course. I'm sorry for prying—"

"I realize you're only concerned, Mr. Reklaw."

"Nonetheless, my sincere apologies. And we'll have lots of fun tonight—that is, if you'll just start calling me Cory."

She beamed. "Cory, it will be my pleasure."

For a few moments they stomped about to "Turkey in the Straw," laughing and cheering with the others. Then Cory tensed as he caught sight of the Hicks cousins trying to cut in on his brothers. He was watching Matt shove Linus away when he felt a tap on his own shoulder.

He turned to see Winky looming in his face, looking rather freakish with his prominent eye twitch. "What do you want?"

"To dance with the lady, there," Winky sneered back. "Don't you Reklaw boys go thinking you can have all the goodies for yourselves. 'Sides, any woman who would hoedown with you no-accounts should be eager to parlay with one of us Hicks boys." He flashed a tobacco-stained smile at Ida May.

As she gasped, Cory fired back, "You get out of our faces, you piece of white trash, before you give Miss Ida May the vapors with your tobacco-breath and cheap talk."

"Cheap talk! I'll have you know I got better manners than you." Again he grinned at Ida May, but it came across as creepy because of his twitch. "May I have this dance, ma'am?"

Before she could answer, Dumpling Reklaw stormed up in a rustle of voluminous gold silk skirts. "Winky Hicks, you quit pestering my nephew and his girl."

"His gal?" Winky jeered back. "Hell, she ain't his woman, and who are you to tell me what to do, Dumpling Reklaw?"

Dumpling sucked in an outraged breath. "I'm your third cousin once removed as well as your elder, and I've been burning in shame over you miserable Hicks boys all my life. You'd all be rotting in the hoosegow now were it not for your shameless Jezebel ma cozying up to the sheriff." Dumpling jerked her thumb toward the fawning couple, who were sashaying about nearby. "In fact, I think I'll go have a word with that scandalous hussy about the way she lets you boys run wild."

Cory gripped his aunt's arm. "Aunt Dumpling, please. Don't go getting in a catfight with Dulcie Hicks on Molly's wedding day. Ma will never forgive you."

"Well, I suppose you're right." Dumpling pursed her lips, then shook a finger at Winky. "But you, make tracks, you slimy little toad."

"Not unless the lady tells me to,"Winky snarled back, turning again to Ida May. "Well, ma'am?"

"Oh, go suck a gizzard," Ida May retorted, and the others burst out laughing as Winky finally turned on his heel and stalked away.

Cory grinned at the sight of Winky off huddling with his brothers and cousins, who had been similarly rebuffed by his brothers and their partners. He winked at Ida May. "Gracious, I didn't realize you had such spirit. Remind me not to cross you."

"Heck, I don't mind keeping you on your best behavior either," she rejoined charmingly.

"Yeah, honey, you make this boy toe the mark," advised Dumpling with a grin as she pounded Cory across his shoulders. She craned her neck. "Well, I think I see my Billy lookin' for me . . ."

As a new reel began, Cory sighed in relief. "At last a moment of peace." He offered his arm. "Shall we dance again?"

"Why, sir, I'd be honored."

Both were about to rejoin the dancers, when they froze at the sound of a loud female voice spewing blasphemies. Turning, Cory cringed at the sight of Ezra Trumble cowering before Grandma as she bashed him over the head with her purple silk parasol. "Oh, no! Looks like your pa asked Grandma to dance, after all. Now our gooses are cooked."

"Sure are," agreed Ida May glumly.

Indeed, within seconds Trumble came storming over to join the couple. Hat askew and face livid, he grabbed Ida May's arm. "Come on, daughter, we're leaving this crazy wedding. Gather your sisters." He shook a fist at Cory. "You Reklaw boys stay the hell away from my daughters. That grandma of yourn is a madwoman."

Ida May gave Cory a pleading glance as her father dragged her away.

With a groan, Cory went over to join Grandma, who was angrily expostulating to her friend, the Widow Allgood. "Grandma, did you have to bash Mr. Trumble over the head like that?"

Eula turned her fury on Cory. "That villain! Why, he had the gall to say, 'Sorry to hear 'bout your dysentery and fleas, Eula.' Where in the name of buffalo turds did he get *that* idear?"

With a massive effort, Cory managed not to burst out laughing. "Grandma, you know he's hard of hearing—"

"Deaf as a post!" she reiterated.

"Yes, ma'am. Well, you see, I just told him you have—well, I knew you needed an excuse not to dance with him, so I said you have dropsy and phlebitis."

"Dropsy and phlebitis?" Grandma hollered. "Why, that sounds even worse. Shame on you. As for sashaying about with that sidewinder, I'd just as soon dance with a three-headed cobra."

"Yes, ma'am." Grimacing, Cory managed to forge ahead. "But couldn't you try to be a sight more civil, so me and the other boys can court his daughters?"

"Hah! You boys need to find yourselves women from decent families, not the fruit of Beelzebub's loins."

"Yes, ma'am." Realizing that further argument with his ornery grandma was futile, Cory gave a sigh and walked away.

Later, while his bride was doing the traditional waltz with her father, Lucky retreated to the edge of the group, only to be joined by Jessica, looking beautiful in her mother-of-the-bride lavender silk dress with braided satin trim.

"You okay?" she asked.

"You come to lecture me on the birds and the bees now?" he teased.

She laughed. "I'll forgo that. I just wished you looked happier, Lucky."

He sighed. "No offense to you, ma'am. I know she's your daughter. But no one has even asked me what *I* want. All of this has been against my will."

"Including when you grabbed my daughter and kissed her?" Jessica asked gently. "You know, that's quite an insult in this day and age, Lucky."

"I've gathered that," he cynically rejoined. He paused a moment, watching his bride laugh as her father spun her about. "You know, everything still seems only half-real to me."

She nodded wisely. "I had that same feeling. It will pass."

"Will it?" he countered, gesturing expansively at the scene. "How do you accept it all, Jessica?"

"I've had time."

"*Time,*" he repeated ironically. "Here we are, living in the year 1911, and with what both of us know about the future, all the implications—"

"Meaning, what will we do about the *Titanic* going down next year, or our country entering the First World War in 1917?" she interjected.

He turned to gaze at her in wonder. "Well, yes."

She touched his arm. "Lucky, don't ponder the imponderables too much. I tried that, and it can drive you crazy. I think we have to take things as they come, prepare where we can."

"And how have you prepared, Jessica?"

A troubled frown puckered her brow. "Well, we've farmed, for one thing, which means the boys should be able to get deferments once the war begins."

"Yes, if they'll accept them."

"I know, *if.*" She regarded him curiously. "Actually, by the time the United States enters the war, I'm betting you'll be too old to serve, since if memory serves, they initially drafted only men between the ages of twenty-one and thirty."

Lucky shook his head. "Hurled back in time and already I'm a fossil. It all just seems so incredible."

"I know. For me, too, sometimes, even after all these years."

"You ever think of going back, Jessica?" he asked wistfully.

She shook her head as she gazed with love at her husband and daughter. "Not anymore."

"But you did before?"

"Well, yes," she admitted reluctantly. "And I did—well, once I was actually offered a chance to return to my own time."

"You're kidding!" he exclaimed with avid interest.

She nodded. "Bizarre as this may sound, the stagecoach that brought me here returned to Haunted Gorge one last time."

"No lie?"

"No lie. When the stagecoach reappeared, I realized that I could use it as my vehicle to return to the present. But I chose not to."

"Why?"

Jessica's luminous smile reflected a soul totally at peace. "Because by then I knew I loved Cole and belonged here."

Lucky hesitated a long moment before asking, "Do you think I might have a chance to return, too?"

She appeared crestfallen. "Oh, Lucky, please don't ask that. There's no way we can know for sure, but I do know that continuing to fight your fate isn't going to help you at all."

"I shouldn't fight?" he countered passionately. "Jessica, this is my *life* you folks are tinkering with."

She squeezed his hand and spoke solemnly. "Lucky, I hope in time you'll learn what I've learned. Everything truly does happen for a reason. You don't really have a life until you learn to share it. Have you heard the old adage 'Bloom where you're planted'?"

"Would that be six feet under?" he rejoined, but more gently.

She chuckled, then inclined her head toward the crowd. "Well, I see folks are starting to leave. I must go help my daughter change for the ride home."

Lucky was lost in thought as she walked away.

Chapter Nineteen

"Ain't you gonna get ready for bed, darlin'?" Molly asked.

Lucky frowned at his bride, who had just pulled off her stylish braided jacket and skirt to reveal all her charms displayed by a low-cut camisole and long, lacy slip. Her grandmother had left moments earlier, after filling the bathtub behind the dressing screen and grinning at them like the very devil.

Lucky was lounging near the bedroom door, primed for a quick exit in his shirtsleeves and trousers, his thumbs shoved in his pockets. "You gonna force me at gunpoint?"

She whirled to face him, curls and bosom bobbing. "What's stuck in your craw now, cowboy?"

You. Gulping, Lucky almost blurted out the word. She looked sexier than sin itself with that hot color blooming in her cheeks, and the lamplight glinting gold in her luxuriant auburn hair.

Somehow he managed to keep his composure. "Other than the fact that I've been forced to marry a woman I can't stand?"

At the dressing table, she leaned forward slightly, flaunting her voluptuous derriere at him, and began pinning up that thick, wicked hair, leaving loose curls dangling about her face and neck with hoydenish allure. "Well, we're hitched now, so you might as well try to make the best of things."

He harrumphed. "Here's the fourth chorus of 'Look for the Silver Lining.' You gonna tell me to bloom where I'm planted, too?"

She flounced about, a vision of feminine sin as she headed for the dressing screen. "If you aren't ornery as a barking squirrel. I'm gonna go take my bath."

"Take all night if you want," he managed to taunt.

Tossing him a glare, she disappeared behind the screen.

During the next few moments, Lucky paced about, doing a slow burn. Despite his anger and frustration, he found his senses tantalized by an alluring aroma rising from behind the dressing screen. Rosewater, wasn't it? A heady scent that seemed to scream, "Seduce me." As if the thought of Molly lounging naked in the tub—her skin glowing, blushing from the warm water—wasn't enough.

Damned woman! Now what was she doing? Singing a lilting, sexy waltz tune—"Kiss Me Again," wasn't it? Seemed like his grandma used to listen to a Frank Sinatra version of that old tune. The romantic lyrics drifted out to torture him:

Sweet summer breeze, whispering trees,
Stars shining softly above;
Roses in bloom, wafted perfume,
Sleepy birds dreaming of love.
Safe in your arms, far from alarms,
Daylight shall come but in vain.
Tenderly pressed close to your breast,
Kiss me! Kiss me again.

She didn't have a bad voice, either. Hell, she didn't have a bad *anything*. Was there no end to the woman's ability to drive him nuts?

Just when he thought he could bear no more, she sashayed back out, dressed in a gossamer-thin handkerchief-linen gown that hugged her damp, curvaceous body. He gulped. Moist, sensuous curls clung to her beautiful face and lovely neck, and the sheer fabric revealed her lush nipples, gently curving belly and the dark curls nestled in her female place. And the scent coming forth from her . . . warm, wet, rose.

Lucky was dying.

With a sly grin revealing that she knew the effect she was having on him, she slinked over to the dressing table, sat down and unpinned her hair, then began slowly brushing the thick strands until they shone like warm copper. The urge to sink his hands into that hair, haul the little tease close and kiss her senseless was all but overpowering now. Lucky's breathing grew ragged, and he was surprised his heart didn't jump out of his chest.

Then their gazes locked in the mirror, his smoldering, hers coy. "You want a bath, too, hon?" she asked, her voice low and intimate, smooth as silk.

"You think I want your leftovers?" Actually, the thought of drowning himself in her essence was enough to make Lucky harden in agony.

"Grandma can bring more hot water."

"I've had about enough of your family for one day."

She turned, her expression impish. "Have you had enough of me?"

He grunted as if she'd knocked the wind from him. He'd never have enough of her—not that he would ever admit it.

"You still determined not to smile?" she cajoled.

"You got that right, lady. I see nothing to smile about."

Now she was angry, her mouth pursed in a pout. She flounced over to the bed, plopped herself down and hurled him a determined look. "All right then, slick. Let's get it over with. I need a young'un."

Lucky's jaw dropped. He didn't know whether to laugh, cry or strangle her. Her gall was unbelievable!

"You actually think I want to sleep with you now?" he asked in disbelief.

"Sure, you do." Brazenly she glanced at his crotch. "Or is that a billy club you've got stuffed in your britches?"

Lucky blushed furiously, quickly covering his privates with a hand. "You leave my britches out of this."

"Cowboy, this is all about your britches."

He gasped. "Woman, for a gal who claims to be a virgin, you got one filthy mouth on you."

"Filthy?" she mocked back, laughing. "So you really think doin' what nature and the good Lord intended for us is dirty?"

"I'm talking about how much you seem to *know* about doin' it," he shot back. "Like maybe you've burned up the sheets with a stud or two already."

Rather than be insulted, she chuckled. "Stud, eh? Cowboy, this is a farm. You think I ain't never seen a stallion mounting a mare?"

At that electrifying image, Lucky could only blink at her, sagging against the wall and beseeching the Almighty to rescue him.

And here he thought he'd lost all faith!

She tried a softer tack, batting her long eyelashes at him and patting the bed beside her. "Now come on, handsome, quit being so stubborn. We're wasting time."

At last Lucky recovered himself. He strode over and glowered down at her siren face. "Get something straight, lady. I'll sleep with you when hell turns to blue ice." He turned and strode for the door.

"Where are you going?" she cried.

"To the barn!"

Ignoring her cry of dismay, Lucky stormed into the hallway and burst out the front door, only to spot Cole sitting on the porch swing, smoking a cigar. "Going somewhere, Lucky?" he drawled.

"Shit." Lucky turned on his heel and reentered the house.

He strode inside the bedroom to find Molly grinning at him. He shook a fist at her. "You hush before I strangle you."

"But why are you back? I mean, if you don't want—"

"Because your father gave me no choice." He stalked over to an easy chair, sat down and blew out the lamp. "Go to sleep."

He heard her gasp in the darkness, then ask more tentatively, "You really gonna spend the whole night there in that chair?"

"Yep. Now are you gonna quit gabbing, or am I gonna hang you by your toenails?"

Blessed silence was his only answer.

In the darkness Molly tossed and turned. She couldn't believe Lucky had done this to her—he had actually rejected her. Indeed, he had only returned to the bedroom because her pa had forced him to.

She had assumed that once she was married to him, getting him to fulfill the rest of his husbandly duties would be easy. She couldn't have been more wrong. And here, she'd really thought he wanted her. Or did men get hard like that when they were angry, too?

Her pride hurt, and though she hated to admit it, she hurt. She realized she wanted much more than a baby from this man—he intrigued her and tormented her. She wanted to get to know him, to know more about his world—and that was scary as hell. For he continued to hold himself apart from her, he'd made his contempt for her clear and her budding feelings for him could lead her only to heartbreak. . . .

She felt a tear welling up. No, she wouldn't cry—she had more pride than that. She would find a way to make Lucky Lamont fulfill his duty if it killed her. She would win—and win without humiliating herself.

Lucky squirmed in the darkness. He knew Molly wasn't sleeping, either. He could hear her tossing and turning.

God, he could still smell her, could see her in his mind's eye, all ripe and beautiful and damp, and he wanted nothing more than to join her in that bed, rip off her nightgown and lose himself in her. But then she would win—win after brazenly using and betraying him, in some ways worse than Misti had.

Was that a small sob he heard in the darkness? Could this she-devil possess a heart after all? Like most males, Lucky could not abide the thought of any woman crying, and he felt a lump rising in his throat, as well as a torturous yearning to go rushing to her side. Good Lord, was he actually coming to care for this spitfire? The urge to comfort her was almost overwhelming. But he knew he couldn't. He refused to be used like a prime stud.

Refuse he might, but his resolve did nothing to diminish his passion. He groaned, wondering if morning would ever come.

Chapter Twenty

Morning came, following a long, sleepless night.

After snoozing briefly, Lucky awakened in the half-light, stiff and sore. With a groan he got to his feet and crossed the room. His bride lay half in shadow, lovelier than words, her features angelically peaceful, one shapely hand curled on the pillow beside her, as if she were seeking him out, inviting him to join her. He caught a sharp breath. He needed to get out of here before his tight loins and roaring blood impelled him to do what he'd been dying to do to her all night long.

Barely bothering to wash up, he changed into a shirt, jeans, and boots, then went straight to the barn and saddled up the brown sorrel Cole had given him permission to ride on ranch property. Dawn was breaking as he galloped out onto the range. Now what?

Lucky rode hard for the next half-hour, as if trying to outrace his raging thoughts and feelings. He found himself inexorably drawn back to Reklaw Gorge, where this nightmare had all begun. The dikes lay softly painted in the half-light, dew-drenched wildflowers emitting their delicate aromas.

Carefully guiding his horse down into the narrow canyon, Lucky could see the wreckage of the old stagecoach still lying there. He pulled up close, dismounted and stared at the pile of rubble. Jessica had mentioned that this very stagecoach had brought her across time, then had returned once again, giving her one last opportunity to leave the past and go back to her own time. She had declined the gift that Fortune had offered her.

Well, he sure as hell wouldn't if given the chance. Did the old stagecoach hold the key to his time-travel experience, as well? Could history repeat itself, as it had with Jessica? Was there really an escape route for him?

But Jessica had not been pushed off a damn dike—and her time-travel vehicle had not been smashed to smithereens in the process. Lucky stared up at the high ledge above him, where the stagecoach had been perched precariously back in the present, right before his enemy had launched him across time. He could haul the wreckage up there, try to reassemble the stagecoach . . .

Then what? Push himself off the dike, hope he survived the fall—surely a hundred feet or more—and got returned to his own time in the process? The whole notion was sky western crazy. How could he dare hope he might endure a second flight, when logic argued he never should have survived the first one? Hell, he'd have about as much of a chance as he'd had yesterday when the Reklaw boys had tried to launch him into space.

Lucky was about to remount his horse and ride away when some instinct urged him not to simply abandon the wreckage. Taking some lengths of rope from his saddlebags, he tied the debris into several large bundles. Mounting his horse, he hauled off the packets one by one, hiding them at the edge of the gorge behind a windbreak of pines.

He would have to think about what, if anything, he should do with the remains of the hussy wagon.

And where should he go now? He was free, actually free. He could ride off for Denver or Alaska or anywhere else he chose in this new world.

Except that he couldn't. Like or it not, he was still bound by his word to Cole Reklaw, bound by his vows to Molly, whether those nuptials had been forced or not. He had to deal with all of that, as well as the unsettling new feelings he had for the she-devil he had wed.

Plus, instinct argued that if Reklaw Gorge was the place where he'd traveled back in time, then this was likely his only escape route. And Jessica was here, a fellow time-traveler, with possibly more wisdom to offer him. Why run away from the only answers he might ever find? No, he had to resolve his problems here.

Which meant returning to his precious little bride . . .

When Lucky stepped back inside the bedroom, Molly lay slumbering in the full light of dawn. She looked so gorgeous with her pink cheeks and sensuous red mouth, she took his breath away. His gaze trailed hungrily over the lush curves outlined by the knitted counterpane. Damn, but she was hard to resist.

He went to sit beside her, inhaling her scent like the most powerful aphrodisiac. Drawing a harsh breath, he pulled down the counterpane slightly and stared at her breasts, so enticingly revealed by sweet virginal ribbons and sheer handkerchief linen. The subtle rise and fall of her bosom, the delicate shading of her nipples, the creaminess of her flesh, all fascinated him. He ached so much he had to touch himself, but even that brought no relief.

His. She was his. Not until this moment had it really sunk in that they were married now, that she was *really* his—and the thought made him drunk with awe and power and an unexpected humility. His wife.

How much longer could he torture himself this way? All at once he knew what he had to do. He had to touch her. His fingertips reached out to stroke her cheek—heavenly soft. He drew a teasing finger down her creamy throat, and heard her sharp little intake of breath. He slid his hand downward to her breast, traced the outline of one dusky areola, watched in fascination as the nipple pebbled against his finger.

Her eyelids fluttered open, she gasped and stared up at him. Her cheeks flamed and her lovely lips trembled.

Lucky couldn't help himself then. His large hand enveloped Molly's breast, squeezing softly, and he felt her nipple go even tighter against his palm.

Her eyes went dark and luminous as midnight ponds. "W-what are you doing to me?"

He grinned. "Maybe what you want me to do, darlin'?"

"Please," she panted, "remove your hand."

She was squirming, and Lucky relished it. "I don't think so," he replied huskily. "I'm your husband now and I'll do what I please." To demonstrate, he moved his hand to her other breast, teasing the nipple with a fingertip.

She shuddered. "You—you're trying to—"

"Get you hot and bothered?" he offered. "Oh, yeah, darlin'. *Very* hot and bothered."

With that, Lucky tugged down the bodice of his bride's gown, leaned over and drew the taut little nipple into his mouth, flicking his tongue over it. Molly screamed, though not with fright. Her hands shoved at his shoulders and her hips writhed up off the bed. "Please, please," she implored.

Lucky knew she wanted him to stop, and perversely he sucked harder, deeper. She yelled and bucked, then moaned and quit fighting, tossing her head and clawing at his shoulders until he felt a shudder rip right through her. Good Lord, had he already given her her climax?

He pulled back and stared down at her face, all aglow with heat and wanton pleasure, her eyes so huge and dilated, her mouth trembling on a pant. The urge to kiss her, to thrust his tongue into that ripe mouth and drive his aching length deep inside her, was almost his undoing.

Instead, with a supreme effort, he stood, smiled and left her.

Even though he still trembled with unassuaged desire, Lucky felt a rare sense of power and triumph as he strode out of the house onto the porch. Why had he not thought of this surefire solution before now—teasing Molly, tormenting *her?* The woman had tortured him long enough. Now it was time to turn the tables on her.

Yes, he'd get his little bride hot and bothered—so hot and bothered that she would soon go crazy and eagerly send him packing. He'd tempt her, beguile her, bewitch her, just as she had done to him. He'd do everything except *do* it, or give her the baby she craved to win the contest.

In this delightfully wicked way, he would surely defeat her.

Yes, this was precisely what he must do. Otherwise, she would win—and soon. She'd snare him just like a hunting trophy and mount him on her wall. It had become a matter of survival now.

Funny how, throughout this whole ordeal, he'd been so blinded by his outrage that it had never occurred to him to use his charm to best the vixen.

And as many a twenty-first-century woman knew, Lucky Lamont's charm could be deadly.

Back in the bedroom, Molly burned with horror and fascination. She couldn't believe what her bridegroom had just done to her. Stroking her in her sleep, rousing her to unbearable desire. Then touching her breasts, taking her nipple in his mouth.

Oh, the stimulation had been unbearable! She was actually wet between her thighs, her womanhood crying out for Lucky's hard length. And he'd looked like the devil incarnate sitting on her bed—unshaven, hair rumpled, something riveting and fierce burning in his eyes. His mouth on her nipple had been hot and wet, his unshaven cheeks had abraded her breasts so deliciously. And his tongue—what pure, wicked pleasure he had brought to her, like nothing she had ever felt before!

But what was on his scheming mind now, avoiding her like the plague all this time, only to charge in like a rutting stallion? Was he actually planning to take his husbandly rights? Then why hadn't he finished what he'd started?

Molly didn't know what to expect next and felt totally rattled. If Lucky did claim his husbandly due tonight, she might win the contest—but she feared she might also be totally undone in the process.

Chapter Twenty-one

Molly was completing her toilette when she heard a ruckus out on the front porch. Glancing out the window, she spotted a surrey with a black horse parked in the front yard. Seconds later, she emerged from the front door to see Grandma at the foot of the steps, confronting Sheriff Hackett and his lady friend, Dulcie Hicks, who looked like a painted hussy with her heavily rouged face, garishly dyed straw-blond hair and low-cut, sleazy gold satin dress. Molly paused to listen to the exchange in fascination.

Grandma's face was purple and she was wagging a finger at the sheriff. "I told you, Hiram Hackett, to get your harlot off our property!"

"Oh!" cried Dulcie, her ample bosom heaving. "You're one to talk, Eula Reklaw. Everyone knows you're the mother of outlaws."

"*Reformed* outlaws," Eula corrected. "There's a big difference, you ignorant bumpkin. My boys saw the light long ago. As for you, everyone knows you're the town harlot and your youngest don't look nothing like his pa. Why, Winky was born a year after Otis passed on, and got that there eye-twitch from Jiggles Jenkins, after you whored yourself with him."

"How dare you!" Dulcie accused, red-faced. She whirled to Hackett. "Hiram, are you going to stand for this?"

Hackett, who appeared miserable as he stood there holding his ten-gallon hat and chewing on his handlebar mustache, barely managed to meet Eula's eye. "Ma'am, just because Miss Dulcie here favored a ride in the country this morning—"

"Oh, yeah? What else has that Cyprian of yourn been riding?"

Hearing this, Molly stifled giggles.

"Hiram, did you hear what she called me?" Dulcie shrieked.

Miserably, Hiram chided, "Ma'am, Miss Dulcie's accompanying me today has nothing to do with—er—my investigation—"

"Don't give me that hokum, Hiram Hackett," Grandma bellowed. "Her bein' here has everything to do with how you favor her no-account boys and their trashy cousins over my grandsons. You're always accusing my boys of thievin' and lawbreaking, instead of looking under your own big nose."

Self-consciously, Hackett scratched that prominent nose. "Ma'am, I just need a word with 'em—"

"Not while I have breath left in my body. For all I know, you been out there yourself, leading the outlaw charge with them lowlifes."

213

"Me?" Hackett protested. "But I'm the sheriff!"

"Then start actin' like one, 'stead of some bull on the prowl, looking for a heifer to mount."

"Oh!" shrieked Dulcie.

By now Molly figured it was time for her to intervene. "Sheriff, what do you want with my brothers?" she asked, coming down the steps to join them.

Hiram turned to her with an expression of intense relief. "Morning, Miss Molly. I just gotta talk to 'em, that's all. Ya see, since during the night, a gang of cutthroats broke into the Dillyville Bank and absconded with the safe."

"And you think my brothers had something to do with this?" she asked sharply.

Before he could respond, Eula snapped, "And did you question all five of them Hickses afore you come out here to hurl false accusations at us good folk?"

Hackett shifted from boot to boot. "Ma'am, Dulcie already told me all five of them boys was at an all-night poker game at her place."

"And you took her word over ourn?" Grandma snarled.

"Ma'am, you ain't even given me your word—"

"And 'sides, Hiram was with me all night, too," Dulcie finished self-righteously, only to blush in obvious realization of what she'd just said.

"Aha!" Grandma sneered, wagging a finger at Dulcie. "And what was you two doin'? Playin' tiddlywinks?"

Even as Dulcie gasped in outrage, Hackett's face went beet red. "Ma'am, I just need to know your grandsons' whereabouts last night, and for someone to—er, vouch for 'em."

"Then you have my word," Eula retorted. "Them boys was in the bunkhouse here, all night."

"Yes, ma'am. And where are they now?"

"Not that it's any of your nevermind, but the eldest three is working the range with their pa, while Cory is helping his ma take chicken soup by the widow Hicks's place. Wilma's ailing again."

"Yes, ma'am. Sorry to hear about Wilma."

"Now get your painted hussy out of my yard."

"Yes, ma'am," said Hackett, donning his hat.

Dulcie's mouth hung open. "Hiram, ain't you got no grit a'tall? Letting her insult me three ways to sundown. And are you just going to take the word of this—"

"For now, yes, I am," he cut in tensely, grabbing Dulcie's arm. "Come along, Dulcine, let's go."

Despite her continuing protests, Hackett dragged Dulcie off to the surrey and hefted her inside. She waved a fist at Grandma and spewed epithets as he drove her away.

Molly shook her head at her grandma, who was grinning like a cat with a field mouse. "Grandma, weren't you a little hard on Sheriff Hackett?"

She waved a hand. "Hard, my butt. How dare that bangtailed weasel just show up here with his whoring floozy—and accuse my grandsons of lawbreakin'."

"But Grandma, the way you were carrying on, you might just make him more suspicious."

"Ah, pshaw! And since when have you cared if your brothers end up in the hoosegow?" Before Molly could respond, she winked. "So how's the little bride this morning? And where ya hiding your bridegroom, missy?"

Molly was frowning at the question when a whistling sound drew both women's attention to the side of the house. Molly watched as her clean-shaven, freshly groomed husband rounded the corner, whistling, "There'll be a Hot Time in the Old Town Tonight."

"Well, there you are," Eula called. "Where you been, sonny? Your little bride here has been complaining you're neglecting her."

"I have not," Molly retorted, her face burning.

Reaching the front steps, Lucky chuckled. "I was washing up in the bunkhouse so my darlin' could sleep." He winked at Molly. "Last night pretty much did her in, I reckon."

Molly's mouth dropped open. "Why, of all the lying—"

"Mornin', angel."

In a flash Lucky hopped up on the porch beside her, taking full advantage of her confused state and parted lips by kissing her heartily. Molly squirmed and protested inarticulately as his tongue greedily explored her mouth, stroking her, teasing her, unnerving her. Her nipples tingled and a hot, staggering weakness swept over her. Again she felt herself go all achy and wet between her thighs.

What was *wrong* with her? Why did he affect her this way, making her weak as a just-born lamb?

At last he pulled back and said wickedly, "Thanks for a night from heaven, angel."

Molly went speechless with shock.

Grandma hooted a laugh. "Oh, praise the Lord!" She pounded them both across their backs. "Good for you, sonny. I'll be expecting that great-grandchild by spring.

And my stars, Molly gal, I reckon you *are* plumb tuckered out."

Molly stared daggers at Lucky. "Just wait till I get done with *him*."

Dodging her insult, Lucky proudly wrapped an arm around her waist. "See how crazy she is about me, Grandma?" Still ignoring his seething bride, he nodded toward the surrey disappearing over the hillside. "Did we already have visitors this morning?"

Eula harrumphed. "Sheriff Hackett came out with that slut of hisn, Dulcie Hicks, to investigate another robbery. He had the gall to accuse my grandsons of raiding the Dillyville Bank, 'stead of arresting them miscrable Hicks boys."

Lucky whistled. "Ah, yes. Heard some talk about the recent robberies at church yesterday. One of the men even mentioned rumors about the Dempsey gang possibly riding again—"

Eula waved him off. "Ah, every time there's a robbery hereabouts, folks are wabashing about the Dempsey gang. Don't you believe that hokum."

Lucky nodded. "Er, do you think Hackett's going after Molly's brothers now because of Cole's—um—history?"

"Yeah, but it ain't right and I told him so."

"Yes, ma'am."

She grinned. "Well, it's Monday and I've tons of wash to do. I'll leave you two lovebirds alone."

"Oh, yes, ma'am." Lucky wiggled his eyebrows at Molly and squeezed her tighter.

Molly surged forward. "Grandma, wait. I'll help you."

She guffawed. "A fat lot of help you'd be, not knowing a wash pot from a scrub board. You tend to your husband, honey."

Lucky grabbed her arm and hauled her back against him. "Yeah, honey, tend to your husband."

Squirming and shooting him a murderous look, she implored, "Grandma, make him stop it."

Eula turned. "Stop what?"

"Grabbing me and kissing me."

She howled with laughter. "Great jumping Jehoshaphat, granddaughter, don't come sobbin' to me. You're the one who wanted this fella, who shanghaied him home and dragged him to the altar. Now he's all yours. If you don't like him kissing on you all the time, then *you* make him behave."

Grandma was still laughing as she ambled into the house.

Molly glanced at Lucky, caught the devilish gleam in his eyes and again tried to wiggle away. "You let me go."

"Let you go?" he teased. "But, darlin', I'm only giving you what you really want, right?" He leaned over and nibbled at her bare shoulder.

"Stop it! Why are you doing this?"

He feigned astonishment as his hand boldly stroked her bottom through her dress. " 'Cause we're married, angel, or have you forgot?"

"But I thought you didn't, didn't want—"

He shoved her up against his hardness and winked wickedly. "Didn't want what?" Looking determined—and sexy—as the very devil, he leaned toward her and brushed his lips over hers, causing her to suck in her breath sharply. "That's better. Now come sit on my lap on the porch swing and I'll teach you more about kissing."

Molly writhed frantically. "I—we'll do no such thing. Why, that's indecent, it's—"

"Come on, now. Boy, that wiggling of yours is getting me hot."

Her jaw dropped in horror.

He was still tugging Molly toward the swing and she was digging her slippers into the porch when she was relieved to hear the sound of approaching hoofbeats. Thanking her lucky stars, she pointed to the west. "Look. Cory's driving Ma home."

"Saved by the buckboard," he teased back. "But don't think you're safe from me, Molly girl." He swept her with a look hot enough to scorch her clothes. "You know what they say: You can run but you can't hide."

Molly could only stare at him, overwhelmed, as the buckboard pulled up in the yard. She didn't draw an easy breath until Ma and Cory had joined them on the porch.

Smiling, Jessica embraced Molly. "Molly, darling, how are you? Why, you're all flushed. Are you feeling well?"

Lucky stepped forward to pull Molly close again. "She's just fine, ma'am. You know, a blushing bride."

Jessica smiled and Cory chuckled. Molly kicked Lucky in the shin and he pinched her behind.

"Ma, how's Mrs. Hicks?" Molly asked, while glowering at Lucky.

"She still has a very bad cough but is slowly mending." Jessica nodded to Lucky. "Well, we'll leave you two alone."

"No," Molly cried. "I mean, why does everyone want to leave us alone?"

" 'Cause you're newlyweds, sis," Cory teased back.

Desperately, Molly tried to conjure up an avenue of escape. "Well, I need to speak with my brother," she told Jessica, "about—about Sheriff Hackett's visit while you were gone."

"Oh, no," fretted Jessica. "Has there been another robbery?"

Molly glanced sharply at Lucky. "Lucky'll fill you in."

She felt intensely relieved when instead of protesting, he stepped forward. "Sure, I will. Later, sweetheart." Quickly, he kissed her lips.

Fleeing inside with her brother, Molly caught a convulsive breath, then turned to see Cory regarding her with curiosity and amusement. "What?" she demanded.

"Molly, you're red as an apple and quivering like a leaf in a storm."

"Oh, shut up."

"Did you bite off more than you can chew with this cowboy?"

"Leave him out of it."

Cory held up his hands. "Sure, sis, whatever you say. Guess a new bride is entitled to be grumpy."

Molly ground her teeth. "Look, I want to talk to you about the sheriff's visit."

"Yeah?"

"Are you boys involved in those robberies?" As he hesitated, she added, "And don't give me that hokum about Dirty Dick Dempsey doing it. I read all about his being killed in a shoot-out in Denver."

Cory chuckled. "Sis, haven't you learned by now not to believe everything you read in dime novels?"

"Quit stalling."

Cory gave a shrug. "You know, Molly, you won't talk about your life, so why should I tell you anything about ours?"

Molly gripped his arm. "Because I'm family."

"Right. Sure."

"All right," she conceded wearily. "Maybe I do care more about you than the others. But the truth is, all of you are my brothers. So, are you four involved in the holdups or not?"

He shook his head. "Nope. The boys and I suspect the Hicks boys are doing it, but Sheriff Hackett's too busy mooning over Dulcie Hicks to see the truth. And maybe she's putting a bug in his ear about us boys to protect her own, and 'cause of her rivalry with Grandma and Aunt Dumpling."

Molly nodded. "Still, are you certain none of you are involved?"

"Molly, I give you my word."

That Molly did believe. "All right, then, I feel better." Biting her lip, she added, "Unless the other three are involved and haven't told you."

That remark left Cory with a troubled frown on his face, a look that worried his younger sister.

Chapter Twenty-two

"What are we doing back in Reklaw Gorge, señor?" Sanchez asked.

At midday, Lucky had again fled the ranch—and Molly—to blow off some steam. Although she'd agreed to let him go riding, she'd sent Sanchez along to keep an eye on him. Lucky had also brought along a large workhorse laden with tools.

During the ride to the canyon, he'd chuckled at the memory of his bride's face when he'd left the house, how relieved she'd appeared to get rid of him. His plan to torment her until she sent him packing was working like a charm. Only problem was, it was working *too* well—he was becoming as hot and bothered as she was. He needed to hedge his bets and make plans to escape this time-travel purgatory, just in case the seduction route became too perilous.

As, indeed, it already was.

Leading the entourage down into the canyon, Lucky

explained to Sanchez, "You and me are gonna start up a little project, buddy."

"*Sí*, señor. Is that why we're carrying all these tools?" Sanchez gestured toward the hammers, mallets and other implements tied to the Belgian Shire.

"Yep. Follow me, now."

Lucky led Sanchez over to the windbreak of pines, where the two men dismounted. He showed him the bundles of debris he'd hidden earlier that morning.

Sanchez crossed himself. "Señor, it's the wreckage of the haunted *coche*. The one used by Señorita Lila Lullaby and her *palomas desgracias*."

Lucky chuckled at the term "disgraced doves." "Sure is. And you and me are gonna reassemble it."

Sanchez was backing away, wide-eyed. "Señor, no. It's bad luck to touch the haunted *coche*."

"Well, hombre, your luck is definitely gonna be bad if you don't help me," Lucky fired back. "I'm aimin' to get out of here, and this here bucket of bolts is gonna be my vehicle. You and me are gonna patch it back together up there on that shelf of dike." He pointed upward at a stone ledge.

"Up there?" Sanchez was wide-eyed. "We must haul these heaps of trash up the mountainside?"

"Yep. And no tattling to Miss Molly either, you understand?"

Although Sanchez was regarding Lucky as if he'd lost his mind, he dutifully nodded. "*Sí*, señor."

"Now let's get started."

Sanchez crossed himself again, then began helping Lucky tie the bundles to the horses.

* * *

That afternoon, Molly sat up in the hayloft, petting Jezebel's newly born kittens and wondering what the hell her bridegroom was up to now. All morning, the memories of his brash intimacies, his kisses, his bold teasing, had been driving her wild.

Why did he avoid her like bad news one day, then try to tear her clothes off the next? And why wasn't she reacting as she should be? She'd gleefully taken the lead before—why should she protest now, when he'd finally responded in kind? After all, wasn't this what she'd wanted all along, for them to get together and make a baby?

She just hadn't expected to become so flustered, so confused—so *aroused*—by the process. Lucky's turning the tables on her had her feeling totally rattled, and vulnerable whenever he touched her. She'd actually been grateful to see him leave for his ride—although she had a hunch he'd be back soon.

"Well, hello, Molly love, what are you doing up here?"

Speaking of the devil! Molly gasped and turned to see Lucky perched at the top of the ladder, sunshine gleaming in his soft blond hair and glinting in his blue eyes. Her cheeks flushed at the realization that he had her cornered, alone, again.

She nervously cleared her throat. "Hi. You gave me a start. I didn't hear you coming up the ladder."

He hopped up into the hay to join her. "Are you hiding from me?"

She rolled her eyes. "Jezebel finally had her kittens."

"Oh, wow." He gazed at the tiny creatures suckling at their mother. "Four of them, eh?"

She nodded. "Yes, one black, one white, one gray—and one calico, like her. They're only a few hours old."

"How'd you know they were here?"

"I didn't. But I got worried when Jez didn't show up for her milk this morning, and had one heck of a time finding her. Why is it mama cats always hide their kittens?"

"Afraid they'll be stolen, I guess."

"Yeah, reckon so."

As the gray kitten mewled, he chuckled. "They look kind of like drowned rats, don't they?"

"They'll get pretty soon enough." She touched the tiny black one. "This one's my favorite."

"Black for the mischief in your soul?"

"Black for the mischief in his *daddy's* soul," she corrected. "Jezebel's a calico, in case you hadn't noticed."

Lucky reached out to stroke her flushed cheek. "And where do you suppose the daddy is now?"

An unaccountable thrill swept over Molly; he just looked so damn sexy, staring at her that way. She cleared her throat. "Oh, I'm sure he's out prowling around, like most tomcats do."

He curled an arm around her waist. "So he just got her in a family way and left her high and dry, eh?"

"Not high and dry. She has her kittens."

Their gazes locked, rife with meaning. "Is that all she wants from him?" he asked huskily.

Molly was on the verge of replying when Lucky drew her closer and kissed her, this time tenderly, without anger. Molly couldn't help herself—she moaned and curled her arms around his neck, loving the way his mouth seduced her and his hard chest crushed her breasts. He groaned, his kiss growing more urgent but still unbearably sweet. Even the scent of the hay seemed stirring, erotic.

"Nice discussion we're having, darlin'," he murmured after a moment, nuzzling her neck. "Mamas and babies—and making 'em."

His words were driving her crazy, sweeping her with dizzying chills. "Lucky, please—"

She tried to protest, but he pushed her down into the hay beneath him, his torrid gaze smoldering into hers. That look threatened to suck her in and devour her, and panic seized her. Then he grinned and reached down with his hand, his skilled fingers slowly stroking up her bare leg, tormenting her.

She grabbed his hand. "Please, stop—"

His hand remained firmly clenched on her bare thigh. "You really want me to stop, darlin'? Aren't you the one always talking about having a young 'un? And driving me crazy with your sexy talk of doin' it?"

"Really? Crazy?" she asked breathlessly.

"Totally out of my mind." He leaned closer and drew his tongue teasingly over her cheek. "Well, sugar, hasn't it occurred to you that we gotta *make* that baby first in order to have it?"

Molly was spinning, drowning in want. Desperately she asked, "If—if we make that baby, will you leave me afterward, just like Jezebel's tomcat did?"

That barb hit home. Lucky cursed and rolled off her. After giving her one last searing look, he left her.

Molly expected to feel relieved. She didn't expect to cry about it.

* * *

Lucky kicked himself as he strode away from the barn. The sight of Molly petting those sweet little kittens had practically unraveled him. The familial scene had been tender, poignant, emotionally loaded. Every fiber of Lucky's being had been focused on possessing Molly, making love to her, giving her his seed.

All the things he *shouldn't* be doing.

Then, when she'd asked if he would get her pregnant and leave her, shame had brought him up short. That was what his own bastard of a father had done to his mother. If not for the coward's betrayal, perhaps his mom never would have sunk into wild ways and gotten killed on a lonely Colorado highway.

He felt guilty for toying with Molly, guilty for going back to the canyon, guilty for being a male with hormones. Yet, as much as her question had smarted, thank God she had asked it, saving him from making a disastrous mistake.

He'd been so close to claiming her sweet body. So close to catching himself in his own trap. So close to trusting again, to regaining his faith, to caring for her. If he had succumbed . . . Well, he knew he could never be the type of lowlife who would give her his child, then leave her. It had hurt him to realize she thought he might, though to be honest, how could he blame her?

Although he felt a certain sympathy for Molly, he'd also known from the beginning what she wanted from him—his name and his seed. Now he found himself wanting more with her, something lasting and genuine. He couldn't expect her to return his feelings. He had to protect himself or he'd get hurt again as he had with Misti.

He had to get control of himself before Molly took control of *him*. After all, he was the one who was experienced and worldly; she was the one who was innocent and naïve as far as sex was concerned—or so she claimed. On that one battleground he had to outsmart her. Surely one more near seduction would be enough to convince her to cry uncle and give him an annulment.

If he didn't cry uncle first.

Chapter Twenty-three

"Ah, these are pretty."

Molly stepped into the bedroom that night only to stop in her tracks at the sight of her husband holding a pair of her lace-trimmed bloomers. Lucky stood across from her at the bureau with her lingerie drawer open, examining the undergarment with an expression of avid interest. The sleeves on his blue-checked shirt were rolled up to reveal his sinewy forearms and several of his buttons were undone, giving her a tantalizing view of his tanned, muscular chest with its covering of tawny hair.

And of course he was grinning like the very devil!

Face red, Molly stormed across the room and snatched the garment from his hand. "Just what do you think you're doing, going through my unmentionables?"

"Oh, I'm just trying to get to know my wife a little better," he teased. He continued rummaging through the drawer and pulled out a pair of pale silk stockings.

Taking a lascivious whiff of them, he murmured, "Ummm . . . sexy. Where are your garters, darlin'?"

"Oh!" Molly grabbed the stockings, shoved them in the drawer and slammed it closed. "You stop that right now."

He smiled patiently and opened another drawer. "I'm just hunting up a suitable nightie for you, sugar."

She shut the drawer. "What?"

"You know, for after your bath."

Molly froze. *Bath?* What did he mean, *bath*? Hadn't his attempted seduction in the hayloft earlier today been torture enough?

Glancing about the room, she didn't spot the tub. But she could see steam curling from behind the dressing screen in the corner, and come to think of it, she'd been smelling the rosewater she used to scent the water ever since she'd entered the room. Her stomach sank.

"You fetched me a bath?" she finally managed.

He winked and stepped closer. "No, your grandma did."

"Oh. So it was her idea?"

"No, it was mine."

Molly gulped.

"So where you been since supper, sugar?"

"Uh—helping Ma with her mending."

"Liar," he accused. "You've been hiding out from me—just like you have all day."

"Have not!" she retorted, though her face flamed.

"Did I make you too hot in the hayloft?"

"I—I don't know what you mean," she stammered. "That—that was about kittens."

"Yeah, and about babies—and a lot more." Laughing, he reopened the drawer and pulled out a long blue flannel nightie. He whistled. "My dear wife, how very unsexy. This goes to the rag heap."

"What?"

Before she could stop him, Lucky rent the garment from neck to hem and tossed it onto the floor.

Molly was livid. "Damn you to hell, Lucky Lamont! That was my warmest nightie. You want me to freeze my butt off in winter?"

Expression utterly rakish, he hauled her close, running his hand provocatively over her backside. "Oh, don't worry. I know plenty of tricks to help keep that pretty backside of yours warm."

Face crimson, she shoved him away.

Undaunted, he turned and pulled a white linen nightgown from the drawer. "Now this is more like it. Demure and virginal, but also lacy and low-cut. Just what I had in mind. I'll lay it on the bed for you, darlin'—although you won't be needing it for long."

Molly was panicking. "I—I just remembered I promised Ma I'd—er—take the slops out to the swine—"

He shook a finger at her, then reached for a button on the low, lace-trimmed bodice of her dress. "To heck with the slops. You're my wife tonight, Molly, not a pig farmer. You're staying right here while your husband undresses and bathes you."

"What?" Eyes huge, Molly jumped back three feet.

He chuckled, while steadily advancing upon her. "We're hitched now, honey, aren't we? Why all this false modesty? Isn't this just what you wanted—a truly *intimate* relationship? Doesn't it say in the good book that the man and the woman were both naked and were not ashamed?"

"B-both?" she managed to stammer.

"You know, that's a great idea," he replied eagerly. "Why don't I join you in the bath? That should help ease another kind of joining, eh, love?"

Molly tried to flee out the door, only to discover she'd headed straight for the wall. As she turned, Lucky easily pinned her there, eyeing her in perverse triumph, pressing his heat into her pelvis. All at once she could hardly breathe.

"Why are you doing this?" she gasped.

"Why?" He arched against her. "Isn't it obvious?"

"But, I thought you didn't—"

"Didn't want sex?" he provided. "Perhaps I've reconsidered. I seem to be trapped here, in this shotgun marriage, so why deny myself certain—er—pleasures? You being the original virgin and all." He leaned over and kissed her cheek.

She panted helplessly. "Lucky, please stop it."

Now he was nuzzling her neck. "Why so coy, Molly? Last night you were trying to climb all over me—today you turn into a skittish kitten. Are you really as innocent as you let on? Or are you hiding some deep, dark secret you don't want me to know?"

Angry, she pushed at his shoulders but might as well have been trying to budge a rock. "Stop it."

He drew back slightly, toying with another of her buttons. "Then madam is ready for her bath?"

Molly's face was bright red as she slapped away his fingers. "Please, I can do it myself."

He grinned. "Very well, then. I'll just watch."

"You'll what? No!"

He pointed at the screen. "It's the only compromise I'm offering, Molly. Either skedaddle into that tub right now or I'll strip you naked and drop you in it myself."

Mortified, Molly dashed behind the screen, grinding her teeth at the sounds of his infuriating laughter.

Removing her clothing with trembling hands, Molly felt a tumult of conflicting emotions—anger, humiliation, fear, but most of all, an overwhelming sense of excitement. Why was Lucky doing this? Pursuing her so hotly, when he'd shunned her until today?

At any rate, she had little time to ponder this. Knowing he might join her at any minute, she hastily finished stripping and settled into the water, which felt warm and soothing but did little to assuage her agitated state. She drew her knees up to her chin to cover her nakedness as best she could.

Then she gasped as her husband rounded the dressing screen and joined her by the tub. The look on his face took her breath away. His eyes were devouring her alive, roving her body intimately. Oh, Lord, she was in deep, deep trouble. When she'd contemplated taking a husband, she'd thought of the marriage act as something mechanical, a path to procreation, a way to accomplish her goals. Never had she imagined that just her husband's burning look could rouse in her such a purgatory of emotion. Longing that made her heart race. Desire so sharp and deep it took her breath away and made her throb inside.

And that was just his look. If he touched her . . .

Just when she thought she could bear no more, he removed his shirt slowly, very slowly, revealing all the glory of his tanned, naked torso. Then he unbuckled and pulled off his belt with that same leisurely ease. His gaze scorched hers as he unbuttoned the top button on his jeans—just that one button. So sexy, with that patch of downy hair revealed at his navel. Her mouth went dry.

If he touched her, she would surely die!

He sank to his knees beside her and did so now, reaching out to stroke her damp auburn curls. She winced in helpless longing.

"Well, Mrs. Lamont," he murmured at last, voice husky with need, "reckon I'm feeling pretty lucky tonight."

The raspiness of his voice, his calling her Mrs. Lamont for the first time, his saying he felt lucky, all conspired to put Molly in a torment of desire. And that was before he kissed her. When his mouth took hers with unbearable gentleness, his lips teasing, caressing her own, she thought she might expire of the emotions consuming her. Then the kiss, which had begun so sweetly, turned carnal, demanding, his tongue ravishing her mouth and enticing her surrender.

Molly was breathless, spinning, wantonly exploring Lucky's mouth with her own tongue. He responded with savage sounds as his free hand began roving her body intimately. For long moments he drew his rough thumb in tormenting circles around one tight nipple, then the other, driving her to distraction. Afterward he kneaded each breast in turn, squeezing almost roughly; the stimulation was shattering, exquisite. Just when she could bear no more, his hand slid lower, stroking her belly, his fingers slipping between her thighs.

Molly clenched her thighs, gasped and tore her mouth from his. "Please, don't."

He only smiled at her. "But you're mine now, darlin'. Here, too. Especially here. Now open to me like a good wife."

Molly could only cry out helplessly, and when Lucky kissed her again, claiming her mouth so masterfully, she did his bidding, easing her thighs apart. When he touched her there her back arched and her nipples tightened in rapture. She heard his moan of pleasure as his fingers explored, finding the tiny nub where so much of her ecstasy seemed to be centered. She squirmed in delicious torment. As he began expertly stroking her, tears of mingled confusion and pleasure fell from her eyes. His free hand gripped her fingers and drew them to his own crotch. She felt his hardness with fingers dampened by rosewater, and heard his tortured grunt as she caressed him, driving him toward a pleasure to match her own.

Abruptly he pulled back and stared at her face—so flushed, rapt and vulnerable. "Damn," he muttered with unexpected vehemence. "Damn it all to hell."

And before her disbelieving eyes, he stood and walked away. Seconds later she heard the bedroom door slam.

For a moment Molly remained stunned. She struggled hard not to cry. What did Lucky think he was doing, driving her insane with desire, then walking out on her? Was this his cruel way of showing her his true feelings, all the contempt he *really* felt for her?

Remembering the loathing in his voice, the heartless way he'd turned and left her, she had her answer.

That realization broke the dike, and Molly sobbed her heart out.

Lucky stood trembling outside the bedroom door. He hated himself. Trying to wreak his revenge on Molly was not bringing him the satisfaction he'd anticipated. In fact, the whole scheme had backfired squarely in his face.

He'd intended to seduce her, only to become seduced himself by her loveliness and innocence. He'd intended to rouse her to unbearable desire, then leave her hanging. Instead he'd visited that very vengeance on himself. He'd become totally snared in his own game—and had taken things much farther than he'd intended.

What was worse, he'd pushed her to tears with his cruelty. *Tears.* So what if she was a pain in the neck and no one's idea of a proper wife? Even she deserved her dignity.

As for him . . . He deserved a good horsewhipping for treating her so badly. Now he would spend a miserable night in the barn, with only himself to blame.

How could he extricate himself from this mess? He wasn't at all sure he could leave, but if he stayed he was bound to make love to Molly any minute now.

One more display of tears and the girl wouldn't know what had hit her. He'd be kissing her, distracting her, loving her to the moon and back. And if he got her pregnant—then he could never leave her. That meant the only possible salvation for him—and maybe her, too—was his escape, retreat.

He groaned. He and Sanchez had best get damn busy rebuilding that stagecoach. . . .

Chapter Twenty-four

At church that Sunday, during the opening hymn, Cory Reklaw smiled across the aisle at Ida May, who looked delicious as a maiden's blush rose in her pale pink Sunday dress. She started to wave back, only to freeze at her father's glower and the venomous look he hurled Cory's way. Cory sighed and turned his attention back to the hymnal, to the Charles Wesley selection "Come, Sinners, to the Gospel Feast."

He and his brothers weren't making much progress courting the sisters, given old man Trumble's unceasing efforts to discourage them. Next to him, his brothers' grim expressions gave mute testimony to their own feelings of frustration.

With a rueful smile, Cory wondered if his sister was faring any better in the romance department. She sat in front of him, all starched up in green gingham and matching bonnet, sharing a hymnal with her husband, though neither was touching the other.

They'd behaved so strangely all week. After the wedding it couldn't have been more obvious that Molly was brazenly flirting with Lucky, pursuing him with every ounce of her femininity, while he bristled and kept his distance. Then the next day, Lucky had started pursuing her, and she had shied away. For the remainder of the week, as far as Cory could tell, the two had avoided each other like a seasonal malaise. Indeed, on a morning or two he'd spied Lucky leaving the barn after obviously having slept there, and he now spent most of his days riding the range with the other Reklaw men, helping them out with the spring calf roundup.

It was all so strange. The newlyweds seemed crazy as a couple of barking squirrels. He couldn't help wondering if they'd gotten together yet, but he rather doubted it. Which meant there still might be hope for the rest of them. Not that Cory really cared that much if he won the contest—truth to tell, he was much more interested in continuing his education than in becoming a rancher—but he did care about Ida May Trumble. He liked her a lot, was very concerned about her, wanted to get to know her better and yearned to help her escape what he felt certain was a bad situation. Every time he remembered Ezra Trumble's shocking displays of temper, it made him crazy to think the tyrant might visit his physical anger on any of his daughters.

He became distracted as Reverend Bledsoe launched into his sermon, loudly proclaiming a passage from Matthew 9:13: "I am not come to call the righteous, but sinners to repentance."

Oh, brother, Cory thought. It appeared Reverend

238

Bledsoe was on another of his redemption benders. As the preacher got into form, alternately whispering, then pounding his fist and yelling, Cory noted that the clergyman's theme quickly evolved from sinners to thieves. Then the parson began expounding on the "evil robberies" in the area, decrying the "servants of sin" and their "wicked fruit," quoting Old Testament passages about fire and brimstone. Indeed, Bledsoe got so worked up that when he screamed, "Repent, ye thieves!" Ezra Trumble stood, pointed an accusatory finger at the Reklaw boys, and declared, "Amen, Reverend! Let's lynch the heathens!"

A gasp rippled over the congregation, and Cory watched his pa and his grandma all but come shooting out of their seats, with only his ma's quick, firm hands holding them back. In the meantime dozens of eyes had focused with suspicion on Cory and his brothers.

Pastor Bledsoe, having unwittingly encouraged the outburst, appeared horrified and hastily turned the congregation's attention to a new hymn. As Ezra Trumble at last resumed his seat, Cory expelled a groan of mingled frustration and relief. *This is great*, he thought. Reverend Bledsoe had inadvertently given Trumble even more ammunition to condemn him and his brothers, even though they'd had nothing at all to do with the robberies.

Nothing? He remembered Molly's question the other day and a chill washed over him. After all, he wasn't with his brothers every minute—indeed, ever since the courting had begun and he'd offered his siblings so much unsolicited advice, more of a rift had developed between him and the others. What if his brothers *had* turned outlaw—and had conveniently forgotten to tell him?

That was easy. If old man Trumble didn't string them up, he would!

After the congregation was dismissed, the four brothers stood in a huddle outside, watching Ezra Trumble lead his daughters back toward their surrey. "Fat chance we got to court them girls now," grumbled Matt.

"Yeah, fat chance," seconded Zach, "after being labeled bushwhackers in front of God and everyone."

"Yes, I must agree he guards those girls like an old miser with his gold," added Cory, feeling quite glum himself.

Vance was about to voice a comment of his own when Grandma stepped up to join them in a rustle of black silk skirts, her mouth pursed in angry determination. "Cory Reklaw, you come with me."

Cory knew better than to argue with Grandma when she had her mouth set that way. "Yes, ma'am." Tossing his brothers a bemused look, he trooped off with her.

To Cory's surprise, Grandma made a beeline for Ezra Trumble's surrey, arriving by his side right as he was about to snap the reins. With a defiant tilt of her feathered hat, she confronted him. "Ezra Trumble, I'll be having a word with you."

He appeared delighted, tipping his bowler. "Why, Eula, I'm honored. Lovely day, isn't it?"

"Hush up that flowery talk of yourn and listen to me. First off, I should string you up for insulting my grandsons at the meeting house."

He scowled. "But Eula, I was only acknowledging what the parson said—"

"Don't Eula me, you old coot! You was accusing my boys of outlawin'! I know you're doin' it out of pure meanness 'cause everyone knows my boys favor your daughters. And I want you to stop your shenanigans right now—and start letting my boys court your girls."

As Cory grinned and the girls tittered happily, Ezra howled derisively. "You think I'd allow these sinners under my roof? How dare you accuse me of judging them, when Reverend Bledsoe all but called them thieves to their faces this morning."

"He did not—and how dare *you!*" Grandma retorted.

"I don't doubt they're the gang that's been robbin' and pillaging hereabouts lately." Trumble sneered at Cory. "Maybe not the runt here . . . but them others—"

"You hush up, Ez Trumble," Grandma cut in furiously. "I'll have you know my boys ain't thieves, and see you remember that. I'll be sending them all by to call this afternoon at three, and you'd best not be receivin' them with that shotgun of yours."

"Oh, yeah?" Trumble had gone livid with anger. "Just who do you think you are, woman, to tell me my business? What kindness have you ever extended my way?"

"Well, I'm not marrying you, Trumble, so git that through your thick head."

Balefully, Trumble turned to Cory. "See what I mean? Your grandma treats me with utter contempt, then expects me to allow you boys to court my girls."

Cory gave his grandma a helpless look, and she turned to scowl at Trumble. "All right, then, you made your point, Ez. What's it gonna take to change your mind and give my boys a chance with your daughters?" As he started to open his mouth, she added, "And don't you dare say my hand in wedlock, 'cause I ain't giving it."

He shot her a long-suffering look. "Very well, then, I'll tell you what it'll take. You come along with the boys today."

"Me?"

"Yes, you."

"When roosters lay eggs, I will." She paused, scowling. "But tell you what—just as a little, er, peace offering, I'll send over one of my molasses pies."

He scowled a moment, then waved a hand in resignation. "Very well, woman, if you're willing to extend some token of friendship—"

Again she shook a finger at him. "Three o'clock, Trumble. And no shotgun."

As the girls tittered happily, Grandma turned and stalked away. Cory caught Ida May's delighted smile and winked back at her before he too hurried off.

He caught up with his grandma as fast as he could. "Thanks, Grandma, you did great."

Eula harrumphed. "Damn that Ezra Trumble to perdition, trying to blackmail me into going along. I'm spiking his molasses pie with plenty of castor oil, let me tell you. The geezer'll never know what hit him till he gets the dysentery."

Cory was aghast. "Grandma, no. You want to get all of us boys shot?"

Eula chuckled and pinched his cheek. "Reckon you're right, darlin'. That codger just gets me so worked up. Guess I'll have to play fair—even if the man is a snake."

Cory beamed. "Grandma, you're earning your stars in heaven."

"Quit tryin' to charm me, boy, or I'll wallop you good."

But she gave him a bear hug as they went off together.

Promptly at three P.M., starched and shining, bearing gifts for the girls and a pie for Ezra, the four Reklaw boys appeared on the Trumble porch.

"Ah, there ya be," grumbled Mr. Trumble as he swung open the screen door. "Ya boys got your calling cards this time?"

Cory was prepared and thrust a stack of four cards at their host. "Ma got them printed up in town for us."

He perused the cards with a frown but didn't comment further. "The girls is inside in the hallway. Mind your manners now, and step inside."

"Yes, sir."

With Cory leading the way, the four removed their hats and stepped into the wide central corridor. Cory grinned at the four girls, who sat in a prim straight row to their left, Sally and Nelly wedged on a small settee, Bonnie and Ida May in Windsor chairs on either side of them. All looked lovely in their Sunday frocks of various feminine shades, their hair gleaming and tied with ribbons. All greeted the boys with coy smiles and giggles.

Zach, always the boldest, stepped forward, extending a ribbon-wrapped box to Sally. "Miss Sally, I brung you this here candy."

"Why, thank you, Zachary," she said, taking it.

Now Vance strode up to Nelly. "Miss Nelly, I brought you these here roses from my ma's garden."

"Oh, how lovely," she murmured.

Matt and Cory followed suit, Matt giving Bonnie a jar of peppermints, Cory presenting Ida May with a slim volume of Elizabeth Barrett Browning's *Sonnets from the Portuguese*. After she lavishly thanked him, Cory turned to Ezra with a cloth-wrapped dish. "Sir, here is your pie."

He took the gift and harrumphed. "You boys park your hindquarters on that there bench across from my girls. You've gotten close enough to my daughters already."

"Yes, sir." Cory glanced with dismay at the long, hard bench on the opposite side of the foyer, at least seven feet away from the girls. "Come on, boys."

Casting him baleful looks, Cory's brothers dutifully trooped across the hallway with him.

Cory watched Trumble walk to a small table just beyond Ida May, which held a curious candle wrapped with a black metal coil. Ezra set down the pie and picked up a box of matches. "Time's a-wastin', boys. I'll be lighting the courting candle now."

All four girls gasped in dismay. "Oh, Pa, must you?" wheedled Sally.

"Hush up, daughter, or I'll send you to your room."

"Yes, sir."

Matt whispered in Cory's ear. "What's a courting candle?"

Cory thought he had a general idea but observed Mr. Trumble to be sure. "See that candle he's lighting?"

"Yep. It's got some spiral metal doohickey wrapped around it."

"Yes. And at the bottom of the candle is wedged a cork to work the metal doohickey up and down."

"What does that mean?" whispered Zach.

Cory winced as the wick was lit. "It means we may be done for before we even begin. See how little of the candle he's exposing?"

"Yep. So?"

As Trumble turned to glower at the boys, Cory muttered, "You'll see."

After lighting the candle, Trumble parked himself in a straight chair flanking the table, then crossed his legs and waved a hand. "Very well, boys. Court away."

With Trumble watching all eight of them like a hawk, the boys glanced helplessly at one another, then at the girls. The girls stared back, appearing equally miserable.

The next five minutes were the most awkward Cory had ever known in his life. First a silence stretched so tautly that Cory feared it would snap all their spines. Then Cory asked Ida May how she liked the weather. She said she liked it just fine. Zach asked Sally if she'd ever been to Colorado Springs. She said no, never. Vance asked Nelly how her health was; she confessed she had a boil on her big toe. When Matt's turn came up and he appeared to go blank, Bonnie took charge, asking him what his favorite color was. He admitted he was color-blind.

No sooner had all this inanity ended than Trumble heaved himself to his feet with a snide grin. "All right, boys. Candle's gone out. Time's up."

"What?" cried Zach, staring aghast at the burnt-out candle. "We ain't been here five minutes."

"Yeah!" seconded Vance. "And you rigged that candle

to burn out quick just to thwart us. Talk about trimmin' the wick—"

"Hah!" Trumble laughed scornfully. "I trimmed yours right smartly, didn't I, young man?"

"Mr. Trumble, why are you being so uncooperative?" Cory asked. "We've tried our best to play by your rules, and our intentions are honorable."

"This from a passel of scoundrels who may be bank robbers."

"We're not outlaws," Matt declared furiously.

"Well, it will take more than idle talk or a molasses pie to move me," Trumble retorted. "If you boys want more lift for your wicks, then tell that ornery grandma of yourn to come along next time."

"Oh, brother," muttered Cory. All of this would go off just swell with Grandma, he mused dismally.

Trumble waved an arm. "Now git out, all of ya, before I fetch my shotgun."

"Pa, please, can't they stay—just for a moment?" pleaded Ida May.

He shook a finger at her. "Hush up, daughter, before I take a switch to you as well."

Cory yearned to punch Mr. Trumble over his last comment but realized that would only make matters worse. Knowing further resistance was futile, he exchanged a wrenching glance with Ida May. He watched his brothers follow suit with their own ladies as the four men turned and glumly trooped out the door.

"I could murder that old tyrant," Matt cursed as the four galloped away.

"Me, too," added Vance.

"The nerve of him, accusing us of bank robbery," complained Zach.

At last Cory dared to voice his concerns. "Unless there was a grain of truth in what he said."

"What?" demanded Zach.

Even though the other three were staring murder at him, Cory went on. "Have you boys been outlawing behind my back?"

"Why, you nervy little snot," snapped Vance.

"How dare you accuse your own brothers of law-breaking?" scolded Zach.

"Now you're sounding worse than old man Trumble," declared Matt.

"But I don't hear you boys denying it."

The others glared again, then Zach sneered, "You go to hell, Cory Reklaw. As for the rest of us . . . Shoot, you and everyone else in these parts already thinks the worst of us. So, come on, boys, why don't we go hold up a bank or two?"

"Yeah!" mocked Vance. "Let's blow up some safes and do some pillaging and plundering while we're at it."

Hooting outlaw yells, the eldest three spurred their horses, leaving Cory to eat their dust.

Later that afternoon, Cory arrived home feeling tired and dispirited. The courting expedition had been a disaster, and as for his confronting his brothers about the holdups—well, now he was more confused than ever. He didn't know whether they'd gone outlaw or not.

Or maybe he did know and was just afraid to face the truth.

He found the house strangely quiet, and strode into the kitchen to see Grandma standing there alone rolling cookie dough. He smiled at the sight of her; with flour dabbed on her nose and generously sprinkled on her apron, she looked quite comical.

"Hi, Grandma, where is everyone?"

She turned to him with a grin. "Howdy, honey. Well, your ma and pa went over to Billy and Dumpling's place to rock the babies—"

"And Molly and Lucky?"

She waved a hand. "I got tired of watching them two mope around the house, so I sent 'em off for a picnic in the buckboard."

He laughed. "Good for you."

"'Bout time they settled their differences."

"Grandma, I wouldn't hold my breath."

She laughed. "So how was the courting?"

He rolled his eyes. "I'm afraid Mr. Trumble outwitted us with a courting candle."

"Huh?"

Cory explained about the tradition. "The upshot is, Trumble gave us less than five minutes with his daughters, then shooed us on our way."

Grandma pounded her rolling pin on the sideboard. "Why, the jackass! And after I made a devil's bargain with him, sending him my molasses pie—"

"Well, this particular devil wasn't satisfied with his lot. He wants you to come along next time."

"What? When mule deer fly, I will."

Cory sighed. "Then I guess our courting days are over."

Grandma gave him a long look, then waved him off.

"Oh, don't stand there pouting like an old maid at a social, Cory Reklaw. If I must deal with Lucifer to see you boys happily wed, then reckon I'll do it."

Cory broke into a grin. "Good for you."

She cackled. "But that old coot may just find he's bitten off more than he can chew with Eula Reklaw."

"I don't doubt it for a moment," Cory concurred with a grin.

Her gaze narrowed on him. "By the way, where are your brothers?"

Cory glanced away guiltily. "Oh, they went for a ride."

She shook a finger at him. "Don't you lie to me, Cory Reklaw. I know you better'n a prairie dog knows his shadow."

He gave a groan. "I'm not sure where they are, Grandma—but maybe they went to the saloon in Dillyville to blow off some steam." Cory hated twisting the truth around but suspected his brothers would end up at the saloon anyway, wherever they might go in the mean time.

Grandma sucked in a horrified breath. "And you let 'em gallivant off alone that way? They're bound to get in all manner of mischief."

Cory felt at his wit's end. "Grandma, how can I stop them? They're three grown men, all bigger than me. I'm the runt of the litter, as my brothers and Mr. Trumble are so fond of reminding me."

Noting his dour expression, Eula stepped closer and enfolded him in a bear hug. "Now, darlin', don't fret. I've always had a soft spot in my heart for you, Cory boy. I'll help you. And we got no time to waste getting them elder three back on the straight and narrow. I'll be speaking with that weasel Ez Trumble the next time we see him in town."

"Thanks, Grandma." With a relieved grin, he nodded toward the sideboard. "Now how 'bout I steal some of your cookie dough?"

She tweaked his nose. "Better that than you rob a bank."

At her words, both went sober. Cory was well aware of the questions both he and Grandma were asking themselves, doubts neither dared to voice aloud. . . .

Chapter Twenty-five

"Well, cowboy, you gonna drive us around in circles for hours or you gonna head somewhere?"

Lucky glanced sourly at his bride, who sat next to him in the buckboard, looking far too enticing in her green gingham Sunday dress. She was right that he'd been rambling about the countryside for a good stretch now. But he was trying his best to postpone the inevitable moment when he'd have to stop the buckboard, pull out the sumptuous picnic Grandma had packed them, spread out the blanket she'd also included and actually talk to his bride, or . . .

Damn Molly's hide!

Meanwhile his wife was growing even more exasperated. "I said, are you gonna keep ambling about like a steer on loco grass—"

"I heard you, woman."

"Then where are we headed?"

"I don't know."

251

"You want to go back to Reklaw Gorge so's you can try to hitch a ride back to the present?" she sneered.

He made a sound of contempt. "You ready to let me go?"

"I'm tempted."

Lucky almost grabbed her bait but remembered in time that there was no way he could take her to the canyon, let alone allow her to see the old stagecoach that he and Sanchez had managed to partly reassemble—although the coach remained quite a twisted sight, even with the wheels reattached to the axle. "I'll pass on Reklaw Gorge. Knowing you, you'd try to push me off a cliff just like your brothers did."

She waved a hand. "What's ailing you, cowboy? First you were all over me like honey on sourdough, then you went all standoffish—"

"And you weren't cold, once I started pursuing you?" he countered.

She turned away, her face hot. "You—you confounded me, I reckon—"

"Well, that makes two of us who are buffaloed."

She shot him a resentful glance. "The other morning when I was feeding the chickens, I heard you snoring in the barn. You enjoying your nights in the hayloft?"

"Yeah. Even with Jezebel and her kittens crawling all over me, it sure beats the hell out of catfighting with you."

Angrily she folded her arms over her bosom. "Oh, why don't you just take me home?"

"No," he retorted stubbornly. "I've been smelling your grandma's fried chicken for an hour now, and there's

252

no way I'm forgoing *some* pleasure from this ill-fated outing."

She spoke through gritted teeth. "Then take us somewhere, before the g'damned horses drop from exhaustion!"

He actually grinned at her mimicking his manner of cursing. "Where do you suggest?"

She bit her lip, then snapped her fingers. "I know. I'll show you the lower five hundred. 'Bout time you saw what's really involved here, and what's at stake in this marriage."

Lucky felt irate again. "Yeah, 'bout time I saw what you *really* want, Mrs. Lamont. And it sure as hell ain't me."

She eyed him mutinously, then went coldly silent.

"Here we are, cowboy."

"My God. *This* is the lower five hundred?"

"Yep."

Moments later, Lucky pulled the buckboard to a halt at the crest of a rise. In awe and wonder, he gazed at the exquisite valley stretching beneath them, where wildflowers bloomed and deer grazed next to an enchanting pond, where aspen and pines grew on a glorious expanse of sheltering mountainside. He stared off at a familiar knoll and his throat knotted.

Molly was observing him raptly. "You like it, cowboy?"

"Like it?" he repeated hoarsely.

Without taking his eyes off the property, Lucky slid to the ground. Methodically, he helped Molly alight. He couldn't believe how beautiful, pristine and pastoral this land was. Untouched, like his bride. Emotion warred within him; his gut twisted and his throat grew even tighter.

"You lost your tongue, cowboy?" Molly asked. "I'm waitin' to hear what you think of my land."

He whirled on her. "Your land?"

She blushed. "Soon as we have that baby."

Lucky seized his bride by the shoulders and spoke passionately. "Woman, this isn't your land. It's *my* land."

"What?" she cried.

Shaking his head in amazement, Lucky murmured, "Mrs. Lamont, you're looking at my grandparents' old homestead."

She gasped. "This is their old homestead?"

"Yes. Their ranch."

"You mean in the future?"

"Yes—well, I guess so." With the same expression of reverence, he gestured at the landscape. "My God, I can't believe I'm actually standing here. This is the land where I was raised, where I loved my grandparents—and buried them. It's so ironic."

She hesitated. "You mean, the land I want turns out to be the same land that you—"

"Lost," he finished in a tortured voice. Swallowing hard, he continued, "When Granddad and Grandma died, I had to sell this land to settle their debts." All at once realization dawned on him, and his gaze settled on her fiercely. "Now I'm taking it back."

"What?" she gulped, backing away.

Lucky advanced on Molly with an intense gleam in his eyes. "Don't look so surprised, Molly. After all, this whole crazy scheme was your idea. Okay then, you've

won, you've got me now. I'm claiming the land I love—
which means I'm claiming you, too."

And before she could object further he closed the
distance between them, pulled her against him and
kissed her long, achingly, his mouth drowning out her
soft protests. His hands roved her body freely, intimately, kneading her buttocks, tugging up her
skirts . . .

At last, with a cry of anguish, she pushed him away.
"You—now you're trying to take advantage of me just
to get what you want."

He laughed bitterly. "Touché, Molly. It was all well
and good when you wanted to milk me like a stud to
suit your own needs. But now that the tables are
turned, you're finally finding out how it feels to be
used, aren't you?"

She began blinking back tears. "Please, Lucky, don't
say such mean things to me. You—you're confusing
me—"

"I'm telling you the truth. 'Bout time you stepped inside my moccasins and walked around, to see how
you've exploited *me*."

A tear spilled down her cheek. "Please stop."

He took in her stricken face, then cursed. "Ah, hell!
You never do fight fair, do you?"

"I—I'm sorry."

"Yeah. Me, too, Molly. Come on, I'll take you home."

With a last longing glance at the land, Lucky
grabbed Molly around the waist and lifted her onto the
buckboard seat. As he drove them away, they exchanged heated, accusatory glances. Just when the

tension seemed ready to shatter, Lucky set his jaw and said adamantly, "Make no mistake about it, Molly. I want the land, too, now. And I'm gonna get it."

Judging from her half-anxious, half-fearful look, she believed him.

Chapter Twenty-six

Late that night Lucky stood in the open doorway of the barn, watching an angry bolt of lightning strike a mountain peak in the distance. The volatile atmosphere seemed to mirror his turbulent frame of mind. He'd been unable to fall asleep in the hayloft, and just when he'd finally dozed, Jezebel had pounced on a field mouse and an unholy fracas had ensued. He'd fled the makeshift comfort of his bed and had confronted the cold night air downstairs.

He craved a different type of heat now. His bride. His lips on hers, his mouth on her breasts, his aching length inside her. Ever since their visit to the homestead, his thoughts, his emotions, had been consumed by Molly.

And now, for the first time, everything she'd told him, everything her mother had told him, was finally making sense. All of that nonsense he'd scoffed at—about Fate and him and Molly belonging together—

had evolved into a blinding truth. There *was* a reason he had come here—a reason he'd survived that harrowing flight through time. This *was* meant to be. He and Molly were irrevocably linked—linked by the land they both loved, bonded by a destiny amazing in its simplicity and significance.

Perhaps he didn't have all the answers yet, perhaps he didn't have every detail resolved, but he knew now that he was supposed to be here, in this place, in this time. He knew he was meant to claim Molly, claim the land they both craved, knew both were deep in his heart now. She might not be the woman he'd thought he'd always wanted, but she was the woman he *needed* now with a fierceness that was gut-wrenching.

And scary. For she'd made it clear she wanted him for only one purpose—to have his name, his baby. She was a creature without pretense; he had to give her credit for that. She'd made no bones about the fact that she was only using him.

Did it matter if her motives were mercenary as long as his were sincere?

It mattered. It smarted like hell. But he was going to have her anyway.

Lightning flashed and thunder boomed, then rain began to pour. Lucky raced across the barnyard, pounded by icy droplets, tearing off his shirt as he went. He'd be warm soon enough.

In the bedroom, Molly, too, had been tossing and turning for some time, jumping at each flash of lightning or boom of thunder. Her nerves were frayed and she couldn't get her mind off those electrifying moments with Lucky earlier today. To think that they both coveted the same section of land—that he'd actually grown up on the homestead she wanted for her own! This seemed the ultimate proof that their destinies were linked.

Yet on an emotional level, the realization was scary as hell. It was enough of a struggle just trying to get her mind around the fact that both their roots lay in the same land. Lucky's revelation had turned the tables on her, making it clear that he wanted her now for the same reason she'd initially wanted him—purely as a means to an end. Yes, now she *did* understand how it felt to be used, to be exploited carelessly and without remorse, and her soul burned with the shame of it. She realized she really was like that other woman who had hurt him so badly—and how could he ever love or trust her under these circumstances?

She also knew her feelings for Lucky had changed and deepened. She cared for him more each day, wanted to get to know him better. But her transformation was too little, too late, she feared. For if she told him now that she really cared about him, believed in him and in their destiny together, surely he would only scoff at her alleged change of heart.

How she had botched things up! Even if they got together now, it would still be for all the wrong reasons—to win a prize, not to begin a life together. How could she have been so immature, so reckless, so heedless of Lucky's feelings, indeed, his life?

As rain began to pour down outside, she huddled deeper under the covers, bereft and miserable. Then she tensed at the sound of the front door banging open and gasped at the sight of a shadow moving into her room from the hallway.

"Who is it?" she cried.

"Me, darlin'," answered a husky voice.

Molly gulped at the sight of Lucky looming in the archway, his tall form backlit by a flash of lightning. He was shirtless, drenched, his naked chest beaded with rain, his hair dripping, his jeans clinging to his trim hips and taut thighs. Even in the darkness she could see something fierce smoldering in his eyes—and even in the cold, she could have sworn she felt his heat.

"W-what are you doing here?" she stammered.

He strode in, his voice quivering slightly from the cold. "I'm your husband, remember?"

"But I thought you were sleeping in the barn."

"Not anymore." He began unbuckling his belt.

She sucked in a horrified breath. "You're sleeping with me?"

"Is there anywhere else I would sleep in this house?" he asked teasingly. "I'm damn cold, woman. There's a spring storm tearing up the earth outside. And we are husband and wife, in case you've forgotten."

Pride and heartache roiled inside Molly. "You're the one who forgot all about that until today, when you saw the land and decided you want it, too."

"Maybe so." He plopped himself down beside her on the bed, inundating her with his hot, earthy, rain-soaked smell. "And maybe it's time for some honesty between us."

She gulped. "Yeah. Maybe."

He hesitated a long moment, then gave a groan. "Molly, I'm sorry I've been so angry at you for so long."

"You—you are?"

"Yes, honey, I am. Hell, I even tried to seduce you hoping it would drive you away—only it drew me closer."

"Closer?" she whispered, amazed. "Is that why you walked out on me last week?"

He nodded. "If I hadn't, I would have made love to you then. In fact, I really don't know how I stopped myself. Then, today, when I saw your land, *my* land . . . much as it chafes my pride, I have to admit I agree with you now."

"You do?" Confused by his words, unnerved by his proximity, she watched a bead of moisture roll down his sexy chest and was treacherously tempted to lick it off.

"All that destiny stuff I mocked before—well, it's all making sense to me now."

"How?"

"It's like I told you today. I lost my grandparents and their spread in 2004. Now I've been sent here to the past to reclaim it—"

"But it's mine, Lucky—"

He pressed a finger to her lips. "It's *ours,* if we win it together—by making a baby." His hand slid beneath the covers, boldly touching her belly.

Molly winced with longing. Lucky's caress was pure torture, and the thought of having his baby aroused her to unbearable desire—even though she still very much feared that he saw this only as a way to accomplish his goal. Sure, he might lust for her, but would he ever want her, body and soul, as she now wanted him? "Lucky, please, don't do this to me—"

His gaze burned into hers. "Isn't this what you've wanted all along—for me to accept my lot and see the silver lining? Well, I'm seeing it now, honey."

"But for all the wrong reasons," she said miserably.

He tenderly caressed her cheek. "At least everything's out in the open between us now. Would it have been better if we'd come together through anger, or under pretense?"

"I—I guess not."

"It's time, Molly," he continued with quiet determination. "You demanded this marriage, and now you're going to get everything it entails." His fingers moved to her breast, causing her to tremble. "You're quivering for me, girl, I can feel it. You want me just as I want you—"

"You don't want me, you just want the land," she whispered back, hot tears threatening to well up.

"I want both," came his vehement reply. "As for the land, can't I accuse you of the same motivation? Haven't you claimed over and over that the land is yours? Not mine, not ours—just yours?"

Abashed, she lowered her gaze.

"Well, the contest is over, Molly," he went on passionately. "Tonight, land or no land, you're mine." He took her hand and drew it to the front of his pants.

Molly moaned at the hot, stiff feel of him against her fingers. Her heart thumped and her insides twinged with a corresponding want. She knew she was slipping, slipping fast. And she knew Lucky was right—she was his now.

He drew a raspy breath and caressed her cheek with

trembling fingers. "Sit up, woman, and take off that gown."

Molly was both scandalized and aroused. "You want me to take my nightie off?"

He chuckled, leaning over to tease her mouth with his lips, darting his tongue at her teeth, torturing her with a promise of the passion to come. "That's how a man and a woman do it, darling, both buck naked. And I sure as hell ain't doing it with you any other way."

Molly gasped in horror and fascination.

He grinned and nestled her closer, tumbling her hair with his teasing fingers. "You know, Mrs. Lamont, maybe you are a virgin, after all. I'm liking the notion more and more by the moment. Now take off that gown before I tear it off you."

Molly's cheeks burned as she watched Lucky stand and begin unbuttoning his jeans. "You're really serious about this."

He shucked his boots and jeans and untied his drawers. "Oh, yeah, darling. I'd love to peel every stitch off that delightful little body of yours."

This decadent and horrifying image was enough to make Molly comply. Lifting the covers to her neck, she tugged off her gown, then dared a glance at her naked husband. Heavens, he was magnificent, all beautiful, chiseled male contours, his flesh gleaming and slick, his body lean and hard. . . .

Speaking of which . . . she gaped at his generous endowments. "Lord, you mean to put that in me?"

He winked. "Don't worry, Mrs. Lamont, you're gonna like it a lot." He slipped beneath the covers. "Now, c'mere."

When he pulled her naked body close, the sensations consuming Molly were so exquisite that she half panicked. She'd never guessed that joining her naked body with a man's would feel so divine. Lucky was soft in some places, rough in others, and solid . . . oh, Lord help her! The feel of his hot, huge shaft pressing against the soft flesh of her belly made her squirm with combined fear and desire.

He seemed to sense her trepidation. "Easy, darlin', easy," he murmured, kissing her hair. "We'll take it slow, okay?"

When she looked up at him helplessly, his mouth seized her own, and at once his kiss told her differently. His lips were passionate, intense, insistent. His tongue probing. She moaned her delight and curled her arms around his neck, and heard his answering groan as her breasts cushioned his sinewy chest.

"Darlin'," he murmured, kissing her cheek, her neck. "You don't know what you're doin'."

"Well, I hope one of us does," she managed dryly.

He chuckled, then kissed her again, his strong hand gripping her breast and kneading it rhythmically. His other hand slid over her body, boldly caressed her belly, her spine. When he sank his fingers into her bottom while leaning over to flick his tongue delicately over one of her nipples, she cried out at the overwhelming stimulation. He groaned and buried his face between her breasts, the roughness of his whiskered face bringing more waves of decadent pleasure.

"Ummm, soft as a baby you are," he murmured, taking her hand. "Now touch me again."

"Lucky—" she pleaded.

"Touch me, woman."

His voice came forth with an urgency she couldn't deny. Tentatively, she touched his hot manhood, loving the feel of his soft yet firm length. His encouraging grunts emboldened her to give in to another wanton urge, and she licked his chest, savoring the salty taste of him. "Ummm—good," she murmured.

"Oh, God," he rumbled. "Keep it up, darling."

She explored him more brazenly with both her fingers and tongue, stroking his shaft up and down, licking his chest and belly. His breathing grew ragged and he pushed his fingers between her thighs, seeking her nub, then probing lower.

"Please!" she gasped, set on fire by his touch, not certain whether she wanted him to keep going or stop.

Too late. He pushed a finger into her, and she cried out as she felt that incredible, shattering intimacy for the first time. Scalding threads of desire tightened relentlessly inside her, demanding that ultimate joining, that uttermost release. She tossed her head and writhed, enhancing the delicious friction as well as her own torment.

"My God, you are so small, so tight—"

He probed deeper and she screamed softly, squeezing his manhood.

He seemed to lose all control then. With a cry he rolled her beneath him and spread her legs.

"Lucky!" Molly was near panic.

His gaze, bright with desire, locked with her own. "Molly. My sweet Molly. Trust me now."

His words melted her utterly and she drew his face

down to her trembling lips, giving him her kiss, her surrender.

He moaned and pushed himself into her. Even though she was wet, ready for him, he was vast, hot, unyielding. She squirmed at the unexpected pain; he shoved his hands beneath her, holding her fast as he penetrated fully.

"Lucky!" Helpless tears spilled from her eyes as she felt rent in two by his rigid heat. But soon the sense of oneness came, a blissful certainty that this was meant to be.

"I'm sorry, darlin'. Just couldn't resist. My God, you are divine." He nuzzled her face, her neck, and waited a moment for her discomfort to fade. At last he began to ease in and out of her, at first tentatively, then more boldly. The sensation was electrifying to Molly—indescribably sensual, brazenly intimate. She moaned as fierce pleasure throbbed and built inside her. She dug her fingernails into his forearms as he pushed harder, deeper still. An ecstasy built within her such as she'd never felt before, and suddenly she had to move with him. When she lifted her hips up to meet him, it drove him mad. Just as she was sobbing her rapture, on the verge of sweet release, he learned over and sucked her nipple into his mouth, biting gently. She cried out and writhed with delight, and with a torrent of consuming thrusts, Lucky spent himself inside her.

Later, Lucky gazed down at his bride in the darkness. Molly was asleep, awash in moonlight, and stunningly beautiful. What incredible ecstasy she had brought him tonight. And she had come to him a virgin—even in the darkness he'd spotted the small stain on the sheet. Her innocence and sweet surrender had touched him deeply. He hoped he hadn't hurt her too badly, but when she'd brazenly licked his chest and boldly stroked him, squeezed him, he hadn't been able to stop himself.

His wife. She was truly his now. The thought made his heart well with bittersweet emotion. The good Lord must have a sense of humor, he thought ruefully. He'd been blessed with an old-fashioned virgin, all right, but his bride had the temperament of a wildcat. She was a thorn in his side, if quite a pleasurable one.

Did she want him, too? Or did she just want the land they both now coveted?

Is it me he wants, or the land?

This was Molly's thought when she awakened later that night to the sounds of Lucky's soft snores. She sat up in bed with a slight wince, still smarting from where he had claimed her body. But, oh, it had been glorious.

Had they made their baby that night?

All at once she wasn't in such a hurry to conceive their child, since her woman's instincts told her she'd want to repeat this delicious process with her husband many, many times.

She brushed an errant curl from his brow, her throat tightening. Lucky was coming to mean much more to her than the land. But how much did she mean to him? She couldn't soon forget that he hadn't come to her bed until he'd decided he wanted the same chunk of range that she did. She was in deep now, so deep. Knowing how badly hurt he'd been before, she wondered if he would ever be able to share his heart fully with her.

Chapter Twenty-seven

Lucky was running late as he led his horse out of the barn the next morning. He practically collided with Sanchez, who was headed inside carrying a saddle he had repaired.

"*Buenas días*, señor." Breathlessly, the little man set the saddle on a nearby stand. "Do you want me to come with you to the gorge today?"

"No, I need to hightail it out to the range. I promised Mr. Reklaw I'd help out with roundup."

Sanchez nodded. "Should I carry on repairing *el coche* by myself?"

Lucky scowled at the conflicting emotion he felt at the mention of the stagecoach, then gave a shrug. "Do whatever you want."

"*Sí*, señor."

Galloping away, Lucky wondered what in hell was wrong with him. Why hadn't he told Sanchez to scuttle that damn stagecoach in the nearest deep hole? Perhaps because his feelings were still mixed about remaining here—perhaps because he still wasn't ready to demolish his one possible escape route. Perhaps because he felt defenseless, falling for a woman who might never return his feelings—especially now that his control was broken, his anger in shards, and he was vulnerable to her. Not that being with her wasn't heaven—their lovemaking last night had touched his soul. And if his seed had taken root inside her . . . never could he become the kind of bastard who would abandon a pregnant wife as his dad had done with his mom.

Yes, he was confused. But he also felt a growing sense of connection—not just with Molly but with this time, this land. As he galloped through fields of young corn and wheat plants, he drank in the dew-drenched air and witnessed the pastoral scene stretching before him through new eyes—the verdant meadow beyond the fields, the stark rise of mountain in the distance. As he approached the range, he chuckled at the sight of the cattle dogs darting about the herd, at Cory and Matt riding their cutting horses, trying to separate out the calves. In the distance near a fire, Cole, Zach and Vance were attempting to brand a squirming calf.

He'd performed these same spring rituals with Grandpa back in the present, and at the Flying T. In a way, he'd been brought full circle in time. He felt a sense of bonding not just with Molly but with her mother and grandma, and with these men beside whom he rode the range.

He felt a true sense of family for the first time in

many years. This realization brought a poignant pain as well as a profound sense of peace.

In town at the library, Cory Reklaw was stamping a due date inside Widow Allgood's selected book when the front door opened and a vision swept inside. It was Ida May, glorious in a white linen dress sprigged with blue flowers, a matching ribbon in her shiny blond hair. She moved gracefully through the dancing patterns of light on the library floor. Cory was so mesmerized by the sight of her that he hardly noticed her three older sisters waltzing in behind her. Then she caught sight of him and waved; he gulped and shyly waved back.

Widow Allgood loudly cleared her throat.

Contrite, Cory glanced up. "Anything else I can do for you, ma'am?"

"No, but it's pretty obvious what that young lady can do for you," she drawled back.

Feeling miserably put on the spot, Cory stood. "My grandma's down at the general store, if you'd like to go visit with her."

The widow laughed and shook a finger at him. "Never mind the hints, young man. I know when I'm not wanted."

Before Cory could protest, she trooped off for the door, her black silk skirts rustling. Cory eagerly went over to greet Ida May, who was still standing in place, raptly regarding him.

"Well, hello. Good to see you again."

"Hi, Cory." She extended her hand.

Cory firmly shook her soft hand, then became distracted by the sound of giggles. He turned to spot her sisters gathered nearby; the three had already pounced on a large wicker basket filled with dime novels. "How'd you girls manage to escape your pa?" he asked Ida May.

"He told us we could have ten minutes at the library while he picks up cattle feed," she confided.

Cory grinned. "Ah, then we've no time to waste."

She nodded happily.

"I'm really sorry about what happened when we men came calling on Sunday," he went on.

She waved him off. "Don't feel bad, Cory; that wasn't your fault. Pa and his darn courting candle."

He nodded. "My grandma promised she'd try to set up another appointment for us."

"Good for her. Hope Pa will listen to reason this time."

"I know. Did you enjoy the volume of poetry I gave you?"

Her expression rapt, Ida May clasped her hands to her breast. "Oh, Cory, I loved it. When Mrs. Browning said, 'And if God choose, I shall but love thee better after death' . . . ah, that was so romantic."

By now Cory had blushed crimson, but he didn't care. "Indeed. 'How Do I Love Thee?' is one of my favorite poems, as well."

"Just to think of having a love like she and Mr. Browning did," Ida May went on with a dreamy sigh.

Cory cleared his throat. "Why, yes, it was—er—extraordinary."

"I can't even imagine how he felt when he lost her."

"They were soul mates, all right."

"Soul mates," she repeated ecstatically. "What a lovely term."

They were gazing at one another giddily when a burst of feminine laughter turned their attention back to the other sisters. Cory chuckled at the sight of the three of them, huddled together wide-eyed, poring over one of the lurid novels. "Well, I see your sisters have selected some meaningful reading material."

Ida May chuckled. "As I warned you, Cory, they're far more adventuresome than I."

He gestured toward the stacks of leather-bound volumes. "Well, our minutes together are slipping away, so we'd best find something for you to read, as well. Since you enjoy Mrs. Browning's poetry, may I suggest her husband's masterpiece, *The Ring and the Book*?"

"Oh, yes!" she cried.

They selected several volumes of poetry for Ida May. Moments later, as Cory was checking out all four young women, he felt amused by the sensational volumes her older sisters had selected. Fingering a dog-eared western, he teased Sally. "So you're braving *Dirty Dick's Downfall* this time? A pretty colorful choice for a lady, I must say."

Before she could answer, Nelly giggled and said, "Sally's already read it five times."

Cory raised an eyebrow. "Indeed?"

Sally grinned. "I just love rereading the account of Dirty Dick getting his comeuppance in Denver—you know, being gut-shot and all, like the low-down dog he was."

Cory whistled. "How very bloodthirsty of you."

The ladies laughed.

"And his funeral was so dramatic," Bonnie added with a lively tilt of her face. "Especially when two of his gang members got in a gunfight and winged the preacher."

Cory feigned a shudder. "You know, ladies, I must tell you what I often say to my sister: You shouldn't believe everything you read in dime novels."

Again the ladies tittered.

"But isn't that the whole point—the 'larger than life' aspect?" teased Sally. "You know, losing ourselves in stories that are a darn sight more interesting than the lives we lead?"

"Granted," Cory replied.

Then he became distracted as the door banged open and Ezra Trumble strode in, his hostile aura accompanying him like an evil wind. "You girls ready to leave?"

Spines were hastily stiffened, dime novels shoved into reticules. "Yes, Pa," the girls answered in unison.

Trumble stepped forward to sneer at Cory. "So you're volunteerin' at the library again, eh, young Reklaw?"

"Yes. Mrs. Schmidt has too much to handle on her own, especially with her husband ailing, so I try to help out where I can."

"Sounds like you're a pure-dee sissy to me," Trumble sneered.

Cory couldn't help himself; that comment raised his hackles. He stood to confront the geezer. "Oh, yeah? Would you prefer I turn outlaw, like you keep accusing my brothers of doing?"

Trumble was poised to reply when the door opened again and Grandma plodded in. She glared at Trumble, then made a beeline for him. "Ez, I'll be having another word with you."

"Hello, Eula," he replied sourly. "Your molasses pie gave me the wind."

"Well, I'm mighty pleased to hear it," she mocked back. "Now, on the subject of my grandsons—"

"Ah, them four," he jeered. "We was just talking about them—three outlaws and a sissy."

Cory heard his grandma's outraged roar and cringed, then watched, appalled, as she drew back her hand and slapped Ezra full in the face. Trumble was so taken aback that for a moment he just stood there trembling, glaring at her.

Eula shook a finger at him. "Ez, you hush up them insults of yourn and listen to me. I want you to let my boys court your girls again this Thursday afternoon."

"And why the hell should I, you damn she-wolf?" he roared back.

"Because if you do, I'll come along this time, trial though it will be. But no short-wickin' my boys, nor bandying foul language neither." She vehemently bobbed her chin. "That's the deal. Take it or leave it."

For a moment Ezra continued to stare murder at her. Then he waved a hand. "Very well, woman. Though I doubtless need my head examined, I accept your devil's bargain."

At this Grandma grinned, the older girls chortled and Cory and Ida May exchanged a delighted look.

Chapter Twenty-eight

By the time Molly awakened, the sun was high in the sky and she was alone. She straightened up the room, changing the blood-streaked sheets on the bed. At last she ventured out to the kitchen to find Ma and Grandma there, preparing chicken and dumplings for dinner.

"Well, you're sure sleeping away the day, aren't you, girl?" Grandma teased.

Before Molly could answer, her mother said firmly, "Ma, that's a bride's prerogative."

Grandma cackled. "Reckon it is. You hungry, honey?"

Molly sniffed the air so redolent with home cooking. "I guess this close to dinner, I'll just wait. May I help?"

"Why, sure, honey, why don't you set the table?" Grandma suggested.

Molly busied herself gathering plates, murmuring

over her shoulder, "What have you two been doing this morning?"

"Well, I started the wash," her mother replied, "while Grandma and Cory went off to town."

"Any news?" Molly asked.

"Yeah," Grandma replied with a grin. "I run across Ez Trumble and his girls at the library and gave the old coot the business, talking him into allowing the boys to go courting his daughters again."

"Gee, that's nice," Molly murmured, oblivious to her mother and grandma's stunned looks. Instead, she smoothed down the tablecloth while reflecting ironically that it was amazing how little the contest meant to her now.

"Also heard tell Buffalo Bill Cody's Wild West Show will be coming through Colorado Springs in a fortnight," Grandma went on, "along with Pawnee Bill's Far East."

"Buffalo Bill Cody?" Molly said eagerly. "Ma, you know I've always wanted to see his Wild West Show. Do you suppose we could go?"

"I'll talk to your father about it." Jessica winked. "And perhaps if you'll promise to read a few volumes of Shakespeare in the meantime . . ."

"Oh, Ma, *really.*"

Grandma was listening to the exchange with a grin. "Also heard tell there was another stage robbed out near Dillyville. The Colorado City line, soon after it left Mariposa."

"Oh, no," Molly muttered. "Anyone hurt?"

"Nope, though the passengers was fleeced right

good. The sheriff said Drew Dalton lost his gambling stake plus his granddaddy's gold watch. 'Course he was up to no good, anyhow, going out there to hell-raise, and—"

Grandma paused in midsentence as the back door swung open and the men trooped in, smelling of dew-drenched greenery and the cattle trail. "Morning, ladies," Cole greeted. "Got some good vittles ready for us?"

"Yes, but you men wash up thoroughly at the sink, now," scolded Jessica.

Cole winked at his daughter. "Your ma and her obsession with kitchen hygiene."

While Jessica tossed a dish towel at Cole, Molly grinned at her pa. Then she watched anxiously as Lucky spotted her and made a beeline to her side. Hot color stained her cheeks as he curled an arm around her waist. He kissed her cheek, and she inhaled the stirring scent of leather and man.

"Well, hi there, angel," he flirted. "How's my little bride this morning?"

Lowering her gaze and grinding her teeth at the sound of her brothers' guffaws, she muttered back, "Fine, thank you."

"You hungry?" Lucky continued. "I've worked up one heck of an appetite myself."

"Yeah, Molly, you'd best chow down," teased Grandma. "After all, you may soon be eating for two."

Hearing her brothers hoot at this gibe, Molly glanced tensely at Lucky, expecting derision from him, as well. To her surprise and relief, she spotted only warm sympathy in his blue eyes.

*　*　*

By sunset Molly discovered she wouldn't soon be eating for two. She was sitting glumly on the porch swing, feeling melancholy, her insides aching, when Lucky came out to join her.

His expression showing his concern, he sat down and took her hand. "Honey, are you all right? I've been worried about you all day."

"You're worried about me?" she asked in disbelief.

His jaw hardened. "I'm not just some heartless jackass."

"I never called you that."

"You called me every other name in the book."

She chuckled.

He tweaked her chin. "I've gotten a smile out of you, after all."

She turned away.

"Molly, what is it?"

She met his eye. "Lucky, I'm bleeding."

He stood, appearing horrified. "Oh, no, did I—"

"No, it's not your fault," she hastily reassured him, grasping his hand. "Last night—well, there was only a little, and it stopped right away. But a couple of hours ago . . . Well, I learned there won't be a baby. Not this month."

"Ah," he murmured. "So it was too soon."

She frowned. "What do you mean?"

"We made love too close to—er—your period—"

"Period? You mean monthy?"

"Yeah. Anyway, it was the wrong time for you to conceive." He winked devilishly. "But don't worry, we'll get it right. In about two weeks' time."

"Two weeks?"

"That's likely when you'll be most fertile."

Her eyes went huge. "How do you know that?"

"We know about such things in the future."

"You mean women can choose when they conceive a young 'un?"

"Yeah, and they can prevent it, too, and still have sex, if they want to."

"Ah," she murmured, cheeks blooming. "Think Ma mentioned something about that. Birth control, isn't it called?"

"Yeah." He grinned.

She hesitated a moment, then went on. "Am I like those women you knew in the future?"

He laughed. "Oh, yeah. You may have come to this marriage an old-fashioned virgin, but you're as liberated as any woman I've ever met."

"You mean women's lib?" Molly asked.

"So your ma mentioned that, too, eh?"

"She even mentioned somethin' called 'corset burning'—"

"You mean 'bra burning'?"

Molly snapped her fingers. "Yeah, that was it. I was fascinated to hear about it, but Grandma got so worked up, Ma had to stop talking."

"Grandma's quite a character, isn't she?"

Molly thought a moment. "So if I'm just like the girls from your time, why don't you like me more?"

A stricken look crossed his features and he squeezed her hand. "I don't dislike you, honey."

"As if that tells me anything," she shot back. "The truth is, ever since you've gotten here, you've told everyone I'm not your idea of a wife. But coming from where you do, what other ideas could you have?"

"Guess that's a fair question," he conceded.

"It's still about your grandma, isn't it? I'm not like her, right?"

He grew thoughtfully silent. "Well, I always did assume I'd marry someone more like her, a woman who truly respects and honors her man."

Molly slowly shook her head. "No disrespect intended toward your granny, but what fun would that be?"

Lucky guffawed. "You do have spirit, Mrs. Lamont, I'll grant you that. And I guess you've made another good point."

She waved a hand. "Well, what do you expect, anyhow, marrying a woman from the year 1911? We females are fed up with being bossed around by you men. Why, women are about to get all kinds of privileges—like the vote."

"That ain't the half of it, darlin'," he added dryly.

She clutched his arm. "What do you mean? What else will women get?"

"Now *that's* a loaded question," he quipped.

She gave him a chiding look. "Come on, Lucky, when are you gonna tell me your stories? Ma used to, but not so much anymore. Maybe it's her way of accepting her lot."

Shaking his head wonderingly, he murmured, "And you're one very smart girl."

"Maybe smarter than you?"

"Never smarter than me." Before she could protest, he conceded, "Okay, then, I'll tell you my stories. Ask me anything you want to know."

In the hours that followed, Molly asked Lucky dozens of questions about the future, and he answered every one in detail, everything from how women became liberated to how space rockets were made and how houses were air-conditioned. She was especially interested in the evolution of culture, what kinds of music and books would become popular, how men and women's relationships would progress and how families would treat one another. She was amazed by the looser moral climate and the high incidence of divorce in the new millennium. Eventually their discussion moved to other subjects such as modern movies, cartoons, computers, children's toys and amusement parks.

On and on they rocked and chattered, as happy as two squirrels in their nest, until at last Molly fell asleep against Lucky, and he tenderly carried her to their bed. . . .

Chapter Twenty-nine

On Thursday afternoon Cory Reklaw sat with his brothers in the central hallway of the Trumble home, each of the four men facing the sister he favored. At the end of the hallway Grandma sat on a stout chair, scowling and tapping her toe while Ezra Trumble babbled on to her about the new brood cow he'd bought at the Clinton County Fair.

Thanks to Grandma's accompanying them, the boys had been allowed to scoot their bench slightly closer to the girls, the courting candle was burning at full tilt and the couples had been happily flirting away for some fifteen minutes now. Cory had especially loved discussing *The Ring and the Book* with Ida May, and suggesting she try some Tennyson and Keats next.

When at last a lull came in their conversation, Ida May winked at Cory and whispered confidentially, "You know, my sisters and I know about the contest."

Her unexpectedly frank statement brought Cory instantly to attention. He floundered for an appropriate response. "Really? What contest?"

She slanted him a scolding glance. "Don't play dumb, Cory. We know all about what you boys are really up to, fighting over your pa's land."

Cory blanched. "But how did—"

"Dumpling Reklaw told Susie Schwartz's mama, and Susie told Sally at prayer meeting."

Cory was crestfallen, running a hand through his hair. "Oh, Lord. It must be all over town by now. I'm so sorry."

"You needn't be, Cory," she replied with a sincere smile.

"But I've behaved horribly—and I should have told you about the contest before now," he said contritely.

"Why didn't you?"

His plaintive gaze beseeched her. "Because I was afraid you'd be insulted, and justly so. That you wouldn't want me to come calling on you anymore."

She reached out to pat his hand. "Cory, you needn't worry about that, not ever. I enjoy your company very much."

"As I do yours," he responded fervently.

"Besides, the girls and I discussed the whole thing, and we decided we don't care."

"What? You mean you don't feel—er, used?"

She shook her head adamantly. "Should we feel used because you boys are fighting for a place of your own? Everyone wants something, Cory. I'd never fault you for having aspirations."

"That's kind of you."

"I'm just being honest, Cory." Glancing warily at her

pa, she added, "As for the girls and me, we want to get away from Pa—"

"Has he hurt you?" Cory interrupted in a low, charged voice.

She bit her lower lip, appearing quite torn. "Cory, please, don't press me. Let's just say you boys need wives, and we girls need to escape."

At this, Cory couldn't contain a very human sense of disappointment. "Believe me, I want you to be free of your bad-tempered father. But—is it all just a matter of convenience to you and your sisters?"

She laughed. "Well, we like you, too, silly, and that makes it all the *more* convenient, don't you think?"

Cory had to smile. Then honesty compelled him to add, "Ida May, there's really something I must tell you."

"Yes?" Her spine stiffened.

He regarded her earnestly. "The truth is, I don't really care about the contest, or the land. Why, before all this competition came up, I'd thought of going on to college in the fall, maybe even becoming a history professor like my moth—well, my ma loves history, too."

"That's wonderful." She hesitated. "But you'd leave me here?"

"No, of course not—that is, if I may dare hope the knowledge of my whereabouts might matter to you."

"Of course it matters, silly," she chided. "Haven't you been listening to me at all?"

"Then—er—I mean, if I choose to go on to college, would you want to come with me?"

She beamed. "Why, certainly. But we'd have to marry first, of course."

Cory blushed vividly, even as his heart sang with joy. "Oh, of course. That goes without saying."

"I'm relieved to hear it."

At her delightfully earnest expression, Cory had to chuckle. He burned to reach out and touch her but knew he didn't dare under present circumstances. He'd have to wait until another time to show her how much she truly meant to him. "I'm so glad to hear of your sentiments, Ida May. I may not care about the land, but I do care about you."

"Me, too, Cory."

"Now if we can just convince your pa . . ."

She sighed. "That won't be easy, I'm afraid. It helps that your grandma came along today, since he fancies her. But he still insists you boys are up to no good—especially your older brothers."

"Ida May, we aren't that gang of bank robbers plaguing the region," he stated firmly.

"Oh, I believe you," she hastily reassured him. "It's just that Pa seems determined to tear you down."

"Or maybe he just doesn't want anyone marrying his daughters?"

"That, too," she conceded unhappily. "Pa does love being waited on." She glanced wistfully in the direction of her father and Eula.

Even as Cory followed her gaze, he was appalled to see his grandma come shooting out of her chair with an expression of stark, blinding rage. Then, before his horrified eyes, Eula attacked Ezra, cursing and bashing him over the head with her reticule.

"You dirty dog! How dare you!" she screamed.

"Stop it, woman!" cried Trumble, trying to shield himself from the rain of blows. "What ails you?"

Matt popped up. "Grandma, what did he do?"

Eula's chest was heaving as she turned to her grandson. "First, he insinuated I'm a cow. Then he asked me how quick I could spit-polish a man's boots. Then the lecher went and tried to put his disgusting hand up my trapdoor!"

At her colorful description, the four couples fought laughter, and Ezra jumped up, his face hot. "I did no such thing!"

"Don't make it worse by lying, you butt-sniffing weasel, or the Almighty will smite you where you stand!" Eula waved a hand at her grandsons. "Come on, boys, we're leaving."

"But, Grandma—" protested Vance.

"You heard me! Rattle your hocks!"

With Eula leading the way, and amid hasty, anxious glances between the couples, the five Reklaws trooped for the front door. Ezra watched their departure in silent wrath, then right as Grandma opened the door, he issued his parting shot. "Woman, you'd best get a rein on that temper of yourn before you darken my door again."

Cory watched his grandma's spine stiffen and came within a hair's breadth of muttering, "Oh, shit!" He noted his brothers had all gone pasty-faced as well.

Features contorted with fury, Eula whirled on Ezra. "Why, you arrogant, conceited pig! You think I'd ever come within a hundred miles of you again, you rutting jackass? Well, you can eat my slipper, Ezra Trumble."

And she pulled off a leather shoe and hurled it square in his face.

All eight witnesses cringed in horror as Trumble shrieked with pain and grabbed his wounded jaw. "Dammit, woman! Are you trying to kill me? Where's my shotgun? I'm blowin' the lot of you to kingdom come!"

"Pa, no!" cried the girls in unison.

Meanwhile, the Reklaw men dared not wait for an additional warning. Even as Grandma would have charged Ezra again, they grabbed her, hauled her out the door and down the steps. Amid her numerous protests and their own considerable groaning, they hefted her into the buckboard. The boys jumped in, and Zach drove the team like a demon.

Fortunately, they were several hundred yards away before Trumble's shotgun boomed out from the porch—but even at that distance Cory winced at the sounds of the ominous blasts and Trumble's lurid cursing.

Fanning herself, Grandma glanced lamely at Cory. "Reckon I didn't help you boys out too much today, did I?"

Stormy silence and surly looks were her only answers.

Chapter Thirty

Matters were decidedly tense on Sunday morning as the Reklaws filed into the community church right as the opening hymn began. Even as Cory saw his grandma shoot Ezra Trumble a withering look, he exchanged a longing glance with Ida May, and she managed a tremulous smile in return.

The entire group squeezed onto the front Reklaw pew—first Grandma, Ma and Pa, Molly and Lucky, followed by the four boys. At once Zach began grousing to Cory. "Just look at old Trumble a-glarin' at us. Grandma's cooked our gooses but good by giving the geezer his comeuppance. Now he'll never let us within a coyote's yell of his daughters. And just watch after church—I'm betting he'll drag all four of them beauties outta here faster'n a cat can wink."

Cory caught sight of his mother hushing them from down the pew. "You'd best hush up, Zach. Ma's staring daggers at us. 'Sides, what can I do?"

"Well, I don't expect a sissy like you to do much a'tall," Zach mocked back. "But as for me and your brothers, we got something cooked up for after church."

"What?" Cory demanded in a fierce whisper. "Please don't start any more trouble."

Zach thrust a hymnal into Cory's hands. "Hush up, now, baby brother, and start crooning with the womenfolk."

Cory had no choice but to wait in anxiety and frustration as the service trickled by, Reverend Bledsoe expounding at length on the theme of "Loving thy neighbor as thyself." At last they came to the final rituals. When Bledsoe asked if anyone wanted to profess his faith and join the church, Cory was stunned to watch Zach pop up.

"I'm professin' my troth right now," he declared, turning to the Trumbles. "I'm saying I want to marry Miss Sally Trumble."

As laughter and excited murmurs swept over the congregation, Vance also stood. "And I'm proposing to Miss Nelly Trumble."

"I'll take Bonnie!" added Matt with a vehement nod.

Catching Ida May's anxious look, Cory also rose, even though he felt ridiculous. "And I'm offering my hand to Miss Ida May."

Now cheers spewed forth from the assemblage. Cory noted the girls smiling back radiantly, their father glowering, Ma, Pa and Grandma shaking their heads in wonderment, Molly muttering tensely to Lucky and the minister grinning broadly.

"Well," declared Bledsoe, clapping his hands. "It seems the good Lord has indeed blessed us with the fruits of His labor. Are we to have a quadruple wedding today?"

Apparently no one else had taken note of Ezra Trumble doing a slow burn. He shot to his feet, face livid, and waved a fist at the Reklaws. "How dare you worthless scoundrels offer to wed my girls! You're nothing but a lot of low-down thieves."

At that Grandma popped up, her bosom heaving. "Ezra Trumble, why don't you go choke on a watermelon? I've had my fill of you insulting my grandsons."

Cole also stood, wearing a murderous expression. "So have I, Ezra."

"Well, I don't care!" Trumble raged. "Those hooligans belong in the county jail."

As the congregation listened in appalled silence, Winky Hicks jumped up, his hastily combed straw-blond hair jutting out at ridiculous angles. He grinned and twitched at Ezra. "Mr. Trumble, sir, if you don't want them lowlife Reklaws to wed your girls, the boys and me'll be right pleasured to take 'em off your hands."

Trumble whirled on Winky. "You shut up!"

Winky wilted back into his pew, while Eula turned her scowl on Sheriff Hackett, who sat stiffly with Dulcie Hicks and the five Hicks cousins. "Hiram, this is all your fault. Why aren't you questioning the Hicks boys instead of always accusing my grandsons?"

Dulcie flounced up in her tawdry yellow satin. "You hush up, Eula Reklaw, and leave my boys out of this."

"When they're in the calaboose I will."

Even as the two women squared off at each other, the sheriff hastily stood. "Dulcie, quiet down now, ya hear? And Miss Eula, please. I got no call to arrest the Hicks boys as they got no history of outlawing—"

"Yeah, it's them Reklaw boys that got that bad bush-whacker blood in 'em!" roared Trumble with a sneer.

Features hard with anger, Cole charged across the aisle. "Ezra, I said heed your tongue regarding my sons."

A gasp rippled over the gathering as the two men confronted each other, obviously on the verge of a scuffle. The sheriff rushed between them. "Gentlemen, please! Let's not have a donnybrook break out in the Lord's house."

"Amen!" intoned Pastor Bledsoe.

The two backed away, although the tension was thick enough to cut. Cory watched, totally dispirited, as Trumble quickly gathered up his daughters and hauled them out of the sanctuary.

Back at the ranch after Sunday dinner, Cory lingered in the kitchen to help his ma with the dishes. His three older brothers had galloped away to blow off some steam, his pa was napping, Grandma was quilting and Lucky and Molly were outside exercising the dogs.

"I'm so sorry about Mr. Trumble's terrible behavior at church," Jessica said as she passed him a wet plate. "Your brothers may have baited him, but *really*."

Cory dried the dish with a thoughtful frown. "I know. All that geezer has done is throw obstacles in our path. And here I was hoping my brothers would grow up and settle down. They do favor the Trumble girls—"

"Just as you favor Ida May." Ruefully, Jessica confided, "I must admit that the sight of my four grown sons proposing to the Trumble daughters, before God and everyone, is not one I'll soon forget."

"Well, Ma, I couldn't let Ida May be the only one who didn't receive a marriage proposal," he protested.

Jessica chuckled.

In frustration, Cory added, "It's just not fair. All we've asked for is a chance with his daughters. We've not done anything wrong."

"I'm sure you haven't, Cory. But as for your brothers . . ." She bit her lip. "I hate to even ask this, but do you think it's possible they've gone outlaw, as the sheriff and Mr. Trumble keep insisting?"

Cory sighed. "Not as far as I know, Ma."

"Well, they are on the rambunctious side, so your pa and I can't help worrying."

Cory couldn't argue there. "I know. And even if my brothers aren't in trouble now, I'm afraid they're headed for it. What can we do to keep them on the straight and narrow? If only they could continue seeing the Trumble girls, there might be some hope."

"I know, and I wish I knew how to resolve this, Cory. Maybe just give it some time."

"And hope my brothers don't do something desperate in the meantime?" he fretted. "Maybe I should have gone off with them today."

But his mother sadly shook her head. "If they decided to break the law, could you stop them, son?"

"I could try."

She touched his arm. "You're outnumbered, Cory. And besides, maybe it's time you started making your own way in this world. It's always concerned me that you've been such a follower. Don't be afraid to decide on your own what's right—and what you believe."

For a long moment he regarded her wistfully. "Like believing you came here from another time, Ma?"

She gasped. "You actually believe that?"

He nodded soberly. "Truth to tell, I always did believe your stories of time-travel."

"You did?"

With a guilty grin, he confessed, "I used to hide outside Molly's window when you told her your bedtime stories. I was every bit as fascinated as she was. But I knew I dared not ever discuss it with my brothers—"

"Well, you could have come to me."

Cory smiled at his mother with deep devotion and love. "Perhaps I could have, but I feared the others would have found out in time. And besides, maybe I was a mite superstitious, afraid to acknowledge the truth. For if you could defy the laws of the universe and come here to us, maybe those same forces could take you away from us, too. Maybe I was afraid of losing you."

"Oh, Cory." Jessica hugged him warmly. "Darling, you're not going to lose me. Love brought me here and love will hold me here—love for your father and for all of you children. Just as love will bind Lucky and Molly together eventually, too. They just don't know it yet."

"They do seem to be getting along better," Cory concurred. "I mean, at first they were fighting like bobcat cubs, but now they act more like a couple of shy colts together."

"They'll get there, son."

"Yeah, and if *they* work things out . . ." Cory brightened. "Well, maybe there's hope for us all."

Chapter Thirty-one

"That was some scene today at church, wasn't it, darlin'?"

Sitting at her dressing table that night, Molly met her husband's gaze in the mirror. He stood a few feet behind her unbuttoning his shirt—and looking sexy as sin in the soft lamplight. His expression was rapt as he observed her brushing her hair.

She smiled at his words. "Yeah, some scene."

"Looks like your brothers aren't having much luck with courting."

Molly couldn't resist grinning at him in the mirror. "Maybe they should just learn to take what they want like I do."

He hooted a laugh and stepped closer, wagging a finger at her. "Are you getting a bit big for your britches, missy? Watch out or I'll take you down a peg or two."

Molly allowed Lucky the small victory of admonishing her; after all, she had been baiting him. Thoughtfully, she remarked, "You know, for a while there I would have cheered Mr. Trumble on in his efforts to thwart my brothers. But now . . . well, he just seems cruel, and I feel sorry for his daughters and even my brothers. Especially Cory. He seems so taken with Ida May."

Lucky shook his head wonderingly. "Are you actually wishing your siblings well?"

She lifted her chin. "I don't hate them."

"You just want to win against them, right?" His expression half wistful, half ironic, he touched her shoulder, toying with the thin lacy strap of her nightgown and making her shiver. "Or could it be you've decided you're actually happy with me and want to spread some of that sunshine around?"

She blushed, for his words weren't at all far from the truth. "We seem to be getting along better lately."

His teasing finger caressed her neck, raising gooseflesh. "Yeah. You know, you look awfully pretty in that lacy white gown, Mrs. Lamont."

Again she met his gaze in the mirror. Though her cheeks now bloomed with high color, she managed to say bravely, "I—Lucky, my woman's time is over."

He grinned and pulled her up into his arms, kissing her hair. "Good. Maybe next Sunday we'll go have our picnic."

"Next Sunday?" Molly felt an unexpected, keen disappointment. Lucky had been affectionate toward her this week but had made no move to make love to her again. Did he not want to do it with her unless they would make a baby together? Much as she yearned for his child—and no longer just to win the land—having him want her only to advance his own interests smarted terribly. And could he control his urges so much better than she? She wanted to do it with him all the time now—though she wasn't about to admit it.

Meanwhile, Lucky kissed her nose and his voice dipped in a sexy way. "Yeah, next Sunday. We'll drive out to the homestead again—*our* homestead. I want to make our next time together very special."

Molly flinched slightly. "Meaning you want to make a baby then—there?"

He eyed her in perplexity. "Don't you? Why sound so unhappy? Isn't a child what you've most wanted all along?"

"Yes, but . . ." Miserably, Molly turned away and confided, "Now you've seen the land and . . . you want the baby just so you can claim it."

"And you don't?" he countered gently, nestling her closer. "Reckon you got caught in your own trap, didn't you, sweetheart? But you never know. I may just have some surprises in store for you."

As he captured her lips with his own, Molly eagerly drank in her husband's kiss, reveling in his nearness, his scent. Perhaps it didn't matter if he didn't want her as desperately as she now wanted him. Whatever had brought them together—whether Fate, a longing for the land or a shared physical desire—she could take heart in the fact that he was here with her now, no longer angry with her, and more accepting of their destiny. Even though the realization that he might never really love her brought exquisite pain . . .

As Lucky sweetly kissed his bride, he reflected that he was the one who had truly been surprised in this marriage. Though he wasn't ready to admit it outright, he was falling for this girl, falling hard. Next to her, even the land he coveted paled by comparison.

But why did he hesitate to make love with her again? He longed to haul her off to bed with him right now, not just to make their baby but more importantly to make them *one*. Was he waiting because he needed to know the precise moment that their lives, their destinies, would become irrevocably linked? Or was it because he was still wary of sharing his heart fully with Molly?

Despite the coolness of the night, Molly felt herself burning as if with fever while she lay next to Lucky. She longed for him to make love to her again and felt confused, bereft. She noted he was squirming, too; when she reached out to touch his warm thigh, he groaned and flipped over, presenting his backside to her. A few moments later she heard his soft snores.

Feeling restless, she donned her slippers and wrapper and went outside. A cool breeze greeted her, scented of evergreen, and above her the night sky was clear and bright, the moon full, the myriad stars glittering wondrously.

She crossed the yard and went over to the barn. It had been a while since she'd checked on Jezebel's kittens, and she needed something to cuddle tonight. First she stopped off at Sanchez's toolbox, took out his tobacco pouch and rolled herself a smoke. Another pleasure she'd been denied lately. Lighting it, she climbed up into the loft. The kittens greeted her with mewls and she petted them with one hand while blowing smoke rings out the barn's front window.

"Woman, what the hell do you think you're doing?"

Molly jumped, then turned to see her husband standing on the ladder, looking good enough to eat in just his jeans. "Thought you were asleep—at least from the sounds of your snores."

"You woke me up when you left—and I repeat, what are you doing here?"

"I'm having a smoke." She wrinkled her nose at him. "And I take it you're feeling as restless as I am?"

He dodged her question while climbing into the hayloft. "Well, it's a good thing I woke up before you set the entire barn on fire." He snatched the cigarette from her fingers. "Haven't you heard that smoking is supposed to be for *after* sex?"

"Are you suggesting something?" she taunted back.

Mumbling a curse, he carefully snuffed out her cigarette on a wooden beam. "I can't believe you were sitting here smoking in the hay. Don't ever let me catch you doing that again."

"Now you're telling me what to do?" she demanded irately.

He plopped down beside her and glowered. "Never mind the fact that you might have set the farm ablaze. Didn't your mother ever warn you of the health risks of smoking?"

"Well, yeah, of course she did, but I'm just trying it, Lucky, not rushing off to have a draw every five minutes."

"Trying it can be deadly," he warned. "Nicotine is highly addictive."

"Nico-what?"

"Many a foolish teenager has become hooked simply by experimenting."

"Now I'm a teenager?"

"Well, you're eighteen, aren't you? And you're sure as hell acting like a rebellious teen at the moment. If I catch you smoking again, you're going right over my knee."

Molly was incensed. "Like heck I am! You don't have to have apoplexy over it."

"Molly, on this issue I won't compromise," he went on heatedly. "My grandpa started smoking before they knew about all the negative effects. He coughed and hacked for decades—then I watched him die of emphysema."

"Emphy . . . ?" She paused, grimacing.

"A lung disease. A very nasty one."

"Oh, I'm sorry," she said sincerely.

"And losing Grandpa—well, that's what ultimately killed my grandma, too. She just couldn't live without him."

Molly's expression was crestfallen. "Oh, Lucky, that's so sad. I hadn't realized . . . I mean, when I came out here, I didn't do it to upset you."

He sighed and wrapped his arm around her. "I know, sugar. Guess I've been kind of hard on you."

"Yeah. But I understand."

"Good." He tweaked her chin. "And besides, you can't possibly smoke if we're to have a child."

She felt her cheeks heating. "Lucky, I already told you, there isn't a child."

"Not yet," he added meaningfully. "But you need to start protecting your health now—and that means no smoking, and not a drop of alcohol, either."

She chuckled. "Now you're sounding like some Baptist preacher at a tent revival."

He grinned. "Maybe I am. You know, my grandparents used to take me to the Baptist Church every Sunday. Then I lost them and . . . well, I guess I lost my faith, too."

She swallowed hard. "How are you feeling about things now?"

He kissed her cheek. "Better. Like maybe there's a purpose to the universe, after all. Heck, maybe I was sent here to keep you in line."

"A man from the future trying to tame a woman from the past?" she teased back. "How old-fashioned does that make *you*?"

He chuckled. "Well, even back in my own time, girls used to call me 'retro' or a 'relic.' "

"I'm sure they did."

He affectionately rumpled her hair. "So maybe being such a fossil, I do belong in a time like this. But the irony is, my bride seems to have come straight out of the future."

"Complaining, are you?" With a wistful smile, she confided, "You know, I used to dream of going there."

"Did you? Guess that makes sense, with your ma and all."

She nodded. "I'd remember the story of how my folks met, then I'd head for Reklaw Gorge and dream of my own hero, coming from across time to rescue me."

"You needing rescue?" he replied drolly. "Now there's a novel thought."

"Oh, hush."

"So, am I your idea of a hero?"

She winked. "You'll do."

He regarded her quizzically. "But I haven't exactly taken you to the future, have I?"

"Nope."

"Do you still want to go there?"

She shook her head. "Reckon I'd miss my family too much."

"Just your family?" he asked with a catch in his voice.

She wrinkled her nose at him. "Well, I allow you're growing on me a bit, too, handsome."

"Uh-huh."

"So, guess I'll just stay here and be a woman before my time—"

"You and your mother—"

"And hope I don't drive you too crazy in the meantime."

He touched the tip of her nose. "Honey, you already have. Only you don't have to smoke a cigarette to prove you're progressive."

She chuckled. "Guess that's my ma's influence." As he raised an eyebrow, she hastily added, "Not that she ever encouraged me to smoke. But she did raise me to believe women can do anything they set their minds to. Why, they can even be spies or outlaws, like Belle Starr or Cattle Annie."

"You read too many dime novels," he teased. "Or so I've heard Cory say."

"And what do you read?" she mocked. "Shakespeare?"

He chuckled. "Well, my granddad did have an entire collection of Ned Buntline novels, and I read those when I was a kid."

Her eyes lit with pleasure. "Oh, I love Buntline and his tales of Buffalo Bill. You know, he's bringing his

Wild West show to Colorado City in a couple of weeks, and Ma says maybe we'll all get to go."

"Sounds like fun." He shook his head. "As odd as it is for me to think of Buffalo Bill as still being alive."

"Which is your favorite Buntline novel?" she went on excitedly. *"Buffalo Bill, The King of the Bordermen or Buffalo Bill's Best Shot?"*

"Gee, that's a heavy question—I'll have to think on it." She pinched his arm.

"But first, hand me a kitten."

She handed him the precious calico one, laughing as it wrapped itself around his large hand, purred and began chewing on his knuckles. "So we're just gonna sit here all night, discussing dime novels and petting these kittens?"

His arm tightened at her waist and his gaze grew unexpectedly tender. "Do you mind our waiting, Molly? I mean, it will give us a chance to get to know each other even better, won't it?"

"Hey, that's sweet," she replied, snuggling up closer to him. "And no, I don't mind."

They jabbered away happily and petted the kittens for many hours.

Chapter Thirty-two

True to his word, the following Sunday Molly's bridegroom took her on the promised picnic. She felt almost shy sitting beside him as he drove the buckboard toward the lower five hundred. She had a good idea what would happen when they got there, and her cheeks bloomed every time she thought about it. Lucky had promised they would make love together again, that they'd make a baby, that this would be her most fertile time. He was more than willing to do his part as a husband, now that he, too, coveted the land.

Be careful what you wish for . . . Now, too late, she remembered her father's admonition. Now she was coming to care for Lucky, and wanted to be wanted for herself, not just as a means to an end. Now she knew precisely how he'd felt . . .

Not that he hadn't been sweet toward her this week, kinder and more charming than ever before. She felt as if they were friends now, united by a shared goal.

But she didn't just want friendship from him, she wanted everything—his heart, his soul, his love and passion.

At least it felt good to escape the house for a while. After last Sunday's debacle at church, things had been decidedly tense at the Reklaw homestead; her four brothers had moped around, having been denied access to the Trumble girls. Molly had also sensed a rift developing between the elder three and Cory, and she prayed it had nothing to do with the outlaw gang increasingly raiding the region. She knew Cory wouldn't be involved but was concerned because her older brothers kept riding off alone. Indeed, on Thursday afternoon the three eldest had gone off hellraising in Dillyville—and sure enough, Friday morning Sheriff Hackett had again come calling. He'd reported a new stage robbery near the town and had questioned the boys, who'd denied all involvement. At least this time Hackett had been smart enough not to bring along his white-trash paramour, Dulcie Hicks, although Grandma had berated him thoroughly nonetheless. Still, Molly had a bad feeling about the whole incident.

"Well, here we are," Lucky announced happily, guiding the team down into the valley, where wildflowers blazed and the scent of nectar was heavy in the air. The day was lovely, slightly crisp but sunny.

"Yeah, here we are," she muttered at last.

In the center of the pastoral vale, he stopped the buckboard, hopped down, then assisted his wife to the ground. Her mouth went dry at the feel of his strong hands at her waist, the ardor glowing in his eyes.

"You look mighty fetching today in that yellow calico," he said.

"Are you buttering me up for the kill?" she managed to tease back.

"Oh, yeah."

She gulped, watching him take out the blanket and spread it on the ground, then set down the picnic basket. He took her hand. "Come on, I'm starving."

"Me, too."

For a while they sat and munched on fried chicken and potato salad, watching chipmunks scurry about near a distant tree, a bighorn sheep eyeing them from a high ridge.

Lucky in particular seemed entranced by each whisper of wind through the pines, each call of a mourning dove or horned lark. Molly found herself longing to know more about his connection to this place. After a moment she cleared her throat. "Lucky, this is the place where you lived in the future, right?"

He laughed. "You know, it's kind of hard to hear the future referred to in the past tense, but I guess that makes about as much sense as anything else that's happened to me here."

"Well, it's the place where you lived with your grandparents."

"Right."

"The other night you spoke about losing them. I'd like to know more about your life with them here."

"Such as?"

"Well, like how you came to be reared by them, and what it was like to grow up here."

Lucky nodded, then spoke at length, telling Molly

how he hadn't known his father, how his mom had gotten killed in an auto accident, how his grandparents had stepped in to rear him and had raised him righteously on this very land. He outlined the character traits he had most admired in Virgil and Bessie Lamont—his strength of character and sense of humor, her old-fashioned values and role as a traditional homemaker.

"You really worshipped your grandma, didn't you?" she asked with a touch of pain.

"Oh, yeah. She was one great lady."

"And she's still the reason I'm not your idea of a proper wife?" she added sadly.

He managed a wink. "Maybe I'm cottoning more to the notion of a feisty bride with each passing day."

Sure he was, Molly thought morosely. To Lucky, she said carefully, "Last week you spoke of your granddad dying from that awful lung ailment—"

"Emphysema."

"Yeah, that. And how losing him killed your grandma."

"Sure did," he acknowledged tightly.

"Tell me more about that time in your life. I mean, that must have been so hard on you. I can't even imagine losing my own folks or my grandma."

He gave a heavy sigh. "Yes, that period was really tough, especially since I was only twenty-two when I lost them."

Lucky spoke of his grandparents' final illnesses and deaths, his words growing gruff and terse. Molly's heart reached out to him as for the very first time she saw him as a man who was not just arrogant, determined and strong. Yes, he was all of those things, and all of those qualities drew her to him. But for the first time she also saw him as vulnerable and alone, especially so far removed from the world he'd once loved, and this endeared him to her most of all, especially considering the courage he'd demonstrated.

She grasped his hand. "I'm sorry, Lucky. I know you must miss them somethin' awful."

Briefly his eyes met hers and she spotted the emotion gleaming there before his gaze moved to a distant hillside. "On that knoll yonder is where they were—will be—buried."

"How sad for you. But, Lucky, I'm wondering—"

"Yes?" he asked tensely.

She squeezed his hand. "If all of that happened— will happen—here, why did you bring me to this place of pain for you?"

He turned to gaze fully into her eyes. "Molly, it may be a place of sorrow, but it's also a place of joyous memories for me. It's the place where you and I seem to be connected, where all of this—my being here— makes the most sense. I want this to be the place of a new beginning for us, a new life."

"A baby," she murmured. "So you can have the land."

"A baby," he repeated fervently, "so *we* can have the land . . . and perhaps be drawn closer together in the process."

"Will we be?" she asked ironically.

"What do you mean by that?"

Molly hesitated a long moment, then forged ahead, asking the question that had been tormenting her for some time now. "I mean, will you ever really be able to trust me after what she—that woman—did to you?"

He gave a groan. "Molly, I apologize for ever comparing you to her. I was wrong to say those terrible things—and to mock you when you said you're honest. The truth is, you are honest, and you're really nothing like Misti. I'm realizing that more with each passing day. I know I've accused you of conniving, when the reality is, the whole world knows exactly what's on your mind. You go straight after whatever you want, and you get it. Maybe that's why I fought you so hard for so long, 'cause I'd never met a woman as determined and tenacious as you. As for Misti, she was weak, stupid, deceitful—and you're truthful and strong."

"But you don't want a strong wife," she whispered in anguish.

"Don't I?"

With those words, Lucky pulled Molly into his arms. She hadn't expected such tenderness from him, to be wooed so expertly. No longer did she feel used by him. His words had brought their worlds full circle and made everything seem right. When his lips took hers, she felt strangely at home.

He pressed her to the ground and smiled down at her, his eyes so blue against the sky. He trailed his lips lovingly over her face, down her neck. She gasped and shivered. When he pulled down the bodice of her dress, it seemed natural to reach up and unbutton his shirt. When she trailed her fingernails over his naked chest, he sucked in a ragged breath and his eyes grew fierce. He covered her, kissing her as his hand slipped beneath her to tug on the strings of her corset.

Though his hands seemed impatient, his lips took their time, slowly trailing down her body, his tongue circling each breast in turn, his mouth taking one nipple, then the other. Molly bucked as a feverish need blazed inside her. Soon her impatient fingers were unbuckling his belt, undoing the buttons on his jeans. She reached inside his drawers and touched his hot hardness, moaning her delight.

His eyes blazed with desire as he spread her legs and pushed himself inside her, inch by throbbing inch. There was no pain this time, only the most exquisite, shattering tension. Soon she was sobbing, "Lucky, Lucky, more . . ."

He heard her plea and with a groan plunged home powerfully. Never had Molly felt anything so sweet, so fulfilling. They mated fiercely, mouths, bodies and loins locked, until their movements reached a staggering crescendo and their ragged cries rose to the heavens. When Lucky spilled his seed inside her, Molly knew with a certainty that they had just made a new life together. But what brought tears to her eyes was the realization that she loved him now, truly loved him. Which meant she was powerless, defenseless against him. But she loved him so much that she no longer cared about the risks. She just wanted them to be together, now and always.

Claiming his bride, climaxing deep inside her, Lucky felt deeply humbled and overcome with ecstasy. He looked down and saw the tears in Molly's eyes. What was she feeling? Happiness? Regret? Perhaps some of both?

He loved her, he realized with a sudden knotting of his throat. Truly loved her. And he knew in his soul that they had just made a baby together. The knowledge rocked him to his core. Just the thought of watching his baby suckle at Molly's breast, a baby with her curly auburn hair and perhaps his eyes . . .

He shuddered, feeling exposed as never before, not since Misti and Bobby had betrayed him. Not to mention scared to death. What if Molly didn't return his feelings? She had asked if he would ever fully trust her. What if he still couldn't?

For the moment none of that seemed to matter as he clutched his bride close to his heart and kissed her with aching tenderness.

Chapter Thirty-three

Holding a pair of binoculars, Cory Reklaw stood on a high abutment overlooking the road to Old Colorado City. For over an hour he'd been hovering here, intently watching the pass below, waiting for the regular stage line to pass through.

Cory was aware that Elk Ravine was a favorite spot for outlaws to ambush both public and private conveyances. And he had a very bad feeling that he might well spot his three older brothers attempting to hijack the Colorado City Line.

Things had not gone well for the family ever since the scene at church two weeks earlier. Cory's brothers had been off hell-raising much of the time, and two more robberies had been reported in the vicinity, one of a train and another of the payroll shack of a local lumber company. Then, when the outlaws had attempted to break into the Mariposa Bank the other night, Sheriff Hackett had been waiting inside with a shotgun and had chased off several shadowy figures. After the attempt on the bank, there was talk in town of a posse being raised to track the offenders, even Pinkerton agents being hired.

No, things weren't going well at all.

Although the prospect was daunting, Cory had decided he must find out once and for all whether his brothers were the culprits. His opportunity had arrived this morning when he'd awakened at dawn to the sound of hoofbeats and had looked out the bunkhouse window to spy his brothers off in the distance, riding hell-bent for leather toward the east. He'd quickly saddled up and followed their trail. Though he'd lost their tracks at a creek crossing, he'd realized by then that they were heading in the general direction of the Colorado City road—and since he'd also remembered the stage's regular route, he'd ridden for the canyon overlook.

He'd been riddled with anxiety ever since arriving here. What would he do if his brothers were indeed the criminals? It would kill his folks to find out. Could he convince the men to stop on their own? Fat chance, he thought glumly. He would have to pray the culprits were the Hicks boys or someone else entirely.

Cory tensed as the stagecoach, pulled by a team of six, with a driver and a guard on top, plowed into view. He drew a relieved breath as the conveyance made it two-thirds of the way through the canyon, stirring up clouds of dust. Then, just when he thought the danger was over, he winced at the sounds of gunfire coming from a distant stand of aspen. Cursing under his breath, he watched three riders in black gallop out from the woods and converge on the stage. When the guard returned fire, one of the riders shot the rifle right out of his hands.

Cory grimaced and lifted his binoculars to have a better look. All three riders were masked, with black Stetsons pulled low, and he couldn't make out their features. Nonetheless, there was something too familiar about these figures. He lowered the binoculars and observed the riders closing in on the stage and forcing it to a halt. He heard muffled shouting as the guard threw down the strongbox. Then, while one of the robbers shot the lock off the box, another retrieved the money bags and tied them to his horse, while the third forced the passengers—three women and a man— outside and demanded their valuables.

Cory felt miserably torn. Should he ride down and try to help the victims? He'd be scant help if the outlaws shot him, which was likely—he might even spook them into harming an innocent party. No, better to pray no one got harmed and track the culprits after they left the scene of the crime.

Within moments the bushwhackers rode off with their prizes, whooping and hollering, firing pistols into the air. After a glimpse through his binoculars revealed that the occupants of the stagecoach were all safe, Cory sprinted back to his horse, intent on tracking the desperadoes.

Later that morning Cory sat perched on his horse on another ridge, gazing in horror at a familiar farmstead in the valley below. He watched three lawbreakers emerge from the barn, now minus their hats and

masks. Any doubts he might have had about the outlaws' identities were at once dismissed.

Damnation! His worse fears were now confirmed.
What a terrible pass things had come to.

Worse yet, Cory very much feared there wasn't a
damn thing he could do about it.

That night at the supper table, everyone was buzzing
with talk of the latest robbery. Grandma had actually
witnessed the bullet-riddled stagecoach pulling into
Mariposa. "I heard the driver telling Sheriff Hackett he's
bringing out another payroll shipment in a fortnight,
and he ain't doin' it till they triple the guard."

"Why do you suppose they let you hear that,
Grandma?" Cory asked. He glanced meaningfully at his
brothers and was rewarded with surly looks. "Sounds
almost as if they're laying a trap for the outlaws."

Grandma waved him off. "Old Hackett ain't got the
brains for that kind of trickery."

Shooting Cory a hostile look, Zach asked Grandma,
"So, is everyone in town still blaming us?"

Even as Grandma had her mouth fixed to reply, Cole
asked sharply, "Should they be, son?"

With a look of angry disgust, Zach threw down his
napkin and stood. "Come on, fellas, let's get out of
here. Maybe see if we can find some folks that trust us."
He stormed out of the room with his two brothers following him.

The remaining diners regarded one another anxiously. Jessica waved a hand at her husband. "Cole, did
you have to get the boys all stirred up that way?"

"I just asked Zach a simple question, Jessica," he

replied grimly. "Was it too much for me to expect him to answer it like a man? Well, I'll tell you, the way my sons hightailed it out of here makes me suspicious."

Jessica started to reply, then bit her lip. Grandma looked sober, too. Cory knew he had to do something. He stood and cleared his throat. "Excuse me, folks. Think I'll go check on my brothers."

Cory dashed out of the kitchen. He caught up with his brothers outside near the barn, where the three stood huddled together, talking tensely, while Zach smoked a cheroot.

Matt, spotting his approach, sneered, "Well, what do we have here? Mama's little pantywaist. Did Ma and Pa send you out here to set us straight, baby brother, or to spy on us so's you can tattletale? Are you gonna accuse us of outlawin', too?"

Joining them, Cory said soberly, "Boys, I think it's about time we had a long, serious talk."

"Oh, yeah?" scoffed Zach, blowing smoke in his little brother's face.

"Yeah." Cory stood his ground.

"And why is that?"

"Why?" Cory asked ironically. "Because I know the truth now. Let's say I've seen it with my own eyes—and it's about time we discuss it."

"You've seen what, you little pissant?" scoffed Vance.

With the other three men staring daggers at him, Cory bravely began to speak. . . .

Chapter Thirty-four

The following morning, Lucky was pleasantly surprised when Cole made an announcement at the breakfast table. "Well, children, your ma and I have been talking, and we've decided we'll take the whole crew in to Colorado City today, so we can all see Buffalo Bill Cody and Pawnee Bill at the Wild West show tomorrow."

As excited murmurs broke out at the table, Lucky said, "Wow, Buffalo Bill Cody. You know, Molly and I were discussing him recently, and I said that it's so strange to think of him as still . . ." He paused at the expectant glances of the others, then quickly amended his statement. "Well, I guess it's pretty amazing that he's still riding the circuit, eh?"

Grandma chuckled. "Well, there's been rumors of him buying the ranch or retiring for ages now, and I allow he's old as the hills. Heard tell he's made half a dozen 'farewell' speeches already. But I reckon the codger is still out there kickin' up dust with his cowboys and Indians."

Cole grinned at her. "You want to come along, Ma?"

"No thanks, son. I seen plenty of Wild West shows in my time. You young folks go on ahead and I'll keep the home fires burning."

"Are you sure, Ma?" asked Jessica. "The poster I saw in town indicated there will be an Indian market, and I'd love to get some pretty blankets and baskets for the house."

Ma brightened. "Well, there's a thought. I reckon I could use a new broom, after I've plumb wore mine out on the hides of these hellions." She glanced meaningfully at her grandchildren, then turned back to Cole. "What about Dumpling and Billy, and their young 'uns?"

"I spoke with Billy yesterday, and the twins are still recovering from the colic. But maybe they'll join us in Colorado City tomorrow." Cole turned to the others. "How about you youngsters?"

"We're in, Pa!" Zach answered.

"Yeah!" seconded Vance.

Lucky glanced at Molly, who tentatively smiled back. "Molly and I will be delighted to attend."

"Good," said Cole. "I reckon we'll need the buckboard and the buggy to carry everyone—"

"Ah, just take the buggy for you, Ma and Grandma," put in Vance. "Us boys can ride."

"So can Lucky and me," added Molly.

"Very well, then," said Cole. "You youngsters go pack up, we'll be leaving within the hour. We'll want to get to Colorado City before all the hotel rooms are let out."

At the mention of hotel rooms, Lucky grinned at Molly and noted her answering blush.

The group made good time riding to Colorado City, Cole and Jessica and Grandma in a light buggy pulled by two swift horses, the four boys, Molly and Lucky on horseback. The late spring morning was crisp and bright, with no signs of rain on the horizon.

Lucky had to admit his bride looked sexier than hell riding beside him in her jeans and checked shirt, her ponytail bobbing in the wind, her bottom nestled in the saddle, her shapely thighs gripping the horse's flanks. He hadn't seen her much the past few days, as the Reklaw men had camped out to finish roundup on the farthermost ranges—and he was definitely in a mood to devour her now.

She glanced up, and her face went hot as she evidently guessed his thoughts. "So, what's on your scheming mind?" she asked.

"Well, I'm excited about seeing Buffalo Bill, of course."

"Right. Sure you are."

"And I was just thinking this is gonna be our first night together in a hotel room." He wiggled his eyebrows suggestively.

"Oh." Her color heightened.

"But not our first night in a bed together, eh, sugar?"

Glancing about them, she lowered her voice. "Lucky Lamont, you rascal. I thought such things didn't matter to you, now that you took me to the home place and had your wicked way with me."

"Yeah, it was plenty wicked, all right."

"Oh, hush."

"But we'll want to keep on trying just to be sure, won't we?"

She glanced away, but Lucky could have sworn he spotted a guilty grin on her face.

"I'm so glad you suggested this outing, Cole," Jessica said. She was happily ensconced beside her husband on the driver's seat of the buggy, while Ma occupied the large seat behind them.

"Yeah, I figured the kids could use some fresh air," he replied, working the reins. "The boys especially need to blow off some steam, with the sheriff constantly hounding them about being outlaws. It'll be a relief just to have them out of temptation's grasp for a day."

"Let's hope so. And I must agree with you that it was worrisome, the way they all stormed out of the kitchen last night. I've asked Cory about whether his brothers might be involved, and he's concerned, too."

Cole sighed. "Well, I've questioned the others several times now, and they always deny any responsibility. But they always get riled, too. Hard to tell if they're guilty or just insulted."

"If only Mr. Trumble would allow them to court his daughters. I think that's what's really eating at all of them."

He nodded. "I know, honey. But Ez always has been ornery as a badger. Maybe I should have a word with him. Who knows—he might even bring the girls to the show tomorrow."

Jessica harrumphed. "Well, I'm not sure you should

even approach that old tyrant. Ma tried—and look where it led."

"Yeah, but he doesn't want to marry me."

"Let's hope not," Jessica teased back.

Laughing, Cole nodded toward Lucky and Molly. "The newlyweds seem to be getting along better—and Lucky seems to be accepting that he belongs here."

"I agree. But there's still some lingering tension between them; I can tell."

He winked. "Another reason I suggested this trip. Maybe some time alone in a hotel room will do them good."

"Why, Cole, you schemer!"

His voice dipped intimately. "It sure helped us when we were newlyweds. Remember when we stayed at the old Antlers in Colorado Springs, back before it burned down?"

She blushed. "How can I forget? I'll bet polite society in Colorado Springs is still buzzing with gossip over that lurid incident."

He chuckled. "Yeah, but that bath we took together was sure worth it."

"Yes, with our shocked audience waiting and listening outside in the corridor," she added drolly.

He playfully pinched her cheek. "You know, Mrs. Reklaw, I hear the Longhorn Inn in Colorado City has bathing rooms on each floor, too."

Her eyes went wide. "Why, Cole, you bad boy! You'd think we hadn't been married for twenty-three years now."

He feigned amazement. "Jessica, I'm shocked at you. I was referring to the newlyweds, of course."

"Sure you were."

He leaned over and kissed her. "On second thought, maybe we'll just beat them to the punch, sugar."

Before long Lucky spotted the familiar, spectacular outline of Pike's Peak, which sheltered the towns of Old Colorado City and Colorado Springs ahead of them. As the first signs of civilization materialized on the dirt road ahead of him, he was thoroughly intrigued. In marked contrast to the popular tourist attraction and antiquing center he remembered from the present, Colorado City was a typical frontier town, with its long central street lined with storefronts, its gaslights and buggies and the occasional Model T rumbling past. A block south, he spotted a magnificent black locomotive of the Denver and Rio Grande parked at the station house, its smokestack billowing steam. Even more amazing, when Lucky gazed beyond the small burg toward the adjacent Springs, he spied only a few multistoried, early 1900s–style buildings, none of the soaring skyscrapers and modern freeways he remembered from the present. There were no jets circling the airport—indeed, there was no airport at all—nor were there any modern automobiles or traffic lights. Now as never before it hit home that he was definitely living in the year 1911. Perhaps some of his prior experiences could have been faked, but no one could have re-created a nineteenth-century version of both towns, then tacked on a replica of Pike's Peak for authenticity!

He did note that the folks strolling the boardwalks of Colorado City appeared a bit more fashionably dressed than those in Mariposa—he spotted ladies wearing form-fitting jackets, long tailored skirts and wide-brimmed hats adorned with silk flowers, gentlemen in much more modern-looking suits with brocaded vests, little girls in straight, long-waisted dresses, stockings and Mary Janes, little boys in sailor or knicker suits.

Cole halted the group before a three-story stone hotel with an arched doorway and a large plate-glass window. "We'll try for rooms here," he announced, hopping down to assist the ladies.

Lucky turned to wink at Molly. "The Longhorn Inn, eh, honey?"

She wrinkled her nose at him. "Don't worry, there aren't any cows inside."

"I'm considerably relieved." He hopped off his horse and helped her down.

Inside, while Cole spoke with the desk clerk and the others milled about, Lucky strolled around the large lobby with Molly, passing a quartet of gentlemen huddled over a card game and a trio of ladies knitting and sipping tea in a corner. He was quite amused by the cowhide rugs and settees he saw everywhere, along with steer-horn chairs, tables and hat stands, even a huge horned chandelier hanging overhead. "Well, there may not be cows in here," he murmured to Molly, "but this is one horny place."

Though she might not have recognized the word, she definitely caught his meaning. "You in a rutting mood, cowboy?"

"Always."

She grinned.

He glanced at a footstool composed of two sets of horns nailed to more horns and added wryly, "Though a fella wouldn't want to land wrong on one of those."

"Don't give me a reason to push you, then."

He chuckled.

Cole left the front desk and gestured for everyone to gather round. As the group assembled near the stairway, he began handing out keys. "Boys, you're up on the third floor where the bunking rooms are. The rest of us have rooms on the second."

"So, you all get the feather beds while us boys get the bunks?" groused Matt.

Grandma swatted his arm. "So you'd have me sleep on some flimsy cot, me with my lumbago?"

"No—sorry, ma'am," Matt muttered.

"Grandma's right," added Cole. "Of course the ladies get the rooms with the best beds"—he winked at Lucky—"which means Lucky and me get some consideration, too. If you boys aren't happy with the arrangements, pay for your own rooms, or better yet, bring your own brides next time. Now go unload the ladies' things from the buggy and get cleaned up. We'll be eating supper early."

Griping, the four men trooped off for the front door, with Lucky following along to help.

Moments later, outside their room on the second floor, Lucky unlocked the door, set down the carpetbag with their things and then, on an impulse, swept Molly up into his arms.

"What?" she cried, laughing.

"Believe I never properly carried you over the threshold, Mrs. Lamont."

Inside the room he kissed her heartily while reveling in the feel of her curves nestled against him, her unique scent of the outdoors mingled with rosewater. She moaned and wrapped her arms about his neck. He felt delighted by the high color he spotted on her face as he set her down. Then he gazed about at the walnut four-poster bed with its burgundy satin counterpane, the richly carved dresser, highboy and armoire. "Well, isn't this nice?"

"Yeah."

Noting with pleasure that her response had sounded breathless, Lucky roamed about the room, pausing to pull a chain on a colorful Tiffany lamp. "Electric light, I see. There's hope for us after all." He pointed toward an adjacent table with an antique wood contraption at its center. "And a telephone, fossil though it is."

"You say the oddest things," she said.

Lucky cranked the telephone, winked at his wife and drawled, "Hey, honey, what year is it?" He scowled a moment, then added, "That's just what I figured. Thanks."

"Hey, no flirting with the operator," Molly teased.

"Jealous?" he countered.

She stuck out her tongue at him.

Setting down the device, Lucky removed his boots, then plopped down on the feather mattress. "Ah, this is heaven after all that riding." He patted the space beside him. "Come join me, woman."

At his wickedly beckoning look, she shied away. "Um, Pa said we're eating early, and I need to change into a dress."

"We're newlyweds. He'll understand."

"First, I—I gotta wash off all this trail dust." She hurried to the dresser and busied herself dumping water into a basin, then cleansing herself with a damp cloth.

Lucky got up and sauntered over to join her. "Maybe I'll just lick the salt off you." He leaned over and delicately stroked her earlobe with his tongue.

"Lucky!" She practically jumped three feet.

"Easy, honey," he murmured, wrapping his arms about her waist and kissing her cheek. "I'll give you a reprieve—for now."

Chapter Thirty-five

Down in the hotel's rustic dining room, Lucky enjoyed the enormous dinner of fried beefsteak, onions and red potatoes, green beans steeped in bacon and yeast rolls flavored with honey and light enough to melt in his mouth. He noticed his bride was eating heartily, as well. Even the boys seemed in a more jovial mood, entertaining the family with the tale of a colorful Irish peddler they'd encountered while on the road to Dillyville.

Wiping his mouth after a last bite of apple pie, Cole remarked, "You know, the desk clerk told me Buffalo Bill has his own special train to carry his Wild West show into town. According to the advance men, it'll be pulling in to the station before dawn tomorrow."

"How exciting," commented Lucky. "We won't want to miss that, right, Molly?"

"Right."

"Indeed," concurred Jessica.

Cole grinned at his wife. "If we all turn in early, we should be able to get good seats, too."

"Ah, you old married couples turn in," scoffed Vance. "Me and the boys aren't ready to roll up our sidewalks just yet"—he paused, sneering at Cory—"except maybe for baby brother here. He'll likely just curl up with *Little Women*, eh, pipsqueak?"

While Zach and Matt burst out laughing, Jessica scolded, "Vance, that comment was totally uncalled for."

"Sorry, ma'am."

"Yeah," added Cory. "And besides, reading a book sure beats the heck out of spending the night in jail."

"Amen!" put in Grandma, shaking a finger at the three older boys. "You hellions listen up to Cory and stay out of trouble. No dancing parlors or hurty-gurty gals tonight."

"Ah, Grandma, we'll likely just go see the nickelodeon over at the Springs," cajoled Matt. "It ain't often we get to see moving pictures."

"And besides, we can take care of ourselves," asserted Zach.

"Like you did the last time you busted up the Mariposa saloon?" asked Grandma.

The three went grimly silent.

"Your grandma's right," added Cole. "Colorado City isn't nearly as wild as it used to be, but there's still plenty of sin in this town to tempt three young whippersnappers."

"Yeah, and you're the man who should know," muttered Zach.

Cole grew stern. "Son, I expect you to learn from my mistakes, not repeat them."

Zach gulped. "Yes, sir."

The three men grumbled a bit, then excused themselves and left.

While Jessica, Cole and Grandma lingered over a last cup of coffee, Molly and Lucky excused themselves. On the way back to their room, Molly asked to stop at the bathroom at the end of the hallway. As she was shutting the door, Lucky caught a quick glimpse of the inside—the old-fashioned toilet with a pull chain, the pedestal sink and, next to it, a huge claw-foot bathtub, with towels neatly stacked on a shelf above it. Suddenly he was inspired by a wicked idea. He hurried back to their room and grabbed their nightclothes.

A moment later he was knocking on the bathroom door. "Molly, honey, you about finished in there?"

He heard the toilet flush, then a moment later the door opened. . . .

Molly was perplexed to see her husband standing in the doorway to the bathroom, especially since he held her nightgown. Quickly, she stepped forward. "Er—I'm done and—you can go in now."

He winked and grabbed her arm. "Not without you."

"What?"

As she gasped in surprise, he pulled her inside with him and locked the door behind them.

"Lucky, what are you doing?" she demanded.

He pulled the ribbon from her hair, burying his nose in her tumbled curls. "Thought it was about time I gave my wife another bath," he murmured huskily.

"Bath!"

He winked. "Either that or we can bob for apples."

"Apples!"

"Yeah." He smiled wickedly. "I've got a couple of round ones you can bob for, any time."

Molly's mouth fell open and her heart hammered with excitement and mortification. "My God! You want to do—such wicked things—in a public place like this? Why, that's scandalous!"

He drew back to gaze ardently into her eyes. "Not between a husband and wife, it isn't."

"Lucky—"

Quashing further protests, Lucky ardently kissed her, and she whimpered helplessly and kissed him back. He sank his fingers into her thick hair, roved his strong hands over her shoulders, back and buttocks. His heat and nearness were dizzying, their risqué surroundings intensely provocative. And his kiss . . . so hot and deep, brimming with the passion that would soon come.

With a groan, he pulled away and went over to start the bath.

Molly could only watch in mingled amazement and disbelief. "You're really serious."

Totally unrepentant, he turned and grinned. "Yeah. Now for you." He returned to her side and began unbuttoning her dress, untying her corset, kissing her neck, then the tops of her breasts.

"Oh, Lucky," she murmured, growing feverish with desire as his mouth teased her aching nipples. When his lips returned to seize her own, she felt emboldened by passion. She unbuttoned the top button of his jeans, then slipped her hands inside, stroking his hard buttocks through his undergarment. He flinched, then groaned, grasping her own buttocks, nestling her against his erection. Molly burned for him, and found herself rocking against him with a woman's wanton need.

He pulled back, his face flushed. "My Lord, woman, you're making me hotter than a volcano."

Molly giggled, delighted that she could torment him so. She was amazed at how quickly Lucky finishing undressing her. She stood proudly before him, hair tumbled over her shoulders, nipples tight with desire.

He raked his smoldering gaze over her body and whistled. "You're so damn gorgeous." He stepped forward, squeezing a ripe breast with his palm, and she cried out at the exquisite sensation.

"Please, get in the tub," he begged hoarsely.

Molly scampered away and got in. The steamy water felt wonderful against her skin. Then her eyes widened as she watched Lucky strip, and viewed his generous erection. "My God, you're really gonna—"

He grinned like the very devil. "Get in there with you, darlin'."

And before her scandalized eyes, he did just that, climbing into the tub, settling himself behind her and drawing her body against his own with a ragged sigh. The sensation was decadently pleasurable, with both of them nestled there spoon-style. And having Lucky's hardness wedged against her lower back felt brazenly erotic.

"This was a great idea your pa had," he murmured.

"What?" she cried, twisting about to stare up at him.

He chuckled and tweaked her chin. "Coming to this hotel, silly."

"Oh." She stretched luxuriously, drawing another

moan from him as her slick body rubbed against his. She raised his hand to her mouth and teasingly drew her tongue along the folds between his fingers. "Guess it's nice to get away."

He clamped his arms around her. "I'll take you away, woman—to the moon and the stars."

For long moments he kissed her hair, her neck, her cheeks, while his hands took the bar of soap and roved her body intimately. Molly thought she might die of the sweet want consuming her. At last she couldn't take any more and turned around, straddling him.

"Why, you vixen," he teased, devouring her with his eyes, from her rosy breasts to her downy slit.

"My turn," she said, applying the soap to him and leaning over to kiss his chest, his belly.

Lucky groaned and pushed his hand between her thighs, plunging two fingers inside her. Molly panted, trembling in ecstasy, and gripped Lucky's manhood, feeling it grow even more turgid in her fingers. With a grunt he removed his fingers and brought her down hard on his distended shaft. She cried out in surprise and pleasure as he filled her utterly. They rocked there, letting the rapture build to a relentless pinnacle, then cried out as they climaxed together.

When they emerged a few minutes later, flushed and breathless in their nightclothes, both skidded to a halt at the sight of Molly's ma and pa standing there disapprovingly—Cole wearing a scowl and Jessica with an eyebrow meaningfully raised.

Molly's jaw dropped and she went completely blank. Desperately, she turned to her husband.

Lucky's face was also bright red. "Sorry—er—folks, but you see—Molly's stopper got stuck."

"Yes, we've heard *that* old excuse before," scolded Jessica.

"Indeed," added Cole.

Jessica clucked to Cole. "What is it about this family and baths?"

"Well, cleanliness is next to godliness, ma'am," Lucky offered lamely.

Both parents fought smiles.

"Sorry, Ma, Pa," Molly finally managed in a squeaky little voice.

She and Lucky exchanged a guilty look, then turned tail and ran off down the hallway.

"You've gone and done it now, Lucky Lamont," Molly scolded, shooting him a murderous glance as they hurried toward their room. "You've totally humiliated me."

"Oh, come on, honey, your folks have been married for ages. I'm sure they've done worse themselves."

She gasped. "Never! They're my *folks*, for heaven's sake!"

"Well, how do you think they got you—and your four brothers—by divine intervention?"

"I'll never be able to face them again."

He pulled her into their room and slammed the door. "Then I'll just have to distract you, darling."

And Lucky lifted her onto the bed, pulled up her nightie, boldly spread her legs and buried his face between her thighs. Molly screamed, but not with fear. Never in her entire life had she felt anything so shocking—or wonderful!

Lucky held her firmly in place as his hot tongue

flicked relentlessly at her most intimate places and his bearded face abraded her with raw sensuality. She tried to buck, to writhe away, but it was useless. She was left to toss her head and moan. When he drew deeply on her, she cried out, then went limp with pleasure, tangling her hands in Lucky's damp hair, her embarrassment lost in the smoldering ecstasy she felt. When at last he slid upward to kiss her, she begged him to come inside her, and he did. . . .

Down the hallway near the bathroom, Jessica and Cole stared at each other, then burst out laughing. "Guess we buffaloed them, eh, darlin'?" Cole asked.

"Well, as their elders we must set the proper example," Jessica replied primly.

He craned his neck toward the bathroom, then grabbed her hand. "Speaking of which, looks like we finally got that bathtub all to ourselves."

She gasped. "Cole . . . you wouldn't!"

"Wouldn't I?"

Laughing, he tugged his wife into the bathroom.

Hours later, Molly awakened in the darkness. The rapture Lucky had brought her to had been so sweet. She throbbed at the memory of his lips between her thighs, his tongue stroking her so expertly. She had felt no shame, only the brightest joy.

Glancing at him, so handsome and peaceful lying beside her, she felt overwhelmed by emotion. He seemed so happy with her now, his anger gone. She felt so grateful for his emotional transformation and sweet lovemaking that she wanted to give him back all the bliss he'd given her.

She burrowed her head under the covers, found his manhood and teased it with her own tongue, stroking up and down, glorying in the sexy taste of him. At once the shaft sprang to life and she heard Lucky gasp.

His fingers twisted in her hair. "Molly. God, what are you doing?"

"Forgot to bob for apples, sugar," she murmured with a husky chuckle. Then she ran her tongue in tormenting circles over his testicles. . . .

Lucked groaned like a man on fire. Molly's tongue was hot, wet, velvety, the purest torture, the sweetest heaven. He loved her so much for abandoning all restraint and giving him such wicked pleasure. She licked and tasted him for long, ecstatic moments, making him grip the sheets until he could take no more. Then, when she drew his maleness gently inside her mouth, a powerful shudder seized him and he pulled her body upward, plunging inside her womanhood, ravishing her with his kiss. She melted, gasping, into his hammering thrusts, and they claimed each other fiercely for much of the night.

Chapter Thirty-six

The tooting of a train whistle awakened Lucky early. He kissed his bride, who appeared so peaceful and beautiful lying beside him in the rosy light. What a wondrous night they had shared!

Quietly, he got up and pulled on his jeans. The sounds of muffled shouts and clanging drew him over to the window. The Wild West show had definitely arrived. He stared out to see roustabouts, Indians and cowboys swarming out of a train parked at the station house, unloading everything from tents and crates to horses, calves and buffalo. He watched the procession move from the station house to the outskirts of town, heard the banging as tents were raised and bleachers set up.

Scant weeks before he would have considered the scene unfolding before him outlandish. Now it seemed right, almost natural. He'd quit fighting his fate, he realized; he was accepting his lot, and grateful for it. After all, as he'd recently admitted to Molly, he did seem to be the type of old-fashioned man who fit in much better here than in 2004.

But the enormity of what had happened to him paled by comparison to his feelings for his bride. Turning to stare at her, he found his eyes misting with emotion. He knew now that it was Molly who had ultimately drawn him here; she was the true reason he had defied time, death and the laws of the universe. They were destined to be together, and he could now hope they'd find their happily ever after.

He turned back to the window and wiped away a tear. He knew one obstacle remained in the path of their storybook ending. He needed to tell her about his feelings as soon as possible—as soon as he could overcome his fear that she might never return them. . . .

Molly opened her eyes to see Lucky standing at the window—shirtless, in his jeans. How magnificent he was, with the rays of the dawn outlining his tall form, his shiny hair and broad, sinewy shoulders.

Last night had been incredibly special, and she longed to tell him her feelings now, burned to reveal to him that her woman's time was now several days late, and she sensed—indeed, she *knew*—she carried his child inside her. She wanted to apologize for her own misdeeds but feared bringing up that touchy subject with him. He'd been so angry at her for so long. Now at last he seemed to be coming around. Indeed, he'd admitted recently that he didn't think she was like Misti, after all—and she could now hope she might eventually win his trust. But she feared if she reached out to him too soon, she might only re-ignite his outrage. What if he still couldn't forgive her for using him so ruthlessly?

What was he thinking now? Was he happy to be here? Or was he looking out, dreaming of the world he had lost and wanting it back?

Then he turned, smiling, holding his arms out to her. "Hey, sugar, come see. The Wild West show is pulling into town."

Lucky felt overcome with happiness as he watched Molly grab her wrapper and come rushing into his arms. He clutched her close, inhaling her wonderful scent. "Morning, sugar. You sleep okay?"

"Yeah, if you can count maybe half an hour's rest sleeping," she teased.

He nodded toward the window. "Look, they're setting up the show."

Molly gazed at the workers milling about on the outskirts of town. "That's what got you up so early?"

"Yeah. I'm surprised the noise didn't awaken you."

She bit her lip.

"What is it, honey?"

She bravely met his gaze. "It's just that . . . when I saw you standing at the window, gazing out . . . Well, I was afraid . . ."

"Yes?"

She drew a bracing breath. "Are you thinking of going back again, Lucky?"

He tensed. "What?"

"It's just you looked so wistful—like you were ready to leave or something."

He gathered her to his heart. "Oh, honey. You shouldn't worry about that."

"But it's what you've wanted, isn't it?"

Lucky felt lacerated by guilt. "Maybe I'm just now learning what I want, sugar."

She still appeared unconvinced. "You know, Ma had her chance to leave once. She told me about it."

"You mean when the stagecoach returned to Reklaw Gorge?"

She gasped. "So she told you?"

"Yes."

Plaintively, she asked, "If it came back again for you, would you go?"

Lucky felt even worse, especially as he remembered his earlier attempts to rebuild the stage. He wanted to reassure her that he would never, ever leave her.

But was that something he could ultimately control? he thought with sudden fear. What if the same forces that had brought him here snatched him away just as precipitously? It wasn't a prospect he'd really considered before now, since he'd been so hell-bent on running, so cavalier about the whole concept of destiny that he'd only considered it in terms of a possible escape route. He'd never flipped the coin and considered the possibility that he might *want* to stay yet not be allowed to. Now the possibility that he might indeed be wrenched away from the woman he'd come to love was scary as hell.

What a fool he'd been.

"Please don't fret about that, sugar," he quietly pleaded. "I'm not planning to go anywhere, believe me." He forced a smile. "Now come on. Let's get gussied up, have some breakfast and go see the show."

"Sure, Lucky."

But he noted her smile seemed forced as she turned away.

By mid-morning when Lucky escorted his lovely bride out of the hotel, the air rang with noise and the main street of Colorado City was jammed with parked buggies, antique roadsters and hitched horses. Citizens mobbed the boardwalks, trooping toward the Wild West show still being set up on the outskirts of town.

The huge sideshow panorama extended along Main Street for several hundred yards. A makeshift arena occupied its center, while bleachers, shaded by massive tents, flanked it on either side. Closer to town, an Indian market was already in full swing, the sounds of chanting and drums and the smells of smoke and barbecuing game adding to the Native American aura, while nearby attendees huddled about a ticket stand. The air rang with the sounds of mallets being pounded, horses neighing, people talking. A huge throng of humanity swarmed the open area between the bleachers—performers in their colorful cowboy and Indian costumes, people from all over the region.

"Wow, this place is busier than a cattle yard at roundup," Lucky muttered.

Molly, looking lovely in a frock of lime green, nodded toward the crowd. "I see Pa over there waiting in line for tickets."

Lucky nodded. "Yeah, and I see your ma in the Indian market with Grandma—she seems to be haggling with a squaw over a broom."

Molly chuckled. "She does prize her brooms."

"Then we'd best behave ourselves." He offered his arm. "Let's have a better look around."

They strolled through the Indian market, perusing the piles of colorful blankets and tooled leather goods laid out, observing squaws grinding pemmican and weaving baskets. Soon they paused before a table crammed with patent medicines in colorful metal tins—everything from "authentic" Indian herbal remedies to chewing tobacco to "Indian Maiden" cologne.

"See something for what ails you?" Lucky teased his bride.

She gave him an unexpected, poignant look. "I don't think there's a cure for what ails me."

Lucky eyed her quizzically. Could she actually be coming to care for him? The very possibility brought an unexpected tightness to his chest.

They moved on to browse at a table of Indian jewelry—colorful beads, bracelets, necklaces and bolos. He observed Molly fingering a handsome turquoise and silver necklace. "You favor it?"

"Oh, Lucky, it's exquisite, but—"

He reached for his wallet. "It's yours." He turned to the Sioux squaw who sat scowling behind the table. "How much?"

She held up one hand with fingers splayed. "Five dollar."

Lucky groaned. He had only the four dollars Cole had given him for helping out at roundup. For a few moments he haggled with the squaw, patiently listening to her broken English. When Molly reached into her own knitted reticule to rescue him, Lucky turned and touched her hand firmly. "No." Lucky turned back to the woman. "Four dollars. Take it or leave it."

The squaw snatched up the money and Lucky grabbed the necklace. He proudly fastened it about his bride's neck. "There."

She beamed. "Thanks, Lucky."

Her parents stepped up. "Molly, how lovely you look," Jessica gushed, touching the turquoise.

"Lucky bought it for me," she declared proudly.

Cole nodded. "Good for him, honey. Well, I've got tickets for everyone, and I see they're letting folks into the bleachers. We'd best grab good seats while we can."

While the performers busied themselves lining up at the end of their makeshift arena, the family settled on second-row bleachers, and the boys soon joined them, sitting just beyond Lucky and Molly. He noted a lot of folks from Mariposa filing into the stands, including the Bledsoes and several other families from the church. He watched the boys crane their necks as Ezra Trumble and his four lovely daughters climbed the bleachers down at the other end, then frown as the Trumbles were followed by Sheriff Hackett and his ever-present companion Dulcie Hicks, along with the Hicks cousins.

Next to him, he heard Zach curse and watched him glare in the direction of the Hickses. "Them damn sidewinders—you don't suppose Sheriff Hackett, his whore and them no-account Hicks boys came here with the Trumbles?"

As Matt and Vance added angry comments of their

own, Lucky quickly scolded them. "Come on, boys, settle down. You don't want to ruin this day for your parents and grandma, do you?"

They fell glumly silent.

The tension eased a bit as Cole glanced westward and remarked, "Hey, I see Billy, Dumpling and their brood on their way over here." He extended a sheaf of tickets toward Cory. "Cory, why don't you go take them these and steer them in our direction?"

Cory vaulted off with the tickets; the boys scowled but made no further comments.

Relieved, Lucky turned to Molly. "You excited about the show, honey?"

She grinned. "Oh, yeah. It's not my first Wild West show, but it'll be my first time seeing Buffalo Bill."

"After reading all those Buntline novels, I'm sure you can't wait," he teased.

"Hey, you read 'em, too, right?"

Jessica, who had been listening to the exchange, remarked to Lucky, "Did you know Buntline's hundreds of dime novels launched Buffalo Bill's career?"

He nodded. "Oh, yes, ma'am. My granddad had a Buntline collection, and he read me some of the stories when I was little. It was pretty wild stuff. Granddad told me Buntline portrayed Cody as a teetotaler, when he was an infamous drunk."

"Still is," Cole put in wryly. "The stories of Bill almost falling off his horse are legendary. Good thing he's had a succession of smart mounts, beginning with Powder Face."

Everyone was laughing over this as a familiar female voice called out from below, "Well, howdy, folks!"

Lucky watched as Billy and Dumpling, each carrying a baby, climbed the stands to join them, with Cory helping along the three older boys. After hugs and hellos were exchanged, Dumpling settled her ample form next to Jessica and declared breathlessly, "We almost never got out of the house this morning."

Jessica reached out to touch Fanny's cheek, and the infant gurgled at her. "Oh, no, are the babies still ill?"

"Pshaw! The babies are fine, but Billy was too busy retching up all the redeye he drank last night."

"I was not, woman!" Billy retorted indignantly, while hastily trying to conceal a redeye bottle in his jacket pocket.

The group was still chuckling when a paunchy man wearing western garb and a silver star on his chest moved out to the center of the clearing and waved an arm. As the crowd quieted, he announced, "Folks, I'm Leroy Lummety, sheriff of Colorado City. I'd like to welcome you all to Buffalo Bill Cody's Wild West show, featuring Pawnee Bill and Chief Wa-Na-Sa-Ga. We're mighty pleased to have Colonel Cody here with us on his farewell tour."

As applause broke out, Jessica whispered to Lucky, "I read in the *Denver Post* that Buffalo Bill has been on his 'farewell' tour for over two years now."

"And no doubt he'll remain there for several more to come," Lucky quipped.

Lummety waved his arms to gain everyone's attention. "Ladies and gentlemen, remember we want you to enjoy yourselves today. But we'll tolerate no misbehavior. No firin' guns, spittin' tobacco or mingling with the performers, ya hear? Now let the show begin!"

Bushwhacked Groom

As another cheer went up from the gathering, the Wild West troupe galloped into view, beginning with Buffalo Bill Cody himself, prancing about on his magnificent snowy horse. Lucky noted that Bill was frontier elegance personified, with his flowing white hair and beard, and wearing an elaborate buckskin costume and hat. The colonel was followed by Pawnee Bill on his brown charger, and Chief Wa-Na-Sa-Ga on his colorful appaloosa; the chief sported full Indian regalia, including a massive war bonnet. The leaders were trailed by dozens of gaudily dressed Indians on paint horses, along with actors portraying soldiers and horsemen.

Following the grand entry, the attendees were entranced by the precision riding of the Rough Riders, demonstrations of cattle roping and buffalo stampedes, followed by a full-blown battle between Indians, cowboys and cavalry. Hearing the harrowing war cries, inhaling the acrid smoke from fake bullets, Lucky was awed, realizing he was truly watching a moment of living history—even if re-created history.

The mock battle was, of course, soundly won by the cowboys. Afterward, Colonel Cody demonstrated his shooting skills, riding about with an Indian companion, shooting at glass globes the warrior tossed into the air.

Then came the grand finale. The crowd stood, cheering, as all the Indians, soldiers and horsemen galloped about in a circle, whooping and firing their guns into the air.

As the throng slowly began to disperse, Cory Reklaw waited with bated breath for the moment when Ida

May Trumble would come down the bleachers. He desperately needed to have a word with his sweetheart and realized this might be his one chance.

At last he watched in mingled fascination and longing as Ezra led his girls down the bleachers, followed by Sheriff Hackett and the Hickses. He managed to catch Ida May's eye, and she bravely waved back.

As his brothers dutifully followed his parents down the steps, Cory seized his opportunity and slipped away. He squeezed his way upward through the masses, trying his best to emerge behind Trumble but near Ida May. At last he reached her side and touched her arm. Tensely he whispered, "Ida May, I really must talk to you—"

Even as she turned to smile at him, Trumble spied him, whirled about and stormed up to confront him. "What the hell do you think you're doin' speaking to my daughter, you little snot?"

Cory gulped. "Sir, may I please have a word with Ida—"

The next thing Cory knew, Trumble slammed him across the jaw and he went tumbling down the bleachers.

Lucky was escorting Molly through the crowd when he heard a gasp ripple through the assemblage. He glanced upward to see Ezra Trumble hit Cory, and Cory come crashing down the steps.

Cory's family had also spotted the altercation and was stirred into an instant frenzy. "Oh, no, Cory!" Jessica exclaimed, her hands flying to her face.

"Dammit!" Cole roared.

"Did you see what that bastard did to our brother?" Vance yelled to Zach.

"I'll go kill the sonofabitch, Cole!" exclaimed Uncle Billy, depositing a plump infant in Dumpling's arms.

"Hey, what about me?" cried Dumpling, trying to juggle both babies. "I'm right good at killin' folks."

"No, *I'll* murder him!" announced Grandma, thundering off with her new Indian broom.

Watching his mother's departure, Cole was aghast. "No, Ma, let me!" he hollered, too late. Frantically, he turned to Jessica. "You go see about Cory. Billy and me gotta go rescue Ma." As the boys opened their mouths, Cole added sternly, "You boys stay out of it."

Billy and Cole rushed off after Grandma, and Jessica ran for Cory. Molly turned to her brothers. "Let's go help Pa and Uncle Billy."

"You bet!" said Matt.

"Hey, you're not going anywhere without me," Lucky scolded his wife.

"Then let's go."

They vaulted up the bleachers, just in time to watch Grandma confront Trumble and roar, "Ez, I've had my fill of you treating my grandsons like the dirt on my broom!" Then, before their amazed eyes, she raised her broom and whacked Trumble square across the face, sending him spilling down the steps.

"Cory, darling, are you all right?" Jessica asked anxiously.

Down at the bottom of the bleachers, Cory winced and blinked, spotting his ma hovering over him. His jaw smarted like hell and his entire body ached from the tumble he'd taken. "Damn, but that old codger packs a punch."

"How badly are you hurt?" she asked anxiously.

"Not too bad, Ma. Don't worry. Help me up?"

Jessica extended her hand and Cory got to his feet with a grimace. His head pounded and he felt as if he'd been battered with a fence post.

But then he became aware of the sounds of enraged shouting, and his pain soon took a backseat to his fascination with the scene unfolding above him. He watched his grandma broom Ezra Trumble across the jaw, watched Ezra tumble down the bleachers. Then Sheriff Hackett surged forward to grab Grandma, and Lucky, Molly and Cory's brothers all threw themselves at him to liberate her. Grandma broke free, only to have Dulcine Hicks shriek at her and tear at her hair; Dulcine only got broomed in the face for her efforts.

With a roar, the Hicks boys leaped into the fray to defend Dulcine and Sheriff Hackett, and a free-for-all ensued. Ezra Trumble crawled back up the bleachers, tottered to his feet, swung his fist at Matt Reklaw and hit Winky Hicks instead. Then he raised his hand at Cole and got knocked back down the stairs by Molly for his troubles. Jeeter Hicks tried to slug Molly and got hurled off the stands by Lucky instead. Bart Hicks launched himself at Lucky, only to have Uncle Billy break a bottle of redeye over his head.

Meanwhile, the Trumble girls and everyone else stood watching the brawl in combined fascination and horror, just as Cory and his mother were doing.

At last Cory cringed at the sound of a rifle being

fired. He turned to see Sheriff Lummety standing nearby, and heard him yell up at the combatants, "Stop that there brawlin' right now or the lot of you is headed for the hoosegow!"

The donnybrook continued unabated, complete with screams and expletives.

Waving his hands in disgust, the sheriff stormed off and began gathering up a makeshift posse to help him break up the fight.

"Molly! Molly!"

In the midst of flying fists and earsplitting curses, Lucky had little time to battle the other side. He was too busy trying to protect his she-devil of a wife.

When she kneed Linus Hicks in the groin, he bellowed in pain, and his brother Jeeter tried to push Molly off the stands. Lucky plunged in and slammed the bastard down the stairs. Then Molly jumped on Sheriff Hackett's back and began pounding him across the head. When Hackett tried to shake her off, Lucky pummeled him in the belly. Then Molly spotted her grandma and Dulcie Hicks rolling around on the bleachers, fighting, hair-pulling and shrieking; she stormed over and gave Dulcie a mighty kick in the rear. She helped her grandma get up and retrieved her broom.

Lucky laughed at the sight, and unexpectedly his heart welled with pride. What a little hellcat he had married! Molly truly was a woman equal to him in every way, he realized. She had her mother's courage, but also her grandma's gumption. She fascinated him on every level. And she was right; how boring his life would have been with a traditional wife. She was the woman he'd wanted all along, only he'd been too blind and stupid and proud to see it.

By now the enemy was in full retreat, fleeing into the arena at the prodding of Grandma's lethal broom. Molly stepped up to Lucky and fanned her face. "Whew! Reckon Grandma's got 'em on the run now."

He tweaked her nose, then straightened the neckline of her dress. "I should whack you but good for getting into a fracas like that."

"Oh, you hush up, Lucky Lamont," she chided back. "You might as well start accepting the notion that I come from a long line of strong women."

"Yeah. Think I may be getting there."

Then, at the sound of a familiar female roar, Lucky glanced downward and grimaced at the sight of Grandma wielding her broom, mercilessly chasing Trumble, Dulcie and Sheriff Hackett around the arena, smacking their backsides at every turn, to the hilarity of the crowd. "Guess your grandma's still a bit riled, eh?"

Eyes huge, Molly nodded. Then she pointed westward. "Oh, no. Look!"

Lucky frowned as the local sheriff and several armed men converged on the combatants—and winced at the sight of Grandma bashing the lawman's butt with her broom.

"Uh-oh," she muttered. "Guess we'd best go help Grandma and the others face the consequences."

"Yeah," Lucky muttered grimly.

"I've a mind to put the lot of you in jail," Sheriff Lummety barked. "Bustin' up this show." He glared at

350

Grandma. "And you, woman, breakin' a broom over my hiney."

"My pleasure, Sheriff," Grandma simpered back, prompting gales of laughter from the spectators.

Ten minutes later, Lucky stood with Molly at the center of the arena, amid a large group of wrongdoers the posse had gathered up, including all of the Reklaw men, Ezra Trumble, the Hickses and Sheriff Hackett. The alleged lawbreakers were guarded by several townsmen with rifles, and surrounded by the enthralled attendees as well as the Wild West show performers.

The sheriff stood at the center lecturing them all, shaking a finger at Sheriff Hackett. "And I can't believe you contributed to this brawl, Hiram."

Red-faced, Hackett hitched up his pants. "But Leroy, you got no call to jail me, a fellow lawman. I was trying my best to help ya keep the peace. And I can always testify to the character of Widow Hicks here, and her boys."

Grandma sneered at Dulcie, with her rouged cheeks, scarlet dress and feathered hat. "Like how they ain't got none, Hiram?"

As Hackett went even redder, several men guffawed. Lucky watched Jessica step forward, Dumpling following her with the two babies. "Sheriff, you have no call to hold my husband or anyone else in our family. My kin merely came to the defense of my younger boy after Mr. Trumble assaulted him."

"Yeah!" added Dumpling, glaring at Trumble.

"That pissant dared to approach my daughter!" Trumble yelled back.

"Which gave you no call to hit him. This is a public event!" Cole shouted.

"He's a Reklaw—that's cause enough," snapped Trumble.

"Cause enough to hang you," retorted Uncle Billy.

"Spoken like a true outlaw," Trumble taunted back.

The gathering thrummed with tension.

"Yeah, I know all about you Reklaws," Sheriff Lummety sneered to Cole, "how you boys terrorized this region twenty-some years back, how you locked up my pa when he tried to arrest you."

"Actually, Joshua Hicks did that," Cole attested. "Your father was a sanctimonious blowhard—"

"And a pain in the neck," added Dumpling.

Lummety turned on her. "How dare you besmirch his name, madam."

Jessica spoke up. "The point is, Sheriff, that all of that is in the past."

"With all the robberies we've been having? I'm not so sure."

Buffalo Bill now wended his way through the gathering, smiling amiably, his imposing presence at once calming the throng. "Sheriff, may I be of any assistance here?"

"Thank you, Colonel Cody, but please don't concern yourself. This is a community matter we can handle on our own."

"But I feel a part of this community—at least for today," the colonel replied eloquently. "And I hate to see our performance end on such a sour note—especially with the potential incarceration of some of my guests."

Lummety snorted. "Ain't you riled to have your show

busted up? And 'sides, these folks added their own sour notes."

"That may be true. But considering how my troupe tends to work folks into a froth of excitement, can't you extend some measure of mercy?"

The sheriff was about to answer when a well-dressed man broke through the horde, screaming, "Robbed! We've been robbed!"

As shocked comments spewed forth, the sheriff swung about to address the newcomer. "Banker Wilkins, what is the matter?"

The brown-suited man rushed up, mopping his damp brow with a handkerchief. "With the show over, I went down to open the bank and discovered someone broke into the safe last night and cleaned it out."

Amid cries of dismay, Lummety turned irately back to Cody. "So I should let these folks go? Knowing there are likely bank robbers in our midst?"

"You have no reason to accuse us of thievery," Cole declared.

"You mean I shouldn't assume your boys are following in your own footsteps, Mr. Reklaw?"

"Sheriff, how dare you slander my sons without proof," Jessica chided.

The sheriff jerked his chin toward the posse. "Well, one thing's for certain: No one's going anywhere until you're all thoroughly questioned and your belongings are searched. Since we can't fit you all in at the jail . . . Men, take these suspects down to the lobby of the Longhorn Inn and let's get started there."

Ignoring the suspects' numerous protests, the posse herded the alleged lawbreakers back toward town.

Lucky squeezed his wife's hand as they moved along with Grandma and the Reklaw men. "Don't worry, honey, we'll be fine."

"You think I'm worried?" she mocked.

"Lucky's right, honey," added her father. "Don't fret. Us men'll protect you."

She rolled her eyes. "How 'bout Grandma and me protect you menfolk?"

"That's right, honey, you tell 'em!" cheered Grandma.

As the men chuckled, Lucky watched Buffalo Bill move into step beside Cole and extend a gnarled hand. "Well, Mr. Reklaw, I'm surprised our paths have never crossed before. I've heard of your exploits numerous times."

Cole grinned and shook Bill's hand. "But not for more than twenty years now—though I do appreciate your efforts to rescue my family, Colonel Cody."

"Ah, there's nothing worse than a reformed outlaw," Bill taunted.

"Only a reformed Indian fighter, eh, sir?" Cole countered wryly. "By the way, a fine show you folks put on today."

"Thank you kindly, though I definitely got upstaged at the end." Cody tipped his hat toward Molly, then winked solemnly at Grandma. "Madam, would you be interested in joining our troupe as our official broom maiden?"

She harrumphed, then broke into a grin. "Thank you kindly, Bill, but I've got enough trouble on my hands trying to keep all these rascals in line."

Amid eye-rolls from the rascals, Lucky tugged Molly

forward with him. "Hey, Buffalo Bill, meet my bride, Molly Lamont."

"A pleasure, ma'am."

"I loved the show," Molly told Bill, "but where's Annie Oakley?"

Buffalo Bill chuckled. "Little Annie retired several years back." Lowering his voice, he added confidentially, "Which I'm hoping the rest of you will be able to do, before Sheriff Lummety sends you all on to that next great roundup."

The group marched on, jawboning and laughing.

Chapter Thirty-seven

Several days later, Lucky walked toward the barn with a spring in his step and a picnic basket in hand. The day had dawned hazy, but surely the mist would burn off soon.

As for his mind, it was perfectly clear—and he was ready to tell Molly what was in his heart. Ever since he'd witnessed her courage and grit as she'd fought fiercely for her family at Colonel Cody's Wild West show, he'd been burning to tell her his true feelings.

That incident had ended in freedom for the Reklaw clan and frustration for the Colorado City sheriff, who'd been unable to recover any loot or usable leads from among the numerous suspects he'd detained. Ultimately, Sheriff Lummety had been impelled to give up and release everyone. Of course, rumors still abounded regarding who the actual robbers were—gossip that unfortunately still placed the Reklaw sons squarely at the top of the list.

Lucky knew he couldn't resolve that issue now, but he could settle matters with his bride. He only regretted that he'd waited so long.

This morning he planned to take Molly back to the old homestead for a surprise breakfast. In the basket he'd packed rolls and fruit, as well as a jar of Grandma's apple cider. He'd profess his love for her there, where their shared future awaited them.

He was ambling into the barn, whistling a jaunty tune, when he spotted Sanchez brushing one of the horses while singing "La Paloma." "*Buenas días*, Sanchez. You're here just in time to help me hitch up the buggy."

"*Sí*, señor. Where are you bound?"

"To the lower five hundred with my bride."

Sanchez grinned. "I'm sure the señora will be pleased. You might also want to take her by Reklaw Gorge."

Lucky frowned. "Why would I take her there?"

Sanchez beamed with pride. "To see Senorita Lila Lullaby's stagecoach, of course. I finished putting it back together yesterday."

A chill washed over Lucky. "What? You didn't."

Sanchez blanched. "*Sí*, señor."

"But why the hell would you do that?"

"Because you asked me to, señor. *No recordó?*"

"Shit! I plumb forgot!"

Lucky shoved the picnic basket into the arms of the astonished Sanchez and raced toward the nearest stall. Never in his life had he saddled a horse so quickly.

* * *

Molly emerged out of the front door to see Lucky riding off hell-bent for leather toward the west. Perplexed, she watched Sanchez exit the barn carrying a picnic basket.

She hurried over to join him. "Sanchez, where is Lucky going?"

"To Reklaw Gorge, señora."

"Reklaw Gorge? But why?"

He avoided her gaze.

"Damn it, tell me why!"

"To see the *coche*."

"You mean that pile of rubble?"

"No, the stagecoach, señora. I put it back together."

"No! You didn't! But why?"

Sanchez lowered his gaze in confusion and shame. "Because the señor asked me to."

"Oh, God," Molly muttered, realization dawning on her. "You gotta help me saddle up Prissy right now."

"*Sí*, señora."

Molly raced for the barn with Sanchez, struggling hard against the hot tears that threatened to well up. So Lucky had been repairing the stagecoach the entire time he'd been making love to her and promising he would never leave her. Had she been an utter fool? Had he been lying to her all along? Did he really plan to forsake her now?

"Oh, God!"

Lucky stood above Reklaw Gorge, staring down in trepidation and horror at the restored stagecoach, which was perched on the ledge directly below him. He instinctively knew he was looking at an object that held the power to separate him from Molly forever. The coach was pieced together patchwork style, misshapen but definitely a reasonable facsimile of the vehicle that had brought him across time. Why the hell hadn't he stopped Sanchez from reassembling it? He knew he must destroy it immediately, or it might well take him away from the woman he'd come to love.

He was about to jump down onto the ledge when he turned at the sound of hoofbeats. . . .

Molly's heart ached as she galloped toward the canyon. Was Lucky still there? Or was she too late? If he hadn't left as yet, could she convince him to stay with her?

And with the child she now knew she carried?

The very thought brought a lump to her throat and tears to her eyes. No, she realized, she couldn't use the baby to keep him. If her love wasn't enough to hold him, she had to let him go.

Then her heart welled with joy at the sight of him standing at the rim of the gorge. Thank God! He was still there.

Molly! She had come after him! Lucky's heart welled with joy at the sight of his beautiful bride galloping toward him. As she arrived before him, he all but hauled her off the horse. "Sweetheart! What are you doing here?"

She peered over the rim. "You—you reassembled the coach! You were going to use it to leave me—go back to your time—"

"No, darling, no."

"Yes, you were!" Trembling, she thrust herself into his arms. "Well, I don't care, Lucky Lamont."

"You don't?"

Vehemently, she shook her head. "I don't care about my pride, or about winning, or about anything but you. Take me with you."

Lucky was stunned as he gazed down into her earnest face. "You would leave this time? Your family? The land you love? All for me?"

She nodded, her feelings shining through straight from her heart. "Of course I will. I'll do anything to keep us together."

He clutched her to his chest. "Oh, darling, I'm not leaving you."

"Then why—"

"For a while I was tempted. I even began reassembling the coach, but soon abandoned the project. I didn't realize Sanchez had actually finished rebuilding it."

"You didn't?" she asked in confusion. "Are you telling me the truth, Lucky Lamont?"

He nodded soberly. "Yes, darling, yes."

"But . . . why would you stay?" she asked in anguish.

He swallowed hard. "Because I love you, of course."

For a moment she just stared at him, features rapt with hope. Then she threw her arms around him. "Oh, Lucky, I love you, too."

Lucky could barely speak, barely breathe. Her admission was like manna from heaven. "Oh, Molly, I'm so happy. And I'm not going anywhere, darling. Not now or ever."

They kissed passionately and held each other close, barely even aware of their surroundings, until the sounds of another approaching rider caught their attention. Lucky turned and blinked, unable to believe his eyes as he spied a misty horseman in the distance, a pudgy man in a familiar sheepskin coat. "On, no! Good heavens, Molly, this sounds crazy, but I think I see Grover Singleton riding toward us."

Molly gasped and stared off at the hazy stranger. "You mean, the man from 2004, the one who hog-tied you, pushed you into the gorge and tried to kill you?"

"Yes, that very one. Damn, I never should have let Sanchez finish reassembling that stage. Now it's starting to happen all over again!"

She seized his hands. "Lucky, we must run. He could hurt you."

"I don't care about me. He could hurt you!"

"Or our child," she added breathlessly.

Lucky's eyes went wild with joy. "Our child? You're carrying my baby?"

She smiled with total love. "Yes, darling."

Quickly, he embraced her. "Oh, Molly, I'm so thrilled. But there's no time to waste. Let's climb down onto the ledge and push that stagecoach into the gorge."

She appeared perplexed. "You really think that will stop him?"

"Yes. Don't argue with me, we gotta destroy it—now!"

They clambered down onto the ledge, shared a smile, then gave the stagecoach a mighty push. Lucky held Molly close as the vehicle slammed and bammed and crashed its way down into the gorge, landing in a blast of spewing wood, metal and dust. Joy filled Lucky's heart to know his escape route through time was finally sealed off—forever.

But afterward, Lucky could still hear the sounds of an approaching rider. "Hell! Molly, come on. If we hurry, maybe we can still get out of here before Singleton reaches us."

He climbed onto the ridge and pulled Molly up, only to be flabbergasted when she pointed to the rider and hooted a laugh. "Lucky Lamont, have you up and lost your mind? That's not Grover Singleton at all. It's my brother Cory!"

"What?" Lucky did a double take at the rider—who was actually much slimmer than Grover, his sheepskin coat transformed into a beige western shirt. "Well, hot damn, Molly, you're right, it *is* Cory—though I could have sworn it was Grover."

"Me, too." At his confused look, she amended, "I mean, I could have sworn it was someone else."

As Cory pulled up before them wearing an anxious expression, Molly asked, "What the heck are you doing way out here, brother?"

Breathlessly, he replied, "Sanchez told me you folks were here. Molly, Lucky, you need to come with me now."

"But why?" Lucky asked.

"Because Sheriff Hackett caught the outlaw gang."

"What?" Molly cried. "He sure enough nabbed 'em?"

"Yeah, he rounded them up. And you're going to have to see this to believe it."

Chapter Thirty-eight

When Molly tore inside the jail with Lucky and Cory, she was horrified to see her worst fears confirmed. In the outer office stood her three older brothers, along with Ma, Pa and Grandma. Everyone seemed to be talking at once, gesturing angrily at Sheriff Hackett.

"Oh, no!" she cried to her brothers. "Are you boys really responsible for all those robberies?"

All at once the room grew deadly silent as the others turned to regard the three newcomers.

"No, no!" Zach denied. He frowned at Cory. "Didn't you tell her?"

Cory shook his head. "I wanted her and Lucky to see this for themselves."

"See what? Is it the Hicks boys?" Molly demanded.

None of Molly's brothers answered her.

Lucky addressed the sheriff. "Sheriff Hackett, what's going on here? Cory said you caught the outlaw gang."

"Sure did. You all want to see 'em?"

"You bet!" cried Molly.

"Lead the way," added Lucky.

The sheriff escorted the group through a passageway into the cell area. Molly was fully expecting to see the five Hicks cousins locked up there, and her jaw dropped at what she actually witnessed in the first cubicle. "My God!"

"Well, I'll be damned!" declared Lucky.

Molly stared at the group in the cell, still not quite able to believe her eyes. For there sat a scowling Ezra Trumble, along with his four very abashed daughters. All five were dressed in the black costumes of outlaws; the women had their hair pinned up under their hats.

"The *Trumbles* were the ones committing these crimes?" Molly asked in disbelief.

Hackett self-importantly hitched up his britches. "Yep. I never would have believed it myself—especially that females would go outlaw like this."

Molly waved him off. "Oh, Sheriff, hush up. Women can do anything."

As Lucky flashed his wife a forbearing glance, Hackett forged on. "Anyhow, ma'am, I hid a posse out near Dillyville this morning and caught 'em all red-handed when they robbed the stage." He gestured toward Trumble. "And that ain't the half of it, neither."

"Yes?" Molly asked tensely. "You mean there's more?"

The sheriff nodded grimly. "Yep. Folks, meet Dirty Dutch Dempsey."

"What?" cried Lucky, staring at Trumble wide-eyed. "Mr. Trumble is Dirty Dutch Dempsey?"

"But you're dead!" accused Molly.

Ezra harrumphed, then glared back. "To paraphrase

Mr. Twain, the rumors of my passing are greatly exaggerated."

"My God, I can't believe this," Molly muttered.

"It's true, folks," the sheriff confirmed. "Ez really is Dutch, and his daughters there is his gang."

"Well, I'll be hanged," Lucky muttered.

"Ez is one sly fox," the sheriff went on. "He's been livin' here under an alias for several years now. Had all of us hoodwinked—until his daughters gave him up after we arrested the lot of them."

Lucky turned to the daughters. "But why were you women involved?"

Sally popped up. "It wasn't our idea a'tall!"

Nelly stood next. "Yeah, Pa forced us to help him rob all those folks."

"We tried to say no, but he beat us!" wailed Bonnie.

Trumble rolled his eyes.

"How horrible!" declared Molly. "Your father deserves to be horsewhipped." She glanced at her brothers. "But why are you boys here?"

"We've been trying to convince the sheriff to let the girls go," explained Cory. "Clearly their father is the responsible party."

"Yeah, you got some nerve, Ez Trumble, accusing my grandsons of your own crimes," scolded Grandma. To Hackett, she added fiercely, "You should hang him by his scrawny neck without benefit of a trial."

Trumble glowered back while his daughters gasped in fear.

"Settle down, Grandma," Cory admonished.

"Why did you do it, Mr. Trumble?" Lucky asked. "You were here, a part of this community. You had everyone fooled as to your real identity. Why not just live out your final years in peace?"

He sneered. "What has this town ever done for me?"

"Well, shame on you," Lucky chided. "And how despicable of you to involve your daughters against their will, and risk their lives, as well. Sheriff, you know Cory is right. You shouldn't hold these young ladies."

"That may be so," conceded Hackett, "but as I was just telling your folks and grandma, that'll be up to the circuit judge."

"But can't you let 'em go until he next comes through?" pleaded Matt.

Hackett scratched his jaw. "Well, maybe if someone will vouch for them—"

"Jessica and I will be delighted to supervise the girls," put in Cole.

The girls chortled in delight.

"Hell, us boys'll marry them!" declared Vance, prompting more grins from both the men and women.

"Well, I guess if they have proper husbands to keep 'em in line . . ." Hackett muttered. "I mean, I have been kind of hard on you boys, seein's how you weren't the real bushwhackers."

"Yeah. You owe this family a big favor, Hiram—and an apology," chided Grandma.

"Very well. I'll release the girls into the custody of the Reklaws." Hiram shook a finger at Trumble. "But I'm recommending the judge sentence you to a good spell in the calaboose, Ez—that is, Dutch."

"Hell, lock him up and throw away the key," pronounced Grandma.

As Dutch growled at Eula, Hackett opened the cell,

and the four girls rushed into the arms of their sweethearts. "Lawdy, lawdy!" Eula laughed. "We'll be having us a quadruple wedding any day now."

Molly felt compelled to speak up. "Um, boys, before you start rushing to the altar, I think it's only fair to tell you that Lucky and I have kind of jumped the gun on winning that contest." She grinned at Lucky, and he proudly wrapped his arm around her waist.

"You're expecting, Molly?" asked her mother excitedly.

She nodded happily.

"Oh, darling, that's wonderful." Jessica hugged them both.

"Yes, that's splendid news, children," pronounced Cole, following suit.

"Congratulations, Molly," added Cory. "And as far as the contest goes, it doesn't matter." He beamed at Ida May. "We're all in love."

"Yeah, in love," added a grinning Zach as he kissed Sally.

While the others chattered away happily, Cory drew Ida May aside and the two shared a long, tender kiss. He was so delighted that things were finally resolved and the girls were safe, their futures secure.

"Are you all right, honey?" he asked raggedly.

She hugged him ecstatically. "Oh, yes, especially now that you're here! Thanks for helping to make things right, Cory."

He shook his head wonderingly. "Dirty Dutch Dempsey. No wonder your pa was always so standoffish. He couldn't risk allowing anyone here in Mariposa to get close enough to learn the truth about him."

"Did you ever suspect it?"

He smiled guiltily. "Actually, for the last week or so, I've known—at least, I've known your father was an outlaw—and so have my brothers."

Her eyes went wide. "You've known?"

"You see, I watched three of you rob the Colorado City stage, then followed you home."

"You saw all that—and didn't turn us in?" she gasped.

"Of course not, honey. My brothers and I had hoped to find a way to stop the robberies on our own. That's why I tried to speak with you at the Wild West show."

She bit her lip, then confided, "Cory, I want you to know that I didn't rob that stage. Bonnie and I were the lookouts. It was Pa, Sally and Nelly who did the dirty work."

"I know. But it doesn't matter—especially not since he forced you girls to participate."

She glanced away guiltily. "Well, I've a confession to make about that, too."

"Yes?"

In a confidential whisper, she admitted, "My older sisters enjoyed playing outlaw a lot more than they're letting on."

He chuckled. "Oh, yeah, I kind of figured that one out, too."

"You did?"

"Well, when they grabbed up all those dime novels at the library, I guessed they were a pretty bloodthirsty lot. And that was quite a hint, too, when Sally admitted relishing the fictional account of Dirty Dutch Dempsey getting gut-shot in Denver. The amazing thing is, she was talking about her own father! Only I didn't see it at the time."

She nodded. "I just hope my sisters will follow the straight and narrow now."

"Oh, I wouldn't worry there. If they played outlaw, I think it was only as an outlet for their resentment toward your pa. With him out of the picture, they'll settle down. Besides, they'll be good matches for my brothers—who are also on the spirited side, in case you hadn't noticed."

"Oh, I've noticed." She glowed with pleasure. "Thank you again for everything you did."

"You think I'd want my future bride in jail?" he teased back. "Besides, I can't wait to hear all about the exploits of Dirty Dutch Dempsey—like how he managed to acquire four daughters, and why he moved here to Mariposa."

"Oh, I've got lots of tall tales to share with you," she rejoined.

Two weeks later Molly sat with her husband in the front pew of the church. She squeezed Lucky's hand and the two of them exchanged a quiet smile. Before them stood Molly's four brothers and their four beautiful brides, listening to Reverend Bledsoe's marriage sermon. The rest of the Reklaw family looked on raptly. Absent, of course, was Ezra Trumble, father of the brides; although the circuit judge had absolved the Trumble girls of criminal liability, old Dutch would be spending the rest of his golden years in the state penitentiary.

With her wonderful husband beside her, Molly had

never felt happier. Time, and Lila Lullaby's stagecoach, had brought her the true hero of her dreams. Even better, she knew Lucky loved her now, and she loved him; he was hers forever. Soon they'd have a beautiful child to further brighten their lives. She felt intensely grateful and only hoped her brothers might know a fraction of the joy she felt.

Next to Molly, Lucky, too, had never felt happier, after finding the woman, and the time, of his dreams. He found it particularly appropriate when Reverend Bledsoe turned to the Beatitudes as part of his wedding oration. With a poignant smile he heard, " 'Blessed are the meek, for they shall inherit the earth.' "

This had been a humbling experience for him, all right, as well as an enthralling one. He'd regained his faith and found the love of his life, a woman who equaled him in every way. He had so much to be grateful for—love, trust, a solid marriage, a family on its way, a future to look forward to.

As the couples began repeating their vows at the parson's urging, Lucky squeezed his bride's hand and gazed into her eyes, seeing his own smile reflected there. The contest that had put him and Molly at odds had made them both winners in the end, and he was intensely thankful for the shared destiny that had bonded them together in love.

Dear Reader:

Recently I was thrilled when my editor suggested I write a sequel to my classic Western time-travel romance, *Bushwhacked Bride*—and *Bushwhacked Groom,* the book you've just read, became the result. If you enjoyed *Bushwhacked Groom* and have not yet read *Bushwhacked Bride,* I do hope you'll read the outrageously funny original work on which *Groom* is based. I'm delighted to tell you that *Bushwhacked Bride* is being reissued by Love Spell, making both books available now!

In *Bushwhacked Bride,* my heroine, Professor Jessica Garrett, is "bushwhacked" back in time to become the captive of the Reklaw brothers, five sexy outlaws looking for a bride. Then in *Bushwhacked Groom,* Molly Reklaw, the daughter and youngest child of my original couple, becomes the feisty heroine. So don't miss *Bushwhacked Bride* to see how all the fun began, including Grandma Reklaw's infamous first swing of her broom! I'm particularly proud to tell you that both stories work in tandem *and* as stand-alone, memorable love stories.

If you enjoyed the humor in these books, I know you'll love my two contemporary romances also available from Love Spell: *The Great Baby Caper* and *Lovers and Other Lunatics.* I hope you'll order these titles from Dorchester or your local bookseller. And please watch for my future releases from Love Spell.

Thanks, as always, for your support and encouragement. I welcome your feedback on all my projects. You can reach me via e-mail at eugenia@eugeniariley.com, visit my website at www.eugeniariley.com, or write to me at the address listed below (SASE appreciated for a reply; free bookmark and newsletter available).

Eugenia Riley
P.O. Box 840526
Houston, TX 77284-0526

EUGENIA RILEY
The Great Baby Caper

Courtney Kelly knows her boss is crazy. But never does she dream that the dotty chairman will send her on a wacky scavenger hunt and expect her to marry Mark Billingham, or lose her coveted promotion. But one night of reckless passion in Mark's arms leaves Courtney with the daunting discovery that the real prize will be delivered in about nine months!

A charming and sexy British entrepreneur, Mark is determined to convince his independent-minded new wife that he didn't marry her just to placate his outrageous grandfather. Amid the chaos of clashing careers and pending parenthood, Mark and Courtney will have to conduct their courtship after the fact and hunt down the most elusive quarry of all—love.

Attention
Book Lovers!